Wings Of The Wind

by

Credo Harris

Double 9 BOOKS

Wings Of The Wind

by Credo Harris

ISBN: 978-93-73401-60-7

Published by

DOUBLE 9 BOOKS

2/13-B, Ansari Road
Daryaganj, New Delhi – 110002
info@double9books.com
www.double9books.com
Tel. 011-40042856

ABOUT THE AUTHOR

Credo Fitch Harris was an American journalist, novelist, and radio station manager whose work reflected both the literary and technological transitions of the early 20th century. Born in 1874 and based in Kentucky, Harris contributed to regional literature while also playing a role in the emerging field of broadcast media. He managed WHAS, a prominent Louisville radio station, during a period of rapid development in American radio. His writing frequently explored Kentucky life, particularly in novels such as Toby, which was later adapted into the silent film One Dollar Bid. Harris's literary range extended beyond fiction, as seen in his travel book Motor Rambles in Italy and his autobiographical Microphone Memoirs, which detailed the early days of radio. His novels often dealt with identity, place, and the intersections between rural experience and broader social changes. Though not widely known today, Harris's combined legacy in literature and media marks him as a contributor to both Southern storytelling and the foundational years of American broadcasting. He died in 1956.

CONTENTS

CHAPTER I
"TO ADVENTURE AND ROMANCE!"

At last out of khaki, and dressed in conventional evening clothes, I felt as if I were indeed writing the first words of another story on the unmarred page of the incoming year. As I entered the library my mother, forgetting that it was I who owed her deference, came forward with outstretched arms and a sound in her voice like that of doves at nesting time. Dad's welcome was heartier, even though his eyes were dimmed with happy tears. And old Bilkins, our solemn, irreproachable butler, grinned benignly as he stood waiting to announce dinner. What a wealth of affection I had to be grateful for!

I did not lack gratitude, but with the old year touching the heels of the new, and Time commanding me to get in step, my return to civil life held few inducements. Instead of a superabundance of cheer, I had brought from France jumpy nerves and a body lean with over training—natural results of physical exhaustion coupled with the mental reaction that must inevitably follow a year and a half of highly imaginative living.

But there was another aspect less tangible, perhaps more permanent—and all members of combat divisions will understand exactly what I mean. When America picked up the gauntlet, an active conscience jerked me from a tuneful life and drove me out to war—for whether men are driven by conscience, or a government draft board, makes no difference in the effect upon those who come through. Time after time, for eighteen months, I made my regular trips into hell—into a hell more revolting than mid-Victorian evangelists ever pictured to spellbound, quaking sinners. Never in this world had there been a parallel to the naked dangers and nauseous discomforts of that western front; never so prolonged an agony of head-splitting noises, lacerations of human flesh, smells that turned the body sick, blasphemies that made the soul grow hard, frenzied efforts to kill, and above all a spirit, fanatical, that urged each man to bear more, kill more, because he was a Crusader for the right.

Into this red crucible I had plunged, and now emerged—remolded. In one brief year and a half I had lived my life, dreamed the undreamable, accomplished the unaccomplishable. Much had gone from me, yet much had come—and it was this which had come that distorted my vision of future days; making them drab, making my fellows who had not taken the plunge seem purposeless and immature. Either they were out of tune, or I was—and I thought, of course, that they were. What freshness could I bring to an existence of peace when my gears would not mesh with its humdrum machinery!

My mother, ever quick to detect the workings of my mind as well as the variations of my body, had noticed these changes when I disembarked the previous week, and had become obsessed with the idea that I stood tottering on the brink of abysmal wretchedness. So, while I was marking time the few days at camp until the hour of demobilization, she summoned into hasty conference my father, our family doctor, and the select near relatives whose advice was a matter of habit rather than value, to devise means of leading me out of myself.

This, I afterward learned, had been a weighty conference, resulting in the conclusion that I must have complete rest and diversion. But as my more recent letters home had expressed a determination to rush headlong into business—as a sort of fatuous panacea for jumpy nerves, no doubt—and since the conferees possessed an intimate knowledge of the mulish streak that coursed through my blood, their plans were laid behind my back with the greatest secrecy. Therefore, when entering the library this last night in December and hurrying to my mother's arms, I had no suspicion that I was being drawn into a very agreeable trap, gilded by my father's abundant generosity.

We sat late after dinner. Somewhere in the hall Bilkins hovered with glasses and tray to be on hand when the whistles began their screaming. In twenty years he had not omitted this New Year's Eve ceremony.

"Your wound never troubles you?" my mother asked, her solicitation over a scratch I had received ten months before not disguising a light of pride that charmed me.

"I've forgotten it, Mater. Never amounted to anything."

"Still, you did leave some blood on French soil," Dad spoke up, for this conceit appealed to him.

"Enough to grow an ugly rose, perhaps," I admitted.

"I'll bet you grew pretty ones on the cheeks of those French girls," he chuckled.

"Pretty ones don't grow any more, on cheeks or anywhere else," I doggedly replied. "Materialism's the keynote now—that's why I'm going back to work, at once."

"Oh," the Mater laughed, "don't think of your father's stupid office, yet!"

"There's nothing left to think of," I grumbled.

"Isn't there?" he exclaimed. "What'd you say if Gates has the yacht in commission, and you take a run down to Miami—"

"Or open the cottage, if you'd rather," she excitedly interrupted him. "I hadn't intended leaving New York this winter, but will chaperon a house party if you like!"

"Fiddlesticks! Cruise, by all means," he spoke with good-natured emphasis. "Get another fellow, and go after adventures and romances and that kind of thing! Go after 'em hammer and tongs! By George, that's what I'd do if I were a boy, and had the chance!"

They waited, rather expectantly.

"Cruising's all right," I said, without enthusiasm. "But it's a waste of time to go after romance and adventure. They died with the war."

"Ho!—they did, did they?" he laughed in mock derision. "What's become of your imagination—your vaporings? You used to be full of it!" And the Mater supported him by exclaiming:

"Why, Jack Bronx! And I used to call you my Pantheist! Don't tell me your second sight for discovering the beautiful in things has failed you!"

"It got put out by mustard gas, maybe," I murmured, remembering with bitterness some of the fellows who had been with me.

What was romance here to the colorful, high-tensioned thing I had seen in devastated areas where loves of all gradations were torn and scattered and trampled into the earth like chaff! Fretfully I told them this.

They exchanged glances, yet she continued in coaxing vein:

"You're such a big baby to've been such a big soldier! Don't you know that romance is always just over the hill, hand in hand with adventure—both lonely for someone to play with? Wars can't kill them! It's after wars, when a nation is wounded, that they become priceless!"

"By George, that's right," Dad cried. "Come to think of it, that's exactly right! And Gates has the same crew of six—men you've always known! Even that rascal, Pete, cooks better 'n ever! The *Whim*, you can't deny, is the smartest ninety-six foot schooner yacht that sails! I say again that if I had the chance I'd turn her free on whatever magic course the wings of the wind would take her! That I would—by George!"

And there was a note of deep appeal in the Mater's voice as she asked:

"Why not get that boy you wrote so much about—Tommy what's-his-name, the Southerner? I like him!"

This plan, which I now saw had been so carefully prepared—fruit of the secret conference—was but one in the million or so of others throughout America nurtured and matured by the brave army of fathers, mothers, wives, sisters, daughters, who stayed at home and gave their all, waiting with alternate hopes and fears, looking with prayerful eyes to the day that would bring a certain one back into their arms. What difference if some plans were elaborate and some as modest as a flower? Who would dare distinguish between the cruise on a private yacht and the cake endearingly made in a hot little kitchen for the husky lad just returned from overseas? Each was its own best expression of pride and love. Each said in its tenderest way: "Well done, my own!"

A lump came into my throat.

"It's rather decent of a fellow to have two such corking forbears," I murmured.

The Mater turned her gentle eyes to the fire, and Dad, clearing his throat in a blustering way—though he was not at all a blustering man—replied:

"Perhaps it's rather decent of us to have a son who—er, I mean, who—well, er—"

"A cruise hits me right," I exclaimed, hurriedly coming to his rescue, for neither of us wanted a scene. "And I'll wire Tommy Davis, Mater—the chap you mentioned. He's a corking fellow! I didn't write you how the battalion started calling him 'Rebel' till he closed up half a dozen eyes, did I? You see, in the beginning, when we were rookies, the sergeant had us up in formation to get our names, and when he came to Tommy that innocent drawled: 'Mr. Thomas Jefferson Davis, suh, of Loui'ville, Jefferson county, Kentucky, suh.' You could have heard a pin drop. The sergeant, as hard-boiled as they come, stood perfectly still and let a cold eye bore into him for half a minute, then gasped: 'Gawd! What a wicked little rebel!'"

They laughed.

"Why didn't you bring him home with you?"

"Same reason he couldn't take me home with him. There were people waiting, and turkey, and—but he won't want to go," I added. "He's crazy about a girl down there!"

"Fiddlesticks," my father chuckled. "Any normal fellow'll want to cruise! I'll wire him myself—this very night!"

Bilkins entered with the tray, wishing us a happy new year. Outside the whistles were beginning to blow. After we had pledged each other, and drunk to 1919, the Mater, a light of challenge in her eyes, looked at me and gave another toast:

"To a cruise and an adventure, Jack!"

"To romance," Dad cried, gallantly raising her fingers to his lips.

There was no use being a wet blanket, so with a laugh I said:

"To adventure and romance!—Mater, if they're still on earth I'll bring them home to you!"

I knew it was a very silly toast, but let it go to please them—for why disillusion those who believe in the actuality of nonexistence?

CHAPTER II
THE MYSTERIOUS MONSIEUR

Ten days later Tommy and I—and Bilkins, whom I had begged of my father at the eleventh hour—stepped off the train at Miami, stretched our arms and breathed deep breaths of balmy air. Gates, his ruddy face an augury of good cheer, was there to meet us, and as he started off well laden with a portion of our bags, Tommy whispered:

"Reminds me of the old chap in that picture 'The Fisherman's Daughter'!"

The description did fit Gates like an old glove, yet his most dominant characteristic was an unfailing loyalty to our family and an honest bluntness, both of which had become as generally recognized as his skill in handling the *Whim*—"the smartest schooner yacht," he would have told you on a two-minute acquaintanceship, "that ever tasted salt."

"We might open the cottage for a few days, Gates," I said, as we were getting into the motor.

"Bless you, sir," he replied, caressing a weather-beaten chin with thumb and finger, "the *Whim*'s been tugging at her cable mighty fretful this parst fortnight! The crew hoped you'd be coming aboard at once, sir. Fact is, we're wanting to be told how you and Mr. Thomas, here, licked those Germans."

"Angels of the Marne protect me," Tommy groaned. "Gates, I wouldn't resurrect those scraps for the Kaiser's scalp!"

"Yes, he will," I promised, smiling at the old fellow's look of disappointment. "He'll probably talk you to death, though; that's the only trouble."

"I'll tell you what," Tommy said, "we'll chuck the cottage idea and go aboard; then tonight, Gates, you pipe the crew—if that's the nautical term—whereupon I'll hold a two-hour inquest over our deceased war, on condition that we bury the subject forever more. We came down here to lose the last eighteen months of our lives, Gates, not keep 'em green. Maybe you don't know it, but we're after the big adventure!"

His eyes twinkled as he said this, and his face was lighted by a rare smile that no one possessed more engagingly than Tommy. While he treated the probability of an adventure with tolerant amusement, such was his inherent love of it and so developed was his capacity for "playing-true," that he sometimes made me think almost anything might turn up. I was quite unaware that my mother had written him, or that he, in return, had promised to keep her fully advised of my improvement—a state which was already beginning.

"I carn't see how you help talking of it, sir—all that gas, and liquid fire, and bursting shells," Gates stared at him in perplexity.

"It's an effort, but I refuse to turn phonograph like some of the old timers—not that I love 'em any less for it, Lord knows!" Then he began to laugh, and turned to me, adding: "One of the first things I did after getting home was to drop in on a very dear gentleman who's been a friend of our family since the Ark. He came at me with open arms, crying: 'Well, Thomas, sit right down and tell me about your experiences!' I side-tracked that—for I hate the word. We didn't go over for *experiences*! But he wouldn't be denied. 'Try to think,' he commanded. 'Why, Thomas, old as I am, I remember when Stonewall Jackson struck that brilliant blow—' and you can shoot me for a spy, Jack, if he didn't keep me there five hours while he fought the entire Civil War! No sir-ee! After tonight, never again!"

But Tommy's talk, to which the crew listened in rapt attention, consumed nearer six than two, or even five hours. These men were hungry for authentic first-hand information—being too old to have sought it for themselves.

It must not be inferred that the *Whim's* crew consisted of the ancient and decrepit. More than once my father had said that if ever he should get in a tight place there was no band of six he would rather have at his back than this one headed by Gates; nor did he except Pete, the prince of cooks. Yet who, by the wildest stretch of fancy, could have contemplated tight places or dangers as the trim yacht rode peacefully at anchor an eighth of a mile off our dock at smiling Miami? To every man aboard such things as death and the shedding of blood had ceased with the armistice, and Gates would have taken his oath, were it asked of him, that our course pointed only toward laughing waters, blue skies, and emerald shore-lines.

Early next morning we were under way when Tommy pounded on my stateroom door, challenging me to a dip overboard. There was a glorious joy in his voice, as far reaching as reveille, that found response in the cockles of my heart. Gates, never happier than when standing beneath stretched canvas, hove-to as he saw us dash stark naked up the companionway stairs and clear the rail head-first, but he laid by only while we had our splash and continued the course southward the moment our hands grasped the gangway.

"We're cruising, not swimming," he said bluntly, as we reached the deck. "But I'll say this," he called after us, "you're both in about as fine condition as men get to be. I'll give *that* to the Army!" Which was true, except for the fact that I might have been pronounced overtrained. Tommy and I were as hard as nails, our skin glowed like satin—but, better than this, his spirit was quick with the love of living, charged with a contagion that had already begun to touch my own.

Half an hour later he mumbled through a crumbling biscuit:

"If Pete ever cooked better grub than this it was in a previous incarnation!"

"Man achieves his greatest triumph but once in life," I admitted. "It's self-evident."

One loses track of time while sailing in south Florida waters. There is a lassitude that laughs at clocks; the lotus floats over the waves even as over the land, and a poetic languor steals into the soul breeding an indifference to hours and days—wretched things, at best, that were only meant for slaves! Neither of us realized our passing into Barnes Sound, and saw only that the *Whim*, sails gracefully drawing, cut the water as cleanly as a knife.

Another day passed during which we shot at sharks, or trawled, or lay on deck smoking and occasionally gazing over the side at displays of fish and flora twenty feet beneath us. But upon the third morning I asked:

"Where are we bound, Gates?"

"Mr. Thomas says Key West, sir, and then Havana."

"Mr. Thomas, indeed," I laughed, for it was exactly like Tommy to take over the command of a ship, or anything else that struck his fancy.

Before leaving Miami he had received a twenty page letter from the Bluegrass region of Kentucky which threw him into a state of such volatile ineptitude that I was well satisfied to let him give what orders he would, sending us to the world's end for all I cared. In a very large measure Tommy's happiness was my own, as I knew that mine would always be dear to him.

During our most trying hours in France, thoughts of this wonderful girl, whose name was Nell, unfailingly kept his spirits high. In moments of confidence that come to pals on the eve of battle I saw that some day they might be eternal "buddies"—certainly if he had his way; and toward this achievement he had been, since graduating from the University of Virginia, directing every effort to build up a stock farm which his family had more or less indifferently carried for generations. Next to winning Nell, his greatest ambition was to raise a Derby winner—according to him a more notable feat than being President.

The sixth of April, 1917, had caught him with a promising string of yearlings, each an aristocrat in the equine world of blue-bloods, each a hope for that most classic of American races. But he had thrown these upon the hands of a trainer and submerged his personal interests six hours after Congress declared war. At the same moment, indeed, all of Kentucky was turning to a greater tradition than that of "horses and whiskey"; and, by the time the draft became operative, the board of one county searched it from end to end without finding a man to register—because those in the fighting age, married or single, with dependents or otherwise, had previously rushed to the Colors. This, and the fact that his state, with three others, headed the nation with the highest percentage in physical examinations, added luster to the shield of his old Commonwealth—though he roundly insisted that 'twas not Kentucky's manhood, but her womanhood, who deserved the credit. After our cruise he was going back to the thoroughbreds, now within a few months of the required Derby age; and of course I had promised to be on hand at Churchill Downs when his colors flashed past the grandstand.

Late in the afternoon the *Whim* docked at Key West and, while Gates was ashore arranging for our clearance, Tommy and I ambled up town in search of daily papers. We were seated in the office of a rather seedy hotel when its proprietor approached, saying:

"'Scuse me, gents,—are you from that boat down there?"

I answered in the affirmative.

"Going to Havana?"

This, too, I admitted.

"Well, there's a feller by the desk who missed the steamer, and he hoped—er—"

"We'd take him over," Tommy supplied the halting words. "Where is he?"

Turning, we easily distinguished the man by his timid glances in our direction.

"Whiz-bang," Tommy whispered. "What the deuce would you call it, Jack?"

Except for his age, that might have been sixty, he was most comical to look upon—in stature short and round, suggesting kinship with a gnome. His head seemed too large for the body, yet this might have been because it carried a plenteous shock of straw-colored hair, with mustache and beard to match. He was attired in "knickers" and pleated jacket, that looked as if he'd slept in them, and his fat legs were knock-kneed. On the floor about his feet lay almost every conceivable type and age of traveling bag, with the inevitable camera.

"What's his name?" Tommy asked, not that that would have made any difference if his passport were in order.

"Registered as 'Monsieur Dragot, of Roumania,'" the proprietor answered.

"Roumania!" Tommy looked at me. "Let's go meet him, Jack."

Monsieur Dragot turned out to be the original singed cat, for assuredly he possessed more attractive qualities inside than were exteriorly visible, and from a first shyness that did not lack charm he expanded briskly. After visiting a "dry" café, to seal this fortunate acquaintanceship—as he insisted upon calling it—he warmed up to us and we to him, with the result that his bags were soon carried down and stowed in our spare stateroom. Leaving him there, we went on deck.

"Dragot," Tommy mused. "Speaks with a slight accent, but I can't make out what!"

"Roumanian, possibly," I suggested, "as he comes from there."

"You rather excel yourself," he smiled. "Registering from Roumania, however, isn't prima facie evidence that he's a Roumanian."

"He's a clever little talker, all the same."

"Right O! Too clever. I'm wondering if we aren't a pair of chumps to take him."

"Why?"

"He may be a crook, for all we know. Did you notice what he said about holding a commission from Azuria, and then hurrying to explain that Azuria isn't on the ordinary maps—just a wee bit of a kingdom up in the Carpathians, yet in the confines of Roumania? I call that fishy!"

"Not entirely so, Tommy. When you said it might now be turning into a republic, did you notice how proudly he declared that the descendants of Basil the Wolf couldn't be humbled?—that, situated in Moldavia, and escaping the ravages of the Bulgarian army, they were stronger today than ever?"

"Sounds like raving, sonny. Who the dickens is Basil the Wolf? No, Jack, that doesn't tell us anything."

"It tells us he couldn't have been inspired like that unless the place and people were real to him!"

"Well, pirate or priest," Tommy laughed, "he'll do if he waltzes us up to the big adventure. You're about fit enough to tackle one now!" During the past forty-eight hours he had openly rejoiced with Gates at my improvement and tried, with the indifferent success of an unbeliever, to play up at top speed that silly idea of an approaching adventure.

We had strolled aft, and now stopped to watch a tall Jamaica negro—or so we thought him to be—asking Gates for a place in the crew. His clothing was too scant to hide the great muscles beneath, and Tommy touched my arm, saying:

"There's a specimen for you!"

Had he been cast in bronze a critic might have said that the sculptor, by over-idealizing masculine perfection, had made the waist too small, the hips too slender, for the powerful chest and shoulders; the wrists and ankles might have been thought too delicate as terminals for the massive sinews leading into them. He smiled continually, and spoke in a soft, almost timid voice.

"I like that big fellow," I said. Perhaps I had been well called a pantheist, having always extravagantly admired the perfect in form or face or the wide outdoors.

Feeling my interests he turned from Gates, looking at me with dog-like pathetic trustfulness. Among the things he told us briefly—for the crew stood ready to cast off—was that he once followed the sea, but in more recent years lived by fishing up sponges and at times supplying shark meat to the poorer quarter of Key West. The carcass of a water fowl tied to his boat, while he occupied himself with sponges, would sometimes attract a shark; then he would strip, take a knife in his teeth, and dive.

I glanced at Gates, but saw no incredulity in his face.

In another hour, at nearly dusk, Key West had grown small and finally sank below the horizon, leaving only its three skeleton-like towers standing against the sky—standing erect with all nerves strained, watch-dogs of the darkening sea; ears cocked, to catch a distressed cry from some waif out in the mysterious night.

Looking back along our wake I imagined the big black man standing as we had left him on the dock, gazing after us with patient regret; and I was glad to have given him the handful of coins at parting, little dreaming how many times that loaf upon the water would come floating in to me.

Monsieur Dragot revealed himself more and more to our astonished eyes as we sat that night on deck. He had been a professor in the University of Bucharest, and hinted at an intimate entente with the reigning house of Azuria. Besides being versed in many sciences, including medicine, he spoke seven languages and read several others. But these things were drawn from him by Tommy's artful questions, rather than being said in boastfulness. Indeed, Monsieur was charmingly, almost touchily, modest.

Of his business in Havana he gave no hint, yet this happened to be the one piece of information that Tommy seemed most possessed to find out.

"You'll be in Cuba long, Monsieur?" he asked.

"No one can say. A day, a week, a month, a year—it is an elusive search I follow, my young friends. May I call you that?"

We bowed, and I deferentially suggested:

"If we can help you in any way?—"

"It is the beautiful spirit of America," he sighed, "to help those in distress, yet there is nothing to do but watch—watch. For you have not yet been here long enough to see a child in these waters—no?"

Tommy, perhaps because he came from the South and was on more or less friendly terms with superstitions, glanced over the rail as if an infant might be floating around almost anywhere. Our strange guest's mysterious hints were, indeed, rather conducive to creeps.

Then, without further comment, he arose, tossed his cigar overboard, ran his fingers through his mass of hair, and went below.

"What d'you suppose he meant?" I asked, in a guarded voice.

"Simple enough," Tommy whispered. "He's got apartments to let upstairs."

"Get out, man," I laughed. "That chap has more sense than either of us!"

"Then he'd better come across with some of it. You remember the freckled lad at Soissons who got fuzzy-headed from too much concussion? Well, he saw children around everywhere, too! It's a sure sign, Jack!" But now he laughed, adding: "Oh, I suppose our little Roumanian's all right, only—"

He was interrupted by Monsieur, himself, who emerged from the companionway door.

"I come again," he smiled apologetically, "because tomorrow our journeys part, and I have shown scant consideration for your kindness."

"It's we who feel the obligation," Tommy murmured. "Now, if we could only help you find the child—supposing, of course, that's what you're watching for!"

Monsieur gave a deep sigh, appearing to be quite overcome by a secret grief; but after a moment he looked at us, asking ingenuously:

"You think my behavior unusual?"

"Well, since you make a point of it," I laughed, and hesitated.

"I see, I see! But, my young friends, you must take my word that I cannot tell you much." He drew us nearer. "This I may say: that, after Roumania dropped out of the war, the new Chancellor of Azuria wired imploringly for me to leave my classes at the University and come to him—because for years I have advised with Azurian statesmen, frequently going on special missions. By the recent death of the old Chancellor a certain paper came to light. This was a secret agent's report sent from Havana in 1914—I may not divulge its contents. But for the war it would have been followed up at once. Whether the same hopes exist now—well, I am here to discover. Ah, my young friends," his voice trembled, "much depends upon this! I must—I must find the child if it lives!"

Tommy's eyes grew round.

"I can say no more," Monsieur added. "Accept my thanks and gratitude for the help you have given me. And now—*bon soir*."

He bowed, backing himself toward the stairs as though leaving a royal presence, doing it so easily, so naturally, that we did not even smile. When he had quite disappeared we turned and faced each other.

"What do you think now?" I asked.

"I think he's a treasure," Tommy cried. His face had lighted with a new excitement. "If we want any fun on this trip, don't let him get out of our sight! Stick to him! I won't deny he has a screw loose, but—"

"That makes it all the better," I laughed, adding: "Looks like the Mater's toast might come true, after all, doesn't it!"—for I had described our New Year's Eve to Tommy.

"Sonny, I've a hunch we won't even have to tiptoe over the hill to find adventures with him around! He's their regular hanging-out place!"

Gates came up, and seemed vastly amused when we told him of our hopes.

"He doesn't look like much of an adventurer, sir, but he's certainly a change from the great run of people I've met. Still, I carn't see how we're going to keep him against his will!"

"Neither can I, Tommy."

"Use a little persuasion."

"But suppose he won't persuade?"

"What's the use of crossing bridges," Tommy grinned. "If he won't persuade, then sit on his head—anything, I don't care! The main thing is—keep him!"

CHAPTER III
THE GIRL IN THE CAFÉ

Next morning began the conversion, or rather the persuasion, of Monsieur Dragot to remain a while longer with the *Whim*. Pete started off with another triumphant breakfast and before our guest had gone far with it his face was agleam with pleasure. Tommy and I put ourselves out to be agreeable, telling him jokes that sometimes registered but frequently did not. Yet we were on most affable terms when, stuffed to repletion, we leaned back and lighted cigarettes.

"Professor," Tommy suggested, "I think if you stay with us you'll have a better chance to find that child!"

Our guest beamed agreeably at the appelative, then looked toward me.

"I'm sure of it," I said. "We've nowhere to go but anywhere, and that ought to fall in with your plans."

"*Pardieu*, you overwhelm me! You mean I may sail about with you, searching?"

"Nothing simpler," I assured him. "We've rather taken a fancy to you, haven't we, Tommy?"

"Double it," Tommy laughed. "We agreed last night that you looked like a million-dollar bill to us!"

"Oh, my boys," Monsieur sputtered with embarrassment and pleasure, "you disarm my power to thank you—see, I blush!"

"Damned if he isn't," Tommy grinned at me. "What d'you know about this little gezabo, anyhow!"

Monsieur's face grew more composed as he showed his interest in a new word.

"You say—gazebo?" he asked, blandly. "Is that not a belvedere?"

"Gazebo is, yes; but I said gezabo—that's you!"

"Your American Indian language?"

"Sure thing. Pure talk. If you're interested in Indians, stick around. Why not get the Havana police to help us hunt the kiddie?"—I had known that before long Tommy would be using a first personal pronoun.

"Bah! They are of no value! But even I have small hope of finding her. The report was written nearly six years ago, and she has been gone upwards of twenty years."

"So it's a she," Tommy looked over at me and nodded. "Well, nearly six years, and upwards of twenty, plus what she was when she left home, leads me to believe the lady's almost old enough to take care of herself!"

Monsieur considered this a great joke, exclaiming:

"It is not so much as that! She is but three—to me, always three! Yet, as you say, I might better find her with you than anywhere! A despairing search, my boys!"

Tommy's eyes were twinkling as he murmured sympathetically:

"If it's a three-year-old you want, there's a place in Havana called 'Casa de Beneficencia Maternidad,' where furtive-eyed damsels leave kiddies at twilight, ring the doorbell, and beat it. You might pick up one there, as a last resort."

"But—but," Monsieur began to sputter, when I threw an orange at Tommy, explaining to our agitated guest that he was a cut-up devoid of ideas, really an intellectual outcast.

"Well," he cried, seeming to exude pleasure, "I will stay with you a while, eh? Maybe we can teach him something—this cut-upping Tommy of yours!"

He had fallen in with our scheme most agreeably, and later Tommy confided to me that he was glad we wouldn't have to sit on the old fellow's head.

Passing that afternoon beneath Morro Castle, the *Whim* tacked prettily through the entrance of Havana harbor and in another scant two miles dropped anchor.

Havana Bay is a dancing sheet of water, as bright as the skies and hardly less contagious than the city's laughter. But when one drops anchor and then hoists it up, one recoils from the black and slimy mud those blue waves hide; and this circumstance, slight as it may seem, held a potent influence on our future.

Riding nearby was another yacht, in size and design very much like the *Whim*, except that her rigging had an old-fashioned cut. Her masts were checked with age and, where our craft showed polished brass, she long ago had resorted to white paint. At the same time, she gave the impression of aristocracy—broken-down aristocracy, if you choose. No bunting fluttered at her masthead, no country's emblem waved over her taffrail, and the only hint of nationality or ownership was a rather badly painted word *Orchid* on her name plate. Taken altogether, she was rather difficult to place.

These signs of poverty would have passed unobserved by us, had we not in coming to anchor swung between her moorings and the Machina wharf. Not that it made any serious difference, Gates explained, nor were we impertinently near, but it just missed being the scrupulously polite thing to have done—and Gates was a stickler on matters of yacht etiquette. So he felt uncomfortable about it, while at the same time being reluctant to hoist anchor and foul our decks with the bottom of Havana Bay. To be on the safe side he determined to megaphone apologies and consult her wishes. Twice he hailed, receiving no answer. Two sailors were seated forward playing cards—a surlier pair of ruffians would have been hard to find—but neither of them so much as glanced up.

"Let the professor try in Spanish," Tommy said.

Monsieur took the megaphone and did so, but with no better success. Then to our profound admiration he called in half a dozen languages; finally growling: "Lascars, likely!"—and proceeded to hail in something he afterwards explained was Lascar gibberish. All of which failed to attract the surly pair who played at cards.

"Now you might try Airedale and Pekinese," Tommy suggested, but this was lost on the serious little man. Yet he did call in another strangely sounding tongue, then with a sigh laid the megaphone down, saying:

"They must be stuffies!"

"Dummies, sir, dummies," Tommy corrected. "Nice people don't say stuffies, ever!"

"Your Tommy does so much cut-upping, eh!" he smiled at me. I had noticed that when preoccupied or excited the idioms of his various languages got tumbled into a rather hopeless potpourri.

Quarantine and customs were passed in the leisurely fashion of Cuban officials, and Monsieur asked to be sent immediately ashore, promising to return at sundown. There was a man, the secret agent, he explained, who held important information.

"I'll have the launch for you at Machina wharf, sir," Gates told him, but he refused to consider this, declaring that he could hire any of the boatmen thereabout to bring him out.

"He's that considerate, sir," Gates later confided to me. "But I carn't make head nor tail of him. Bilkins says he went in to lay out his clothes, and the things he's got stuck in those bags would astonish you!"

Nearing six o'clock a skiff drew alongside, being propelled by one oar—a method much in vogue with Havana harbormen—and when Monsieur came aboard we saw at once evidences of disappointment. His arms hung listlessly, and his large head drooped forward as if at last its weight had proven too great for the squat body.

"What's wrong?" I asked.

"How do you know there is anything wrong, my boy Jack?"

"You look so killingly happy," Tommy said, joining us.

Monsieur's pale eyes stared for a moment, then blinked several times before he murmured:

"The man I went to see is dead—murdered, just after he mailed that report. So I have no information. These police called it suicide because a knife lay in his hand. Bah! I could place a knife in the hand of any man I kill!"

"Was he a friend of yours?"

"No. I have never seen him. But he knew something!"

"He evidently knew too much," Tommy suggested.

"You speak true, my boy. It seems to be a dangerous thing here to know too much of certain matters!"

"Well," I laughed, trying to put a heartiness in my voice and drive away his depression, "let's go ashore for dinner! Then the Opera—and afterwards another bite where the high life eats? What-say, Professor?"

As it turned out, however, neither the dinner, nor all of Tommy's banter, nor Madame Butterfly sung in Spanish (as if it could!) succeeded in restoring Monsieur to a normal temper.

"We've simply got to make him laugh," I whispered to Tommy. "It's a matter of principle now!"

"Then wait till we have supper, and get him soused," my confederate cautiously replied. "That'll do it. But you'd better not drink much," he added. "How are the nerves this evening?"

"I've almost forgotten them," I answered.

But Tommy was persistent at times. Unknown to me he was now preparing a report to wire the Mater.

"Sleeping better?" he asked.

"Lots."

"Lying to me?"

"A little," I laughed outright. "But honestly I'm in heaps better shape!"

"Oh, I've seen you improving from day to day, but we want to put it over right. So don't hit the asphalt too hard tonight."

And in all justice to myself and my friendship to Tommy I really did not intend to. What place was it that some one said is paved with good intentions?

Leaving the Opera House we mixed with the laughing tide that flowed along the Prado, and by the merest chance—destinies of nations, much less our own, sometimes rest upon a merest chance—dropped in for supper at a fashionable place patronized by those who wish to see the brightest of Havana life. There were other places, of course, that might have offered quite as much, but this one happened to be on the route we had taken.

Midnight passed, but still we lingered, seated on the latticed balcony that encircles an inner court where cabaret features are held—suggestive of a bull ring. One rather piquant Spanish girl, playing her accompaniment on a guitar, gazed softly up at Tommy while singing about some wonderful Nirvana, an enchanted island that floated in a sea of love. It was a pretty song, even if more intense than temperate, and pleased with it he tossed her a coin; whereupon she tilted her chin and raised a shoulder, asking in the universal language of cabarets if she should not come up and drink a health with the *imperioso Señor*. But he, whose heart was beating against a twenty-page letter from a nymph in the Bluegrass region of Kentucky, laughed a negative, this time throwing her a flower that she kissed lightly and put in her hair.

We had supped well, the mandolins were now tinkling, incessantly, and this, mingled with the silvery tones of glasses touched in eager pledges, created an ensemble of sounds dear to the heart of every true Bohemian. Effects were good here. The ceilings and walls of our balcony were lighted by vari-colored electric bulbs artfully placed amidst growing vines that drooped in festoons above the tables, producing a fairy-like enchantment. And, indeed, the café proved to be a mart not only of enchantments but entertainments, including a popular gambling salon.

At last, in desperation seeing that Monsieur refused to be cheered, Tommy sprang up, saying:

"Come, gezabo, let's court Dame Roulette! Join us, Jack?"

This I declined, and watched them move off arm in arm. But a strange thing arrested my attention for, as they preceded down the corridor, I saw a man in yachting clothes—the uniform of a captain—draw quickly back into an alcove as if wanting to escape discovery. When they had passed he looked out, more fearfully than curiously, and after a moment of indecision slowly followed them. Urged by a suspicion that this was in some way associated with the professor, I arose and also followed. Yet upon reaching the salon the stranger was nowhere to be seen. Tommy and Monsieur were each buying a stack of chips, the place seemed quiet and orderly, so without being observed I returned to my table.

Now left alone I leaned back, idly twisting the stem of my glass, looking over the sea of merry people who made a picture that quickened interest. For I am particularly fond of sitting apart and watching an assemblage of handsomely groomed men and women laughing, talking and making love. I like to guess whether fears or tears or desperate courage hide behind their gayety; whether the rapidly wagging tongues are uttering inanities or planning naughty things; whether the love-making will stop with coffee and liqueur, or, lighted by them, burn into eternity.

All phases of human banality and human enigma seemed to be represented. There were languid beauties of the Latin type whose drooping eyes might have expressed *ennui*, passion, pride—anything, in fact, that one's humor chose to fancy; the blonde by adoption was there, with heavy ear-rings of jet, whose habit was that of looking slant-wise through her cigarette smoke and raising one black, though carefully plucked, eyebrow; also there were a few American women, by far the most smartly dressed. Great was the throb of life in this discreet and fashionable café. I felt its tremendous emphasis, and was content.

Then, quite without warning, I caught my breath as my glance fell upon a girl dining with an old chap but three tables away. Among the habitués of the Ritzes of two continents there could not have been found another like her, for never had I beheld a face as exquisite—and I've seen many. It possessed a beauty that left me helpless—yet there was an indefinable sadness in it that might have suggested a haunting fear.

One of the lights among the vines hung close to her, and I could see these things. Even could I see the color of her eyes, deep purple eyes—the tone the wild iris takes at twilight. When she leaned one way I might have thought the rich abundance of her hair contained spun copper or deep red gold, and again I would have sworn it matched the mellow brown of chestnuts; in all forming an arrangement of waves, each refusing to stay in place yet never really getting out of order, each coquetting with a subtle mischief that found an echo in her lips. Her neck and shoulders were of that perfection that men realize but can not analyze; and her mouth, laughing or in repose, was maddening.

And there was an added charm quite apart from hair and eyes and lips. This I had never before seen in any face. Animation? Yes, and more. Interest in the life about her? Assuredly, to a very marked degree. Wildness? That was it!—a wildness, subtly blended with refinement, that found expression in every quick look; as if someone had put a fawn there from the forest and it was trying, half humorously, half confidently, to keep itself from running away in fright. It was this glory of wildness that she typified which made my cheeks grow hot with watching.

But who has ever made a picture worthy of his dreams! How, then, can I describe this girl, when painter, sculptor, writer—all—would miserably fail at attempting to portray a beauty whereon imagination might gaze in frank amazement and admit itself surpassed! Here, indeed, was all the vital, colorful magnetism of a type that men are quick to die for!

Her gown—yet how can man describe a woman's gown? It was a very rich affair and added to the picture. But this I did observe distinctly, that in revealing her arms and shoulders there was no slightest hint of that abandonment of *décolleté* which denotes the approach of feminine despair, nor was the color in her cheeks a result of anything less pure than the kiss of air and sunshine.

Her *vis-à-vis,* almost too old to have been her father, was one of those whose nationality is difficult to place. His hair, mustache and Vandyke beard were gray; he was tall, thin, and perhaps seventy-five years old. His complexion impressed one most unpleasantly because of its sallow, almost yellow, hue; and although I had not yet had a full-face view of him I intuitively knew that his teeth were long and thin and yellow. A slight palsy never let his head be still, as if some persistent agent were making him deny, eternally deny, an inarticulate accusation—as accusations of the conscience perforce must be.

Despite his grumpy silence he showed an air of repressed excitement, sending frequent, shifty glances over the room; and that he possessed the temper of a fiend I did not doubt after seeing him turn upon the waiter for some trifling omission and reduce that usually placid individual to a state of amazed incapacity. Then a quick, really a pitiful, look of terror came into the girl's eyes as she shrank back in her chair. It lasted but a second before she was again making herself agreeable—acting, of course—and I wanted to cross to him and demand: "Why is this lady afraid?"

I hated the man; at first sight I loathed him. It was one of those antipathies sometimes observed in dogs that see each other from a distance—hair up and teeth bared. The feeling is spontaneous, unpredictable, and the usual result is fight.

Up to this time she had not seen me, or even known of my insignificant existence; but suddenly, as though it were a sally of banter whose blade he parried in the nick of time, her laughter-bathed eyes darted past him and squarely met my own; her lips sobered into a half parted expression of interest and, some strange thought—perhaps unbidden—coming into her mind, sent the blood surging to her cheeks. As quickly as this happened it had gone, and again she seemed to be absorbing the attention of her *vis-à-vis*.

Once, years ago in the Dolomites, I thoughtlessly struck my staff upon a piece of rock when, lo, a wonderful tone arose therefrom. And the memory of that rich, unbidden sound was re-awakened now as the contact of our glances stirred something which thrilled me with a maddening sense of harmony. As an E string vibrates when another E is struck somewhere near to it, so my being vibrated with each tilt of her head, each movement of her lips. Yet however much I conjured the magnet of my will to make her look again, she successfully, if coquettishly, resisted.

The Spanish waiter came up softly to refill my glass; an attention I permitted, murmuring happily:

"Right, kiddo! Stay me with flagons, comfort me with champagne, for my heart is faint with love!"—only Solomon didn't sing it quite like that, the fickle old dog, nor did my waiter understand me, which was just as well.

Engrossed with watching her I saw a new look come into her face as she quickly whispered something across the table. Her *vis-à-vis* turned impatiently as a man approached them, who to my surprise was the yacht captain—the fellow who had apparently followed Tommy and Monsieur. He was a well-built blond, with a bullet-shaped head, high cheek bones and deep set eyes—pig eyes. His right cheek bore several scars which, considering his type, strongly suggested a German of University dueling experiences. So I looked on him with a livelier suspicion, even as she seemed to be doing.

In an undertone he now said something that brought the old man to his feet. With fear written on their faces they talked for several minutes, during which the blond jerked his head once or twice toward the gambling rooms. The girl had leaned forward watching them intently. Then with a peremptory order the old one sent him away and sank back into his chair; but a moment later, clutching the tablecloth, he spoke a few words that made her recoil in evident horror.

I did not know what to do or what to think, so I merely watched with every sense alert. I saw him call the waiter for his settlement, I saw him take out a large roll of money and with trembling fingers peel off the outside bill—a new and crinkly fifty-dollar note. I saw the girl idly marking on the winecard with a small gold pencil, though her eyes were veiling an intense excitement; and when the waiter returned with a pile of change which the old man began to count, I saw her furtively slip the winecard to her lap. A moment later it fell to the floor as she arose to leave.

Together they started toward the exit, but having taken a few steps she left him with a brief word and returned, presumably for her glove. Partially free from his eternal vigilance, she raised her eyes without dissimulation and looked quickly, appealingly into mine; then down at her hand, on which she leaned, whose fingers were unfolding from a little ball of paper. Again into my eyes she looked—a look of infinite appeal.

Across the void from her world to my own she was signaling—trying to tell me what?—and frantically my fancy sprang to translate the message. But as the man, with growing agitation, had been watching narrowly throughout this—a condition of which I felt sure she must be acutely aware—I dared not make the slightest sign. Yet she seemed to understand and, joining him, they passed out.

I pounced upon that crumpled ball of paper and was back in my chair unfolding it with nervous fingers. Feverishly pressing out the creases I saw that it was, indeed, a corner torn from the winecard, and written upon it—nothing. Absolutely nothing!

Perhaps I should have laughed, but as a matter of fact I cursed. Deep in my soul I cursed. Her little joke, her pretty bit of acting, had left a stinging sense of loss. As suddenly as this ruthless comet swept into my orbit it had swung out and on; for one delicious moment we had touched across the infinite, but now my harmony was shattered, the strings of my harp were snapped, curled up, and could not be made to play again.

But the Spanish girl was playing her guitar, once more singing her impassioned song of the enchanted island in its sea of love, which made me pity myself so much that I permitted the waiter again to fill my glass. What a wondrous adventure this night might have brought!

Such thoughts wore not to be profaned by the companionship of Tommy and Monsieur, so I slipped away, hailed a cab and alighted at the Machina wharf. The boatman there, whom I aroused to take me out, was one of the most stupid fellows I've ever encountered. At any rate, someone was stupid.

Going aboard the yacht I stood for a moment listening to the lonely sweep of his oar sculling shoreward through the murky night. Over the castellated walls of La Cabaña raced low, angry clouds. Was it a storm brewing, or had some supernal madness touched the night?

The watch forward called in a guarded voice: "All right, sir?" to which I answered, "All right," then went cautiously across deck and crept down the companionway stairs. The cabin was dark so I felt for my stateroom, passed in and closed the door. Somehow my fingers could not locate the light jet, but what matter? In three minutes I had undressed and was fast asleep.

CHAPTER IV
NIRVANA

A pleasant sense of motion came over me that suggested cradling waves, and I was sleepily wondering why we had gone out on a day that portended storms, when a tapping at my stateroom door was followed by someone whispering:

"Aren't you ever going to get up, you lazy old dear?"

It was a girl's voice.

Gradually and cautiously I drew the sheet about my chin, feeling no little confused to have a girl five feet away whispering pet names at me through a thin partition.

"Aren't you?" she repeated, more sweetly imperious.

"You bet," I stammered.

"Then do hurry! It's almost ten, and I've been waiting such a long time!"

Whereupon I heard her moving off, pressing her hands against the panels for steadiness, and there struck me as having been an endearing pathos in the way she said: "such a long time!"

This was, no doubt, some of Tommy's doing. He had invited friends aboard for luncheon, and was now daring one of them to play this joke. But my glance turned to the room, to its equipment and toilette articles which were large and curiously shaped, and the numbing truth crept into my brain that the stupid boatman had put me on the wrong yacht.

I had known some tight places in France, but this one simply squeezed me all over. There was nothing for it, of course, but go out and explain—yet how could a chap appear at noon draped in a sheet! The situation confused me, but I decided to search the wardrobe, of my unknown host, to borrow his razor, appropriate a new toothbrush that should be found in a box somewhere, and select flannels and linens in keeping with the hour. Still balanced between confusion and panic I must have done these things because, fittingly attired though with no very good fit, I opened my door, stepped softly along the passageway, and entered the cabin.

On a wide couch built in at one side a girl lay reading. Her head was toward me, but as I advanced she arose with a low cry of gladness, saying:

"So you're here at last—!" then with a little gasp drew back, facing me in the most entrancing attitude of bewilderment.

It was the girl who had left that ball of paper!

The sea, always my friend, at this moment did a rather decent thing; it gave the yacht a firm but gentle lurch and sent us into each other's arms. Perhaps nothing else in all the world of chances could so effectively have broken the ice between us, for we were laughing as I helped her back to the couch; and, as our eyes met, again we laughed.

"I didn't know," she said, "that Father brought a guest aboard last night!"

"Awkward of him, wasn't it?" I stammered, sparring for time.

"One is apt to be awkward in weather like this," she graciously admitted.

"You don't know how profoundly aware I am of—of how terribly true that is," I stumbled along. "Is he on deck?" For, oh, if I could only get to see him five minutes alone!

"No, he's unusually lazy this morning; but I've called, him, the old dear!"

A chill crept up my spine—crept up, crept down, and then criss-crossed. But she must know of her mistake before we had gone so far that putting me ashore would be a serious inconvenience—for I knew he would put me ashore at the nearest point, if not, indeed, set me adrift in an open boat. Therefore I suggested:

"Wouldn't it be a good idea to call him again? It's rather important!"

"Oh, you think we shouldn't have gone out in a storm like this? I've been dreadfully uneasy!"

"No danger at all," I declared, with affected indifference, adding: "The weather isn't half as rough as 'the old dear' will be, take my word for it!"

A shadow of mystification passed over her wonderful face, yet she smiled with well-bred tolerance, saying:

"You are quite droll."

"Drollery is the brother of good fellowship," I replied, helping her across the reeling cabin. As I had feared, she went directly to my room where the door had swung back showing an empty bunk.

"Why, he's up, after all," she glanced over her shoulder at me.

"I believe he is," I idiotically affirmed.

"But where?"—this more to herself.

"Hiding, maybe," I ventured, taking a facetious squint about.

"Hiding?" she asked, in mild surprise.

"Er—playing a trick on us! He's a funny old dog at tricks!"

"Funny old dog?" She drew slightly away from me. "Do you mean my father, Mr.—er?"

"Jack," I prompted, more than ever embarrassed and wishing the ocean would come up and swallow me; for I realized, alas, that my gods, by whom I was reasonably well remembered in so far as concerned physique, had been shamelessly remiss in their bestowal of brains.

"Jack?" she slowly repeated. "What an odd name!"

This made me feel queer.

"Where do you live," I asked, "that you think it's an odd name? The States are crawling with Jacks! It's even the Democratic emblem!"

Her perplexity was fast approaching alarm when we heard a muffled report above, followed by a trembling of the yacht. Someone called an order that sounded far away in the wind.

"Hold tight," I said, "while I see if anything's wrong!"

But I did not leave her side, knowing exactly what had happened. We had snapped our mainsheet, that was all; letting the boom swing out and putting us in the trough of the waves where we might expect a few wobbly minutes until the sailors could work in a new line. There was no danger and I reassured her at once, but she merely asked:

"Was my father on deck?"

"I didn't look," I answered, wondering why she thought I knew.

"Won't you see?" Her patience was becoming exhausted.

"I'm crazy to. But first let me help you back—you can't make it alone!"

"Oh, yes, I can," she murmured. "I always make things alone!"

I tried to fathom the meaning of this, but gave it up and started to go on deck. If I could take her father off to one side and explain, well and good. He would perhaps sympathize with my mistake when he understood that it was partially the result of a desire to fill Monsieur with spirits. Considering this, I spoiled everything by asking:

"What does he look like?"

"My father?" she gasped, in a wondering way.

"No—yes—certainly not! I mean—oh, this is intolerable! I don't know your father, never saw him in my life—unless he was the one with you last night when you drove me frantic with that ball of paper trick! But what you did has nothing to do with my being here. I've not wilfully followed. A stupid boatman mistook your yacht for my own when I was—I mean to say, when I was too engrossed with the memory of you to notice his mistake."

From alarm her look gave way to wonderment, then almost to mirth. It was a hard place for a girl to be in, and I expected her to leave me now, find the old chap and promptly have me hanged to a yard-arm. The fact that there are no yard-arms on schooner yachts made no difference. And I do believe she was considering that when a sailor passed us, looking enough like Tommy to have been his twin brother.

"Jack," she said to him, "tell Mr. Graham to come below!"

The fellow saluted and left, and I stared at her in surprise, saying:

"Then my name can't seem very odd to you, Miss Graham!"

She was regarding me as though trying to discover what kind of a species I was that had got on her father's yacht, when the sailor came back followed by a husky brute in uniform. Intuitively I stiffened to meet the crisis, but even at this eleventh hour a respite came.

"He ain't aboard," the other Jack whispered, and the captain—for the burly one was only the captain, after all—saluted, saying:

"I've just now found out, ma'am, he ain't aboard!"

"Not aboard? What do you mean?"

"After bringing you on last night he went ashore again to get a little ball of paper, but told me to sail the minute he returned. I don't understand it, ma'am, for later the watch woke me to say Mr. Graham had come."

"Good Lord," I groaned. "It was I, and not your father, who answered the watch."

For several minutes we stared blankly into each other's faces, but it was she who broke the deadly silence.

"We must hurry back," she calmly told him, adding with a nervous catch in her breath: "What a joke on Daddy!"

"A scream of a joke," I muttered, "—one he'll roar over till God-knows-when!"

"We can't go back, Miss Sylvia," the captain now said. "When our mainsheet parted the boom gybed so hard that it opened a seam. It may hold on this tack, and it may not, but we'd sink if the weather hit us on the other side. So I'm making for Key West."

A suspicious quiver played over her lips as the big fellow turned and went upstairs, and I began to hate myself rather cordially.

"Do you happen to have that—that ball of paper?" she asked, when the threatened storm of tears had been controlled.

"No, I threw it down."

A look of terror came into her eyes as she gasped:

"Then he'll find it!"

"It won't matter if he does! You hadn't written anything on it!"

"Did you look on both sides of it?"

"I—I think so; of course, I must have. Did you write on the other side?"

"I don't know which the other side is that you refer to," she answered with some show of anger. "There were two sides, you know. Still, it can't much matter now whether it had any sides or not."

This was very perplexing, the words no more so than the way she looked at me while pronouncing them. Yet I hardly thought it should give her as much concern as our leaky boat. The storm had grown worse, and more than once she glanced anxiously at the portholes whose glass, over half the time, were submerged by swirls of greenish water.

"It'll turn out all right," I said, gently. "And you mustn't be afraid of this storm."

"I'm not afraid!"

"Yes, you are," I tenderly persisted, "but your skipper looks like a man who'll bring us through."

"Your concern is most flattering," she frigidly replied. "But fear of storms, and distress over the unhappiness one may be causing others, are quite different phases of emotion."

"I stand corrected and rebuked," I humbly acknowledged. "Yet I want you to know that my concern springs from a deeper source than flattery. I want honestly to assure you—"

"Of course, there's less danger here than in port," she continued in the same icy tone, utterly ignoring me, "for here, at least, we can't be boarded at night by irresponsible people."

I winced.

"By people who drink," she added.

I winced again, for I seemed to be getting the winces now, and couldn't stop.

"That isn't fair, Miss Graham! Circumstances are against me, but you might suspend judgment till you know me better!"

"The circumstances require no further evidence," she said, with supreme indifference.

"But circumstantial evidence," I felt pleased at turning her phrase, "often wears the cap and bells, instead of the wig and gown!"

"I'm discovering that," she murmured, and added with a touch of sarcasm: "The knack of making a catch phrase is often very agreeable, but presupposes no presence of an idea."

Now I thought this most unkind of her, because I had been quite set up by my retort; so, arising with as much dignity as the waves would permit, I buttoned my coat, remarking:

"Then I'll go on deck, and leave you."

The coat was tight and, while fastening it, I felt something in an inner pocket press against my side. There are few impulses more natural than to investigate anything that has a curious feel in one's pocket, so thrusting in my hand I brought forth a small round frame of brass, made in the imitation of a porthole, encircling her photograph. This would not have happened had I remembered being in her father's clothes, but it was done, and I stood looking first at the picture and then at her.

"Give it to me," she cried.

"I don't see why," I temporized, not at all loath at having this chance for revenge.

"It's mine," she imperiously announced.

"It may be a picture of you, but, as you perceive, not at this moment your picture," and my eyes lowered again and lingered on it, for it was indeed a wonderful likeness, moving me strangely by its amazing beauty. The frame, too, gave it added charm, as she seemed really to be looking out of a porthole.

"Give that to me this instant," she said, with such a show of passion that I passively surrendered it, and started to walk away. Yet some cruel power held my feet. I tried again to move, but could not.

Overhead the men were working desperately at the pumps to keep us afloat. One of them left his place and passed us, whispering:

"It's no use—we're gone!"

The cabin was in twilight as I again turned to her. She had crawled to the far corner of the couch, and lay staring at the ceiling—waiting. Here in this dismal room, alone and facing death with a courage amazing to behold, she made a picture which so stirred me that despite earlier wounded feelings I went to her side. The little hands were cold and inert when I took them, but her fingers tightened ever so gently.

"Did he say we're going down?" she quietly asked, without turning her head.

"Yes," I answered—though both of us spoke in whispers.

"I'm sorry to have been unkind," she said, withdrawing one of her hands and laying it on the back of my own—for Death is a great leveler of conventions.

The pathetic resignation in her voice brought hot tears to my eyes and, raising her fingers to my lips, I murmured:

"You're the sweetest angel I ever knew!"

For a long time we sat in the gathering darkness, holding to each other as two little children lost in the night. Finally I heard her whisper:

"Why am I not afraid—now?"

I turned and looked down at her; down into those eyes gazing back at me through a magnetizing moisture that drew my face nearer, nearer.

"Because," I said, "we've found something which outlives death!"

"Yes," she whispered, as her arms moved sweetly up around my neck—but the next instant they held me off, as she gasped: "Look! Look! The end is here!"

Quite a foot of water was swashing back and forth over the cabin floor, while a steady stream poured down the companionway stairs. Yes, the end was here!

"Take this," she hurriedly pressed into my hand the round brass frame that held her picture—the frame fashioned after a porthole. "Keep it—then come to me! Swear!"

"I swear," I gasped. "But where shall I find you? In what strange land will you be?"

Her eyes were wide with a frightened look that even in our extremity gave the lie to fear. Through parted, expectant lips a trembling sigh of inexpressible sweetness seemed to carry her answer; it was brought by the mystery of her look, by the clasp of our senses—for I know she did not speak a word:

"I'll wait beneath the palms on one of many, many
islands,
Set as emerald jewels in an ever-changing sea;

> My hammock swings beside a pool of purling, crystal water Whisp'ring to the shadows of a lonely Arcady;
> The Spanish moss hangs solemn in long streamers from the cypress,
> The paths are soft and noiseless with dead needles of the pine,
> The nights are still and fragrant, and I'll wait—

Ah!" she broke the measure with a despairing cry and struggled to get from my arms, as another voice, far away but familiar, began to call my name. Then slowly my eyes opened and beheld Bilkins looking down at me, in my own stateroom, where my clothes were lying as I had thrown them off the night before.

"I've called you twice, sir," he was saying. "It's almost ten o'clock, and I'm afraid your bath is cold."

"I want it cold," I murmured, staring up at him. "God, Bilkins, I've had a most extraordinary dream!"

"If it's bad don't tell it before breakfast, sir, whatever you do! Just hold on a minute, and I'll bring your tray right in!"

CHAPTER V
"TO THE VERY END!"

I dressed hurriedly, wanting to be on deck and get a more searching view of the yacht near which we had anchored. Stepping out into the cockpit, therefore, I looked hungrily toward her mooring place, but it was vacant.

"Where has she gone?" I asked Tommy, who was the only one about.

"The etiquette of this yacht requires its owner first to say 'good morning' when he comes up at break of day," he grinned at me accusingly. "The little professor won eight hundred dollars from the proud Castilian last night—I hope Dame Fortune was as kind to you!"

"She was diverting," I admitted. "Where's Monsieur now?"

"'Sleep. We didn't turn in till an unholy hour. He got up at seven from force of habit, fussed around a while, took some pictures of the neighborhood and developed them, but by that time the poor old door-mat couldn't keep his eyes open. Do you know he wept all the way home last night, telling me how good we were to him?"

We laughed.

"But, Tommy, where's the yacht that was over there yesterday?"

"Her? Oh, she cleared this morning—and listen to me, boy, if you want to see a dream just cast your eye on that last film of Monsieur's!"

See a dream! Great heavens, if I wanted to see a dream!

He led the way aft to a ribbon of freshly developed film hanging from the boom to dry and, as I gingerly raised it to the light, he went on to explain:

"It was boorish of him, but I'm to blame. We were standing forward after breakfast snapping the harbor when that yacht weighed anchor and swung across our bow less than thirty feet off; and, Jack, with the prettiest girl I ever saw—barring Nell—looking out at us through a porthole. 'Shoot her,' I whispered. So he swung his camera and shot, and she gave a darling little gasp and ducked."

I had come to the last negative and there, with the porthole in exact imitation of the round brass frame, was the same beautiful face of the same beautiful girl I'd left in that wondrous dream!

"Sylvia Graham," I cried.

"The devil," Tommy straightened up. "Graham's the chap who owns that boat! Gates found it out this morning, but how did you know?"

My eyes were glued to the negative.

"They cleared for Key West, Tommy?"

"So Gates said. Has he told you?"

"I haven't seen him since yesterday," I murmured, still unable to look away from that strip of gelatine which held the image of my world.

"He didn't know anything about it yesterday, either," Tommy announced, and I felt him regarding me in some slight amusement, as though he thought I had a secret up my sleeve that I was trying to keep from him. "What's the cute little idea, son? I've told you where she cleared for, now clear me up!"

"Tommy," I let the film swing back and caught him by the shoulders, "Miss Graham's father carries a photograph like that in the inside pocket of a white flannel coat which hangs behind his stateroom door!"

He looked me up and down, this time more seriously, and murmured:

"Whiz-bang!—but you must have been heroically decorated last night! Still, I can't see that it hurt you much, for you look about twice as fit as when we left Miami."

"I'll bet I didn't drink an ounce more than you, or Monsieur," I declared. "The facts of the matter are, Tommy, that there's a lot mighty curious about this picture!"

"Really?" he grinned. "You go below and take something with a dash of bitters in it."

"Dry up," I snapped. "I tell you I'm going to catch up with that yacht if we have to follow her around the world!"

He gave a low whistle, saying with good-natured tolerance:

"Looks like the big adventure's on the wing, doesn't it! Well, I don't mind chasing the old tub, or doing any other damphule thing in reason, but what's the game? Put me next! When was this earthquake that loosened all your little rivets? Speak up, son—I'm your *padre*!"

"It's hard to explain," I turned again to the negative, feeling too serious for his asinine humor. "But I'll honestly try to before night. This girl needs me. I don't know why or how, but she does. What's more, I'm going to find her. It's the most unheard-of situation, old man."

"I'd be ashamed to belittle a situation like this by the mere term 'unheard-of,'" he now laughed outright. "Anyhow, she doesn't need you at present quite as much as you need scientific attention—and I hear the professor moving around!"

Stepping to the companionway door he bawled some nonsense to our guest about bringing up his medicine chest and a rope, then turned back to me.

"You see, Jack, I consider this to be serious. As long as I've known you that lady in the porthole is the first female you've ever thought of with any sign of, what I might call, *ardeur*. Where you met her is your business, but how you're going to get her must naturally concern us all. Hence Monsieur to consult with!"

We could hear Monsieur's grunts and wheezes before he appeared, and on catching sight of me he actually skipped to us. It was a grotesque exhibition that made me burst out laughing. His hair was tousled, his eyes were half closed, and he looked about as much like a scrambled egg as anything I could think of.

"We lost you last night," he cried. "You ran away from us?"

"He was poisoned," Tommy blandly answered, "and now his heart's kind of upside-down and twisty."

"Upside-down and twisty?" he gasped.

"Tommy doesn't mean it's anything dangerous, just an affection; a kind of—a kind of—"

"A kind of affectionate affection," Tommy put in. "You see, he was stung there, and it itches, and he can't scratch it."

"Stung on the heart? *Sacré nomme!*" The old fellow clasped his head in both hands and stared at us.

"You fascinating little ass," Tommy murmured, "did you ever hear of love?"

"Love?" the professor's face beamed into twice its usual breadth. "You, my boy Jack? Is she a Spanish mademoiselle?"

"Good Lord, whoever heard of a Spanish mademoiselle! No, Jack says that she's a lady in need, who lives in the pocket of her father's white serge coat that hangs behind his stateroom door; and she's in a helluva lot of trouble, but Jack doesn't know where else she is, so we're going to comb out the universe and find her! Get the idea?"

"I will drink some coffee," he stammered, and disappeared.

Tommy and I decided that we must be after the *Orchid* without losing a minute, as there was still a chance of drawing in sight of her before she could leave Key West. Yet I first had a mission to fulfill at the café, nor did I confide this at once to him lest he brand me a total wreck. I knew that he was delighted at the prospect of this bizarre chase, however chimeric it might seem to him, for he possessed the faculty of "playing-true" even in the veriest of fairy-tales. So for the moment I let the other matter rest, not realizing at the time that he had read more of it in my face than I meant to show.

Gates, also, had caught the excitement and was waiting with the launch to push off; and thus, while he concluded official duties at the port, I entered the café—in the present unfriendly light a changed place from the night before. As luck would have it, my own waiter was the first man I saw.

"Do you remember finding a small piece of crumpled paper on my table last night?" I asked.

"*Si*, Señor; the mad *caballero* came for it."

"Did he get it?"

"But, no, Señor," the waiter lowered his voice. "Yet he came near to, being much angry, and calling you—pardon me!"

"Well, what? What, man?"

He still hesitated, so I carelessly took out my wallet. It's amazing, the power of a wallet!

"He demanded the paper of our *maître d'hôtel*, saying you, Señor, were a pig of a detective—and as we admire the detective not at all, everyone searched for it. But I had seen other things, Señor," he smiled knowingly.

"You have it?"

"*Si, si,*—but not so loud! Could I give it to the old one? Even a poor waiter may sometimes observe! *Mas vale saber que haber, Señor*," he shrugged and smiled as the ancient proverb slipped from his tongue.

"You've a mighty level head on you, kid," I agreed; a metaphor he may or may not have understood. There was no doubt in my mind that his words, "wisdom is better than wealth," were never more aptly spoken.

"I saw it after you left, Señor, and put it away—so! The mad *caballero* soon came—he was not happy. We searched the floor, and all the time he was shaking his head and mumbling that Mademoiselle had confessed to writing it—and to a detective! He was quite crazy. Ah, with what care and sympathy did I help him, Señor, and how generously did he reward my careful search!"

He shrugged and smiled, then drew the paper from his pocket, and I slipped it into mine—passing him back another kind of paper that he slipped into his with a grateful bow.

"Do you know who the man is, or if that was his daughter?"

"No, Señor. I have seen them, but can not remember where. Carlos served their table—but Carlos is stupid," he shrugged compassionately.

The moment my cab turned the first corner I feverishly took out that precious paper. Sure enough, on one side were marks *I* had not seen, but the pencilling was very faint—having had the soft tablecloth for a desk, perhaps—and showed only a meandering line, curving in and out through a group of dots. From every angle I studied it, coming to two conclusions: first, that it could mean nothing; and second, that I must have imbibed more freely than I thought to have overlooked this.

But now I saw, fainter than the dots, something that resembled written words. They were so obscure, indeed, that although the light was excellent my jostling cab made it impossible for me to decipher them. Telling the driver to stop, I bent over again, and laboriously read:

"I am on Mr. Graham's yacht in great da—"

At this place, as I looked back upon last night, the old chap had indicated his wish to leave, and she, tearing off a corner, had let the wine card slip to the floor. It explained the broken word, the sudden interruption; and this much was not a dream, neither was the disturbing message in my hands—for what else but "danger" could the "da" mean?

All was ready to weigh anchor when I stepped aboard, and when we were outside the harbor, drawing nicely toward the north, Tommy came up grumbling.

"This mystery's getting heavy," he said. "Put us wise!"

So I pushed him into a chair, and called the professor and Gates; then when the four of us were comfortably settled, the cushions fitting our shoulders, our pipes alight, our spirits glowing with that exhilaration which a yacht can bring as she lays over and cuts the waves, I told the story from beginning to end—sparing Sylvia where I should.

For some minutes they smoked with their eyes downcast. Then Monsieur looked up in his mild way, asking:

"May I see the paper?"

I passed it to him and we drew together, studying it.

"This is the most singular part of the affair," he said, leaning back, "because it first came to you in fact, although the man's returning for it was told in the dream—and later verified. The dots and line mean nothing, perhaps, but that interrupted message!—ah, truly it spells danger! What danger? She spoke of no danger in the dream?"

Now, it may seem strange or not, but I had begun to lose track of the places where the dream came in and where they left off. The actual was so woven with the unreal that I had to stop and consider this question. The paper episode, the vividness with which Sylvia had appeared to me, the brass frame made in the imitation of a porthole, and the camera's film, all contributed to a confusion not unshared by my three friends.

"It's a darned funny coincidence," said Tommy, in an awed voice. "But, Jack, you don't think more seriously of it, do you?"

"Would we be chasing these people if I didn't?" I temporized with another question.

He seemed to be troubled, glancing toward the thoughtful professor as if expecting him to speak, and when this was not forthcoming he asked again:

"Well, friend gezabo, what do you think?"

The little scientist lowered his pipe, sighed and impressively answered:

"It is not given to all men to see this invisible agency at work."

The profoundly solemn way he said this made Tommy's eyes grow round. Ghost and mystery tales imparted during his childhood by black mammies and other negro servants had endowed him with a considerable amount of superstition that not infrequently prevailed against his better judgment. So now, when the erudite Monsieur treated my experience with reverence, even introducing an element of mysticism, Tommy wavered.

"Whiz-bang! You don't really believe that spooky stuff, do you?"

"To my knowledge," Monsieur answered, "I have seen one case. You have heard me speak of Azuria. Well, many years ago a friend of mine, daughter of our King Christopher, fell to worrying about her cousin, a profligate who divided his time between the palace and Paris. As a punishment for various escapades the King had curtailed his allowance to a mere pittance, yet he seemed in spite of this to have as much money as before. It was this fact that worried my friend—the fear of a scandal.

"One night she dreamed that her child, a girl of nearly three, was being kidnaped. She arose in her sleep to follow, walking the length of the palace, and awoke to find herself in the cousin's room—standing, indeed, behind his chair as he bent beneath a shaded lamp earnestly working on a plate for spurious money. Instantly she threatened to expose him to the King.

"Well, to shorten a long story, that night he did actually kidnap the child, leaving a note to my friend in which he suggested a compromise.

But there was no compromise with villainy in her make-up. The old King was much affected. Yet there were things in the air at that time, delicate situations of state, which demanded consideration. The kidnaping, if made public, would have produced a most disquieting effect in certain quarters. Our treaty with a powerful state had just been signed, based on the little princess' betrothal—you see? Therefore, her disappearance must be kept a secret for a while, so the police of the world were not notified. But that night ten men—a few of them loyal subjects and the others paid agents—left the capital. Thus a relentless search began, being carried to the ends of the world. A noted rogue, that fellow was—yet, strange to say, in earlier life a man of parts, an esthetic, an artist and musician of great ability; but *mon Dieu*, what a scoundrel!"

"Where did they find the little princess?" Tommy asked, after a pause.

"She was never found," he answered softly. "Word once came that she had died; again that she lived—but this I begin to doubt. So her mother reigns as regent, and in sorrow. Old Christopher had two daughters, the younger of whom—" but he stopped in confusion, his face turning very red. Later I remembered this.

We fell into a silence, a mutual sympathy for the bereaved lady who had been so wronged. At last Tommy asked:

"Do you cross your heart that Jack's dream was anything like the one she had?"

"Dream?" Monsieur ran his fingers through his shock of hair. "Who can say? Was she dreaming, or did she see a vision? If a vision, why did it mislead by urging her into the very step that brought disaster? That scoundrel might never have considered kidnaping the child had the mother remained unsuspicious of his occupation! Yet visions are sent to warn against, not to court dangers. Again, some hold that he happened to be contemplating this step as a means of escape should discovery come, and so it was his thought transmitted to her."

"For goodness sake talk sense," I cried. "What difference does it make whether they were dreams or nightmares, or how much the cousin was thinking! What we want to know is where does my dream come in!"

He looked so hurt that I apologized by saying his fairy talk had sent me off my head. Small wonder, for when our guest attempted to explain a theory he proceeded on the assumption that we were as well versed in it as himself. Anyway, we smoothed him down and now, looking at us solemnly, he said:

"Latter-day English-speaking psychologists to the contrary notwithstanding, we know in the East that souls do travel abroad; that they will speak, one to another, while our bodies sleep—while we are steeped in that mysterious period of mimic death which leads us so uncannily near their twilight zone! Some men hold that our dreams are vagaries, as a puff of air or a passing breeze; others that they are unfulfilled desires; still others that they are the impress made by another soul upon the subliminal part of us, that leaves to our active senses but imperfectly translatable hieroglyphics. Does that show you nothing?"

"Well," I temporized, "I can't say it shows me much. How about you, Tommy?"

"Smell a little smoke, but don't see any bright light yet. Elucidate, professor!"

He sighed, giving us a look of pity, I thought.

"If I call to a man, and the space is great, my voice may fail before reaching him. Yet if it hangs its vibrations on a puff of air, a passing breeze that blows in his direction, he hears me! So does the soul employ the passing breeze—by which I mean the capricious thing called dreaming—to enter our consciousness that might not otherwise be reached. The impossibility is to say which is which—that is, which is the unfulfilled desire, which is but the capricious passing breeze, and which is the message from another! If in the dark an uneducated fellow sits at a piano he might play several lovely chords, yet while they sounded well there would be no intelligence behind them. Such is the chance dream! But a master-player could produce a rhapsody, expressing to one who listened hope, love, desire, warning—everything. Such is the harmonious blending of soul and soul in sleep! And how can we tell which is which?"

He paused and gazed out at the water, and I saw in his face the peculiarly wistful expression that so often accompanies thoughts which are both elusive and far away. The index finger of his right hand was slightly raised, indicating a subconscious impulse to point upward. Slowly turning back to us, he said in a tone of solemnity that lingers with me even now, a year later, as I write of it:

"In the Psalms we find these merciful words: 'He giveth His beloved sleep.' Yet they are but an imperfect translation of the original, which reads: 'He giveth *to* His beloved *in* sleep.' Do you not see here a greater meaning? Do your minds not at once grasp the corollary?"

"Then you mean," Tommy asked, "that every dream is intended to express something?"

"I will not go quite that far, although there are men highly practiced in the science of psycho-analytical research who stoutly affirm it. Ah, the great difficulty is in drawing the line—in determining which dreams are but passing breezes and which are sent to us upon the wings of angels!"

"You've studied those things," I ventured. "Which was mine?"

"Study!" he cried, with a fine degree of scorn. "Yes, we study! We gather around the brink of a black well and steep ourselves in thought; we wrinkle our brows and tear our beards. Cries one: 'I know what is down there!' Another turns to him: 'You lie!' A third challenges: 'Prove yourselves!' And thus do professors, students, psychologists, churchmen, laymen, infidels, and fools, gather about the pit! This much for study," he snapped his finger. "Unless a man have faith, he is in darkness to the end of his days!"

"All the same, I believe someone tried to warn the princess," Tommy insisted. "And it couldn't have been anything less than a master-player that got off that rhapsody to Jack last night!" There was a note of teasing in this that the others did not detect.

"Well, Mr. Thomas, you're wrong, sir." Gates, who had been listening attentively, now uncrossed his legs and spoke. "There isn't a single curious thing in Mr. Jack's dream. Anyone can see how it came about—with my apologies to you, sir," he bowed to Monsieur.

We laughed, because Gates had not impressed us as being much of a psychologist, and Tommy said:

"If you explain how he knew what Graham's name was, I'll listen."

"Why, sir, he saw it on the paper the night before—for it was there, as sure as you live, and he says he looked at the paper. The only thing is, he didn't know he saw it—being a little gone in his cups, as you might say. But he did see it, and it soaked into his head, waiting till arfter he got to sleep before stirring around."

"That's my first clear idea," Tommy's face brightened; and Gates, thus encouraged, added:

"The reason he dreamed the old man went ashore for the paper was because he saw the lady being watched when she came back to her table—and I'll venture he thought right then that the old one was about to come back, too, and see what she was doing. Didn't you, sir?"

"I believe I did," I murmured.

"So that stuck in his mind and came out the wrong way, just like dreams sometimes will. As for the photograph and brass frame—why, Mr. Thomas, you and the professor took on so about that picture when he'd developed it that Mr. Jack could have heard you in his sleep, and got that part of his dream from what you said!"

"It does fit, doesn't it," Tommy cried. "And, Jack, the poetry Sylvia breathed at you—wasn't it about the same thing our little Spanish girl sang?"

"It had the same general idea," I admitted.

"There you are, sir," Gates announced, with a satisfied air. "So there isn't a thing unusual about your dream, arfter all. It's as reasonable as the general run."

Monsieur did not relish having his big occult smoke blown away in this fashion; he looked at us with rather a sickish expression, as a boy might have if someone stuck a pin in his toy balloon. But it was such a relief to get back to practicalities that we let him sulk.

"Jack," Tommy asked, "do you think her real name is Sylvia?"

"Yes; I'm sure of that, anyhow!"

"How're you sure of it?"

"It fits her so absolutely," I answered with decision.

"But Revenge would fit her, too, wouldn't it? That's sweet," he grinned.

"Or Constancy," the professor smiled, for once becoming inspired as he threw off his grouch.

"Try Ignorance!" This again from Tommy, who made an attempt to look blissful and only succeeded in making himself ridiculous, I thought.

Old Gates now stretched, cocked an eye up at the weather and, in a drawl, asked:

"Would it be supposing a great deal, sir, to suggest that the lady might be named Much-Learning?"

Whereupon we laughed uproariously, and Tommy slapped him on the knee, exclaiming:

"Papa Gates, you've hit it! Truly, she hath made us mad!"

"All the same," I cried, arising and laughing down at them, "there's one thing you can't explain away! The big adventure's come at last!—the wildest chase—"

"Love chase," Tommy interposed.

"Chase," I repeated, "that man ever started! Are you fellows game enough to see it through—to the very end?"

"*Are* we?" Tommy yelled, springing to his feet. "To the very end! What say, Gates?—Professor?"

"To the very end, sir," the old skipper's face beamed happily.

"Why, yes, my boys," Monsieur declared. "To the very end,—*certainement!*"

And Gates must have confided this to the crew, for later, as I passed the mate, that worthy gave his forelock a pull and whispered:

"To the very end, sir!"

It pleased me immensely.

CHAPTER VI
A VOICE FROM THE WATER

A perfect tropical night crept down on us, with the sky a deep and velvety blue, and the stars low enough to touch. Brilliant phosphorescence dashed from our bow and a silvery streak trailed in our wake emphasizing the enchantment as the *Whim* rose, leaned, and dipped over the bosom of the breathing Gulf. So, also, were my hopes; now up, now down, on the breast of another fickle monster. Love and the sea! Have they not always been counterparts? Do they not span the known and unknown in each man's world, carrying some in safety—others destroying?

It must have been nine o'clock when the forward watch called and, springing to the rail, peering through the darkness, we saw down upon the horizon the fixed white eye and three red sectors of the Key West light.

"A good run, Gates."

"Nothing of our size can beat it, sir."

"You think the *Orchid* will be in harbor?"

"I carn't say, sir. She had six hours' start of us, and could have left."

"How long do we lay off this burg?" Tommy asked, sauntering up.

"That depends. If the mysterious yacht's here we'll stay till something happens."

"And if she isn't," he nudged the professor, "we'll comb out the universe. You get that, don't you? A nice fat job, I'll say it is! How'll we know which way to start? Gates, couldn't you get a peep at her papers in the port?" But the skipper solemnly shook his head, saying:

"It carn't be done, sir."

"Well, Jack, when customs are finished we'll take the launch and comb out the harbor, anyhow! She'll be anchored nearby, like as not."

Not caring to tie up at the dock we chose a berth far enough out to escape the electric glare ashore, and had hardly swung-to when Gates was off in his gig to clear our papers. The port officials were astir and accommodatingly looked us over without loss of time, for the skipper had mentioned our wish to leave whenever the spirit moved us. Those, indeed, had been his identical words, and I wondered if they were prophetic—whenever the spirit moved us!

They were a nice pair of fellows, those American officers, and before going into business—a mere formality in our case—we gathered in the cockpit for a long straw and a bowl of ice. The occasion was more agreeable for possessing that sense of aloofness one feels at being on the edge, yet safely beyond the reach, of a little city's night diversions and excitements.

"I suppose you've nothing dutiable," one said, knowing we had left Havana unexpectedly soon.

"Nothing," Tommy volunteered.

"But, yes," Monsieur exclaimed. "I shall declare!"

"About the only thing he brought away was a wad of money from a roulette game," I laughed.

"Ah, I surprise you," he cried, in high good humor, ducking below; and was soon heard struggling up the stairs, crying: "Give me help!"

Into our hands then he began thrusting packages of cigars; packages containing a dozen boxes each, until the cockpit looked like moving day in a tobacco shop. Behind the last of these, he came.

"Oh, *là là*," Tommy's jaw dropped. "Where did you tie up with this stuff? We've been together all the time!"

"Not all the time," the professor chuckled. "Before you were awake this morning I was in town for camera supplies, and brought back, also, much of that most genial and ameliorating of influences exerted upon us in life—cigars! How much do I pay?"

"How many have you?"

"Ten thousand."

"Ten thousand cigars!" We stared at him.

"That's a lot of ameliorating influence," one of the officers laughed. "But, in spite of it, I'll have to charge you on nine thousand, nine hundred—unless a hundred belong to each of your friends. Everyone's entitled to bring in a hundred free."

"A hundred are mine," Tommy spoke up at once. "I haven't won cigars so fast, ever! Jack, you for a hundred. Gates, you, too. Colonel," he turned to the officer—out of the Army he scattered the titles of Colonel, Judge, Governor and Parson with a free hand—"suppose you all take a hundred each. It'll be a whole lot cheaper for Sir Walter, here!"

The professor was giggling.

"They have cost me nothing," he cried, "for last night I have won almost a thousand dollars at that wretched place—see, here is plenty with which to pay!"

And a fortunate thing it was that he had, being called on for something in the neighborhood of three hundred dollars.

The officer—Hardwick, by name—and his associate were good fellows, as I have said. They had greeted us as congenial spirits and, probably on this account, I noticed some embarrassment on his part when he leaned into the light and slowly looked over the money Monsieur had given him. The rest of us were conversing in a more or less distrait fashion till this unpleasant duty should be finished, when he took an electric torch from his pocket and flashed it on one of the bills; then on another, and so through the lot. Hesitatingly he touched Monsieur's arm, asking:

"Is this the money you won last night?"

"That? It is just as they paid me."

A moment of silence, then:

"I'm sorry to tell you, but these two fifty-dollar bills are counterfeits."

There ensued an absolute hush, and before my eyes arose the vision of Sylvia's father paying his supper check with a crisp fifty.

"Counterfeit," the professor mused, putting out a hand for them and moving nearer the light. "Strange! Just today I was speaking of a counterfeiter!" And Tommy, in an awed voice, asked:

"You don't think it's more dreams?"

The officials, I rather suspected, were beginning to look at us askance. Our various attitudes at this discovery were scarcely in accordance with the usually accepted actions of innocent people; on the contrary, with but a grain of imagination, we might be branded as a trio of rascals trying to stall out of a tight place. My apprehension was more confirmed when Hardwick, a shade less cordial, said:

"As a United States official, I should like to hear your views about these."

Now Tommy looked across at me and I saw that he was awake. Monsieur, on the other hand, remained blissfully indifferent that anything might be out of the ordinary—except, of course, being loaded with a hundred dollars of bad money, which does not happen every day.

"My counterfeiter?" he smiled innocently. "Yes, he could have done these. His plates are all but perfect. And these bills—you will admit they almost fooled you!" Whereupon he laughed.

Tommy fidgeted, saying:

"Have a care, gezabo, or you'll be sending us to the rock pile!"

"My friend is cut-upping," Monsieur beamed on the official, but met with no more hearty response than the dry acquiescence:

"I've no doubt of it. But suppose you tell me more of your other friend—the counterfeiter!"

"Friend? *My* friend?" Monsieur's face now became the picture of horror. "I was telling these boys of one who disappeared years ago, and afterwards the police showed me some plates found in his rooms! *My* friend!"

Hardwick began to laugh.

"Please accept my apologies, but, really, for the moment—"

"Don't mention it," Tommy interrupted him, handing across a newly opened box of cigars. "I understand you—the professor couldn't!"

Returning to the important subject, Hardwick said:

"Whoever put these out is probably in Cuba. You got them at the café—?"

"Quite so," Monsieur exclaimed, warming up with the notion of doing detective work. "I was playing roulette—but, pardon me, you have heard."

"Do you remember any one around the table who showed new-looking bills?"

"No. We were the only ones playing, and but a few were looking on."

"The restaurant was crowded," Tommy said, "and connects with the gambling rooms. Mightn't they send money back and forth if needed?"

"Quite probable."

In the silence that followed I started twice to tell him that Sylvia's father had used a new bill of that denomination, yet the words would not come. It seemed a sneaky thing to do, after she had turned to me for help. Yet, if she were in danger, what quicker way to safety than arrest the old vulture who had her in his power? So I said:

"Mr. Hardwick, last night in that restaurant I saw a man—" but this time something stopped my words. It was a voice, a girl's voice, beautiful with an impassioned ring of protest, that cried from some place near us on the water:

"It isn't fair!"

It isn't fair! Oh, the just and pleading accusation of that cry! I sprang up, loudly calling her name:

"Sylvia!"

There was not a breath of sound. Those with whom I had been conversing were as mute as graven images, but in the black pall just beyond our taffrail drifted the magnetic presence toward which every nerve and fiber of my body pointed;—pointed, aye, tugged and wrestled with my poor flesh to be free! Yet, silence; all silence. No sound, no vision, no anything to guide me, other than my flashing brain and thumping heart which spoke of her.

I saw one of our sailors staring at the water with strange owlish eyes, and yelled at him:

"Into the gig, man!"

But this was frustrated before he moved, for some black shadow, showing vaguely, glided out from beneath our rail and disappeared. I could not be sure that I saw it, but the sailor did because he crossed himself.

"It ain't no use—now, sir," he managed to say.

My own eyes were trying to follow the eerie, silent thing which had passed so spookily into the night, leaving the merest suggestion of phosphorescence after it. Then an arm slipped affectionately about my shoulders, and I felt that Tommy was also standing by, looking along the trail of deadened sound. His face showed excitement, but he whispered steadily enough:

"Come and sit down."

Indeed, now that the thing had disappeared, I felt like an ass; and, resuming my seat, attempted to make the best of it.

"Really," I laughed, "you fellows mustn't judge a man too critically. There was something in the voice of that young lady which took me off my guard, and recalled—well, it recalled what you've all probably had recalled by one means or another, at some time or other, during your—er—lives." And I gave a weakish smile, waving my hand toward any old thing in sight by way of saying: "You know, old chaps, how just that one girl plays the devil with a fellow, sometimes!"

But the government officials received this in a different spirit than that which I had hoped to arouse. They looked at me with a gravity most disquieting, and Hardwick, suspicion written in every line of his face, asked:

"Is the young lady a member of your party?"

"Heavens, no," I answered quickly. "Oh, no," I vigorously repeated. "We don't know her, at all—none of us!"

An ominous silence followed this emphatic denial, and I could actually *feel* him making up his mind about us. It was an awful moment. At last Tommy flecked the ash from his cigar and, with great deliberation, asked:

"Colonel, do you believe in ghosts?"

"If you're serious," Hardwick snapped, "I certainly do not!"

"I'm serious, all right," Tommy purred, and I knew, from the unusually soft quality of his voice, that, indeed, he was—"for, if you don't believe in ghosts, you believe we're a bunch of damn crooks—oh, yes you do!—and I may say that if you don't, you're a damn fool. *Now* you see how serious I am, and how serious this affair is! This man was telling the exact truth when he said that none of us have ever heard that voice. If we actually did hear it just now, the coincidence that brought a small boat past us at this time of night, and prompted some woman in it to speak when and what she did, is more inexplicable to me than you think it is to you—because you've made up your mind to understand it. I can, however, understand how any sweet voice on a night like this might make my friend skid off his usually sane and normal track, because—" he hesitated, adding slowly: "Hardwick, I can't go into my friend's private affairs, but I wish to tell you that he's had a hell of a jolt, and on account of a memory—a memory, Hardwick—we're at Key West tonight. I trust, sir, that you won't misjudge, but rather fit these fragments and supply the needed others; for I know that your appreciation of—er—things is too delicate to allow me to proceed."

Be it noted that Tommy did tell but the simple truth; and, what is more, he told it with such sincerity that, in a large measure, our embarrassment became shifted over to our guests. Personally, I felt like a howling ass to be staked out and exhibited as somebody's jilted Romeo, but this was a welcome compromise; thrice welcome, since Hardwick's next words showed that he had forgotten, or dismissed, the prelude to my burst of confidence about "a man in the restaurant," for arising he said:

"Well, we've kept you longer than we should. If this gentleman will give my government good money for its revenue we'll bid you *bon voyage*. I suppose there's no objection to my keeping those?" He pointed to the spurious bills.

"I have paid dearly for them," the professor remonstrated.

"I'm sorry, but you won't lose any more than you've already lost—nor gain more, as you won't think of using them!"

"Why should I not use them? I will use them—*certainement!*"

"Be explicit, or forever hold your peace," Tommy laughed. "Can't you see the man reaching for his handcuffs?"

But Monsieur, thoroughly aroused, waved the crisp bills with a great show of indignation, crying:

"If there is a way to run this cheat to earth I, alone, will know it! Then you will want me to be telling you! For my own pleasure I have made a study of counterfeiters and their methods. Perhaps it may surprise you to learn that the police of Europe come to Bucharest and consult with me, eh? Thus, if I may also help you, I must retain my bills!"

We laughed, although I felt tremendously proud of the professor, having had no idea he was such a wonder; and Hardwick said, bowing:

"Then help yourself so I, also, may be helped. But let me take one for my government and, when you finish with the other, mail it to me with your report. I shall appreciate your assistance, really."

Monsieur was delighted.

They left us then, and again we settled about the cockpit; each waiting for one of the others to begin. My own thoughts were like a whirlwind, and my ears strained with listening toward the black Gulf—listening for a voice, or the unnamable noise of the gods knew what, that might float to me across the water. I think Tommy half expected me to suggest that we take one of the small boats, and went to his room to put on darker clothes. In a few minutes Monsieur yawned and followed him—though I rather suspected that his yawn was caused more by nervousness than the want of sleep. A moment later Gates, standing near the wheel, softly called my name, so I arose and went to him.

It must be remembered that Gates was absolutely dependable. There were no frills about the old skipper, he shared not one superstitious sentiment in common with Tommy, and it is extremely doubtful if he knew the sensation of fear; therefore, when I saw his face, I was astonished, and in alarm asked:

"Are you ill?"

"No, sir, but I'm sore upset. Please come a bit more aft, sir."

Taking a few steps till we were abaft the traveler, he turned and whispered:

"Mr. Jack, someone's been trying to blow us up!"

CHAPTER VII
A BOMB AND A DISCOVERY

It seemed that either Gates or I must be out of our senses.

"Blow us up!" I gasped, staring at him.

"As sure as you're born, sir! 'Twas about the time you called over the rail. A little before that, as you gentlemen were talking, I heard a small boat. She came near, and she came up sneaking. First I thought it might be a sponge fisher with more curiosity than manners, but as she didn't start on again I begun to cock my ear. Then something gave a rub against our rudder post. I didn't like it. I was sitting back there, anyhow, so just got to my hands and knees, and peeped over."

"Why didn't you challenge?"

"Because there's been strange doings these twenty-four hours parst, and I knew your affairs might be taking a serious turn. I thought you'd be wanting to know their play, 'stead of scaring 'em off. So I peeped and listened. With my eyes getting fair used to the dark I made out a dinghy with four men, and think they'd bent a line about our rudder post, for the for'ard man seemed to be working at us silent and farst. The middle one had the oars, ready to pull away. In the stern sheets sat the one I guessed was boss and, kind of squatting down in front of him, was a lad. To tell the truth, sir, I felt squirmy, for those night-hawks were up to something mysterious."

"Wait a minute, Gates—did you recognize them?"

"Not me, sir. As I was saying, the fellow aft now parssed up a bundle to the for'ard chap, who took it gingerly and began farstening it on to us somewhere—I couldn't see. The young lad leaned over and looked at it, then he up and sings out: 'It ain't fair!'"

"Yes, yes," I caught him by the shoulders. "Go on, Gates!"

"Mind out this thing under my coat," he warned. "Well, sir, the one that was boss made a grab for him—Lor', how he did jerk him!—and the others froze like stone. They stayed that way while you were calling, then the dinghy glided off—the one aft still holding his hand over the lad's mouth and kind of choking him with the other."

My blood was fairly steaming, and I cried out what was uppermost in my mind:

"That wasn't a lad, Gates! It was a girl!"

His jaw dropped and he stared at me, but slowly shook his head.

"No, sir, it warn't a girl, or the fellow wouldn't have handled her so rough. Besides, sir, he wore—the lad, I mean—a jacket and cap like you or me."

"That doesn't mean anything. I tell you it was a girl—I'm sure of it!"

"Well, sir, you're wrong; for when they got out five fathom or so they stopped—to listen, maybe. You were back in the cockpit by then, and I guess the fellow must have let up on the young-un; for, all at once, he—the lad, I mean—raked a match along the gunnel, for to take a smoke, d'you see! My word, but the way he was grabbed this time would have shocked you. I couldn't see it, but you could hear the youngster gurgling. That shows it warn't a girl, sir!"

"What shows it? Because you think she wanted to smoke? Girls do, Gates!"

"They do that, sir, and I'm not gainsaying it; but they do it sociable, arfter dinner, setting 'round the cockpit, as you might say. It's seldom any of 'em has such a mortal craving for tobacco as to have to take a suck at a little cigarette every time a man chokes her by the throat. My word, no! It's the male sex that wants the weed under those conditions—not a girl, sir!"

But I was seeing an entirely different version of the affair, so far as the smoking went; and Gates would have seen it, too, if he hadn't been so excited. She had not wanted to smoke, at all, but to signal us! I knew it! I was never more sure of anything in all creation!

"And besides, sir," Gates now added, "no one would push his fingers into a girl's throat like—"

"Stop," I cried, for I could not listen to more of this. If ever I wanted to kill it was then. I wanted to get my own fingers on that scoundrel's throat as he had dared touch hers; and in my heart I swore by all the gods, by all the stars and moons and other things in the heavens and under the sea, that I would strangle out his miserable life by inches, or leave my bones to bleach on the shore of her unknown island. Wherever it was, I would find it; wherever she was, I would find her!—and God help him when he came my way! It was a classy oath, and I felt a lot better for it.

"Now, sir," Gates's voice began to tremble with passion as he held up a black thing that had been tucked under his coat, "this invention I took off our rudder post when I rowed 'round to see what they'd been up to. It's a dirty bomb, fixed to start us off for Davy Jones's Locker sometime tonight, sir!"

"You're sure it can't start us off now?" I asked, taking it from his hands.

"Not lest you get too familiar, sir. I've disconnected the clock part of it."

"Have you any idea what those men looked like?"

He solemnly shook his head.

"You can't guess who they were, or why they wanted to blow us up?" I persisted. "Shall we notify the port, or what?"

He stood a while silent before answering.

"Mr. Jack, God knows who they are. It was too dark for me to get any satisfying squint at 'em; but I never saw 'em before—that I know. Three things are sure: they're either lunatics, or they've taken us for some mortal enemy, or—"

"Well?"

"Or I'm wrong in those two guesses, sir."

"But you think they're from the *Orchid*, don't you?"

"On another guess, I'd swear it, sir."

"And you're positive you never saw the yacht till yesterday—in any port?"

"Never, sir. I even made inquiry about her in Havana before we cleared to-day—that is, without exciting comment. A one-eyed stevedore said she drops in there maybe once or twice a year, but he didn't know from where. *I've* never seen her, and I've sailed close to thirty year most everywhere in these waters during winter seasons!"

"Well, I'm stumped," I admitted. "Let's take this to the professor and see what he makes of it." So we went down together.

Monsieur, in his stateroom, sat bent over his counterfeit bill when I quietly shoved the bomb in front of him. He sprang up with a broadside of expletives that in the sunlight would have cast a wondrous rainbow. It was a way with the little professor, and we had learned to keep respectfully distant during such periods of effervescing energy.

"Tied to our rudder post," I told him.

He seemed to grasp the entire situation at once. I have never known such a genius for corraling facts! In an instant his mind apparently galloped completely around the boundary of our discovery, and then circled in.

"You have made it harmless," was his first oral observation.

"Gates did, yes; he disconnected the clock-work."

"It is quickly made, and crude," he mused, turning it over in his hands, "but the work of one who is not a novice. Give me the other part!—um! Very pretty, very pretty, indeed!" Then he looked up, calling: "My boy Tommy, come! We are to see what we shall see!"

"See what?" Tommy sauntered in; but as we explained the situation he looked positively hopeful. For the chief quality in Tommy that made him so likable was his abiding love of danger. He would rather flirt with death than a ravishing coquette—though I will not deny his preference to play the pair.

"Oh, boy!" he now chuckled, giving my arm a squeeze.

As we gathered about the table, Monsieur took a knife and began to press its blade into the covering of the bomb, saying:

"I have known the builder of one of these to leave his tracks inside, trusting the explosion to obliterate them. But sometimes the machine does not go off."

"Let's hope this'll be one of those times," Tommy murmured, "or we'll pretty well leave our tracks all over the Gulf. Don't use any bad judgment, Professor. Centuries are looking down at you!"

"I shall try not," he smiled, pushing the blade deeper and giving a gentle twist.

"I should say he ought to be doing that ashore, sir," Gates whispered. "Lor' knows this is no place—"

But Monsieur was speaking again.

"The gentleman who left it with us may have used bad judgment by not exploding it himself. So much the worse for him. Steady!" he grunted, peeling off another slice of the wrapper. "Yet, if criminals did not sometimes use bad judgment, a sorry plight would be ours, eh? Moreover, it is natural that they use bad judgment, for, being criminals, their judgment is bad—primarily bad, or they would not be criminals."

"Please work without your tongue or talk without your hands," I said, with a touch of irritation. "That thing's nervous for undivided attention!"

The professor may not have heard, and in a monotone continued:

"The man who made it knew his business; therefore he is a student of this type of explosives; therefore a police agent, a—what you call—crank like myself, or a destroying criminal—that is, an anarchist. Therefore he is the last named, since neither of the others would want to blow up a gentleman's yacht. It seems clear to you?" he asked, without raising his eyes; but none of us cared to divert his attention by answering.

By now Monsieur had peeled off several pieces of the wrapper, and was sprawled over the table with a powerful magnifying lens. For some time he minutely studied them, finally squinting closely at a particular one and beginning to show increased excitement. Arising and pushing by us, he went to his many boxes and returned with a small glass-stoppered bottle. It must have contained an acid; at any rate, he touched a drop of it to a piece of the inner wrapping, then bent over to watch results. Finally, with very bright eyes, he looked up announcing in a voice of triumph:

"This paper is the kind they use for printing money on!"

We stared at him, but he volunteered nothing further, having again bent over his search. For several minutes we watched in silence. Then he sat up with a snap, as a steel spring might be released.

"The man who made this bomb made my counterfeit bank note," he cried.

Tommy and I jumped.

"Just so," he continued eagerly. "The bomb is a hurried affair, impromptu, constructed of materials happening to be at hand when needed. That necessity, we assume, arose within the last few hours, since we have been in these waters but shortly. Here is a piece of the wrapper. You make nothing of it, yet to my experienced knowledge I see the identical paper on which my money is printed. The counterfeiter, possessing a good resisting paper and suddenly desiring to make a bomb, employs it. So much for so much! Now we have him a bomb-maker and a counterfeiter;—then we shall eliminate the anarchist!"

"Why?" I asked.

"Because a counterfeiter of such skill—and this engraving is the work of a master—implies long and intense application; therefore a secluded life rather than one of following the red flag. Moreover, an anarchist would be tempted into this risk, such as tried upon us, only to destroy someone of great importance—which I may conclude no one of us is. And irrespective of these reasons counterfeiters do not sympathize with anarchy. The psychology of each must be diametric, for if there is no government to make money there is no money to counterfeit. So the anarchist in our case lacks motive, but the other finds it if he suspects us of knowing his secret. So much for so much. Do we know any counterfeiter's secret? No. Then a final theory: the placer of this bomb has mistaken us for an enemy—he thinks we are whom we are not!"

"That's what I said," Gates interposed.

"But he does suspect us of knowing it," Tommy exclaimed, "or why did he tell the waiter Jack was a detective?"

The professor, obviously disappointed, turned again to the bomb that was fast reaching a state of *déshabille*—if bombs can be said to reach that state.

"You assume this to be the work of people on that yacht," he said, with a touch of annoyance. "Can you sustain that theory?"

"Why, of course, sir," Gates declared.

"A mere presumption, *mon Capitaine!*"

"But the voice," I challenged. "Don't you suppose I recognized it?"

"Tut-tut, my boy Jack! You have never actually heard the lady's voice!" And as this was true I had nothing further to offer; but he brightened up, adding: "We shall now go to the stomach of the bomb, if only to enjoy ourselves."

"You've a curious idea of fun," I grunted.

"Just go easy," Tommy said. "She may be ticklish."

"Why not sink the wicked thing at once, sir," Gates urged. "We've seen enough now to keep us awake nights, and I haven't any craving to look at its stomach, Lor' knows I haven't!"

But the professor would not listen. Already he had recommenced the exploration, gingerly removing some wires wrapped about the explosive center, while we almost held our breaths lest he touch the wrong thing. Once he smiled, and murmured: "*Le capitaine* is right—it was made on the *Orchid*!" Yet he did not stop work for this, and soon brought to view two half sticks of dynamite, one of them ingeniously capped. Leaning above this now, with his elbows on the table and his head in his hands, he sank into a profound study, then startled us by giving a snort and springing up, jostling the table so violently that the dynamite slid gracefully toward the edge. Most happily Tommy grabbed it in time.

"Lor', sir, 'twas a close shave," Gates whispered, wiping his forehead.

But Monsieur remained blissfully unconscious of the mess so narrowly averted. He was staring, breathing heavily, blinking and thinking. As though walking in his sleep he again went to his mysterious bags, took out something and began to study it through the lens. Then with a yell he rushed at me, hugged me, kissed me on the cheek, held me off, and hugged me again, crying over and over:

"I am right—I am right—I am right!"

He now caromed from me and in the same manner embraced Tommy, and after this he tackled Gates. But Gates did not understand the continental fashion of masculine salutations, and sternly disengaged himself, saying:

"You carn't be right, sir! I don't know what's the matter, but it's easy to see you carn't just be right!"

"*Sacré bleu!*" Monsieur stepped back, actually weeping with happiness. "What stupid idiots we are! Can't you see?"

"I can see one," Tommy grinned at him sweetly.

"Ah, but look!" He thrust before us the thing he had taken from the bag. It was that precious kodak film of Sylvia. "Look!" he cried. "You say she is near to twenty—he, to seventy-five! But, more than all, I see with my lens that here is the breathing likeness of the mother! Where are your eyes, my boys? *Ciel*, must I tell you? She is the kidnaped princess of Azuria!"

You who read may have surmised this; so might we, had we been reading instead of making history. The human mind that leans above a printed page possesses a more concentrated grasp of facts than the human atoms who run over the earth collecting them. So I caught my breath and simply stared, too dazed to speak. It seemed as though something had given me a surprising whack that sent a thousand sparks before my eyes. But then slowly the whole structure began to unfold. Each step of evidence we had picked up since the memorable night but twenty-four hours ago, now took its place as the panorama—not flawless, but with inviting possibilities,—and passed across my brain.

It was very late when we pushed back from the table. In its center were the counterfeit bill, the magnifying glass, parts of the thoroughly dissected bomb, several pages of writing pad with the professor's deductions; and by these were some of Gates' charts, the paper I had procured from the waiter, and another page containing those mystic sentences Sylvia had spoken for finding her island—because I thought it fair to her that this should be laid before my friends, especially as she had only said them in a dream.

Strangely enough the professor was willing to admit them to his scheme of carrying on our pursuit—a chase which he now seemed determined to direct—when even Tommy, the superstitious Tommy, declared they would throw us off the track a thousand miles. I could think of no plan, for altogether it did seem like combing out the universe for two human atoms.

"We have one sure way, of course," the professor leaned wearily back. "Keep the *Orchid* in sight. If we do this till she reaches her lair, all is well."

"I wouldn't doubt she sailed, sir, right arfter placing the bomb," Gates ventured.

"Then we can't keep her in sight," said Tommy dolefully.

"Do not thwart me," the little fellow cried, with a sudden flare of anger that made us smile in spite of the serious work at hand.

"We'd better go ashore first," I suggested, "and get authority to capture her. The government can deputize us by sending along an officer."

"Authority!" Monsieur puffed out his cheeks and snapped his finger. "That for your government's authority! I have the authority with me!"

"You!" I exclaimed.

"*Certainement!* I was one of those true friends who left the palace years ago, with the old King's authority in my pocket! It is in that bag now! It is absolute—absolute!—protecting me against anything I may do in effecting her rescue and return. It is by far more powerful than anything your government could give us! A King's order makes the police of the world my underlings! Besides that, she is my special charge, and no power this side of Azuria can abrogate my authority over her!"

A cold hand wrapped its fingers about my heart. The hopelessness of our search would have been depressing enough had it not contained the spice of chase, but to feel that it might be fruitful only to have her snatched off into a world as unknown, as impossible to me as this far off kingdom, was crazing. To me it would be like seeing her transported from one star to another, while I remained on earth to gaze my eyes out and eat my heart out with endless longing.

"Her mother is regent, you say?" Tommy asked, intuitively sympathizing with my state of mind.

"Yes. In Roumania a woman may not ascend the throne alone, but in Azuria, where the Ruman blood has never mixed, she may act as regent if her heir is a girl too young to marry. But now," he clapped his hands joyfully, "we can complete the alliance with a neighboring prince—and, ah, what joy there will be!"

"You've got to catch her first," Tommy said, not without a trace of spite. "Even if we get near enough to see him, at all, he can see us, too; then lead us off the track till night and make a run for base."

"So he will, my boy Tommy. And if his lair is to the west, he will doubtless lead us to the east. But we must sail at dawn—then we shall see what we shall see!"

"Good night," I said, abruptly kicking back my chair.

Thus our meeting broke up; Gates going first to sink the dynamite and then leave orders for all canvas to be stretched at peep o' day. Tommy came on deck with me, and we stood a while looking into the black water. Off in the town, in a side street near the wharf where sailors' amusement halls are clustered, some tipsy fellow was bawling a love song at the top of his voice. He seemed to be the only thing awake in Key West at this hour. When the song, or his voice, gave out the silence settled heavier than before. A ship's bell, far over the water, began to strike, and we counted five mellow strokes: one-one, one-one, one!

"Half-past two," Tommy whispered, "I wonder what Nell's doing!"

"Dreaming of you, no doubt," I tried to laugh. "Maybe you and she are wrecked on a desert island at this blissful moment."

"I wish we were," he murmured, without looking around. "And you and Sylvia, too!"

"Cut it," I growled. "She's a princess, Tommy, and that puts the kibosh on my dreams."

"Nell's a princess, too," he said gently, "and I still hang on. Tilt up your chin, Jack, and things'll squeeze through for us! We'll ship the old counterfeiter to prison, or kill him, and then—"

"And then," I said bitterly, turning to go below, "Princess Sylvia goes to the arms of some popinjay prince!"

But I had taken only a step when his hand fell on my shoulder like a piece of steel and whirled me around. There was nothing gentle in his voice this time as he sharply commanded:

"Look at me, you damn slacker, and let's see if I'm talking to the man I fought the Boche with!"

I must have appeared rather well indignant with him, for he gave a low, reassured laugh, adding:

"That's better. Now I want to say, once and for all—and I swear it on each of these stars, both for myself and Nell—that if we catch up with Princess Sylvia, and you let her be taken away, I'll punch your face into a jolly good pulp, so help me old Kentucky! Good *night*!"

"If you're man enough to do it," I yelled after him.

Fine old Tommy! I believe I loved him then better than ever before.

CHAPTER VIII
THE CHASE BEGINS

I slept like a log and was awake, anxious to turn out, at the peep of dawn. But Gates was ahead of me when I reached the deck. Our anchor had just been hoisted, and every sail was set, though nearly limp with a negligible breeze.

"What news?" I asked.

"Nothing, sir; leastwise nothing of the *Orchid*. She's gone."

"We expected that. Any idea which way?"

"I talked to a sponge fisher who came by a while back, sir, and he said a schooner yacht sailed about midnight, or maybe later; north, he said. But she carn't have got far, as there hasn't been hardly any air stirring all night till this little one now. If it wasn't so heavy off there we might see her, I farncy. The mate's aloft, sir."

I looked up and saw him steadily sweeping the distance with his binoculars; but, as Gates had said, the horizon in all directions was heavy, and in such weather our search, indeed, seemed next to useless. With the world a playground, how could we find this vagrant yacht.

Then I let my eyes rest on the tinted east, marvelling at what a curiously beautiful, dangerously sweet old world this is. The sky and water were beginning to be touched by the first faint tones of rose, the dawn was bringing its enchantment to this marriage-time of the black and white. Over in the Key West barracks a bugler would soon be blowing reveille; down in the sleeping town stumpy little street cars would squeak from their sheds and clang their discordant gongs through the narrow thoroughfares. But farther yet to the northeast, in the Florida I best knew and loved, a whooping crane would startle the solitude with its uncanny cry, the alligators would croak their guttural grunts at waking time, while, here and there in the shadowy forest, the whine of a skulking panther would strike terror to the hearts of gentler things. Ah, the trackless wilderness of dreamy Florida, where nature moves on padded foot and silent wing!

Gates had hoisted even the topmast- and maintopmast-staysails, but these did not help much; and when Tommy and Monsieur appeared half an hour later they were in wretched humors at the way matters stood. The only slight hope we nursed had been one cry of "Sail-ho!" from the mate, but he could not tell what kind of a craft had rested on his lens, because she was almost at once swallowed by the distant bank of mist. At last, with a squint into the southwest, Gates prophesied that something worth while would be coming before long, and with this crumb of comfort, seasoned by his promise to call if anything appeared, we half-heartedly went down to breakfast.

Healthy man is ever cheered by breakfast, especially if Pete has prepared it, and gradually our departed spirits came lumbering back. I remembered Tommy's promise of the night before to mutilate my countenance on certain conditions, and began to laugh. Then he laughed, doubtless because I had, and pretty soon Monsieur showed signs of warming up.

"This is what my boy Tommy would call hot-stuffie, eh?" he cried. "To be chasing a scoundrel who has kidnaped a Princess is fun, you think so?"

"And such a princess," Tommy rapturously exclaimed. "Eyes more deep than the mysteries of twilight shadows in a woodland pool!—oval cheeks more damask than the rose which steals its fragrance from her hair!—lips whose Cupid's bow—"

"Here," I good-naturedly protested. "Don't make her so wonderful! You won't have an adjective left for the beautiful Bluegrass flower!"

"But isn't she wonderful?—I challenge you, isn't she perfect?"

"That is a perilous assertion," Monsieur chuckled, "since there is a Persian proverb that 'to be perfect is to be damned.'"

"Well, she'd rather be damned than ugly, if I know anything about girls—and I do!" Tommy declared. "Isn't that right, gezabo?"

"Isn't what right? That you know so much about girls? Bah! It is a young rooster's foolish talk! Woman, my boy, is as the law of gravity—difficult to understand, and I may add difficult to disobey. But to comprehend her she must first be stripped—"

"Why, you wicked old thing," Tommy, in mock astonishment, gasped at him.

"You do not let me finish," he blushingly protested. "What I mean is stripped of her inexplicable—"

"Oh, come off," his tormentor burst out laughing. "That's as transparent as a girl buying cigarettes for her brother! I didn't know you were so curious."

"Please—you shame me! I am curious of nothing, and you will someday learn that curiosity is the root of tragedy."

"There's an epigram worthy of you: 'Curiosity is the root of tragedy'—and the blossom of delight!"

"I said nothing of delight," the professor blushed. "I said tragedy! And—ah, I see! You are cut-upping! I will not talk. Your conscience should hurt you!"

"Not conscience, old fellow! The wages of conscience is *ennui*, and the gods know how I hate that. Give me your epigrams on delight and love, and the Princess of Azuria!"

"Love! Bah!" Monsieur now stormed in disgust. "A mythical invention of diseased minds to explain away our follies!"

"Wait till she hears that," Tommy warned, "and your head's as good as in the sawdust. I hope to heaven she makes me her lord high executioner, and darned if I don't lop it off with a single whack!"

"And I hope you have a chance to tell her, so smart!"

"I'll have a chance, all right, never you fear. I'm the only one who will, for after you're disposed of, and Jack has gone moony, this expedition will need a clear thinker. There's where your uncle Tom comes in."

"He understands himself so well," the professor indulgently smiled.

"It requires no concentration, really," I murmured.

"Ah, Mr. Brutus," Tommy grinned at me over a fork-load of buckwheat cakes, "can it be your cooling blade I feel?"

"It is; and you'll get it in the neck, good and properly, if you don't leave me out of your silly nonsense," I warned.

"Here's a touchy one for you, gezabo! Yachting with royalty the other night made him too good for us."

"You close up," I growled.

After a few minutes devoted to breakfast, he asked:

"Are princesses like other people, I wonder? Jack ought to be put wise, so he'll know how to behave when we get her aboard."

"Why, yes, my boy Tommy," Monsieur answered, taking him seriously, of course. "They are the same as other young ladies, except more highly cultured, more of education, more of that—what you call—indefinable chasteness."

"Indefinable chasteness," he puckered his lips and repeated the phrase in a ruminating way. "D'you know, a philosopher once told me that if ever I heard an old lady call a girl anything like that, to put the young one down for a kissable, artful little flirt; for in this present day of ours, he said, woman understands everything on God's green earth—except the mind of her succeeding generation."

"But I am no old lady," the professor bristled.

"Sail-ho!" came the far off voice of the mate from his perch aloft.

We held our breaths, intently listening.

"Where away?" Gates called, and I could picture him: legs apart, head thrown back, hands cupped around his lips.

"Dead ahead, sir," came the answer: "I got a better look at her this time, and she's a schooner yacht like us!"

We bounded from the table and dashed up the companionway stairs out into the cockpit. The old skipper was laughing gleefully, and our spirits were as high as the masthead.

"We're on the right track, Mr. Jack," he cried. "Just wait till arfter a breeze springs up—she won't stay so far ahead!"

But the breeze did not pick up and we continued to poke along at about six knots, hardly consoled by the knowledge that she was doing no better. Time seemed to be creeping on its hands and knees. The *Orchid*, if such were the yacht ahead of us, continued beyond the fringe of mist, now mixed with a fine drizzle, showing herself at rare intervals which served to keep us from going astray.

The slickers of the crew were dripping and shiny, and we, too, soon looked like a flock of wet, disgruntled hens. To add to my discomfiture the professor brought up a newspaper and began consulting the shipping news, blandly telling us that if we captured the princess within forty-eight hours he could have her in Azuria in twenty days. I was glad when the paper got so wet that he had to throw it overboard.

At luncheon we could not help being downcast, largely owing to the drizzle which, aboard a yacht, is indeed a spirit breaker. The few sporadic attempts we made at cheer did not get very far. But after a little, happening to glance at Tommy, I saw a look in his face that put me on my guard for something. There was no hoax about this, no "cut-upping."

"Our conversation was interrupted this morning," he said, in answer to my unspoken question. "There were things I wanted to talk about—for instance, what'll we do when we catch up?"

I had thought of this a hundred times without finding a very definite solution, as my fancies refused to reach beyond the moment I should stand face to face with Sylvia. But, after a fashion, I made answer:

"We'll hand the scoundrel over to the law, I suppose, and take the Princess—"

"That's just it," he interrupted me. "Take her where? That's the point I want to make." His voice was almost purring now—a sign with him of deadly earnestness. He was continuing: "Suppose she has a perfectly good home where she is! Suppose she doesn't see the virtues in our interference that we see! How do we know the man's a scoundrel, anyway?"

"Bah!" Monsieur cried. "She wrote a message of danger! The man tried to blow us up! He made bad money that I have here!"—whereupon he thumped his breastpocket half a dozen times. "How do we know? *Pardieu,* I tell you!"

"She wrote the message," Tommy admitted, "but everything else you say is guess. Even suppose you're right about it, where are our warrants? Where are the sworn officers to serve them?"

"I have told you that I have the authority, the absolute authority!"

"Oh, that doesn't amount to a damn," Tommy replied with supreme indifference, and for a moment I feared Monsieur was going to have a stroke of apoplexy. "Don't you see that we must possess proofs? And then we've got to board his yacht, don't we? Is he going to take a siesta while we stroll over the old tub? Your authority, gezabo, is a scrap of paper unless, first, he's the man who kidnapped your princess, and second, we can lay our hands on him. Now try to think!"

"Think! There is nothing to think—only to do! You speak as a child! We must take that girl to her throne, to her rightful heritage! By every law of conscience, justice and humanity, there is nothing left for us to do! Absolutely we must obey!"

A silence fell upon Tommy and me. I saw him moisten his lips and dart the professor a quick glance. I knew how inherently strong that little fellow was in his loyalty, but had not been prepared for such an appeal as this. Conscience, humanity, justice! He was calling on my manhood to send her back to Azuria, out of my arms, out of my life. And she would go; I felt it, I knew it. I realized now that Tommy, in preambling up to this point, intended to settle it once and for all. And I realized how much farther his clear vision had penetrated the situation than my own poor addled mind.

Leaning forward, he said in the same soft voice—though Monsieur did not recognize the deadly purpose behind it:

"Professor, if you seriously want to see Azuria again I think we'd better arrange this thing, somehow. You came here to look for a princess; Jack came—pardon me, Jack, but it's unavoidable—for a sweetheart. Every man to his trade, you know!"

"Yes, and if I find Her Serene Highness I shall most certainly restore her to—"

"You'll most certainly do nothing of the kind," Tommy interrupted him. "You see, old fellow, we couldn't trust her to you—it wouldn't be fair. The fact is, you've been acting mighty queerly of late, saying all kinds of strange things!"

A puzzled look came into the professor's eyes as he glanced at me and then back at Tommy, who now leaned confidentially nearer.

"Do you realize," he soothingly continued, "that you thought someone was trying to blow up our yacht?"

"Trying to blow it up? Did I not have the bomb in my hands?"

"He still believes it, Jack," Tommy sighed. "There's nothing to be done, I reckon, but take him back to Key West. They've a pretty fair hospital there."

Monsieur's face turned so livid and looked so weird in its frame of straw-colored hair that I began to think all the hospitals on earth could not save him. Sputtering, he appealed to me:

"The truth, my boy Jack—he is cut-upping?"

But Tommy was saying:

"We're awfully sorry, you dear old manatou; we'll miss you, take my word for it."

"You boys dare do this," he sprang to his feet, too angry for further protest.

"Sit down, sir," Tommy spoke now in a different tone. "Of course, I don't believe it, nor does Jack; but others will if we take you to the Key West hospital tied up in ropes and say you've got that blowing-up bug in your bonnet. Get the point?"

"I get no points," he furiously pounded the table.

"Well, here it is, and its name is Compromise! Either compromise, or the wow-wow house. We won't force the issue; you must decide nicely, without being pressed one way or the other. But these are the facts: you're sailing on an American yacht; Jack's the owner, Gates is captain, I'm the boss. We're hoping to overhaul the *Orchid*, board her, capture the princess, and all that. Then for one entire week Jack's to have an uninterrupted tête-à-tête while you make yourself invisible. Come along if you want to and turn the old rascal over to your consul when we get home, plead with the princess after Jack's week is up, recover a hundred good bucks for your bad ones—but he has to have his chance first, and we sign articles of agreement *right now*!"

"Children," he cried, with a great show of disgust. "Should you return to Key West, how would you ever find the *Orchid* again! Ah-ha, you have tripped yourselves!"

"Not on your life, we haven't. We'll keep on now and locate her hiding place, then deliver you to a guardian, and come back."

The professor thought a moment, breathing fast and blinking.

"What are those bucks you spoke about?" he asked.

"Bucks? Hell, man, they're beans, bones—the things you won at roulette!"

"I won no such things at roulette," he gravely shook his head, adding slowly: "So I must agree, eh? *Tres-bien!* Yet I warn you that she will go back with me in spite of all my boy Jack can say in a week, or a year. It is inevitable—she can not possibly disobey! Come! You win for the moment, so we will drink, standing together for Azuria!"

"Standing for your grandmother," Tommy laughed. "No, you jolly old filbert, we stand for Jack and Sylvia, and don't you forget it! We'll use your vaunted authority, too, when the time comes to make that scoundrel surrender. Now let's get our arsenal in shape!"

Monsieur approved of this, entering into it with a boyish spirit, and for a long time we went over rifles and automatics, showing him their virtues, explaining the accuracy of their range, occasionally throwing one up to the shoulder and taking a quick aim over the sights, as fellows will who find them good companions.

"I'll lay you odds, Professor, that the barrels of some of this hardware get hot before night," Tommy said.

"Ah, I will not bet on such bloody business. You think we fight today?"

"Two to one on it," he answered; then giving my shoulder a slap that felt like the kick of a mule, he cried:

"So romance and adventure died with the war, did they? Oh, *baby*, what a shame!"

CHAPTER IX
A SHOT FROM THE DARK

During the first few hours of the afternoon we had looked on deck several times, but felt better satisfied to remain below, out of the drizzle. Now the captain's big voice rumbled some kind of good news, and each of us made a dash for the stairs.

Even as we piled out into the cockpit the mate gave a yell and sailors sprang to haul down the topmast-and main-topmast-staysails. Off in the southwest, which had been leaden from horizon to meridian showing no distinction of water and sky, appeared a spot of light, a glow, growing rapidly brighter. Before it the misty rain was being wiped as if by magic from the air.

Looking toward the northward I beheld the other yacht standing out in bold relief upon a blacker, more dismal background. She was beautiful at that moment—her sides and sails unnaturally whitened against the gloom, suggesting a cameo set on a piece of slate. Our blocks began to creak, sails bulged into huge scoops, masts tilted majestically, and the *Whim*, freed from her enforced idleness, bounded in response.

"Wind!" Tommy shouted, his arms held skyward. "Aphrodite, sweet and mighty, send a gale before the nighty!"

"But," Monsieur looked at him reprovingly, "Aphrodite is not goddess of the wind!"

"Who said she was?" he innocently asked.

"You conjure her for the gale—bah!"

"That's because she rhymes with nighty, gezabo! When my Muse sings, to hell with mythology! Come join the clouds—you're sordid!"

"These have been sordid clouds," the little fellow laughed. "I would rather join you in other, but a more genial, wet."

"Gates, how long before we catch her?" I called.

"I carn't measure her speed yet, sir, but should say we won't be far behind in an hour and a harf."

"Then," Tommy announced, "we'll go below and drink to the safety of our sweet Princess—for, unless I'm greatly mistaken, this day will see the finish of one good yacht! Give over the wheel and join us, Captain!"

It was a hilarious four that touched glasses in the cabin, and after Gates went above we set to work in good earnest on our arms and cartridge belts. Having seen that each piece worked perfectly we followed him up, and the sight which greeted our eyes made us laugh for joy.

How we accomplished it only Gates could have told, but now in the late afternoon light the *Orchid* seemed to be less than half her former distance. Looking over the rail at the flying water I felt a great pride in my father's craft, for she fairly skimmed along. Monsieur began at once to hug the captain, and this time the old skipper did not mind—at least, he permitted it.

There was, of course, some concern along with our happiness; first of importance being the declining day that held scarcely more than an hour of light. Had it been otherwise, had the blessing of good sailing weather come to us earlier, we might have held an immediate council of war; but this for the present could be left. It was a profound disappointment, though, and showed in our strained silence. Gates stood at my elbow.

"How'll we find her in the morning—if we don't catch up pretty soon?" I asked.

"I was thinking of that, sir. Now, as she sees we can sail circles around her with a good breeze, she won't hold the same course, and can give us a mighty slip during the night. We're almost in—" he hesitated, and again ventured: "We're almost in close enough to send a shot across her bows, sir, if you wish to bring her about!"

Tommy, overhearing, let out a yell of joy. The old skipper's suggestion electrified us all, particularly myself, for it promised that he would see this affair through at any and all costs—and I had been apprehensive regarding the attitude of Gates, lest his love for me, or for the *Whim*, cause him to balk short of the danger line. So, hastily imploring Monsieur to hug him again, I dashed below for one of the rifles. This arm was a neat high-power sporting model, but I thought it might persuade our kidnaper to look around.

Coming up, however, I found that another plan had been adopted. Gates and Tommy were busily unlacing the canvas cover from our brass cannon. While it was only used for signaling, it could make a stunning racket. Bilkins was holding a box of blank shells, each containing somewhere near twenty drams of black powder. As I approached, Tommy was excitedly arguing with Gates who, this time, seemed to demur.

"It's not of the *Orchid* I'm thinking, sir," he turned appealingly to me, "but ourselves! Miss Nancy—as Mr. Thomas calls this young howitzer, here,—won't stand much fooling. She warn't built for it, and if we go pressing her too hard she'll bust a stay—which is the same, sir, as sending harf of us to the sick-bay!"

"What I want to do," Tommy explained, "is load her up with sinkers and truck like that, and touch her off right! Just a blank won't tell those devils anything, but if we pepper 'em with a hat full of old junk they'll haul-to in a jiffy!"

"Surest thing in the world," I cried. "Suppose she does bust a stay, Gates! We can huddle in the cockpit and fire her with a long lanyard—then let her bust!"

"That's easy, sir," he still remonstrated, "but suppose Miss Sylvia's looking out a porthole and stops one of the sinkers!"

The thought of it made me shiver. Tommy, however, his enthusiasm undampened, acquiesced at once, saying:

"Righto, Gates! Blank it is! Cartridge, Bilkins! I'm ready—say when!"

"Wait! Let's get a bit closer, sir," Gates urged.

Several minutes passed. We were only four hundred yards from the *Orchid* now and cutting down the space. She stood off our starboard quarter and, although a great deal more obscure in the gathering dusk, her cabin lights came on changing the portholes to a line of golden disks. Then another solitary light appeared, being carried aft by a sailor who fastened it to the taffrail. It was the stern lantern being swung out for the night, and I could not help smiling at this delightful display of audacity, deliberately to put up that tell-tale beacon, right in our faces, as it were.

"It's a good bluff," Gates chuckled, "but they don't intend leaving it there for long, sir. I'd say we'd better fire now, Mr. Thomas, and when they stop we'll have a little chat with 'em."

Tommy sprang up and pulled the string, and our eyes were dazzled, our ears jarred, with a perfectly glorious explosion that lighted up the sea for a hundred yards.

"Whiz-bang!" Tommy yelled. "I wish I had this thing in Kentucky! It'd work wonders for the Democrats!"

Nothing happened aboard the *Orchid*. She did not vary her course an inch. The sailor at the helm had given a frantic jump when Miss Nancy went off, but resumed his place evidently aware that no missiles had been fired.

"Load her up again," I urged. "Let's keep on till they get mad!"

Bilkins passed out the shells and the piece was loaded and fired, loaded and fired, till we seemed surely to have waked old Nep himself. I do not know how many rounds we shot but it must have continued for some time, thoroughly engrossing us. Now suddenly the stern light went out, and immediately afterwards the portholes, losing their glow, became as nothing. The tropical night, always swift in coming, had fallen more stealthily than we realized, and the yacht melted into darkness.

"*Sacré bleu!*" Monsieur raged—for the night was overcast and as black as sin.

But Gates was already stripping the searchlight of its cover. When he had swung open the big lens Tommy struck a match, which blew out. His second was blown out by a hiss of air that preceded the flow of gas, and the professor jumbled matters by trying his hand. But these efforts scarcely took more time than the telling, and when the powerful streak of light finally pierced the darkness the very first thing it showed us was a white sail.

"I shouldn't have worried about night catching us, sir, if I'd thought of this before," Gates laughed. "And there's plenty of extra acetylene tanks, too, so she carn't get away now!"

"You'll have to haul down some sail, though," I replied, seeing that the *Orchid* lay nearly abeam of us.

"No quicker said than done, sir."

He went to direct this, while we held our light squarely on the fleeing outlaw. Nobody was astir about her deck; indeed, so undisturbed did she appear that the sailor standing statue-like at her wheel might have been the only living thing aboard.

I breathed fast with thinking that maybe Sylvia might come up, and my senses were so alert, my mind, eyes, ears so intently reaching toward her, that now I heard what was indeed a most unexpected sound: a piano. Grasping Tommy's arm I whispered this to him, and he nodded, saying in a low tone:

"Yes, I hear it plainly. Reminds me of Monsieur's master musician playing a rhapsody in the dark, d'you remember? Listen! Gods, it's '*De puis le jour*,' from Louise!" Yet in the next breath he added: "Cheerful girl you have, Jack,—she's switched off from her love song to Chopin's funeral march!"

I dolefully smiled to myself, not at the funeral march but at the realization that dreams are only dreams and nothing more, that Gates's common sense had come nearer hitting the mark than all of our professor's psychology; for

I had seen no piano in that cabin, and five minutes ago I would have sworn its interior was as well known to me as the *Whim*. But an instant later my smile had given way to a cry of rage, as a little streak of fire spat from one of the portholes and the big lens of our searchlight, with a bang, shattered into a thousand pieces.

"The nerve of it," Tommy yelled, violently shaking his hand that had been resting on the brass frame. "Damn his hide, he nearly shot off my finger!"

"Are you hit?" I asked quickly.

"Hell, no; but my hand feels like a pincushion! Say, he knows how to shoot, though! I'll give him that much!"

"Those people are prepared for all that comes, I tell you," Monsieur vigorously nodded his head. "They must even have violet spectacles for looking into search-lights, else that fellow's eyes could not have stood the glare."

Again the *Orchid* was invisible. For a moment I thought that out of the dark sky my gods were derisively mocking me; but it was a human sound, a long, triumphant laugh, doubtless from the coarse-throated creature who had made the lucky shot.

Gates, fearing we might answer it in kind, came forward to counsel silence, at the same time sending a sailor for the megaphone and ordering another to extinguish our own lights. With his knife he then hastily cut the megaphone in half, keeping the large end whose openings now tapered from about eight inch to eighteen inch diameters. As we stood, not understanding what he meant to do, I heard across the water a rattling of blocks and knew the *Orchid*, free of pursuit, was changing her course. Gates cocked his head and listened, then whispered to the mate who went back and changed the *Whim's* course.

"Now, Mr. Jack," he said, in a guarded tone, "we're behind her, and dark, too; so keep all hands as quiet as mice, sir! Take the wheel and steer as I signal from under my coat with this electric torch, like this: one long, means put your helm up a point, two long means two points; but a short flash means down a point, two short down two points. D'you understand, sir? We've got to keep close to her, or daylight'll find her gone! I'm going out on the bowsprit and, with this piece of megaphone to help, think I can follow by sound. They're apt to make some noise, believing themselves safe. And their blocks are bound to rattle when they change their course—which they'll be doing before long as we're both headed for the coast of Florida, twenty-five or thirty miles off. Now go back quiet, sir, and watch for my lights."

God bless old Gates, I said to myself.

Till well into the night that indefatigable sea dog sat astride the bowsprit with the crude sound magnifier over his ear, while I, alert and watchful, gripped the wheel as though I were driving a speed boat. In the beginning he had sent a few signals, and we jockied this way and that, but after perhaps an hour we settled down to another straight course—though I could not tell how near we were, or if we were sailing right, or if they suspected us.

Tommy had come aft to keep me company, and now asked in a whisper:

"What do you think about that piano?"

"I think she played like an angel."

"Son, you don't get the point. What do you think about changing suddenly from that exquisite Charpentier love song to a funeral march—just before the rifle went off?"

"You don't mean she was signaling?" I asked in surprise, for the idea knocked me a little bit silly.

"I mean just that; of course, she was signaling, and taking a big chance, too. You may put your own construction on the first piece she played, but the instant she saw what they were up to she sent us the flash. The only trouble about it was that we weren't anywhere near as quick."

"But look here," I said, alarmed by another thought, "suppose she meant it would be *her* funeral march if we keep up the pursuit?"

Tommy considered this.

"I reckon not," he finally replied. "They might threaten us with her death if we don't turn back, but there'd be no reason to kill her otherwise. No, she saw them preparing to shoot—which you can't deny that they did, jolly good and well."

"She's a queen," I murmured.

"Queen! That girl must be a royal straight flush in hearts, and if it weren't for Nell I'd adore her to the tips of my teeth!"

At midnight I sent the mate to relieve Gates and gave the wheel to a likely sailor, and after making sure they understood the signals we went below for a bite to eat. Although the day of suspense had been wearing, my brain was too active to permit much thought of sleep; but finally Gates nodded, awoke with a jerk, and started off to bed. He had had no easy time of it on the bowsprit, good old Gates!

Tommy and I talked in low tones while the professor sat to one side, humped over and buried in thought. He was a strange looking spectacle when buried in thought. His countenance then became all wrinkles, with a kind of turned-up nubbin in the middle that I knew to be a nose, only because I'd previously seen it—otherwise it might have been almost anything that one does not expect to find in the center of a man's face. Tommy regarded him a moment in silence.

"Monsieur," he whispered, "come join this confab. We're up against the real thing in the morning, and may as well begin to lay pipe. The old catamount who shot out our searchlight won't have any more regard for our personal lights, let's keep that in mind. What's more, he has a real excuse now, because we fired those blanks at him which he'll find it convenient to say weren't blanks. So the business is coming off to a certainty. What's your idea?"

"My idea?"

"I meant to be that flattering, yes. What do you think we'll be up against when ordering the *Orchid* to surrender?"

"I do not know; but something we are not expecting, you may be sure," he dolefully answered.

"That sort of gloom won't get us anywhere," Tommy retorted. "Try another thought!"

"It gets us very far! If we expect to experience what we are not expecting, then we are expecting it! How can we be surprised when we are prepared for the thing we are not prepared for? It is obvious. That is my idea."

"Then you ought to keep it in a less fragile place. Try still another, gezabo!"

But he was inclined to pout now, and would neither talk nor listen to our entreaties.

"Well," he exclaimed at last, with a superior smile as he struck the table smartly, "I will tell you this: I have nothing more to say!"

It was a lot of preparation for a mighty small result, I thought, and Tommy smiled at the childish gentleman, murmuring sweetly:

"If you really mean that, and stick to it, pray accept my congratulations upon having reached the height of conversational charm. Now, Jack, let's plan!"

But Monsieur, while unwilling to talk, was also unwilling to be ignored. I think he wanted to be coaxed. People get that way, sometimes. So he petulantly exclaimed:

"You think I am what you call an old crank!"

"No I don't, honest!" Tommy gave me a wink. "Even if I did, it's a compliment in America to be called a crank, because cranks make things move. Now help us out, like a good sport. By this time tomorrow you'll be shot to pieces, for all we know."

He said it solemnly, but his humorous mouth showed how much he wanted to laugh. I believe Tommy would have walked to the gallows joking with his executioner. That infectious smile, sometimes the flash of his teeth, but always a snap in his honest gray eyes, were invariably quickened by the imminence of danger. I knew Tommy; therefore I also knew that beneath his jocose raillery were nerves stretched to concert pitch that meant music for whoever stood in his way tomorrow.

The professor sat up straighter and blinked at him.

"Why do you say I get shot to pieces?"

"Why not? The fellow'd be a fool to sit by and let us go aboard—and we've got to go aboard!"

"It is nonsense! You want my advice? Then leave him alone!"

I think that Tommy's eyes narrowed slightly. I know that my teeth clenched at this evidence of quitting; yet what could we expect from a chap who did nothing but teach in a University?

"You won't be in any danger," I said, arising. "We'll manage all right. Come on, Tommy!"

"You will not manage—that is just it," he angrily retorted. "You two boys will strut about like roosters showing what good fighters you are, and get blown up through the insides! Have I not seen it often? Bah!" He ran his hands through his hair. "Why is it, when brains are as easily cultivated as biceps, that young bloods think only of a strong arm! You stay in the cabin and leave the man to me; then I will take him before your eyes, and nobody get hurt!"

"I don't think we quite understand!"

"Of course! But there are no ladies on the *Orchid* whom I desire to charm, therefore I will be rational. Your *Capitaine* Gates will lower a boat, we row to the scoundrel's yacht, I present my authority, he surrenders, and we bring him back. There is no bloodshed, and my two young friends who are disposed to ridicule me will not get hurt!"

Tommy flushed, and I felt uncommonly like a pup.

"But suppose he won't come?—suppose he begins to fight?"—we asked these questions simultaneously. They were quite unnecessary, for the man would not come and, moreover, he would fight; but Monsieur's earnestness and visionary assumption had completely disarmed us.

"In that case, your Gates and I will shoot him," he answered, as a matter of course. "Such grizzly alternatives must sometimes be the means of peace and harmony."

Some might at times have called him an idiot, and on occasions I have found myself wondering if he possessed a scintilla of common sense, but no one after this could call him a coward. He would have gone single-handed to the *Orchid* with the same beautiful faith that a wee child would crawl into the kennel of a vicious dog. It was not in Monsieur to consider that anyone would dare disobey his Azurian authority.

"Gezabo," Tommy said tenderly, "I'm going to lock you up tomorrow, for if anyone so much as rumples your noble topknot I'll cut him to ribbons—so'll Jack. Now kick us, and go to bed. We've been a pair of braying asses, and you're a sure-nuff Prince!"

And, although I thought that Tommy had done most of the braying, I was willing to let it go at that. A lack of discriminating accuracy on his part might have been pardoned when we were faced by issues of so much greater portent. The dawn was but six hours off, and with it would come—what?

CHAPTER X
A SILENT ENEMY

Bilkins rushed into my room at daylight announcing perfect weather and the *Orchid* sailing some twelve miles astern of us. While dressing I wondered how she could have fallen so far behind, but assumed that our men on watch must finally have lost her. As this seemed to be a reasonable explanation, since the later the night the more probability of her company having settled down and become quiet, I dismissed these speculations of no consequence for a feeling of thankfulness that she had not escaped us.

Gates was on his way to call me when I came out, and one look at his broad smile required no further augury of good news.

"We're arfter her hard, sir," he said, "and have been drawing up farst this hour gone. We'll be in hailing distance in another two hours, or less."

"There's a good wind?"

"Fair, sir. The mate, who's aloft, says that for some reason she's hauled down everything but mains'l and jib, and carn't be making any speed to speak of. Still, she's going along. We've quite some canvas set. He says there was noise enough to follow till about five bells of the morning watch; then she grew so still he wondered if she'd sunk. You'd better have breakfast, sir, for we'll be on her, as I say, in two hours or less."

This was Tommy's idea when I met him with Monsieur in the cabin, but Tommy was always ready for breakfast. They had become reconciled—or, perhaps, I ought to say the professor seemed to have forgiven both of us handsomely. Gates sat down with us for there was much to talk about. In fact, the professor, in his uncontrollable and passionate appetite for grapefruit, had scarcely extruded a spray of its juice in our direction—the usual evidence with us that breakfast had seriously begun—when the question of how we should board the *Orchid* was raised. The old skipper listened to my plan, then to Tommy's, and after these he turned to our little scientist, who waved a hand with no small degree of impatience, saying:

"One is visionary, the other is crazy. One wants to blow her out of the water—with what? The other wants to do something no one can understand—and why? But they both agree upon killing everyone on board except a privileged lady. It is school-boy tomfoolery!"

"Tomfoolery your grandmother," Tommy flared up. "What do you suggest that's any better—the utopian scheme you sprung on us last night?"

"How do you know we have to board her?" Monsieur thrust half a biscuit in his mouth and took a long drink of coffee. "I have been thinking since; I have been on deck, and observed. There is wind, and we are catching up. Off there," he pointed toward something the cabin walls prevented us from seeing, "is land; low, gray-blue land. Now it can be done with cattle, but can it be done with yachts?"

"Can what be done?" we asked.

"We shall sail out, head her back, and drive her into the land until she sticks!"

Never having heard of such a silly idea I looked at Gates, who was chuckling.

"Oh, it might be done, sir," he laughed, "if she stood close enough to the islands. We might jockey her that way, foul her a bit, and make her go aground—or fight. But, Lor' bless you, she's sailing straight west across the Gulf, with nothing but a thousand miles of good water between her and the mouth of the Rio Grande!"

"Get in front—butt her around," Monsieur cried. "If she does not like it, then let her, as you suggest, fight!"

"Well, you've said something at last," Tommy grinned. "How about it, Gates? And, by the way, what are those islands you spoke of? We're looking for a certain

'—one of many, many islands
Set like emerald jewels in an ever changing sea.'"

Though with his sincerity there was also the bantering tone of the unbeliever here.

"It's the Ponce de Leon Bay, sir, with the Ten Thousand Islands—and I'd say there're all of ten thousand, or quite harf, anyway."

With his fork he quickly drew on the tablecloth a sketch of southwestern Florida, outlining the waters northeast of Cape Sable and with little jabs indicating the island area which extends up and down the coast, as well as into Whitewater Bay. Gates was used to doing this kind of thing and he did it well, with the result that we got a very clear idea of what he meant. No one knew the exact number of islands, he said, because they had never been charted. Government surveys had been considered useless, in all probability; and, of private interests, there were none. No boat, except perhaps at rare intervals a very small craft of adventurous spirit, ever tried to enter—but, as to that, twenty small boats might spend a month's playing in that maze and never meet. The mainland, for many miles in all directions, was without habitation, and these conditions had isolated this entire section as completely as though it were in the heart of a South American jungle.

Difficult as it was to believe that on the "Playground Peninsula" of eastern United States an unsurveyed primeval wilderness of perhaps three thousand square miles had remained absolutely detached from inquisitive civilization, I was soon to learn that Gates had not in any way exaggerated. It was there; it is there today in the same unbroken solitude, for any to see who will.

"Why didn't she duck in there and hide last night?" I asked, coming out of the charmed spell his description had cast over me.

"She daren't, sir. Nothing but a dinghy, or the like of that, has ever gone in very far. Leastwise, I don't think so. The islands are just a lot of oyster-shell bars covered with sand and overgrown with red mangrove trees. I've been told the channel between 'em sometimes isn't more'n a foot deep; but in other places there may be good water. What I mean to say is that they're not charted, and I doubt if any man living could find his way through 'em the same way twice. They lay in a bunch stretching about forty miles north and south, and maybe fifteen or twenty through. Some are good sized—we'll say a mile long—but others run down to the size of the *Whim*. Oh, he wouldn't dare to run in there, sir! Now we might try to tease him close to 'em and crowd him some way, as the professor says—or let him do the other thing!"

"That sounds like some plan," Tommy sprang to his feet. "We'll tease him, all right, if we shoot fast enough!"

"But they must be let to begin that shooting first," Monsieur insisted.

"I'd like to know why?" Tommy turned to him.

"Why? What right have we to come and start such a business?"

"What right have we to crowd her out of the ocean?" Tommy answered with another question. "What right have they to blow us up?—or steal a girl?—or counterfeit our money?—or darn near shoot my finger off and then laugh at me? To hell with rights! We've got more than that scoundrel has, if we haven't any!"

Gates got up with an oath.

"Yes," he said, "and shoot out my searchlight! No, Professor, I'd say the shooting's already begun. But they won't stand for too much fooling, not if I know anything!"

"Oh, well," Monsieur sighed, "give me the gun."

"Give him Miss Nancy," Tommy laughed. "Now, fellows, suppose a couple of us entrench on top of the cabin, to get the advantage of altitude—the superiority of position, as it were—and command their decks!"

"You'll need a fair protection, sir, as they'll be shooting from the portholes," Gates said. "And we carn't fire back at the portholes because of the lady!"

"Righto! But the man at their wheel's our meat, and anyone else who comes to take his place. Minus a steersman they're helpless; and then, Gates, if we can run alongside and batten down (is that what you call it?) their hatches, they're ours."

"Suppose they send the Princess out, herself, to steer?" Monsieur asked.

The suggestion gave me a turn.

"Still, they may not think of that," he continued, "and our two shooters may command their decks quite easily. It is good. If a man comes out to steer you will shoot him till he runs downstairs again, then we go aboard and sail home. Yes, it is a good plan."

"Shoot him till he runs downstairs!" Tommy gasped. "What d'you think we're going to do—just spank him with lead?"

"I'll say that professor is in a clarss by himself, sir," Gates turned to me, chuckling.

The next half hour was a busy one. Our sailors, singing with happiness, brought up from the cuddy rolls of extra sails that were lowered overboard for a good wetting, then mauled into a neat rifle pit on the cabin roof—as snug as I'd want anywhere, and quite able to stop high-power bullets. Gates then showed another bit of generalship that called anew for Monsieur's nods of approval. Since our own helmsman would be as much exposed as the man on the *Orchid*—whom we intended to "shoot until he ran downstairs"—the mate brought up some line, bent it several times around the wheel drum, passed it through newly fastened blocks, and let it run into the cockpit. By this arrangement he could lie on the floor, as safe as you please, and steer according to orders sung up by the old skipper who, stationed below with a shaving mirror—suggesting a trench periscope—would take his bearings without showing any portion of his face. It was a nice piece of work.

"One carn't be too cautious, sir," he explained. "Harf our chance of coming out ahead is being ready beforehand, and harf our satisfaction is to keep from having any burials at sea—which are gruesome things, any way you take 'em, sir."

Bilkins had acted as armorer and laid out rifles, bandoliers bulging with filled clips, and a few automatic revolvers; then in a low tone he said to me:

"I'll never go back, sir, if anything happens to you today."

"Yes, you will," I replied, touched by his show of devotion. "You'll have to tell them why it happened. But don't be a raincrow. We'll come through."

Gates now sent the men to stations for we were within a half a mile of the *Orchid*. Then Tommy stepped into our rifle pit and laid down. I followed. Quietly each of us beat a crease in the soaked canvas through which we could fire without showing too much head.

The mate, crouched below, tried his new steering device as Gates sang up an order, and swore a jovial oath at the ease with which the *Whim* responded. Within his reach was an automatic, and he looked the very picture of contentment.

Along the side of my rifle barrel now resting in the crease I took a good look at the *Orchid* sailing with apparent unconcern but a short way out from us, but I could picture the activity and hatred seething below her deck. I wondered what Sylvia might be thinking about all this; if she associated our pursuit by the slightest imaginative thread with a fellow who impolitely stared at her in a Havana café, yet to whom she had been willing to cry: "I am in danger!" Presumptuous fallacy! Then other thoughts began to race through my brain. Now that we were face to face with action, how were we going to come out? Had I a right to imperil those who were sailing with me? Was it not my duty, even at this eleventh hour, to order the *Whim* back?

I turned to Tommy, saying:

"You didn't ship for this kind of thing, old man. If anything happens to you I'll feel like the devil."

"So'll I," he grinned. "Don't bother about how you'll feel if anything happens to *me*; keep those regrets for the moment a hot pill investigates your own honorable insides, Mr. Jackass! I wouldn't miss this party for a million dollar bill. Settle down, now. Gates is pointing closer." Then, peeping along his rifle, he crooned one of our regimental paraphrases: "Stick your head up, Fritzy-Fritz, while I plug you in the gizzard," adding: "I don't see anyone at their wheel!"

I took another squint and, just as he had said, their deck was deserted—not a man in sight.

"What d'you make of it?" I asked.

"Get down," he warned. "Don't forget that anyone who could center our searchlight, as some crafty boy did last night, won't have much trouble peeling a scalp at three hundred yards! They've probably made a steering rig like ours, that's all. The first thing we know bally hell will spit out of those portholes, if my guess counts! Beats a trench raid, doesn't it, old man?"

"All hollow," I agreed. "We've got 'em this trip!"

"We have unless they carry a ten-pounder—in which case we'll take a bath. Freeze close, buddie!"

Nearer and nearer we drew, but no bally hell came from her. She showed absolutely no sign of anyone, not even a pile of canvas or a box that might hide a sharp-shooter. That, then, was the old counterfeiter's ruse: to tempt us into taking the initiative when, more than likely, he was ready with the probable ten-pounder to sink us. Still, it felt rather snug to be lying there elbow to elbow with Tommy.

Gates had steered so close by this time that any skipper on the other yacht, not endowed with stupendous nerve, would certainly have gone about; for we had maneuvered to get the right of way, and a collision would have been entirely the *Orchid's* fault. But no one ran out, nor did her course change, and at the very last minute Gates called an order that brought us off a few points.

We were now sailing parallel, not more than ten fathoms apart, and could have thrown a biscuit on her deck. I glanced out the corner of my eye at Tommy. His cheek rested snugly against the stock of his rifle and his finger stroked the trigger, I thought affectionately.

Had either of us been more conversant with nautical matters we would have noticed something that Gates now came crawling up to tell us. He did this without being much exposed, by creeping along until abreast of us and then projecting himself, headfirst or any other way, into our midst. It was an active accomplishment for one of Gates's years.

"D'you see what they've done?" he excitedly asked. "That wheel, there, is lashed over; they've paid out the mains'l enough to starboard, and set the jib properly to port. That's why the fores'l isn't up!"

"What of it?"

"Why, sir, she'll sail that way all day in a wind like this, and nobody have to touch her! They knew we'd be popping at their helmsman, and they fixed it so we carn't! Now it's our turn to start something!"

"Then start it," Tommy said. "Run alongside and we'll climb over!"

"Mr. Thomas," he demurred, "that's rank piracy, unless we're the law. I wouldn't say no, understand, if there warn't some other way. But if we try it they'll have every right to shoot us down—which they can easy do, being hid and ready!"

"You forget, Gates, they haven't a right on earth. They don't want to face the law with the best justification ever known—they'd be mortally afraid to!"

"Then they wouldn't be any less particular about shooting us," the old skipper replied.

There was no denying that Tommy had impaled himself upon his own point; not that he cared a hang whether they began shooting or not, but the anxiety of Gates caused him to temporize, and he said:

"Bluff it! Sing across that we're the U. S. A. ordering 'em to stop. Say it strong enough to make us believe it, too, Gates—so we'll feel self-righteous when the scrap comes!"

Gates grinned and, cupping his hands, shouted:

"*Orchid,* ahoy! This yacht's chartered by the U. S. Secret Service, and you're ordered to come about! Delay one minute and we blow you out of the water!"

"Accomplished old liar," Tommy chuckled. "See anything?"

Gates, so earnest was he in this rôle of Uncle Sam, had his watch out, marking off the seconds. When the sixtieth had ticked he called again, in a more ferocious tone:

"Time's up, but I'll give you harf a minute longer! This is the larst word!"

"Now," said Tommy, having waited the thirty seconds which brought no response, "let's see you make good! Will you fire a torpedo, or one of the fifteen-inch guns?"

But Gates was seeing no humor in the situation; neither was I; neither was Tommy, if the truth were known. Our position was in a sense desperate. We had bluffed and the bluff had been called. Five minutes ago we might have turned back, but such a course now would make us laughing-stocks even to ourselves. And there was Sylvia. What sort of a quitter would she think me!

I saw that someone had to board that yacht, even though such a course, almost to a certainty, meant a test of the professor's surgical skill—a skill we knew he possessed along with his other attainments. But I could not—I simply would not—risk any of our fellows on an undertaking so hazardous. Conscious, however, of Tommy's utter pig-headedness I saw the futility of merely asking him to stay behind; so my mind became instantly made up and, turning to Gates, I sharply asked:

"Who commands here?"

"Why, I'm the captain, sir," he answered, surprised at my tone.

"But whose orders are absolute?"

"Yours, Mr. Jack, sir."

"Then take this man below and keep him there while you run your rail alongside the *Orchid*. Nobody follows me until I call, or shoot. Be lively, Captain!"

He looked his horror, but stiffly saluted, saying "Come" to Tommy who had turned white with anger and murderously glared at me.

"Do you mean this dirty trick?" he asked, and I did not meet his eyes when admitting it.

In a few minutes he and Gates were safely in the cabin—Gates having dived nimbly out of our canvas fort; while Tommy, oozing rage, had walked erect, shaking his fist at the *Orchid* and calling me pretty much every kind of a lizard that crawls the earth.

Perhaps the mad that this aroused was good for me. I had charged into an enemy's face once or twice under a certain amount of unpleasant fire and most uncomfortable sensations. A fellow's *savoir faire* is far from being faultless on such occasions, but if he's mad—damn mad—he gets along rather well, and Tommy's insulting words turned the trick for me.

We had luffed a bit to let the *Orchid* draw out ahead, and now all I seemed to see was her slowly nearing rail; twenty feet away, fifteen, ten. My rifle had been laid aside, and I felt to see that my automatic was snugly nested in its holster. Five feet, four, three—we were about to touch! With a bound I cleared my shelter just as the rails were within spanning distance, and vaulted over.

CHAPTER XI
A STRANGE FIND

My feet had no more than touched the new deck when I became electrified with a glorious feeling of possession, of mastery. Immediately I seemed to know just what to do, where to go; and my first move was another headlong rush at the companionway door, bursting it in with a kick and springing quickly aside—ready, listening; being for the time shielded from a fusillade of expected shots. And, because these were not forthcoming, I felt momentarily confused.

Yet in times of white hot action it is impulse that succeeds. This door ahead of me was the only way below, except perhaps a hatch, offering greater danger, somewhere forward; it was the only way, therefore, through which Sylvia might be brought up to safety. She was now below, and I would reach her if it were my last journey! Three bounds down the stairs took me into the cabin, my pistol forward, my nerves on hair-trigger, ready for anything that moved.

Silence!—that sickish silence which permeates places of death! No human sound could be detected—no sound of any kind, except an uncanny creaking beneath the floor where the old masts rested in their steps, and a gentle swish of water outside the hull.

There were two doors from the cabin, each opening into a separate, though parallel, passageway that doubtless led forward to about the same general arrangements we had on the *Whim*—one past three staterooms, through a galley and into the sailors' quarters; the other, also past a stateroom or two, but opening to the ice-box room and galley. Both of these doors now swung slightly ajar, at a suspicious angle that almost without doubt told me where the men were crouched, and this rendered my position so inexcusably exposed that swift and vigorous action was the only choice. With finger tightening on the trigger I dashed at the nearer of these, giving it a kick that sent it banging against the wall. The passageway was empty, and thus encouraged I rushed the other door. Here, again, no foe had lain in ambush.

I was crouched now, sheltered by a strip of paneled wall between the two doorways. The staterooms on one side must come next, and after them the galley, with the forecastle beyond, and even beyond this, perhaps, some kind of a cuddy.

Where the men were hiding God only knew, but hiding they were with cocked weapons, firmly gripped knives at some point of vantage that had been carefully chosen—as they expected nothing less than half our crew. I could almost feel their nearness; so alert were my senses that I fancied I could smell their sweaty clothes.

Again action spelled success and, marking the first stateroom, I bounded into it covering the interior with a quick sweep of my automatic. Nothing! From this I sprang to the second room, showing myself in the passageway only long enough to cover the space. This, also, was empty.

A third was on this side before the galley should be reached. By my tactics of quick rushes I had doubtless made too fleeting a target to draw their fire, so I dashed at this third door. It was closed but yielded to my shoulder. As I entered, and became instantaneously aware that it contained no foe, my nerves were fired by the sound of rushing feet behind me.

Trapped! At such a time a man will ask an awful price for his life—when he is trapped by merciless villains to whom quarter is an unknown tongue! Springing behind the door, keeping only my pistol hand and eye beyond its thin partition, I waited with leveled weapon, ready to drop the first man who came in sight. He did not keep me long in suspense. It was Gates, while behind him pressed several anxious faces.

"Thank God, sir, you're not killed," he shouted.

I was glad to see him, there's no denying it!

"Mr. Thomas said he heard you call, so we came a-biling, sir!"

My mind was working rather fast; indeed, it seemed to be thinking at the rate of a thousand miles a minute—clear thinking, too—so even before Gates spoke the second time I had seen through Tommy's ruse. Bless his old scalp, I was a dog not to have taken him in the first place, now that things were nearer equal. But I said hastily:

"Look sharp, Gates, I haven't been farther than here! They're in the galley!—I'm rushing it!"

So I splintered the door and charged through, with the others tripping over my heels. Then my revolver swung across and covered a crouching form.

"Hands up," I commanded.

Although darker here, we could see a huge, partially clothed figure on the floor, reclining very much as The Wounded Gladiator. Leaning above him, with an arm passed beneath his shoulders, was another man.

"Hands up, you fool," I called again, ready to fire at the first suspicious move. The man lowered his burden and turned. It was Tommy.

"You'll forgive me, Jack," he grinned. "We thought I heard you call—and that was to be the signal, you know!"

We thought I heard you call!

"I know about that, you prince of liars. Who's this? But hold him!—we're going on through!"

"You needn't," he said. "I took a speedy trip down the other passageway while Gates went to you. There isn't a soul on board, except this poor devil who's got a crack on the bean."

"It isn't possible," I cried. For, indeed, it was not possible, and we hurried forward, leaving him as he was.

But a two-minute search revealed the truth of Tommy's words. There was not a sign of anyone. The yacht was as absolutely deserted as if it had been sailed by spirits—except, of course, the wretch in Tommy's charge.

"You're sure we've looked everywhere, Gates?" I asked, stunned at the disappearance of Sylvia and mystified by the whole affair.

"Everywhere, sir. To tell the truth, Mr. Jack, a minute ago it was as complete a mystery as I ever saw. But I understand it now. They've taken to the small boats and escaped, sir. They've just sailed in close to shore and done that during the night, sir; and all morning we've been chasing a boat with nobody on it. I should have noticed the small boats gone, if I hadn't been so sure the people were here."

I leaned against the wall too utterly disappointed to move, vaguely wondering if this were another dream from which I should awake and find the *Orchid* sailing out ahead of us. But it was no dream. In dreams one can not always know that one is dreaming, but there is never a doubt of knowing when one is awake.

"They couldn't be under the floor?" I asked, absurdly clinging to a straw of hope that Sylvia might be there.

"Lor' bless you, no, sir! I tell you, Mr. Jack, they just sailed as close as they dared to those islands, and skipped—the hull pack of 'em; first having headed the *Orchid* out as we found her. That's why everything was so quiet the larst part of the night—there warn't anyone here to *make* a noise!"

Passing back to the galley we saw half our crew, in a circle, looking down at the wounded man.

"Who is it, Tommy?" I asked. "Not the old scoundrel himself, by any good luck?"

"Stranger yet," he said, waving the others back and standing up, "It's your black giant of the Key West docks!"

"How the devil did he get here?" I cried, pushing between the men and also looking down at him. "How did he get here?" I asked again, but Tommy had gone.

Someone had put a cushion under his head. His eyes were open, gazing up with their former gentle expression; more sad now, I fancied, since the great human machine he had controlled was wounded.

"How did he get here?" I repeated my general question, this time straight at him.

His lips moved with a curious, rather horrible, inarticulate sound, and his glance swept our crew as though in search of a face. Then he seemed to give it up, and passed a hand slowly over his forehead. I was about to order him carried on deck when Tommy called through the galley portlight:

"Fetch your wounded, Jack! The professor's here with his outfit!"

As our men stooped to obey the big fellow surprised us by quietly arising; and, when cushions had been arranged in a shaded place above, he laid on them as obediently as a docile mastiff. Monsieur, very much in his element, became busy at once.

The *Whim* and the *Orchid* were still at grips—or rather were it more correct to say the *Orchid* was in the *Whim's* grip. Lines had been passed through the chocks of each, sails had been hauled down, and both yachts rode inertly side by side.

The part of our crew that had stayed behind to attend these matters now came over the rail like monkeys, grinning broadly and crowding up to shake hands with me—a wholly uncalled for proceeding which charmed me, nevertheless.

"Lie on your face," I heard Monsieur saying to the big black. He had become excessively busy and his fingers were feeling everywhere over the man's cranium, yet as tenderly as a woman's. "What struck you?" he asked.

"I've told you he can't talk," Tommy, who was also kneeling by him, explained.

"And I did not ask you," the professor snapped. "What if he can not! May I not see him make the effort?"

"But what's the use of having the poor beggar make the effort when you know he can't put it over? Why not get down to cases and cure him, instead of monkeying?"

"Down to cases! Cure him!" Monsieur sputtered. "How great a surgeon are you to direct me in this impertinent manner?"

Really, he was quite a great deal put out.

"You fellows cut it," I interposed. "While you're squabbling the chap might click it, and then what?"

"I'm not squabbling," Tommy looked up earnestly. "I'm only saying it's a rotten shame to put a *blessé* through a lot of unnecessary paces that hurt him, and I stick to it! But go ahead, professor!"

"I shall go ahead, have no fear of it! You think me cruel—but see: if I am aware something is wrong with a machine, how better to find out what than by trying to make it run?"

He turned again to his examination, while Tommy lit a cigarette and sat nearby, looking on. At last Monsieur gave a sigh, indicating that his diagnosis was ready. I waited until he, too, had lit a cigarette, then asked:

"Well, doctor, how serious?"

"Perhaps not serious, as there is no fracture. He has suffered a concussion over the third frontal convolution, resulting in an aphasia—aphemia we are sure of, and doubtless also agraphia—"

"Hold on! This isn't the University of Bucharest," Tommy cried. "If you insist on telling us, instead of putting this man to bed where he ought to be, tell it nursery-fashion!"

"Already I have said it for children," he witheringly replied.

"Then God help 'em!" This in a whisper from Gates, but with no thought of levity.

"Go ahead and cure the man," I implored. "We couldn't understand you, anyhow."

"But, yes, you will understand—I desire it! This blow has produced the aphemia. If he were not illiterate we could, by asking him to write, say if agraphia also is present. But he can not write, therefore we do not know whether he can or not; so, therefore, we only know that he can not speak."

"You know he can't write, too—you just said so!"

"Exactly, my boy Tommy, you have the correct idea. Yet we do not know it by the test."

"I begin to see what he's driving at, Jack. He knows he can't write because it's a known fact, but he doesn't know it by the scientifically known test known to him—and that's agraphia. If it isn't, it's near enough. Now, he knows he can talk because we all know he can, but no one knows it at present because he can't—and that's aphemia. Do I get you, Professor?"

"Yes, as you say, you get me. The motor area has suffered a concussion; perhaps a slight hemorrhage, perhaps not. It may pass in a few days, or longer. We will keep him quiet, with ice bags to the head and blood pressure low, and see what we shall see. A hundred years ago they would have bled him and made him well. But we shall see!"

"If he'd got well a hundred years ago by being bled, why not now?" I asked.

"He'd be too old now," Tommy whispered; but the professor, not hearing this, looked at me as though I had committed an unpardonable breach of etiquette, and again witheringly replied:

"We have more advanced methods."

Having thus been put in my place, he ordered his patient taken aboard the *Whim* and ran ahead to superintend the construction of a bed. Scientists are a curious lot, Tommy says, but I doubt if there is another like the professor. I hope not, for the sake of the sciences. But let that pass. In half an hour the big black was resting easily in the midst of paraphernalia especially designed, and Bilkins had been assigned the place as nurse.

I fancied, when this latter suggestion came up, that our old servant might not readily take to it. With twenty years of his life spent as major domo and general valet in my father's household, a sudden transformation into trained nurse for a dusky African must, peradventure, have been a shock.

But in this I was mistaken. The last forty hours of common peril, of a central interest, had lifted Bilkins from that pettiness usually burdensome in servants of his type. He was, as a matter of fact, cheerfully alert to take the job, accepting it with the same enthusiasm that Gates, and later the mate, had straddled the bowsprit. So I realized that Bilkins had doffed the uniform of servitude to put on one that fit a man. True, indeed, there is no such potent melting-pot as common peril! It had been the same in France—banker, lawyer, merchant, beggar-man, thief, perhaps—all one. Common peril, common necessity!—O thou molders of men!

When everything had been arranged, and a sailor put at our ice machine to supply packs for the wounded man's head, Tommy, the professor and I climbed back aboard the *Orchid*, this time to give her a thorough search. We held to the hope that there might be a note, or little clue, from the girl whose extremity had once led her to send the other message. Monsieur thought this most probable, and our hopes ran high.

Beginning with a writing desk in the cabin, we examined the book shelves and every nook and corner, then passed to the staterooms. These gave the same impression of having been swept clean—cupboards, presses, all were empty. Only in one drawer, delicately scented, was there a single item—a hairpin. Here, then, must be Sylvia's room, but otherwise it was devoid of any article. Equally unproductive did we find the galley, the crew's quarters, and a small cuddy forward.

Monsieur sat down and pursed his lips.

"They have anticipated our intention," he said, thoughtfully. "Doubtless the things were emptied into sheets, then either weighted and sunk, or taken in the boats. But she must have exerted her ingenuity. There absolutely must be some word left for us. Wait!"

Hurrying to the *Whim* he returned with his lens, while from the mate he had borrowed a caliper, a two-foot rule and a sail needle.

"Now we shall search scientifically," he cried. "Remember, that as no personal belonging remains, even the books being gone, we must infer they made a great effort to destroy everything that would leave a clue. They suspected the girl, too, and that made them doubly careful. What would she do then? Exactly as we would do—hide her message so the others could not discover it! Now, my boy Jack, you take the sail needle and probe cushions, pillows and mattresses! My boy Tommy, take my lens and look for places where the glue has been disturbed on furniture joints; I will measure the desk, piano, panels—everything—for a secret hiding place!"

"Well, I'll be darned," Tommy grinned. "You're some cop, professor!"

When each of us had finished and reported failure, Monsieur did not seem at all discouraged.

"Now we go to the second phase," he said. "Keep in mind, whenever you search for anything, that it may be under your nose. That is the place to look, not off at the clouds—and nothing is too insignificant to escape investigation. For see: I can write on a very thin piece of paper, roll it into a string, thread it into a bodkin, and weave it into a rug, curtain, quilt, and so forth; or press it lengthwise into a crack in the floor. A favorite way is to tie it to a real piece of string, and throw them carelessly into a wastebasket, thus making them appear to have been cut from a bundle. But there are a thousand ways! Now we proceed with this. Later we probe down gas jets, water spouts and outlets, empty lamp reservoirs, unscrew the backs of mirrors, search key holes, unravel carpets—"

"Heavens," I cried, seeing that in his zeal for doing this professionally he was making himself absurd; and Tommy burst into a hearty laugh, saying:

"Gezabo, there isn't a girl in a million who'd think of those places, and if she did she wouldn't credit us with enough sense to find 'em. Call off your bloodhounds! There's no message for us, that's a cinch! Let's get busy at once on something practical!"

"That's what I say," I chipped in. "It's only eleven o'clock, and we have eight good hours of daylight. Let's go back and call Gates for a conference, without losing a minute!"

"You may be right," he sighed, "but—well, let us go, as you say. With eight hours of light we can accomplish everything. Today may bring success!"

CHAPTER XII
THE HURRICANE

Tommy's spirits were sky high. While treating our situation seriously he found in every phase of it some new sense of humor, whereas the professor looked on with grim purpose. Gates occupied rather a neutral ground, I think, perhaps alternately leaning one way and the other. But I was gripped by a single idea, a deep and growing love for this fugitive girl to whom I had never spoken, who I did not know, but had sworn to rescue.

As we climbed back to the *Whim* and summoned Gates it was understood that haste meant everything. Yet we could not very well move before knowing whither the outlaw crew had gone. That they made for Florida was, of course, self-evident, but where upon that vast stretch of coast? Would they entrench and wait? Were they even now watching with binoculars from a pine tree top to discover our next move, or had they set out at once for the security of the Everglades, the prairies, or the forests? Any of those trackless vastnesses to the eastward might hide a battalion of men for months; therefore, in case they had run, what hope of finding them?

These and other facts I put before my friends while they listened in glum silence—indeed, with hardly a move except the pipes carried mechanically to their lips or down. Tommy's brier was empty, but his teeth were tight upon the stem and I saw the muscles of his jaws working, as though grinding up my conclusions.

"So that's how it stands," I said, at last. "Personally I lean to the Ten Thousand Islands. Gates tells us the location is unexplored; it offers ten thousand hiding places and, in the circumstances, they couldn't ask for anything better."

Monsieur stretched back in his chair and blew out a volume of smoke, adding:

"It is the Islands, of course. And I think there is little doubt what they did after landing. They did not start inland. They feel secure where they are, and there they will remain to watch us. It may also be their lair, their home, for they must have a home ashore somewhere! *Mon Capitaine*, you know with certainty there is not a channel deep enough for our yacht?"

"I never heard of one," Gates answered. "Of course, there might be; only I never heard of it."

"If there were, why did they abandon the *Orchid*?" Tommy asked.

"It will bear looking into," the professor mused. "Now, that paper with the dots and rambling line! Could it represent a chart to their stronghold?"

"From what I saw in it, as a sea-faring man," Gates answered, "the bearings on that paper didn't tell enough. No one could sail in new water without a plainer chart than that. No, sir, if it means anything at all, I'd say it meant something else."

"We're wasting a lot of golden time here," I said. "What if there is a channel, and what if the paper does mark the entrance to it! That doesn't get us anywhere. How could we tell which were the right two islands to go between, when there're thousands of 'em on the water and less than fifty on the paper, and not even a landmark of any kind indicated! As Gates says, it isn't plain enough."

Monsieur seemed to be unconvinced, and Tommy began to laugh at him, saying:

"Gates would be an idiot to sail into a lot of treacherous oyster bars guided by that poor excuse of a thing! Sylvia drew it for a subterfuge, anyhow, not a chart. I've got the right dope, so listen: Those crooks are ashore watching us right now—it's a cinch they are, because any of us, placed in their position, would be doing the same. Now if we sail in and push things, they'll run off and we couldn't find 'em again—probably never. So let's divide our crew and sail both yachts straight out across the Gulf—like we're going home. Then they'll think we've given up the chase and be off their guard. But when we get over the horizon we'll make a circle back, and after dark anchor in some cove north of this island area—if Gates knows a good one. From that point, being well hid and unsuspected, we'll conduct operations by land as we think best. How about it?"

It was the most sensible thing I could see, and said so. The others quite enthusiastically agreed, and in a few minutes the two yachts were sailing prettily westward. Lower and lower sank the Ten Thousand Islands, and sometime after we finished luncheon a sailor aloft reported them gone. Then with a will we changed our course and began the big circle back.

Gates had been making observations. His chart showed a cove about ten miles north of the island area, but too shallow for the *Whim*. Yet ten miles farther north of that was another inlet with fairly good water. Some thought this would be the logical place to anchor, while others insisted it was too far from operations.

"We might establish an outpost in the little cove," I said, at last, "making a camp there and keeping the launch with us, while the *Whim* stays in the larger cove as a base to fall back on in case of necessity."

"The launch won't do," Tommy corrected. "In a quiet place like that its put-put could be heard for miles. Paddles, oars or sails for these still waters, Jack!"

He was right. Moreover, one of our small boats did have a center-board, thwart and portable mast, so that obstacle was easily crossed.

"Now," he continued, "I approve of Jack's plan, and suggest that tonight we slip into Big Cove—hereinafter to be so called—and anchor the *Orchid*. Then with a whole crew we'll sail down outside of Little Cove, land provisions, ammunition, and stuff like that for the scouting party. After this the *Whim* goes back and waits alongside the *Orchid*. The thing now is to decide on signals. Who knows the Morse?"

Gates answered promptly that he did; but I did not, so Tommy wrote the alphabet on a card, saying:

"You've this afternoon to memorize it, and tonight I'll drill you. It'll do between ourselves, Jack, if we get separated. But how shall we reach you, Gates? Have you any black powder for smoke balls?"

"Lor' bless you, sir, we've only what's in a few shells belonging to Miss Nancy. It would take a fair sized keg to signal that far, sir!"

I will not recount the hours I walked back and forth along the deck, with a flag in one hand and Tommy's card in the other, making what to the uninitiated would have seemed a perfectly ridiculous spectacle. But I had got quite well along, and was standing near the foremast wig-wagging a message to an imaginary pair of violet eyes—for man can be silly and serious at one and the same time—when a little puff of hot air struck my face. It was the second puff of this kind I had noticed. Gates now came up and joined me.

"There's a howl of something coming, sir," he said. "I've had suspicions of it all day, but now the barometer's touched bottom."

"The sky's clear," I suggested.

He laughed, though without humor.

"A sky isn't always clear because there're no clouds in it, Mr. Jack."

"But what do you expect, Gates? We don't have storms at this season!"

"You're right, sir. But once in a long while there'll be a howler, and that's what the barometer is trying to tell us now. As we have only harf a crew on each yacht I think we'd better make a bee-line in. 'Twill take us twenty miles north of where we were, and those fellows carn't see us."

I never disputed conditions of weather with Gates, so the course was changed and we started on our run to land, which he thought might be reached by dark. In this he was right, for as the sun, like a strangely weird greenish ball, touched the horizon our prow, leading the *Orchid* by half a mile, entered the protecting waters of Big Cove.

Just at this moment Bilkins dashed up from the cabin, looking scared and yelling:

"He won't stay quiet, sirs; I can't make him!"

We would have thought a delirium had seized the big black had not he then appeared from the same doorway, regarding us with an air of rationality. I have never seen a smile more broad, or more expressive of relief. It simply radiated happiness, and Tommy, staring at him, began to hum a song that had cheered us many a time in the trenches.

"By Jingo, Tommy," I cried, "we'll name him that!"

And thus he was christened Smiles—which, however, through some fatuous process of fabrication so soon grew to Smilax, that as Smilax he shall henceforth be known.

The frown of displeasure that had gathered on Monsieur's brow fled as the fellow spoke. For he did speak, telling in his own style that the concussion had been a mere bagatelle, that his faculties had returned quite unimpaired after their brief absence, and that he was hungry but ready to serve us. What he did actually say to express this—to which the professor would have devoted five whole minutes of scientific phrasing—was:

"Me well."

Monsieur sprang forward and imperiously commanded him to sit facing the western glow. He then proceeded to squint closely into the patient fellow's eyes, he felt of his head, his pulse, and looked at his tongue. At last he stood back, pondering with an air of deep solemnity.

"It is true," he sighed. "The man is well."

"You look like we ought to put the flag at half-mast," I said. "What's the objection to a little snicker?"

"I do not understand," he murmured, ignoring this flippancy, "how he got well so soon."

"Of all the funereal old bugs!" Tommy began to laugh at him. "If you ever doctored me, gezabo, and I happened to recover, darned if I wouldn't turn around and die out of pity for you! Come here, Smilax, I want to ask some questions!"

The result of Tommy's probing showed that late the previous afternoon, while this negro was fishing sponges, the *Orchid* deliberately ran him down.

She would not have stopped, but luckily he grasped the bowsprit stays and climbed aboard of her. Here he was met and roundly cursed by angry men who were, for a while, at least, in favor of throwing him back. He had seen the *Whim* following. No, he had not seen a lady. Yes, he had heard strange music that, with our shooting at them, decided him to swim off to us during the night.

To Tommy's further questioning we learned that he knew nothing of the Ten Thousand Islands except through hearsay. As to his wound the recital was brief: he had been put to work wrapping up many things in old sails; two men came into the galley and stood by while he finished the last bundle, then one of them who wore a cap like—he pointed to Gates—stepped behind him, something crashed upon his head, and that was all.

Tommy drew in his breath with a sharp hiss, saying:

"That's a cold blooded bunch!"

"They're on those islands, sir," Gates cried. "I just feel it!"

The mate and his half of the crew had come aboard after making the *Orchid* snug for whatever weather the increasing sultriness portended, while Tommy took Smilax forward to coach him in the manipulation of an automatic revolver—for this modern arm puzzled the big negro who was, however, nicely skilled in the use of older models.

That something brewed in the way of a storm did not require a barometer or the eye of a seaman to determine, so I insisted upon speeding up preparations for the landing force. This met the approval of all, since the skipper thought it likely that we could be put ashore and the *Whim* get well on her way back to Big Cove before the disturbance came.

While we ate a hasty supper, therefore, Bilkins saw that the things we should want were stored in the small boat: food, ammunition, canvas for a lean-to, matches, utensils of sundry kinds—in fact, the necessaries. He had attended to my camping outfits before, and possessed a genius for knowing what to include. Only when this was under way, and the mate had thrice assured Gates of his ability to navigate the *Whim* on her ticklish course down the coast, did the old captain feel satisfied to join us at table.

He brought with him a large chart that he pinned to the wall and, nodding to it as he tucked a napkin under his chin, said:

"You should take that, sir. It shows scarce more'n the shore line, but the shore's where you'll be, and not far inland. Here's Little Cove," he touched the spot with his fork. "In harf an hour we'll lay outside it, not being able to get in, and there we'll anchor to put you off. Who'll you be taking with you, sir?"

"Tommy and I thought we'd make a sort of reconnoissance first, and Bilkins says he wants to go as cook," I answered. "In a day or two, weather permitting, we'll sail the small boat up to Big Cove for a council of war."

"Well, sir," he said, shaking his head, "just go slow, that's all I arsk. Don't start anything. There's no use two young fellows kicking up a racket without their friends, that's what I say. So just poke around, but keep out of sight; learn all you want, but don't start anything. If you carn't learn it all, be satisfied with harf; then the rest of us will take that and make a whole of it in no time. Am I right, Professor?"

"You are right, *mon Capitaine*, if they will mind you. But will they? A chance comes for to—what my boy Tommy calls plug—that old sinner, and so they will jump to a fight. Fight! Bah! How many fools give a life for one who cannot give a reason!"

"There's reason enough here," Tommy laughed. "But we'll promise to be careful, if that satisfies you."

When at last we dropped anchor half a mile outside the entrance of Little Cove our deck became active. I went off first with the supplies to choose a spot where they should be stored, although in such a black night this might have been left haphazard to the men. But one never believes, on occasions so momentous as pitching camp, that others know a jot about it but oneself—to this there are practically no exceptions.

While being rowed shoreward I noticed that the wind had quite died down, leaving a suffocation in the air that is difficult to explain; but I've felt something like it on a sultry summer day when the sky is black with slowly advancing clouds, when the birds have become too awed to chirp and every leaf in the trees hangs motionless. It is in these suspenses of unpleasant expectation, when at any moment the heavens will open with a hissing smash of fire and nature be turned to fury, that one breathes heavily. There is no other feeling like it, except the drag of torturing minutes before being called to make a speech, or to be whistled over the top into No Man's Land.

Our prow grated on the sand and in silence we began to unload. Back from the sloping beach grew a fringe of small machineel trees and palms; the beach and they, as well as I could judge, forming a kind of amphitheater to the water.

My men wanted to raise the canvas into a make-shift tent before returning for the second load, but I thought better of this and had them leave it as it was, wrapped about our guns and stowed with the other things beneath the palms. Until daylight showed how well our position might be screened from the islands, it were a short sighted business to stretch a tell-tale piece of white duck that could be seen for miles.

Already there were eerie whisperings of some disturbance in the sky. From the black forest far behind us could be detected faint restless noises, as if a myriad agitated spirits were scurrying hither and thither whipping their wings against the branches. Something more than an ordinary man's size blow was coming out of the southeast, so I tumbled the crew into their boat, charging them to pull right heartily and bring back Tommy, at least, before too late.

They must have got close to the *Whim* when a force, as sudden as it was at the moment unexpected, almost lifted me off my feet. Indeed, had I not possessed the presence of mind to fall flat upon the beach I should have gone kittering. In half a second the heavens were cluttered not only with screaming and tumbling winds but branches of large trees driven along as straws. I dug my toes and fingers into the sand, flattening out for dear life. Close upon the head of this hurricane came the deluge of rain, cloudburst after cloudburst. Then lightning was unchained, veritable shocks of fire, and no thunder out of hell could have been more appalling.

For perhaps a minute I had not been given a chance to think of the small boat, or the *Whim*, but struggling to raise my head I stared through the inky space eagerly awaiting the next flash. It came almost at once, bringing into image the Cove as if a million green calcium lights were focused there. This was but for an instant, yet such is the peculiar effect of lightning that in the following blackness each detail of the scene remained photographed upon my retinæ. I saw the turbulent waters apparently sweeping, as a mill race, out to sea; I saw a lone palm, that had formerly stood in dignified solitude upon a nearby point of land, now bent in the wildest agony, its leafy top resembling an umbrella turned inside out. I saw the *Whim*, greenish white in a greenish foam, heeled over till her masts were all but on the waves and her mainsail, half torn from its boom, snapping in the wind. In this fashion she was being driven at breakneck speed across the Gulf. I thought—I tried to think—that I had seen a small boat being dragged behind. Surely my men had reached her!

But another flash, and still another, brought no greater assurance of this. Each showed the yacht farther away, more blurred by rain, until the distance became too great for me to make her out at all.

And then another sky-splitting flame photographed a sight that made my blood congeal. I got but an instantaneous glimpse of it from the corner of my eye before the world became wrapped again in darkness—but something had been there, some huge, horrible monster was rising out of the water and waddling toward me. I had seen two long dripping arms, or feelers, extending in my direction. Crouched, with my nerves on fire, I waited. The rifles and revolvers were wrapped in the canvas and could not be reached in time; there was nothing to do but wait till this thing touched me.

It seemed an age before the heavens split again, and then I gave a yell wilder than the lashing rain, a yell of joy; for, staggering up the beach was Smilax, true to his name with a grin so broad that the greenish glare flickered on his teeth.

His sense of direction was either extremely acute or he possessed the eyes of a cat, for in the following darkness I felt a hand grasp my shoulder and push me toward the trees. Obediently I yielded. Then above the storm I heard him tearing leaves from the smaller palms until, by overlapping them against some bushes so they would be held by the wind, he constructed a lean-to—in the circumstances a most creditable achievement—beneath which I crawled.

The rain drumming upon this shelter made conversation an effort, but in half an hour the storm had all but blown itself to pieces and then I let fly a string of questions—the first being of our small boat.

He told me, in his taciturn way, that her crew had made safe just in time. As they scrambled aboard the hurricane struck. The mate, knowing with laudatory foresight that the masts were in danger of destruction, had rushed forward and chopped the anchor cable. Even that had not saved the mainsail from being torn away.

As to the fate of our yacht neither he nor I felt much concern. I knew her to be a staunch craft, handled by able seamen, and felt that she would come out on top even if upon the coast of Mexico. Then, with a simplicity that deeply touched me, he added that as she was about to be blown off for an absence of, perhaps, some days, and he realized that I would be in need of help, he dived overboard.

"But," I cried, remembering the anger of that seething water, "you took your life in your hands!"

"Me swim all over," came his quiet reply; but whether he meant all over the world, or all over as might apply to his personal self, was left in doubt.

Anyway, I do not believe there is another man living who could have breasted that hurricane-lashed sea for such a distance. I could judge something of what it cost him by the way he had gasped for breath—and since then I have seen him finish a fifteen-mile run, breathing little faster than normally. This gives an idea of his task that night, and the risk he took—and the indifference with which he took it; yet about his stupendous strength I can not write, but only marvel.

Wet clothes are not conducive to sleep, but I was thoroughly tired, healthily drowsy. There were more questions to be asked, plans to be discussed, but my gods descended; and, lo, when I looked again the sun was shining in all its glory.

CHAPTER XIII
ON TO DEATH RIVER!

Some day I shall write an ode, not to sleep but to the pleasure of awaking when the sleep has been deep and dreamless, when the day is ushered in by smiling skies, a laughing earth, and a forest of joyous songsters. More especially beautiful is the face of nature after a storm-swept night, for then, indeed, the blinking dawn itself reflects the gratitude of mundane things for their deliverance. In the forest one hears a water-drip—aftermath of rains; a gentle, almost noiseless fall of crystal drop on crystal drop tapping the loamy soil, and imagination sings in whatsoever key the soul is tuned.

But with what reaches of farther imaginings do we greet the day, and how variously! Our eyes do not require a visual picture of the lone wild turkey on his cypress roost to know that he is ruffling his feathers, craning his neck inquisitively downward in all directions, before chancing to descend to earth and breakfast; nor need we see the panther skulking from his lair to know that he has stopped to lick his paw and pass it over his face—the feline morning ablution. Each creature has a particular mode of resurrection after its hours of mimic death; and so I, on a bed of whatsoever it may be, yawn hideously and stretch my arms and grumble: O, Lord, how I hate to get up! Indeed, how variously do we greet the day!

Smilax had opened our duffle and hung out several things to air. But the provisions, ammunition, matches and—glory be!—my tobacco, had been packed in tins and were dry. I could not say as much for the clothes I wore, and quickly stripped them off to hang before the fire he was building.

As these and the coffee pot were steaming I walked to the beach and followed it to a westernmost point, being curious to see if from there we could get a glimpse of the islands, and also if our camp were securely hidden from anyone passing the entrance of the Cove. Most of all, of course, did I want to search the horizon, and for several minutes stood beneath the solitary palm that had resumed its majesty. So white was the sand, sloping from a violet-tinted fringe of sea-grape stalks to the lapping waves, so green and sparkling, yet so drowsy, was the Gulf, that I could not realize, were my present nudeness less constantly a reminder, that since the setting sun these peaceful things had been lashed with a devil's fury. No sail showed anywhere; only the palm and I seemed to be alone in this balmy wilderness. But my faith in Gates whispered that the *Whim* was safe. Looking back, I realized also that our camp lay well concealed; to the south the islands were cut off by an opposite strip of land; eastward and northward stretched primeval forests, swamps and prairies for half a hundred miles. I seemed to be the only human animal upon the earth.

A hungry osprey circling in the sky dropped as a plummet, struck the water and, after a momentary struggle, arose with his fish, ingeniously holding it head-foremost to facilitate flight. From another point now came a scream, well known to me, and I turned to see an eagle approaching with tremendous speed. Here before my eyes was to be committed "an overt act of piracy" that has for untold centuries caused a strained relationship between these birds. By feints at darting, but with no real intention to harm, he drove the osprey upward—for in aerial combats amongst the feathered tribes advantage lies in the higher altitude, and the hawk excitedly strove for this while the eagle coolly permitted it. In such a manner the fight was carried skyward until the combatants looked small. Then it entered its second, and last, phase.

Quite master of the situation the eagle now rose to the upper plane and began his attack from above, whereupon to save itself the hawk released its fish and took to flight—which was, of course, exactly what the eagle wished. Here was his opportunity for the spectacular. Diving straight downward—first, however, increasing his speed with two swift strokes of his powerful wings which then became set in a half curve—he overtook the falling breakfast in mid air, seized it, swung gracefully outward and disappeared over the forest.

Shame, thought I, that our National Bird, secure from discovery at Washington, should be practising this thoroughly un-American might-makes-right business! Yet through my being came a sympathetic whisper. I had never felt it while in contact with other people, but here I was stripped as a savage—alone with the woods and the ocean. If the Florida peninsula had been formed when my ancestors went naked, one of them might have loitered near this very spot, and I smiled as I wondered if he, too, had been planning to carry off some female from her watchful tribe!

It was good to be in the wilderness, good to be savage, good to be unclothed beneath God's high heaven and know that by my muscle and my cunning I was king. No ordinary king who went about with a jeweled crown upon his head could ever feel this exuberance of being, and in pure delight I plunged into the water.

Out, out and out I swam, joyously diving for handsfull of shells that I held aloft as a pagan offering to the gods. I put in bursts of speed, then rested on my back upon the cradling waves, watching the streaks of feathery clouds that stretched across the sky—streamers, flying far behind the tempest. And then, with tingling blood, I would flip my body and swim down, down for more shells. I was King of the great out-of-doors; a reincarnated primordial monster, holding high carnival with the elements!

Smilax, having come in search of me and seeing my head far from shore, followed at once. It was then, as he approached, that I received my first disillusionment of being king by the right of muscle, because he sped through the water as an oiled torpedo, putting to shame my skill that had been somewhat thought of in the Athletic Club tank at home. Almost immediately followed my second jolt, as he glanced over his shoulder, saying:

"Lookout, maybe whole lot shark!"

King or no king, I went shoreward like a scared cat. Anyone could have had my crown then for the mere trouble of picking it up. Curiously, there flashed into my mind a game I used to play as a youngster: What-Would-You-Rather-Be-Eaten-Up-By! We boys would pompously answer lions, puffing ourselves out bravely and pretending we didn't care, but I remembered one little girl who aroused our contemptuous laughter by answering "goldfish." And now, after all these years, for the first time I found myself marveling at her sagacity. Indeed, she was off and on in my thoughts until I had clothed myself in dry garments and partaken of a grown man's breakfast; after which I dropped into a state of retrospective contentment, divided between the annoyances that beset kings, Azurian princesses, and the culinary skill of Smilax.

That ebony giant of strength was not aware of my mission here, nor, indeed, of anything that had passed aboard the *Whim*, so when he had cleaned the dishes I lit my pipe and called to him. It seemed but fair that he should know the dangers of our expedition before joining it. His perception was quicker than his speech, and more than once he anticipated my narrative with some word suitable to its climax.

"We get lady," he said, at last.

"After a while," I corrected. "Just now we're to see where she is, how she's guarded, and how many guards there are. But we're not to start anything till the others get back. You don't happen to know this country, I suppose?"

"Not right here; but two day walk there," he pointed a little east of north, "yes, good. Mother live with Seminole one time, over there."

"I thought you were from Jamaica," I said; for, indeed, we had got that impression.

"No, me nigger raised by Seminoles. Been to Jamaica on ship, heap time."

"Then you speak Seminole?"

"Some," he answered, modestly.

I should have recognized in his way of talking, which was neither Jamaica nor American negro, the Seminole influence. Now this further light upon his past accounted for the many ways he had shown himself a woodsman; things that had astonished and pleased me, since I had not looked for them in a seafaring man who later became a fisher of sponges. It brought me a feeling of greater assurance for the task ahead of us, because Smilax, with an Indian training added to his stupendous strength, would be scout, warrior, pack-horse, all in one; really, an invaluable asset.

The chart that should have come in the second boat—with Tommy, alas, and Bilkins—was missing, but I remembered pretty well the lay of the land and knew that the island area began only a short distance south of our Cove. This I discussed with Smilax, who added light by his general knowledge—hearsay, for the most part. Yet when I suggested leaving our things cached where they were while we made a reconnoissance, he strenuously objected.

"Lady maybe fifteen, twenty, mile 'way," he said. "We take camp 'long."

"That's very well if you take it," I laughed, "but I've no idea of lugging that stuff half over Florida. Why not carry the things we need?"

"Maybe need all," he answered, then smiled: "Camp light."

At this he arose with a subtle power that reminded me of a huge black leopard and began making our things into a pack. Never had I seen, anywhere from Newfoundland to the Rockies, a bundle of duffle more skillfully arranged, and I said with no small degree of admiration:

"I'd take off my hat to you, Smilax, if the storm hadn't blown it away!"

He grinned, feeling the praise if not understanding its medium; then asked:

"We go now?"

"Let's wait half an hour to see if the *Whim* comes in sight," I told him. "There's a lot to talk over, anyway, before we start. For one thing, if we get separated how shall we find each other?"

"If you lose me, you hunt good place to wait, and wait. Me find you."

For some time we discussed other details. Finally I asked:

"How far down in those islands do you think they are?"

He was sitting with his knees drawn up, his arms crossed upon them, and now let his forehead, too, rest there in meditation.

"One place," he slowly answered, "no white hunter ever get. Injuns know it, but 'fraid to go 'cause evil spirit live there—near mouth of river Seminole call Il-lit; in white man tongue, mean Death. Me think maybe find 'em there."

"Death river's a good place for that old scoundrel to hang out," I agreed. "How far?"

"Maybe fifteen mile, maybe ten, maybe twenty; no can say. We see."

"By the way, Smilax, how do you say 'damn old scoundrel' in Seminole?"

He raised his head and appreciatively grinned, answering:

"Hal-wak esta-had-kee, mean 'bad white man.'"

"That's neither bad nor short enough. What else?"

"Host-cope-e-taw, mean thief."

"Good but too long. I want something I can remember; to christen him, understand? What's your shortest word?"

"Shee."

"That's more like it. What's 'shee' mean?"

"Feathers."

"But, hell, Smilax," I burst out laughing, "there'd be no sense in calling him feathers!"

"Efaw," he said again, "mean dog; kotee, toad; chesshe, rat. Maybe him dog-toad-rat!"

"That only begins to be him," I declared, with the same glorious contempt for pronouns. "In the prospective waters of Death river I christen him Efaw Kotee, the dog-toad!"—But in my heart I offered an apology to the canine family, many of whose sons and daughters have been among my most loyal friends.

“We go; maybe find him,” the black giant grinned again, bending backward to get his shoulders beneath the ropes and then straightening up as though two, and not two hundred, pounds of weight came with him.

I walked quickly out to the point and took one more look, a searching, lingering look across the green water. Nowhere was the *Whim*, nowhere even a speck of sail or any other craft. Except for a pelican of sober mien, rising and falling with the waves, the Gulf seemed barren of any life. But something told me that the yacht was safe.

A scrub jay, in a near-by thicket of mangroves, mocked my solitude with a raucous note; yet it gave me heart, for I saw in it the call of the land and knew that thoughts of the *Whim* must be put aside. So I went back to Smilax, and together we strode through the fringe of palms into a shadowy jungle; our faces set toward a mysterious place, unknown to us, where Death river meets the sea.

CHAPTER XIV
SMILAX BRINGS NEWS

Intuitively I dropped behind and walked at the heels of Smilax who, as if he were treading a well-defined trail instead of unknown jungle land, moved with a free stride that challenged my endurance. Clinging vines pulled at my clothes as things alive, causing both noise and annoyance. Silence was a virtue on our present expedition.

After an hour of this we came to a cypress swamp, and for several miles waded through water ankle-deep although on a bottom of firm sand. Hardly any undergrowth was here, but in all directions stood gray, dismal cypress trees, coarsely buttressed at the water's edge and tapering to slender tips. Draped in long streamers of Spanish moss which were delicately swayed by an almost imperceptible current of air, this was a ghoulish place—suggesting a rookery for shrouded spirits which perched along the bonelike branches awaiting their resurrection. Here, too, upon some convenient root of these gray ancients—perhaps the longest lived of our southern trees—lay coiled the dozing moccasin. And from this grim place we merged once more into the jungle where my clothes again became the prey of clawing things.

But Smilax, never faltering, moved with the ease of a shadow. At last, by watching him I, too, came to learn his secret and was charmed to find that it made my pace both quiet and swift. Indeed, I took great care to practice this silent trail walking—a knack that can be acquired only by the closest observation; for a hundred books could not teach a hundredth part as much as a ten-mile hike at the heels of a trained woodsman when he is trying to go noiselessly. Finally he turned and looked at me, saying:

"You do good now."

Noon brought us to a higher country whose beauty could not be surpassed. Dark and cool it was, even dismal without bringing depression. The mid-day suns of a hundred years must have been tempered to the aisles of this wild cathedral by venerable specimens of mahogany and black olive trees; and, where the branches of these did not touch, rose the slenderer red ironwood. The mahoganies, alone, stood as a proof that we were entering a region which had escaped the eyes of white man for—how long? It was even seventy years ago that bands of wood pirates, known as "the mahogany cutters," invaded southern Florida from the Bahamas and ruthlessly pillaged this desirable wood for foreign markets; so here, at least, was a spot that had remained undiscovered, where perhaps a white foot had never trod.

Charmed as I was, a greater enchantment awaited, when the next few steps brought me to a pool; a pool of crystal transparency, though dark for reflecting the black bowl of earth in which it lay. Without a ripple it nestled close against the roots of a golden-fig tree—an unfruitful parasitic giant of squat stature and tremendous girth; while, pendant from one gnarled out-reaching branch, and almost touching the mirror-like surface into which it looked, hung a solitary streamer of Spanish moss.

One might have fancied that this pure water slept in the tranquillity of being forever blessed by a gaunt old friar, the gray sleeve of whose cowl hung from an arm perpetually outstretched in silent benediction. Around the bank, and leaning their purple flowers above the more purple depths, grew a fringe of wild iris; while sprinkled at random farther out were a few blooms of "bonnet"—the yellow water-lily of southern ponds. And then, in a darker nook, erect and motionless upon one leg, a pink flamingo stood. I caught my breath in amazement at the beauty of this place!

To me it possessed a soul; and the soul, arms, that were amorously held out, inviting, pleading. This was the spot, and not by the green waves, to strip my mind of culture, to tear a club from nature's forest and do battle for existence! Here, in the very birthplace of silence where I could smell the loam of untouched wilderness, would be the haunt of my re-created, or pre-created, self. Throughout the days I would hunt—and slay; in the nights I would sleep among the branches. But there would come dawns and sunsets when in some corner of this wild temple I would raise a pagan altar, light a tiny wish-wood flame, and conjure the forest's soul of many arms to reach across the earth, bringing me a living, breathing Psyche with iris-colored eyes to gaze into the limpid pool!

In the contemplation of such an Eden I had forgotten Smilax, who now shattered my illusion by swinging down the pack and saying, as he turned to me:

"We eat."

O, mundane worm, that he could think of food while my spirit was communing with our common ancestor! However, without much reluctance, I arrived at his point of view when, filling my pipe, I stretched out to watch his savory preparations. And now to my surprise, but increasing admiration for his woodcraft, he raised a hand as I was about to strike the match.

"Wait," he said. "Wind wrong; maybe some one smell; me go see."

"Never mind," I protested, wanting to spare him additional work after the amount he had already accomplished. "I don't care about smoking."

"Cook fire smell," he said, rather pityingly that I should have overlooked this obvious fact. "Me go see; get good wood." Then, grinning broadly, he added: "Maybe Efaw Kotee somewhere."

I knew that if he went for wood he must mean buttonwood, because there was no end of other kinds about; but buttonwood is the only fuel in Florida—dry mangrove being a close second—that, burning slowly like charcoal, is both very hot and smokeless, and he was evidently taking no chances. I knew, too, that he would have to go far toward the coast for it, since only on tidewater shores may it be found; and with a pleasant feeling of excitement I wondered if he would also bring back news of—her; some sign, a thin line of smoke above the trees! It was not the excitement of battle, or a skirmish; no, it was the approaching reality of a dream that had gripped me with soft fingers since the moment I entered this forest. Since my eyes had rested on that pool, my heart had called afresh for her. The arms of the place were about me.

Softly I arose and went back to it. The pink flamingo was there, but as I approached, nearer this time, he gave signs of uneasiness and at last clumsily took wing for some other sanctuary where his solitude might be untroubled by strange beings.

Standing on the flowery bank, I looked deep into the water. No fish, nor life of any kind, disturbed its sweet serenity. So like her soul, I thought, was the soul of this! Yet could her soul be undisturbed? Was it not, indeed, turbulent with apprehensions? Did it—I asked the question eagerly—did it sometimes hope that I would come? And something in the water answered yes. So I picked a blossom of the iris—that had taken its color from her eyes—and put it carefully away. By the spirit of her glance, by the unspoken message of this place, I swore—oh, why put down here all I swore? Men have stood beside solemn pools before, and women, too. Those who commune in the woods think more sublimely than they speak, so I can not speak now, in written words, my immeasurable longing.

Soon Smilax, grinning broadly, emerged from the shadows.

"All right," he said. "You smoke; me cook."

"Did you see anything? How far did you go?" I asked, and he answered in the curious way he had of dealing with one question at a time.

"No see signs of Efaw Kotee. Long way."

While the combined aroma of bacon and coffee was for the moment throwing its cloak of materialism about the romance of my forest, I asked again:

"Why are we heading so far inland, when they must be somewhere along the coast?"

"Best go this way. All right; you smoke."

I was smoking, but that seemed to be his way of telling me to put my mind at rest. Yet I persisted with another question:

"How do you know we haven't passed them already?"

"Me know," he grinned. "All right; you smoke."

He was a funny cuss, but I let it go at that.

Biscuits, bacon and coffee might properly be called the Woodsmen's Ambrosia, but it is not a feast over which man is inclined to loiter, and Smilax was soon re-wrapping the pack.

Up to this time I had walked practically empty handed, yet now I conscientiously rebelled, insisting that a share of the load must rest upon my shoulders. But here he showed himself as obdurate as a mule until, arbitrarily, I strapped on our second automatic, took out our second rifle, and filled my pockets with extra cartridges. He raised no objection to this; he even approved it. We were getting down into the Death river country and ready fire-arms made agreeable companions. Furthermore, at his direction I tied the rather goodly supply of buttonwood into a bundle and swung it to my back.

Toward evening we saw on our left evidences of open country and bore in that direction, for when one has walked many hours in the shadows of interlocking branches it is as natural to be drawn toward a spot of sunlight as it would be to approach an open window after having been confined in a dismal room. So we bore in that direction and came to the edge of a vast prairie stretching before us as a sea of lifeless grass.

Except for a gray line on its horizon, marking, I afterward learned, the boundary of the Great Cypress Swamp, there was but a single break on this expansive waste. That was a rich growth of trees about two miles out, to the southeast of us; an oasis, it would have been called in the Sahara, but in the Florida prairies known as an "island." Whether this term of "island" finds origin in the similarity of these verdant places to real islands, seeming as they do to float upon an inland sea of grass, or whether because, being of higher ground, they actually become islands during rainy seasons when much of the prairie land is inundated, the native "cracker" is unable to explain. At any rate, fanned by the prairie breeze, they afford agreeable shelter where, in perfect seclusion, one may look out upon the surrounding country for great distances.

"We camp there," Smilax nodded.

"A good place," I affirmed.

"You stay hide," he said again. "Me find out if nobody 'round to see us go."

"Why can't I look with you?" I asked, wanting to study more of his methods, but he squelched me by answering:

"You look whole lot; no see anything."

I would have given him a good piece of my mind had he not suddenly disappeared; returning soon with his usual smile and saying:

"Come."

Single file, as before, we pushed into the breast-high grass, and the walking was easy. Once we crossed a patch of oozy turf from which arose a score of jack-snipe; again we skirted a drying pond whose boggy edges were the hunting ground of marsh hens. Yet other trails could be read here: deer, wildcat, raccoon, and innumerable wee things. And here, too, around the "bonnet" leaves, the silent moccasin lay coiled, so it was well to step with caution in a place like this.

A wound by the cotton-mouth moccasin, if treated properly, may not result in death. Like other viperine bites, however, it so affects the surrounding flesh that blood poisoning may follow days after the first crisis has been passed. Yet, even with this two-fold menace lurking in its fangs, it is not the most feared of Florida snakes. Preëminent in that capacity stands the diamond-back rattler, largest of the world's venomous species and second to none in point of deadliness. Smilax insisted—on I do not know what authority—that more dangerous than either of these is the beautiful little coral snake, *elaps fulvius*, whose victim becomes ravingly insane and invariably dies. That he possessed some uncanny knowledge of the creature must be admitted because of its close relationship to the Cobra-de-Capello, of Asiatic fame, whose poison, we know, flies directly to the nerve centers and almost entirely ignores the tissue. Four days later I had good reason to remember this.

"Are there many snakes hereabouts?" I asked.

"Winter, not much; summer, heap."

However, at that very moment he held his hand back to stop me, then beckoned me forward.

"Look!" He was pointing tensely ahead of us, moving his arm leftward and indicating a circle of perhaps thirty feet in diameter.

Whatever it was, I could see the tops of the grass shake as their stems were slightly jostled by this unknown creature's progress, which continued with incredible speed and was circling back toward us. Then, with a slightly swishing sound as its body glided through the dry grass, that friend Florida woodsmen—the king snake—passed before our feet like a brownis green streak.

"Rattler! You watch!" Smilax whispered. His eyes were wide with interest, for it is not permitted many men to see a duel between these mortal enemies.

Somewhere directly ahead of us a diamond-back rattlesnake must have awaited the attack he sensed, though we could not yet see him. Time after time the king snake swept by in front of us, decreasing the circles and, I thought, increasing his speed. After each revolution we stepped in a little nearer, being careful not to interfere with his course nor distract his attention from the serious business at hand.

Soon the viper became visible. His flat head, elevated a few inches above his heavy coil, turned anxiously with the sounds in the grass. He knew what was coming, I think, but did not rattle until the king had reduced the circles about him to a diameter of six or seven feet. Then he became electrified. The rattles sounded viciously, and his head began an ominous swaying motion, out and in, as he searched for a vital spot at which to strike.

The king, although keeping just outside the danger line, was also watching for an opportunity. He may have realized his immunity to poisons, yet did not care unnecessarily to suffer the laceration of fangs. Rather did he choose to rely upon the further protective gifts that nature had given him: length and strength, speed and agility, and a skin that blended elusively with the ground colors; therefore, revolving in these smaller circles, he seemed to make almost a continuous line, without beginning or end, and the rattler was at a loss to act. Now, profiting by a moment when the venomous eyes were turned away, he darted in and caught the viper close up behind its head. Wrapping himself about the squirming body he ruthlessly straightened out. We heard the vertebrae being torn until his victim lay crushed and stretched into a helpless mass.

For several minutes the sleek avenger remained perfectly quiet. Then, uncoiling warily but not releasing the hold with his teeth, he worked his body aside. Last of all he dropped the head and drew suspiciously back as if alert for a sign of life. Of course, there was none, and soon he glided into the grass, not seeming to have noticed us at all.

"Whew!" I said, taking a deep breath. "I wish we had king snakes around us all the time!"

"Heap good friend," Smilax grinned, stooping to cut off the rattles that were large and perfect.

"I thought you said there weren't any snakes out in winter!"

"Not much; maybe no see any for long time."

He told me now as we proceeded across the prairie that the Seminole Reservation lay about fifty miles north of us, and I wondered what our chances would be of getting a squad of "braves," should the *Whim* not show up and we found ourselves on the eve of a fight against rather big odds. It was worth keeping in mind.

The "island," when we reached it, was by far the largest I had ever seen, and proved to be an ideal place to camp. High pines and stately palms grew here in great profusion, while there also might be found a sprinkling of hardwoods; and yet in some parts there was enough sunlight to permit the growth of really luxurious grass, as trim as if it had been cut by the hand of man. Smilax, pointing to a number of tracks I had not observed, said the deer kept it short by grazing. One's first impression here was of a well-kept park, intersected by green avenues that stretched beneath the best specimens of trees which a landscape architect had carefully planned to leave standing. But there were wilder portions; perhaps three acres of heavy jungle. About midway, festooned with vines, was the pool I had hoped to find, of quite good size and cool. It, like the other that had entranced me, nourished a few stalks of iris, but there was no "bonnet" or other place on its closely cropped bank for the wily moccasin.

"My private bath," I declared, feeling at this sundown hour the call strong within me.

Smilax had remained behind. His reconnoissance as we entered the prairie must be completed by another as we emerged from it; and I had left him standing behind the trees looking back across our trail, searching for any distant movement. At last he came up, saying:

"All right; you smoke."

"I don't want to smoke," I laughed. "I want to get in that pool, if we can find another supply of drinking water."

"No need um," he grinned. "Big spring come up there," he pointed toward the farther end. "Me know island now; been here one time."

I afterwards saw that he referred to one of those unique springs, occasionally to be found in Florida—a transparent water of bluish tinge, bubbling up through the bottom of its deep, self-made reservoir; keeping the sand in a subdued state of agitation, and bringing pleasure to the eye of man.

By the spirit of Pan, my pool felt good after the long day's hike!

The wind had changed with the waning afternoon and now blew gently from the southwest, promising a period of fair weather. It gave us, also, the advantage of greater freedom in noises; for, when living in the wild, one comes to realize how potent a carrier, or muffler, of noises is the wind. A fire at night, or smoke by day, may be tempered with human ingenuity, but nature bandies the sound waves with her breath.

I dined in the elegance of simplicity, and Smilax extinguished our small fire of buttonwood. Leaning my back against a stalwart pine, I watched the shadows stealing through our avenue of trees. Somewhere above my head a whistling owl, one of those lovable little feathered cavaliers that showers his mate with unstinted adulation, fluttered and courted. Later the mournful call of a whooping crane floated across the prairie.

I heard these things in a lazy, contented way, but my thoughts were on another island—a real island surrounded by water, where waves lapped the beach and two eyes, that had given color to the iris, watched for deliverance. Then with a jerk I sat up. Smilax had turned his head to listen, and in his attitude dwelt a note of agitation.

"What is it?" I whispered; for surely I had heard a sound that did not belong to these creatures living in the forest about us.

He raised his hand to caution silence. Then came the sound again, slowly: one—two—three—four—

"Axe," he said, his eyes shining as beads and his finger pointing into the southwest from where the breeze was coming. "You wait; me go see."

"I'll go, too," I announced.

"No; maybe make too much noise. Smilax go."

"Who d'you suppose it is that close to us?" I excitedly asked. "Not them, surely?"

He looked at me with grave eyes and answered:

"No can say; maybe hunters find way in here. You smoke; me go see."

Yet his sudden gravity left little doubt in my mind of what, at least, he suspected; for he well knew that hunters did not find their way into this unsurveyed wilderness! Then, too, there was something in the stillness of the night that seemed to portend great things. The leaves transmitted their restlessness to my yawning nerves, as iron dust springs to a magnet.

Intending to wave good luck as he melted into the darkness, without being observed I walked silently behind him to the prairie's edge; but there he stopped, opened his arms, raised his face to the sky, standing motionless. And a great peace came over me, for I saw that, in the simple way of the old-time Seminoles who invariably turned to their Great Spirit on the eve of hopes or fears or dangers, Smilax was praying.

Religion is the poetry of the savages' existence. Alas, that we are civilized! He does not spend his nights poring over The Laws and The Prophets, and his days peppering a neighbor across the head with a new-born creed. No, he puts an abiding faith in some Great Spirit, be it the sun, the moon, the stars; or fashioned of stone, or clay, or wood. But his soul looks into the Infinite as his physical sight, less far reaching, feasts upon the Symbol. And what does he lose? He loses the privilege of bickering with evangelists; he loses the acid frequently to be found in church organization—the feeling of pity or contempt of one denomination for another, each of which stands upon the Holy Rock searching for motes and waving a princely disregard to beams. And, because he remains benighted and in darkness, he also loses doubt; wherefore, as a trusting child, he touches the hand of God.

I had long since finished my second pipe when Smilax returned. He came out of the darkness as he had gone into it, with the stealth of a panther, and was close to me before I knew it. But a striking change had taken place in him. His breathing was fast, though not from exertion, and pointing back he hurriedly whispered:

"Efaw Kotee there! Lady, too! Me see!"

CHAPTER XV
EFAW KOTEE'S DEN

Sylvia there! I bounded up as though some one had sent a galvanic current through my body, exclaiming:

"Good Lord! How far, Smilax? Come quick, let's go!"

He answered each of my exclamations in sequence, a peculiarity he had:

"Yes, Lord good. Two mile, maybe some more. Plenty time, we go back soon."

"But we couldn't have heard that axe two miles," I said incredulously.

"Still night, when wind on prairie right; yes, sometime."

"How are they camped? How many are there? Come, man, don't keep me waiting!"

He drew himself up to full height and, with one arm pointing toward the southwest, spoke deliberately as if realizing his importance, seeming to choose his words—seeming, rather, to grope for them.

"Over there forest is little strip thick, maybe half mile; then come water—Gulf. Me know um is Gulf; taste and find um salt. Close by shore big island, close by um little island. More island all 'round. Too dark to see much, but Efaw Kotee live on big island. Many cabin. On little island Lady live. One cabin. She come to door and me get good look, for light in cabin. Old woman live with her; Injun squaw; me know by way she walk. Before day we go hide in good place on shore. Watch all day and see. Must watch all day, or they see us if we leave 'fore dark. Now you smoke; then we go 'sleep l'il while."

Sleep! How could I sleep while she was within three miles of me, surrounded by ten or a dozen devils the combined virtues of whom would not fill a gnat's eye! Of course, she had lived in this situation for years, but I had not heard of it until very recently, and that makes a world of difference.

But after we got back to camp and I had stretched out on my blanket to let the telescope of my fancies pierce the realm of hopes, sleep did come. I would not have believed it, but it did; for soon I realized that some one was shaking my arm, while a voice said over and over:

"Time we go; time we go!"

It was yet night when I opened my eyes, but Smilax had lit a small buttonwood fire and breakfast was waiting. While I stumbled to the pool to drive the cobwebs from my brain he took the canteens and filled them at the spring; for, in the all-day strain ahead of us—and few things are more trying than to lie concealed and watch from the gray of dawn till the black of night—we should need a liberal supply of water.

"Shall we take rifles?" I asked, when everything was ready and each of us had our snack of food.

"No," he answered. "Too hard to crawl like snake. They no see us to-day. We take l'il crack-crack."

"Little crack-crack" meant an automatic revolver, greatly admired by Smilax and, since Tommy's coaching, handled by him with no mean skill. So I swung one of these to the small of my back, into position when we should begin crawling, and handed him the other; whereupon, without further ado, we traversed the "island" and melted into the prairie. Forty minutes later Smilax moving slowly and cautiously ahead, entered the narrow strip of forest. Another ten minutes, and we got to our hands and knees. In this way we proceeded perhaps a hundred yards when, putting his lips close to my ear, he whispered:

"We hide here; come still like snake."

I put out my hand and felt the ragged edge of saw-palmetto, then slipped in behind him, moving scarcely more than a yard a minute. Heaven help us, I thought, if we had to lie on that torturous stuff for fifteen hours! But Smilax was equal to every occasion. When we reached the far side of the patch, leaving only a fringe of leaves to shield us from those we came to watch, he worked a while with his hands, then whispered: "Now lay down." Lo, the uncomfortable roots had been pressed in other directions and the soft sand received my body. He remained, however, long enough on his knees to make sure that none of the fronds had been twisted out of line, else uncompromising daylight might show our enemy that all here was not right.

The night remained very still and impenetrably black, though I think that Smilax could see a little with his extraordinary catlike sight. Then came a first sleepy bird note. The day, at last, was on the wing!

When from obscurity the saw-tooth stems took shape before my eyes and the distance receded farther, I saw that we were near the edge of a steep bank. Perhaps twelve feet below us lay the water, as a mirror on which some one has breathed. A mist hung over it—and in that gossamer shroud a little island floated whereon my Sylvia dwelt—where now she slept.

A minute later the forest awoke with bird life; dawn came rapidly. Islands took shape, trees stepped out from their obscurity and small details drew into focus. First I sought her home and could hardly take my eyes from it. Low and rambling, it stood two hundred feet away, nestled in a most inviting shade of splendid trees. Flowers and climbing vines were everywhere, touched with the rich coloring of poinsettia and bougainvillea—although this very approach of day began to close the fragrant moon-flowers and spelled death to the night-blooming cereus. The walls of her bungalow seemed to be tinted red, varying to purple, which gave a strange yet most pleasing effect in the setting of blossoms. Not till later did I learn that this was the rare Cat's Claw wood, nowhere to be found but in southern Florida.

On the larger island, not over a hundred feet from us, were perhaps ten buildings of about the same size and plan, and presumably sleeping quarters. But in their midst stood a structure of some pretensions that we afterwards knew to be a dining hall. Quite off in the background were two small bungalows whose air denoted quality, but the roof of one had been fitted with a skylight which gave me the impression that here Efaw Kotee worked his trade at counterfeiting. Still beyond this was a tower rising above the low trees, perhaps intended for a lighthouse, although there had been no light burning when we came. But these were at best surmises that arranged themselves in my mind while noting everything in sight and awaiting a further sign of life.

Soon a hinge squeaked. A man stepped from one of the smaller huts, looked at the sky, yawned and stretched. A second appeared from another hut, walked away and came back with an armful of wood that he took into the dining hall. As they passed there was scarcely a nod of greeting. A surly pair, I thought. After this smoke issued from the chimney, and other men, one by one from other huts, came dribbling out into the day, until altogether we had counted seven. The six now before us, after make-shift splashes in the basins beside their doors, went as the chap with the wood had gone; and shortly we heard sounds of knives and forks rattling on china.

It was at this moment that a thin line of smoke arose from the chimney of Sylvia's bungalow. Longingly I watched it; tingling to my finger tips I blessed it. A side door opened, but it was an Indian woman who emerged with two pails and walked back of the house—doubtless to a tank of rain water, because she returned with them full and went in, taking care to close the door softly. The deference of her manner, the affection with which she apparently guarded her mistress' sleep, strongly appealed to me, and I knew that the Indian woman would be my friend.

The next move came again from the dining hall when a swarthy fellow emerged wiping his mouth upon his sleeve. His hair was long and black, reaching below his shoulders. With a rifle nested in the hollow of his arm he disappeared toward the tower, and Smilax whispered:

"Him Injun."

Now to our surprise some one appeared to be looking down from the tower, and a few minutes later the Indian was seen above the mangroves climbing up to him. There must have been strips spiked crosswise to one of the uprights, making a kind of ladder.

"So that's a watch tower," I said cautiously. "And he makes eight."

Smilax nodded.

The fellows talked a while, then the one who had been relieved came down, going for his breakfast.

"What do you think of it?" I whispered.

"No see him before," Smilax looked grave. "Maybe one up in tree 'round here."

"Gee, you think so?" It was not a comforting suggestion.

"No, maybe not," he answered, after a moment of thought. "They no look for us by land; all by water. We all right. Look! Efaw Kotee have breakfast!"

Two men left the dining hall, each bearing a tray of food, and we watched until they entered the rather exclusive house next to the work shop. This without doubt was the old scoundrel's headquarters, but why did he have two trays? Could by any chance Sylvia be kept beneath the same roof with him? Had Smilax been mistaken? The weight of my automatic felt good just then.

When they came out, empty handed, one turned toward the watch tower but the other went for still a third tray. This, which he carried with an air of deference, was covered by a white cloth. He came to the boats across from us and got into a punt, balancing his tray across the bow while he paddled, standing, toward the little island. Now I became more than ever tense, and perhaps I moved, for Smilax pressed my arm in caution.

As the punt touched at the landing platform below Sylvia's house the fellow did not get out, but gave the call of an ibis—a weird, beautifully mystic call that is rarely heard and almost impossible to imitate. Smilax appreciated this, for he grunted: "Good."

The door opened and the Indian woman looked out.

"Hey, there, Echochee," he said. "I got a present from the boss."

She slammed the door, and I do not know when in my life I was ever so charmed by this simple act.

"Then you go to hell," he drawled. "But I tell yer this: the boss said if no one come down to git it, for me to leave it in yer parler."

While Echochee had slammed the door she was evidently listening; for now she came out again, a picture of fury, crying:

"Don't you put foot here!"

"Then come an' git it," he carelessly replied.

She hesitated.

"Lay um down, then go back. Me get um."

"Naw, old hatchet-face. Jest come on down an' git it yer own se'f, or I'll bring it up."

"My Lady no let any one come here," she warned. "You go back quick!"

"That's all right 'bout yer Lady, but the boss says fer me to hand this right in myse'f, an' what the boss says—goes! Yer git that, don't yer? So come on down an' git this, an' that'll make two things yer git," he laughed boisterously, adding: "It's a weddin' present, an' if yer don't git a move on maybe the boss'll come his own se'f!"

I could see from the woman's face that she was in a towering rage, but she went—lithely as a girl, for all her years—to the landing.

"That's what I call sense, old hatchet-face," he sneered, stepping gingerly over the seat—for a punt is a tippy thing—and holding the tray out to her.

With a snarl she jerked it from his hands, raised it quickly and brought it down on his head. Of course, the cloth and everything beneath it went scattering to the winds, while he tumbled backward into the water. Not content, she picked up several of the various fruits the tray had held and began to pepper him with such good aim that he hastily and profanely splashed back to the other shore. Then the tray, its cover, and the spilled fruits not already used in the form of ammunition, were contemptuously tossed in his direction. After this she tied the punt as though nothing had happened, went back into the house and closed the door. Smilax was shaking with silent delight.

"Bully," I whispered.

"Good," he said. "Look—water not much deep. We 'member that." Though at the time I did not see how this held any advantage for us, being distinctly of less protection for Sylvia.

The man dragged himself up the oozy bank, cursing roundly, and started post-haste for Efaw Kotee's bungalow. We could hear the water sloshing in his shoes, and knew that he was quite as uncomfortable in mind as in body. He did not go upon the porch, but stood below, hat in hand, calling. Then I saw the old chief—the same man who had paid his supper check with a new fifty-dollar bill. Smilax squeezed my arm, saying:

"Him boss on yacht."

I felt well satisfied at this identification, which was the first definite assurance that the owner of the *Orchid* and my neighbor in the café were one and the same. He came out scowling, listened unmoved to the fellow's recital and turned back without a word, while the aggrieved one walked sulkily to his quarters.

But soon Efaw Kotee reappeared, this time with another man, and Smilax became excited.

"Look," he whispered. "Him name Jess. Him bust Smilax head!"

It was the fellow who had drawn back when Tommy and Monsieur went to the gambling rooms, but now without his uniform he seemed coarser and more cruel.

"That makes ten, all told," I whispered.

"Whole lot," was the black's only comment.

They came slowly, talking in low tones. At the water's edge across from us they halted and Jess, pointing to the punt, said something whereupon the older man's face turned dark with anger.

"Echochee!" he called.

No answer; the door of Sylvia's dwelling remained closed.

"Echochee," he called again, and his voice grated hatefully on my nerves, "bring that punt over here!"

Then the door did open, I thought reluctantly, and the Indian woman came out.

"What you want?" she asked.

"Say: 'What you want, *Master*!'" he yelled at her.

"Why I say that?" she asked, a dull fire of hatred kindling in her eyes.

"Because it's so," he thundered, stamping the ground in fury while his palsied head shook more noticeably.

"You lie," she replied. "You no master of my Lady or me, any more. We go to Great Spirit any time now."

A chill ran over me. What, in God's name, did she mean? Was Sylvia dying? Again Smilax touched my arm to caution prudence.

Efaw Kotee was, I think, trying to control himself, yet his long arms and veiny hands were swinging, pendulum-like, to and fro across his body. It was an uncanny indication of anger, suggesting rather a beast than a human being. The captain was standing silent, with his arms folded.

"Echochee," said the chief, "bring us that punt. We must see your Lady."

"My Lady see no one."

"I want that punt," he bellowed at her.

"You got plenty punt; me go in house," she replied stoically.

There were, indeed, three or four punts tied to the shore near by.

"Hold on, there," he commanded, "or it'll go bad for you! I want that punt, there, understand?"

"Then get that punt there," she said indifferently.

"You damned old hag," he screamed, now quite beside himself, "one of your rotten tribe's in that lookout tower, d'you understand? If you don't bring that punt across I'll have him crucified before your eyes! Hear me, hag?"

"All right," she said quietly. "Him no 'count; do him good."

She turned back to pass through the door, but was stopped by some one coming out. Sylvia! Never more beautiful than now! Echochee put up both arms to stop her and I noticed—for in tense moments one's eyes retain some of the most insignificant details—how incongruously her brown old bony fingers sank into the dainty folds of her lady's morning gown. But Sylvia would not be stopped. She placed a hand on the woman's shoulder and spoke a few hurried words, then raised her head and looked imperiously at the men, saying:

"You shan't hurt any one because Echochee obeys me. Is the punt all you want?"

Jess moved uneasily, but there was no trace of embarrassment in the bearing of Efaw Kotee.

"No, it's not! We want to cross to you!"

"No one comes on this island," she said.

"I've had enough of your nonsense," the old fellow cried. "I believe yet you steered that bunch of pups after us, in spite of hell I believe it; but, whether you did or didn't, I've had enough of bowing and scraping like a nigger, and begging to be allowed to go over there! Enough, I tell you!"

"Then don't try any more," she indifferently replied, turning to go in; but he checked her with another threat—and by the way she flinched I knew that he meant it.

"If you go in that door till I'm through," he bellowed, "that crucifying comes off in ten minutes—right on this spot where you can hear the beggar squeal!"

She stopped and looked at him, and I realized that we had come in the nick of time for some great crisis which was enveloping her.

"Now, see here," he continued, in a calmer voice, "you've kept this up since yesterday morning, and it's unreasonable. Why don't you let us come over and have a talk? I've been a good father to you! You've had everything you want—and just bought six trunks full of clothes in Havana last week! Why do you keep us—keep me—away?"

While absorbedly listening, I was struck by the oddity of a girl in this wilderness buying six trunks full of clothes; but it then occurred to me that Efaw Kotee would encourage extravagant buying of all things, when the *Orchid* visited a city, in order that he might get bona fide change for his spurious bills. At least there was good reason for her gown to be modern, smart, and becoming, as Havana's best Americanized shops are quite continental.

"I keep you away," she answered icily, "because you're planning to marry me to an unprincipled scoundrel."

"A what?" Jess yelled.

"Shut up!" the old one snapped at him.

"An unprincipled scoundrel," she answered evenly, "who's as loathsome as an ape. And I shan't be married to that kind of thing, or any one else. You've had my warning. If you, or he, or any of your beastly men come to this island, you'll get only my dead body. And Echochee, dear soul, is going with me. What's more, if you start any tortures, we'll die before witnessing them."

"Then, by God," he screamed, "you and your damned hag'll begin to starve from this day! With no more provisions sent over we'll see who obeys me! And in three more days if you don't come to your senses I'll crucify an offering to your dead body—head down on the spot I stand!" He had been raving, but now his tone quickly changed to one of whining entreaty, as he added: "I hope you understand how it pains your dear old father to threaten you, my child!"

It was so maudlin an exhibition that I wondered if he were sane.

"Dear old father," she repeated, giving a short laugh of contempt.

I did not know how much of this was real and how much acting on her part, although it did seem genuine enough when she could not be looking for relief. Yet, as she stood there calmly mistress of herself while Efaw Kotee writhed beneath her scorn, I was reminded of an angler who had hooked an ungainly fish—she with intellect at one end, he at the other representing brute strength, fear, cunning; both connected by a barely visible thread that in this case was not a line, but Fate. For another moment she let him writhe, then turned and went in.

Jess laughed.

"Shut up, you clown," the old chief turned on him.

"Clown yourself," the captain snarled. "I'll have you know I won't take any of your lip!"

"Then I back out of our bargain, that's all!"

"If you say that again I'll twist off your palsied head with these two hands," Jess held them under Efaw Kotee's nose and wriggled his fingers, until the old man shrank back, cowering. "The men'll follow me when I tell 'em you play double, an' you know it! You swine, I'm sick of this place! I'm going to take my share of the stuff, an' the girl, an' clear out! It's been fifteen years since we raised these cabins—more'n that! An' what have we got? Plenty of the slickest money ever printed—an' the other stuff, too—an' you afraid to take a chance. Three times I've stopped a mutiny for you, an' you'd be dead an' buried if I hadn't. Then came this last when things went wrong. You say the girl peached, but 'tween you an' me I say you tried to turn State's evidence—don't deny anything," he held up his hand when the other would have interrupted. "That's passed now. But I've agreed to forget it, to keep the mutinies stopped for keeps—by marrying the girl. You agreed, too. Now you talk of backing out. Is killing too good for you?"

"I don't want to, Jess; I don't, honest," Efaw Kotee said, with a whine. "But you see yourself how she is! If we rush the place, day or night, she'll kill herself. Tell me what to do, and I'll do it!"

"You've done about all you can for a while," Jess grumbled, adding: "If she don't run away."

"Where'd she run to?" the other sneered.

"Well, some kind friend might show her!"

"You're crazy," the chief contemptuously exclaimed.

"Crazy or not, you just see that she doesn't. Then, if starving three days doesn't bring her, maybe crucifying *you* head down might do the trick."

"Wha—what d'you mean?" The old fellow sprang around and stared at him, seeming to have grown hollow and gray.

"Oh, nothing," Jess grinned. "Just a little idea I had—worth keeping in mind, though. It might be healthy for you to see she can't run off, that's all."

Efaw Kotee looked at the captain suspiciously, and said:

"I'll guarantee she doesn't run off—and your other little ideas aren't pleasant. Let's go back and have a drink."

When they had entered the bungalow a silence fell over the settlement. I did not see a man anywhere. But I drew a long breath of relief because Sylvia was for a little while safe, even while I raged at the realization of her danger. My body was cramped, and cautiously I stretched my legs. Smilax had not moved.

"It looks like we got here just in time," I whispered. "But what shall we do?"

He relaxed then, and slowly answered:

"Me think 'while. Echochee good old woman; always kind to l'il black boy."

"You know her?" I could hardly have hoped for that stroke of luck.

"Me know all Seminole; not many left. 'Echochee' mean what white man say 'li'l deer.' She old woman when me l'il black boy in Reservation. Me think 'while; you, too."

Schemes of every wild kind, daring and impossible plans of rescue, raced through my brain; seeming reasonable enough at the time, but Smilax quickly found the flaws in each until I had exhausted my supply. Finally he spoke, and I knew that he spoke with judgment.

"To-night," he said, "we watch and see if they put out guard. Maybe they do, after what Jess said 'bout Lady run off. When dark come, me swim to l'il island and give owl call—two times, then stop soft in middle. Long 'go in Injun village that mean: 'panther, come quick, gun,' Echochee will hear and 'member. Good. Then we talk and fix all up. First we see if Efaw Kotee put out guard."

This was so different, so tame, to the brilliant, suicidal dashes into the thick of rescue and glory—and doubtless destruction—as my plans ran, that I almost felt ashamed. Smilax could neither read nor write; his vocabulary might have been held in the hollow of one's hand, but in many respects he was the sanest creature I ever met.

"Do you suppose Echochee will trust us to get them away?" I whispered.

"If Lady say come, she come," he answered.

This set me thinking, and I decided to write a note that Smilax could deliver. Sylvia might then feel assured that she was not being abducted by a negro whom Echochee had known only in childhood. But, on second thought, I wondered if she would risk escape with an unknown white man; if she would not rather face the supreme issue, once and for all, than perhaps be forced into it later by an over-zealous stranger! In her distracted state of mind I feared she would find the rescue too precarious—too easily offering the same danger that beset her now, and lacking her present weapon of defense. Yet if she refused to come—what then? I could always rush the camp, if but to die with her. Having gone over these possibilities, I whispered to Smilax:

"She'll come easier if she doesn't know I'm here. Echochee will remember you, and reassure her. You might tell Echochee that you were hunting this way and saw her beat the chap over the head with the tray. Understand? After that you saw the rest and realized how much trouble she was in. How about it?"

"Good," he grunted. "That good. To-night me tell Echochee get ready, and to-morrow night we run 'way—maybe to Reservation. But we come by camp and find you; then all work 'round to yacht. Good."

"Well," I demurred, "that isn't the way I meant, for I intend to stay here and help. Some of those devils might get busy!"

"That good, too. Now we eat; then you go sleep."

While tackling our rations we discussed the plan again and again. I did not want to leave Sylvia another night within the grasp of those fiends, but Smilax insisted; explaining that she was practically safe for three days, at any rate. Of course, each twenty-four hours would make her and Echochee weaker from starvation and, as they would need strength, we dared not wait too long. Immediate help from the *Whim* was all but a forlorn hope. The rescue had come suddenly up to us, and it must be met without a thought of failure.

But as the tiresome afternoon wore on without further incidents to keep us aroused, my fancies drifted from rescues to the rescued; and after a while I whispered:

"I'll take that nap now,"—scarcely hearing him reply:

"Good."

CHAPTER XVI
THE CAVE MAN SETS FORTH

Close to my ear I heard a warning: "Sh!"—at the same time feeling a hand squeeze my arm. It was dusk. While I slept the shadows had lengthened and blended into those soft gray tones of twilight that give mystery to forests of the South. Cautiously I raised my head and, following the tense stare of Smilax, saw the cause of his agitation.

Three men were standing on the larger island, at the spot where Efaw Kotee and Jess had stood, and one held a piece of coiled rope tied to a grappling hook. They were whispering and chuckling. Then he with the iron hook began to swing it back and forth, finally letting it fly across the water into the punt, whereupon they chuckled again. Now they began to haul in the line at a lively rate, doubtless fearing that Echochee, aroused by the noise, would rush out and frustrate them. But the house remained quiet, even dark; and, since the boat's painter was of slim material, there could be only one result when they gave a hard pull—the punt was theirs.

This procedure disturbed Smilax, no less myself. There was deviltry afoot, yet hardly a plan for capturing the girl as other punts were available. But the next moment we breathed easier, for the men broke into a boisterous laugh, and one called:

"Ole hatchet-face, yo're done out-punted this time!"

Another, bending over and slapping his thigh in mirthful ecstasy, guffawed:

"Bill says she's done out-*punted*," whereupon they again laughed, and a third called:

"This here busts yo' chance of makin' a git-away to-night, yer ole she-devil! The chief's on to yer, he is!"

"They expect an escape," I whispered.

Smilax nodded. His face was grave.

Then came a most exasperating moment, when I hugged the ground so close that my body felt no thicker than a playing card. The men, each picking up a rifle, stepped into the punt and paddled to our side. Two of them climbed the bank, one going about a hundred yards to our left, and the other, passing within ten feet of us, went the opposite way. We could not follow him with our eyes but knew, by counting his steps, that he stopped at about an equal distance. Then the punt glided back and disappeared behind the little island. Guards! Sentinels! We were trapped, as well as those whom we had come to save!

The firm fingers of Smilax had never left my arm, a continuous caution for silence that I minded well. Ten minutes passed, and the trees had all but lost their shapes. In another ten minutes the night wholly enveloped us, and then the black man moved so that his lips were at my ear, while he barely whispered:

"Me go; noise in camp will help. You wait still like dead; me come back soon."

I did not attempt to answer, for there was nothing to say. Flanked by the two sentinels, I was pretty sure to wait, and wait like dead, too. He began to move then, yet he did not seem to move. But as I watched—more with my senses than my eyes—I knew that he had worked his head and shoulders out of our shelter, and was edging himself along at the rate of perhaps a foot a minute. Soon I realized that he had entirely gone; that, free of the saw-palmetto—a most difficult stuff in which to move silently—he was topping the bank. I could imagine how he glided now, alligator fashion, head downward to the water; and I could almost feel the moment he slid noiselessly into it. I waited for the owl call—"two times, then stop soft in middle."

And now an electric torch flashed where the sentry on my right was posted, and I froze, wondering if it were directed at Smilax. But no challenge came. In a very short interval it flashed again, and the fellow called in military style:

"Post one, seven o'clock, and all's well!"

The voice at my left took it up:

"Post two, seven o'clock, and all's well!"

From somewhere beyond Sylvia's island the third guard called post three, and silence followed. I was glad to find that they called their posts. It told us that there were only three, and gave a very fair idea of their positions. Of course, we could not hope, with this military precaution, to have one of them fall asleep at a convenient moment. Especially would this not happen with a newly placed guard—and these fellows were on watch to-night for the first time, else we would have seen them, or they us, when we came that morning. Smilax, also, would have discovered them the night before. Sylvia and Echochee, therefore, had just come under suspicion of intending to escape—and we were in the nick of time, although I felt staggered by the job ahead of us.

After another wait the fellow at post one again flashed his torch—on his watch, no doubt, because from time to time there were other flashes and, after the last of these, he called half-past seven. That was good for us, too—the half hours! Eight o'clock came, then half after, then nine. The lights in the camp had been extinguished. A real owl hooted mournfully somewhere back in the forest. I was waiting for post one to be called again when a voice, not twelve inches from my face, whispered:

"All right; come; slow like me. When you think you can no go more slow, then go two times as slow."

Had it not been for that last piece of advice I might have made a mess of things, but by moving at first scarcely more than an inch a minute, by distributing my feeling sense to every part of my body, detecting the slightest pull at my clothing, the merest contact with any little twig that might traitorously snap—in fact, by almost wishing myself along—I came at last free of the palmettoes and lay beside him. From there our progress was easier, and shortly we got to our hands and knees.

After following in this manner for two hundred yards Smilax stopped and sat down.

"You do good," he said. "Wait; me go back."

"What for?" I asked, in surprise. "Tell me what Echochee said?"

"After 'while," he answered. "Me go fix pine needles where we crawl out; then take look at all's-well-men. You wait."

I should never have thought about obliterating our trail in the pine needles, yet now saw that it was a very necessary thing to do, for men can not crawl on their stomachs without mussing the ground if it is at all soft. In the morning those fellows would see our tracks leading from the palmetto patch and, to a certainty, be waiting for us when we returned.

He was back sooner than I expected, and we took a good swinging pace to camp. Not till he had made a mere handful of fire and warmed over some coffee (gods of good things, how delicious it was!) and I had lighted my pipe (O, goddess Nicotine, what a pipe!) would he speak. Then suddenly he said:

"We no lay out to-morrow."

"Why?" I asked, quickly alarmed that Sylvia had refused to come.

"No use. When men on guard call, we find 'em easy. No much palmetto; we slip up good."

I laughed; not at what he said, but because to laugh was irresistible. My nerves were just a little drunk on relaxation.

"Come across with what Echochee said," I told him.

He grinned and nodded.

"Echochee know me. Me no call like owl, for 'fraid all's-well-men no be fooled; so crawl close and scratch on wall. She come to place inside, then me put mouth to crack and say in Seminole: 'Echochee, me Tachachobee.' She squat down by crack and whisper back: 'You lie. What your father name?' Me say: 'Black boy got no father; Echochee friend, Wanona, squaw of Kittimee, raise him.' Then she ask back quick: 'How many pickaninny Kittimee and Wanona had?' Me say: 'Boy child.' She whisper quicker: 'What wigwam stood in morning shadow to Kittimee?' Me say: 'Echochee wigwam.' She say: 'Who next?' Me say: 'Pattawa, him shoot long gun.' She wait 'while, and say: 'If you Tachachobee, what scar you got on left leg?' Me say: 'No scar on left leg, scar on right leg; four teeth of Pawpawloochee spotted dog what wildcat kill.' She know then me tell no lie, and unlock door and come out, and take my hand. 'You big man now, Tachachobee,' she say. 'Me got big man job, Echochee,' me say, and tell her how me take 'em 'way."

I was charmed with the way Echochee had put Smilax through the third degree, so to speak, because it proved that Sylvia had a shrewd protector; one who would at least not be outmatched except by force—and, judging from the tray episode, even force would have to be considerable.

"She go in," Smilax continued, "and tell Lady, then Lady come out and say: 'Good. We be ready. How we know when you come?' And me tell her this, Mister Jack, so you listen for you have to do um. Me say: 'You hear men call what time?' She say she do. Me say: 'You hear 'em call all's well?' She say she do, and me say: 'When you hear one call all's-er-well, unlock door for me come quick.'"

"You want me to call all's-er-well, instead of all's-well? Is that the idea?"

"Good. We slip up on guard; you take man at One, me man at Two; we kill 'em quick and make no noise. Man at Three far off; him no count. Me wait then till time for next call. If me hear all's-er-well, me know you no dead, and go in water. Then you come quick and quiet to place where Two is dead and make call for him. Then Three will answer; we no care 'bout Three. If me take long, and come time for 'nother call, you do um same as first. Soon we be over."

"You won't have a punt," I suggested.

"No need um; water so," he drew his hand across his waist. "Tote Lady, then Echochee."

"She doesn't know I'm to be there?"

"No; plenty time."

That night I slept heavily, as a man who has regained the bloom of health, and awoke with the rosy dawn. A few fiery bars shot across the sky, which the trees, brush and grass reflected. Red, everywhere red; and I thought how much more red the night would be after Smilax and I had silenced Posts One and Two. I raised my head and looked for him. The fire was burning, our breakfast was cooking. He had doubtless gone to the spring for water, so I rolled out of my lean-to and started to the pool; but stopped, listening.

Somewhere ahead of me I heard his voice, deep and musical, droning a weird kind of chant that seemed to be utterly everlasting. It was not loud, but rather like a deep organ note that carries a long distance. In a while he came nearer, walking unconcernedly with his face to the sky. Over and over and over the chant continued; truly a sort of world without end.

"Do you know the second verse?" I cheerily asked, as he was about to pass.

He stopped, swung around, and showed his teeth in a smile that was as free from worry as the day.

"Me sing askabee," he explained. "Enemy go down when me sing askabee."

"Then pray continue, by all means," I said hurriedly, "Maybe after breakfast we can manage to knock out a duet."

"We build fort after breakfast," he replied, unmindful of my banter. "Breakfast 'bout ready. Get wet quick and come back soon." It's a wonder he hadn't told me to smoke.

On the southern and western edge of our "island"—thus being nearest Efaw Kotee's settlement—were a lot of fallen palms; trees that many years ago had been killed by fire and now lay partially rotted. The best of these Smilax had planned to make into a fort; not an elaborate affair, but a shoulder-high hollow square, around which was to be built another hollow square, a three foot space between their walls to be filled with sand. It was a good idea, and would stop a Krag or modern Springfield bullet with ease.

We worked on this till noon; he trimming, lifting and placing the logs—and elephants have never swung teak more splendidly—while I, with our jointed camp spade, filled in the sand. The use of an axe could not possibly betray our position as Efaw Kotee had been betrayed, because the breeze continued from him to us, and also for the equally good reason that the bite of an axe in soggy palmetto does not sound with anything like the ring that is caused by hardwood. So our walls grew, being fitted with nice precision that gave them more than enough strength to sustain the filling of sand—

which, in turn, was kept from sifting through the interstices by a double lining of palm leaves.

After an early luncheon we went back to add a few finishing touches, and then stood off admiring it.

"Oughtn't we put in a stock of provisions?" I asked.

"No stay long 'nough in there to get much hungry," Smilax shook his head. "One night and they pull um down and got us. Good to keep 'em off in daytime; after dark we run in grass."

There was something in what he said.

With the approach of evening a curious calm came over me. Perhaps it was the nearness of action, perhaps because I had accustomed myself to the thought that before another dawn I must deliberately slip upon a fellow man and destroy him. In France, with a battle raging, men lost their identity, and if—or when—we killed one, we rarely knew it. But in this peaceful country it seemed a more murderous thing to do. Yet perhaps the truest reason why my nerves had turned to steel was the dominating thought of Sylvia.

Twice I rehearsed before Smilax what I was to do. I stood apart and called: "Post One, nine o'clock, and all's-er-well!" to let him judge if my voice differed materially from the one we heard last night. This was most important, as the suspicion of the guard at post Three must not be aroused. I then called the next post in an altered voice, and felt well pleased when Smilax said the tones were near enough to pass.

It was an uncanny rehearsal, this imitating the voices of those whom we should have made forever silent, but if there existed anywhere on earth a justification for the taking of human life it rested with Smilax and me. We were not killers, but defenders; we did not go so much to destroy as to save. Our way was the only way to rescue a helpless girl and a faithful old woman from destruction. Two men, or two hundred, made no difference now; I would kill all, or any number, who stood in the way of that beloved girl's safety.

We looked over our firearms. I had given him Tommy's "l'il crack-crack" which, with my own, were the only weapons we intended to take—I mean the only explosive weapons, for Smilax carried his long, keen-edged hunting knife, a thing he was never without; and I, likewise, strapped on my own. After this we went about putting the camp in order; building a shelter tent by the spring for Sylvia and an adjacent lean-to for Echochee. Joyfully I robbed myself of bedding, arranged comfortable shake-downs with moss and leaves of the cabbage palm, and did everything conceivable to make the place attractive.

I had demurred at first about coming back here for a day or two; wanting, instead, to travel as speedily as possible to Big Cove, where the *Whim*—and if not the *Whim*, at least the *Orchid*—would be at our disposal. But he showed me the futility of this. In the first place, that was exactly what Efaw Kotee would be suspecting when the escape became known. The dead sentries, certain to be discovered when they failed to call the next half hour, would reveal the story of outside help, so the pursuit would be swift and directly up the coast—swifter, indeed, than she might be able to travel.

"Why shouldn't they think we'd taken her off in a small boat," I asked, "and escaped through the islands?"

"Then Efaw Kotee want to know why kill guard on mainland."

"That's so. But, Smilax, suppose we hide the guards?"

He thought a moment over this, but finally shook his head.

"No good. Then Efaw Kotee say guard run off with Lady, so he come back 'cross prairie same as up and down shore. That make our chance ve'y bad. No. They find men dead, then hunt quick through forest up beach; maybe down beach. After 'while, maybe they find sign where me and you camp in L'il Cove; then they know small boat been there and gone. Then they come home mad, and when all quiet we make big circle to *Whim*. Some day we come back; maybe kill 'em all. Me want Jess; him crack Smilax head. That good plan; you smoke."

I lay on the ground and smiled. Kill 'em all! Gods, but I was going back into the primitive by leaps and bounds! I wondered if that girl would trust herself to me, were she to know!

"Me big fool," Smilax suddenly cried, smashing a fist into the palm of his hand.

"What's the matter?" I sat up, asking.

"Me ought to be in L'il Cove and make fresh signs. Me big fool!"

It would have been a cute move, but now too late, and I told him so.

"No too late," he sprang up. "Three hour more sun."

"But, Smilax, it took us the best part of a day to come here! You can't do it!"

"Me go short way back, and fast." He pointed to the western sky, at an angle of about twenty degrees above the horizon, asking: "When night come you see big star there?"

I nodded. It was Jupiter or Venus, I didn't know which; but it was large and beautiful, and I had seen it many evenings.

"When um touch top of trees you start. Me meet you on far side of prairie."

Feeling to see if his weapons were securely holstered he was off without another word to make signs in the sand at Little Cove that would look as though this very afternoon a landing party had been there, and I wondered if real Indians could possess the foresight of this big negro. In amazement I watched him growing smaller and smaller across the sea of grass; going north-by-northwest now, and not the way we came. The prairie in this direction must have extended five miles before it met the forest, and as long as my eyes could follow him he was jogging at a good free trot. By this more direct route he had perhaps ten or twelve miles to go each way; and his return would be at night, lighted by a partial moon. I knew that he would make it, and be at our meeting place when I arrived, but how he could possibly do so was in a realm beyond my comprehension.

When the evening star sank and touched the forest I quietly left our camp. The night air was delightfully mellow, but my soul, my nerves, my determination were as cold as the long blade of my knife. In our present days of railroads, telegraphs and institutions of learning I was merely a chap setting out to take a girl from a den of rogues; but in this night-bathed Florida wilderness civilization had been stripped to the bone. I was a man going forth to steal a female—I had come from my lair at dusk, set off with a snarl on my lips and a firm grip upon my stone axe; so completely dominated by this feeling that human pawns who might stand in the way would be of no more consequence than ants.

From the lighter prairie I cautiously approached the black shadows of the forest, made impenetrably dark by a network of branches and a mat of leaves which no ray from the half grown moon could pierce. As I was about to enter Smilax arose from the ground in front of me.

"Good," he whispered. "We rest li'l while; then go fix 'em."

CHAPTER XVII
THE RESCUE

We lay in silence till at last, faintly, came the call of post one. I listened, trying to catch the quality of his voice, knowing I soon should have to imitate it. To the call of the next man I also listened. The third did not concern us more than to know he was on duty. No others called, so the guard had not been strengthened. These voices seemed to arouse Smilax, for he raised himself up on one elbow, whispering:

"What time they say?"

"Ten o'clock," I answered.

"Good. We fix 'em 'leven; come."

So the game was on! I followed silently—and savagely; for, as I have said, the human pawns who stood between me and my maid held no more value than the ants.

For about ten minutes our progress went reasonably well, then Smilax slowed to a pace of extreme caution and finally sank to his hands and knees. In this manner we crawled a few hundred yards farther.

"Here your place," he put his lips close to my ear and whispered. "First man not ve'y far; straight. You find out when he call once more, or flash light. Watch when Two man call so you know where go next. No let 'em call 'leven. Good. Me go now." And he was off like a snake to take up a position behind post two.

I felt about me and, finding the ground clear of any growth that might produce a noise, moved stealthily forward, still on my hands and knees; but, after each step, pausing and feeling ahead until my fingers seemed to have grown as long and sensitive as antennæ. In this way I must have gone another two hundred feet when I saw a glimmer of white light. It was the electric torch, and I knew the sentry must be looking at his watch.

Fleeting as it had been it showed me that between us lay a patch of saw-palmetto, and this was awkward as I could get no idea of its depth. But since he did not call the post I knew that he would soon be taking another look at the time, and kept warily on, my eyes alert to ascertain the dimensions of that patch the instant his torch should flare. For I must crawl around it; to go through would be impossible. Smilax could have achieved it, but Smilax was a wonder.

The light showed again. I was within fifty feet of the patch now and saw with a feeling of relief that it ended almost at the spot where my man stood, or sat, or whatever he was doing. Still, the time had not come for him to call the half hour, when I should be able to advance more rapidly during the few seconds that his voice would make him insensible to other slight sounds. Inch by inch, almost holding my breath, I crawled. The pine needles let me slide along as though on a greased floor. My left hand touched a saw-toothed stem, so I veered slightly to the right, getting closer, all the while closer.

At the next flash I heard him clear his throat—that had ever been his prelude to a call—and by the time his sing-song "Post-one-half-past-ten-and-all's-well" ended I had made good progress. Now, close up behind the point of palmettoes which acted as a screen but was too sparse to offer interference, I realized that he could be not more than ten feet away; and this was the best I could hope to do, surely as close as I dared get.

But ten feet was too great a space to be crossed at a bound before he might utter one cry that would alarm the camp. One cry, even half a cry, meant ruin to us. It was not enough that this sentry die; he must die without having uttered the merest sound. I determined, therefore, to wait until his senses became focused, his breathing centered, on the eleven o'clock call; for, so occupied, his mind would be a fraction of a second slower in responding to an outside thought which came unawares to him than if he were standing on the alert for sounds. This seemed to be good psychology. When he cleared his throat to call eleven, therefore, I would spring—and the gods be with me!

I own that for a little while my heart did pound unmercifully, but with even less mercy I willed it to be calm. For the moment I almost regretted having come so near, because it seemed preposterous to suppose that he would not discover me. I could distinctly hear the slightest move he made—but it must be remembered that I was listening to him, whereas he did not suspect my existence. Once he knocked the dead ashes from his pipe against the heel of his boot; then I thought he was getting ready for a smoke, and soon after this he struck a match.

As the flame, sheltered by his two hands held cup-wise, flickered above the bowl I got a look at him. He impressed me as being a well put up fellow of considerable strength, who would not be conquered without trouble. But never have I seen a face present a pantomime of more brutal indifference. It was seamed with lines of cruelty; the coarse lips were hideously puckered about the pipe stem; his eyes drooped in bestial satisfaction as he sucked at it. While he was getting the light, thus creating a noise in his own ears that would drown a slighter noise from me, I took the opportunity to arrange my position somewhat, and now felt satisfied. With clean ground beneath me, with only a thin screen of palmetto leaves between us, how better could I have planned!

Minutes sped, and my senses seemed to have accumulated into a little ball between my eyes. I may have trembled; I know that my nerves were stretched to the very highest fighting pitch, they were in tune with my determination. The next half hour would decide the salvation or destruction of the girl I loved.

The electric torch flashed on a silver watch in his huge, dirty hand. I held my breath, ready—but he did not call. Again I had to will my heart to stop its sudden thumping; again I settled down to wait—though with my legs crouched and my fingers resting on the sand, as I had "set" many a time for a hundred yard dash. All I needed now was the word "Go!"

More minutes sped. At last he moved, and I guessed that he was reaching into his pocket for the torch. It flashed, shining on the silver watch as before. I heard the cover snap to with a click of finality; he cleared his throat—and I bounded into the air.

He had no time to cry out before my fingers locked upon his throat as jaws of iron. He staggered and caught my wrists, but did not immediately begin the frantic struggle I expected. His rifle fell to the soft earth with hardly a sound and, like a dead weight, he crumpled up; falling so quickly that I nearly came down on top of him.

At first, suspecting this might be a ruse to break my grip, I squeezed the tighter, holding his head up as far as my knees and shaking it with the savageness that a terrier would shake a rat. There was no room for compromises here. Grimly believing him to be beyond the point of giving an alarm, I was not prepared for an attack when he came to life with an energy born of desperation, wrapped his arms about my legs and with tremendous strength jerked me forward, at the same instant striking me in the back with his knee. Thus, to keep from pitching over his head, I involuntarily lost my hold—the last of all things I would have done!

Yet the effect to so violent a choking seemed for the moment to have paralyzed his power to call, and swiftly, as a darting hawk, I made another grab for the throat that must at all costs be silenced. He had covered it with his own hands and I could not pry away his fingers. Again and again I tried, and now, with growing strength, he caught my wrists and held them. Maddened by the specter of failure, I heard him drawing in a labored breath that I knew would come out in a hideous yell.

Success lay upon the fraction of a second. In a frenzy jerking one of my hands free, and throwing the full weight of my body across his face to momentarily smother the outcry, I twisted around, drew my knife, and plunged it deep into his side. There was a convulsive tremor, and silence. Yet, as the king snake had done, I also drew back warily, listening. It had been enough.

Springing up, and trying to calm my breathing, I called:

"Post one, 'leven o'clock, and all's-er-well!"

The last word had no more than been pronounced when I was moving swiftly, silently on post number two. True to his intention, Smilax had prepared the way.

"Post two, 'leven o'clock, and all's-er-well!" I called in an altered voice.

The sentry at post three, doubtless having a vein of humor or finding any variation of his tedious duty agreeable, dwelt in his turn long and almost lovingly over the "er-well," making it sound "e-e-er-well."

"How you like that?" he called, in a guarded tone, and receiving no answer, laughed: "Then go ter hell with yer perlite manners."

A few minutes elapsed before I was conscious of a movement in the water, slight, barely distinguishable. But my eyes had grown more and more accustomed to the darkness and I thought that I made out something coming toward the shore. Creeping a little forward and listening, I felt that it was Smilax carrying Sylvia, and became certain of this when someone was deposited there who began cautiously to climb the bank. Smilax, evidently, had turned back for Echochee. But along this section of the mainland the bank was steep, and the climber came with difficulty—once slipping and making what I thought to be an awful racket. Even the humorous sentry on post three heard it and, providentially unsuspicious, called:

"Yer ain't bit yerse'f, have yer?"

I made no answer to this, trusting him to be satisfied with his own wit. Yet now, following a most natural impulse, forgetting in our extreme peril that Sylvia was unaware of my presence, I leaned above the top and reached down to her; when, to my utter consternation, she gave a piercing scream of terror. Quick as a flash the sentry at post three yelled and fired his gun, and the sleeping camp became a bedlam of cursing men.

"For God's sake," I whispered—but Smilax had turned back to us and was beside her.

"Him friend," he said, hurriedly. "Only friend we got! Go with him quick! Me get Echochee!"

While saying this he was pushing her up to me, at the same time holding out a bag, or kind of traveling case, that she had dropped. I seized it with one hand, and her arm with the other.

"Quick; go to camp," Smilax was saying. "Me get Echochee and give 'em chase up coast. Be back soon; you wait there."

He had taken to the water again and was making for the Indian woman, who I thought had started out to meet him. So I knew he would rescue her, as surely as he was six and a half feet of muscle and endurance. The camp had become thoroughly aroused by now, and lights were everywhere. Hoping to reassure Sylvia, I whispered as Smilax would have spoken:

"Me friend; come quick!"

Above the confusion we could hear the voice of Efaw Kotee bellowing:

"Get the punts, you fools! Which way is she?"

"On the mainland," someone yelled.

"Then catch her," he bellowed again, with a string of blasphemous oaths.

This decided her, and she whispered wildly:

"Hurry! Take me where Tachachobee said!"

We dashed through the forest, I leading, she close behind. Nor had we any time to spare, for before we had gone a hundred yards two quick shots rang out. It was "li'l crack-crack" speaking, I felt sure of it.

Shots answered rapidly in threes and fours. The automatic spoke again, this time farther to the north, drawing more shots from the angry pursuers; but I knew that among trees so thick and in darkness so impenetrable Smilax and Echochee ran little chance of being hit. At the prairie, made vaguely lighter by a hazy, half grown moon, we crouched in the grass and waited.

You have never, I suppose, been afraid to breathe, flattened against a wall, or huddled in a shadowy place, listening to the growls and grunts and sniffs of the man-beast hunting you? No, of course not.

Men were now tearing through the forest like a herd of stampeded horses, shooting, yelling, cursing, while at brief intervals the automatic told them which way to go. Farther and farther the chase went, all the time following the coast and leading away from us till, after twenty minutes, the yells were hardly discernible and the shots sounded like faint little pops of a nursery gun. But they were as rapid as ever, telling us that the pursuit had in no way diminished. Smilax, undoubtedly master of the situation, would lead them on and on; either close by Big Cove so those aboard the *Whim*—had she made harbor—could take a hand, or finally lose them somewhere in the treacherous Everglades. Then he would came back for us. I felt no great uncertainty for Smilax and Echochee.

I now straightened up—taking care that she should not see my face—and listened to satisfy myself that no one had stayed behind to be roaming in the forest near us, then whispered:

"Come!"

In silence, she following, we crossed the two mile space, and I drew a deep breath of thankfulness when we at last stepped beneath the black trees of my "island."

I knew that she had taken me for a Seminole—at least, the probability seemed to be strong in that direction. The darkness again was too intense for her to see my features, and, since I had been fairly successful in speaking the choppy English of the Indian, I determined to continue the deception until morning. For she had become somewhat accustomed to the "trusted friend" by now, whereas re-introductions at this hour would be exceedingly awkward, if not quite disastrous to her peace of mind. So, without a halt, I walked on through the trees until we came to her tent. At the door of this I put down her bag, then stepped back and for a second at arm's length flashed my electric torch on it, again being careful to keep my face in shadow.

"You safe here," I said. "Tachachobee make this camp for you. Me and him camp little way off. To-night me watch to see when him and Echochee come. No one find you; you sleep well. Tachachobee good man; me and him friends. You no be 'fraid."

"Thank you," she said wearily. Ah, how tired her voice did seem!

"There water; good to drink. You hungry?" I asked.

"No, thank you,—what is your name?"

This was a poser, for I had not thought up a name. But, of course, Jack came first into my mind, so I answered:

"Jackachobee."

"No, thank you, Jackachobee," she said, "I'm not hungry."

"You want gun?" I asked again.

"I have one," she answered.

"Good. Then you sleep; no one find you here. In morning take time; when ready for breakfast walk back this way a hundred steps and whistle like plover. Then me come and show you way. Sleep good."

Thus, feeling very well satisfied with my Indian impersonation—which, nevertheless, had its faults—I left her; turning and going to the fort, there choosing a place where I could keep guard all night against possible danger.

Long and earnestly did I listen for some sound of the chase, but the night had grown absolutely still except for a soft breeze rustling the palm fronds above my head and the prairie grass in front of me. Yet I felt secure in the belief that Smilax had not been taken. Without question, he and Echochee were still in flight, heading toward some safe refuge; coaxing, by shot or cry, the furious pack that tore hopefully after them. I knew that my vigil here was unnecessary—that with all senses focused on the chase no straggler would by any chance be coming this far out into the prairie—but I had told Sylvia it would be kept.

As I sat there, joyous over the conquest we had made, but more supremely happy because she was safe and near me, thinking tumultuous things which were a credit to mankind, hoping hopes that man has never realized, I raised my face to the sky and thanked God.

Creature of incongruities! I thanked God for putting her safely into my keeping, when my fingers had not yet been washed after their bath in a fellow creature's blood! The cave man had gone abroad at dusk to find a mate, and human pawns who stood in his way had been of no more consequence than ants!

Thus it has always been for the women we love. Thus it should be.

CHAPTER XVIII
DOLORIA

With the first glimpse of dawn I arose and faced the East; my arms out, my palms up, and across them my rifle as a kind of offering to the day. I do not know why I did this—this spontaneous though semi-pagan act—except that on my "island," and in my power, slept the girl I loved; she whom I had stolen from her watchful tribe, whom I would have as mate. By all the laws of the wilderness she was mine, and I wanted to tell someone, to challenge the wild, that these arms and hands and this rifle would protect her till the end.

A thin mist hung low upon the prairie, a faint tint of salmon touched the sky, and to my lips sprang the words of that inspiring "Salutation of the Dawn" which found expression in the Orient many thousands of years ago:

Listen to the Exhortation of the Dawn!
Look to this Day!
For it is life, the very life of life.
In its brief course lie all the verities
And realities of your existence:
The glory of action,
The bliss of growth,
The splendor of beauty:
For yesterday is but a dream,
And tomorrow is only a vision;
But today well-lived makes
Every yesterday a dream of happiness,
And every tomorrow a vision of hope.
Look well, therefore, to this Day!

Then, as the light increased and the mist began to dissolve, I swept the prairie in all directions for a sign of enemies. Everywhere was peace.

Assured that Efaw Kotee would never find us here I turned and went to my lean-to—to the place my lean-to had been before we moved it beside the spring—gathered up my knick-knacks and repaired to the pool, emerging half an hour later a more presentable man. After this I built a small fire of buttonwood and set about preparing breakfast.

But this proved to be a perplexing ordeal. Bilkins had packed in a lot of stuff that he might have manipulated, though to me it was worse than Greek. Of course, I could cook up coffee and bacon—the kind of meal Smilax and I were used to—but Sylvia must never be subjected to that! And it would be insane of me to go out on the prairie after snipe! There was nothing for it but prepare a dainty concoction from what we had, so, wishing heartily that Bilkins had come off in the small boat with me, I dived into our stores on a tour of inspection.

Tea!—who wanted tea for breakfast! A pot of butter!—appropriate enough, though it might have been fresher. A can of beans!—worse than tea. A can of finnan haddie came after this, and several cans that only Bilkins could have understood. But in the end I carried a number of them to the fire and had a general opening, arranged them in a row, and began to cook. The chief trouble was that I did not know which should be done thoroughly and which merely warmed up. Anyway, I emptied something, inviting if unpronounceable, into the skillet and as it began to sizzle it smelt really good. So I crouched lower, stirring vigorously to keep it from scorching, and thought of the surprise it would be to her—for, to be quite frank, it was a surprise to me!

Then a voice at my back, making me forget the sizzling stuff, the fire, the breakfast, said with a note of extreme anxiety:

"Good morning, Jackachobee! Oughtn't Echochee be here by this time? You don't think any thing's happened to her, do you? I can't whistle like a plover and had to come to breakfast unannounced. I hope it's ready. You've seen nothing of those men?"

I did not move under this rapid fire of questions and statements. To the contrary, I lowered my head and was afraid to move; afraid to face the rebuke, or the fear, or whatever it would be, that might naturally follow her discovery of my deception. But more potent than this dread was the thrill of joy I felt in knowing that she stood close behind me; that when I turned I should see her there, face to face. Yet the very thought of turning again started the chill of apprehension. Without doubt she would wither me like a parched leaf for having played so silly a part as Indian. I began vigorously to stir the stuff in my skillet which now had stuck to the bottom and was smelling like the very old devil. Of course, my face would have been red, anyway—leaning over the fire as I was!

"Are you keeping anything from me?" she cried, I thought on the verge of "nerves," so hesitating no longer I arose and turned to her.

"Oh!" she gasped, drawing back and putting one hand to her breast—while the other, I noticed, fell mechanically to the butt of a revolver swung to her waist. Her eyes were wide with surprise, as her lips were parted in fear and utter wonderment. Truly, she was the incarnation of girlhood standing at bay!

I had known her beauty; I had been astounded by it in the Havana café, in my dream, in the little kodak film of Monsieur's, and last, when she stood in her doorway less than forty-eight hours before. But here was something that transcended all that I had previously seen in her. Perhaps the young sun, golden in the morning atmosphere, cast the spell as it sought out spun-copper strands amongst her waves of hair; perhaps the days of anxiety, terminating in a night of unfearful sleep, had put the dew, the mystery, in her eyes; or it may have been the color, smouldering beneath the attractive tan on her cheeks and tinting her pure throat, that held me charmed; or the indefinable spirit of wildness that showed through a natural poise. I saw, too, in a hazy kind of way, a most bewitching costume—at least, admirably suited to her: a waist of olive-drab, not unlike our service shirts but of delicate material, open at the throat and fitting her snugly; quite a short skirt to match, and laced tan boots.

"Please don't shoot," I said, trying to smile.

"Where is Jackachobee?" she demanded.

"I'm Jackachobee."

"But you're not an Indian!"

"No, but I really am the friend Tachachobee told you of."

I could see that she was growing more alarmed, and now spoke frankly, saying:

"I pretended to be a Seminole last night because explanations would have taken time; and I thought, too, that you'd feel safer with a good Indian because he's easier to boss than a white man."

Her eyes narrowed, subtly suggesting that she might take this as a challenge. At last, having looked me over—but not once removing her hand from the revolver butt—she said, with a little pucker between her eyebrows:

"I've seen you somewhere. Were you ever in our—in that place over there?"

Now, of course, I could hardly expect her to see a resemblance between a chap wearing breeches and puttees in a Florida wilderness and the dinner-jacketed yachtsman who dined near her table off yonder in Havana. It would be asking a great deal—although I did feel disappointed.

"No," I answered, "I haven't been in that settlement; but I watched it from a hiding place all of day before yesterday. You see, I've come two hundred miles to take you away from it."

"You've come to—to take *me*?" she slowly asked, and I thought the color began to smoulder again; while from her eyes flashed a look that might have been a struggle between gratitude, resentment and fear. Wanting only the first to prevail I continued hastily:

"Yes; I followed ever since you wrote that you were in danger, and I've sworn not to return to my yacht without you."

"Oh!" she gasped, stepping back and staring at me through the swiftly changing lights of her awakening. "Surely," she caught her breath again, "surely you're not the—you *can't* be!"

"I am," I smiled, holding out my hand. "The man you gave the paper ball to."

Impulsively she clasped it in both of her own, swaying slightly toward me and looking her gratitude through eyes brim-full of tears—but the angels be my witness that spoken words have never been so eloquent! Then she began to laugh—a little wildly, a little hysterically—so I said:

"It's all right—you're safe here, absolutely! I watched last night and there wasn't the slightest sign of anyone. You see, Smilax—that's Tachachobee, but we call him Smilax because he smiles—well, he and Echochee purposely led those fellows up the coast, and they'll keep on leading them any-old-where until it's safe to join us here. It's been carefully planned out. However, I'll tell you everything after—after—" I looked ruefully at the shriveled black stuff now incinerated on the bottom of my skillet, adding: "but there isn't going to be any after; it's all burned up!"

She had pluckily taken herself in hand by now and, following my dejected stare, cried:

"Is *that* our breakfast? Heavens, what a calamity! But show me where the things are and I'll cook another!"

"You'll soil your fingers," I hesitatingly protested.

"Soil my fingers! Of course, I will; but there's no scarcity of water, nor of my appetite, either—and we can't possibly eat what you cook!"

"Oh, I don't know," I said, just a little touchily. "I'm a pretty good sort of a cook, I am!" Often have I noticed how the majority of men get touchy about their cooking.

"The evidence is convincing," she laughed. "Where do you keep your stores? Hurry, please do, if you don't want a fainting woman on your hands. I'm starved!"

Now I saw that some of this was being put on; that it was the slackening of tightly pulled nerves; so I encouraged her as far as I dared without being suspected, knowing that it is best to open all vents when one's feelings have been dangerously pent up. As to my ability to cook!—why, there were extenuating circumstances governing this breakfast that should have excused it. Some day I'd surprise her.

I changed that idea quickly enough when she took charge, however, for in ten minutes there were two or three things sizzling and sending out an aroma that might have brought Epicurus himself back to life. What's more, she did not seem to be worrying over them; she did not even seem particular about stirring them, nor did she burn her fingers, nor get red in the face and hot, nor suffer any of those agonies that I had supposed were a necessary part of culinary science.

"You're a wonder," I exclaimed. "Darned if I've ever seen such a swell cook!"

"Thank you, sir," she tossed her head and mimicked. "I'm glad I please, sir."

"Like your new place?" I asked, gravely.

"I've seen worse, sir."

"Like your new master, too?" I ventured.

"Marster, is it!" She sent me a look with which there was a most fetching little curve at the corners of her lips that she seemed unable to control. "I'll 'ave you understand that queens of the kitchen know no marster!"

"But you won't be in the kitchen all the time."

"That I will," she replied. "In the woods, all the world's a kitchen!"

"I rather wish it was," I sighed, looking toward the savory skillet and coffee pot; whereupon she gave the brightest of laughs, telling me to set the table as things were about ready.

But Smilax and I had never bothered about a table. We did not even possess a cloth, or napkin, or anything like that. So I cut some palm leaves, arranging them on the ground; then ransacked the duffle for a small kit of aluminum plates and cups, with also knives and forks. Neither had Smilax and I deigned to use this kit, principally because our meals had been taken on the move. At best palm leaves do not make a good table, as their ridges cause the dishes to wobble; so in the end we spread our steaming feast upon the grass.

My word, but that was a breakfast! I don't remember what we had, but it did taste good. When it was over, right down to the last crumb—for she had complained of starvation, too—I looked across at her, saying:

"If I can move, at all, and you're willing to go slowly, I'd like to show you over your new possessions!"

"Right away? Mercy no," she stood up, brushing her skirt. "I'm going to get a cigarette, and you're going to wash the dishes!"

"But Smilax washes the dishes," I protested.

"And he may be thirty miles from here," she announced.

"Will you come back and watch me?"

"I will if you want me to," she laughed, "but you'll look awfully silly."

"Then you needn't," I agreed, less reluctantly, "and I'll call in half an hour. By the way, I've deeded you all the 'island' east of those two big pines. The other side is mine."

"Thanks. I'll take possession at once." And she left me for her spring and bailiwick and cigarette—although I never saw her smoking one before, or after. In a few minutes I heard her calling and, straightening up with some feeling of alarm, answered:

"What's wrong?"

"Nothing; only don't forget to use very hot water!"

Later we walked to the south-western edge of the "island," so she could see how it stood in relation to Efaw Kotee's settlement; and I showed her the fort, purposely exaggerating its ability to withstand a siege and minimizing its chances of having to do so. We sat down there upon the turf, where the breeze and shade were refreshing. It was a fortunate location, also, for keeping an eye on the prairie.

"Have you named this beautiful place of yours?" she asked.

"No; we merely call it the 'island,' after the native fashion. Will you name it for me—for us? It's half yours, you know."

"Let's call it—" she thought a moment, "oh, let's call it The Oasis; for that's cool and comfortable and suggests safety from all sorts of things!"

"The Oasis it is, and we'll put it on the map some day, see if we don't!"

After a while I told her pretty much everything from the beginning of our cruise: of Tommy, Monsieur, and Gates, of Smilax, of seeing her in Havana. I scrupulously avoided any mention of having been bowled over by her beauty, or of the dream, and was inclined to treat the paper ball episode with a laugh; but here she interrupted me, saying:

"But I was very serious, really, and scared almost to death. You surely know I must have been to've done it! The whole thing came so suddenly—like a frightful storm!"

"Then you hadn't always been at outs with him—or forbidden him to cross to your little island?" I asked.

"Mercy, no—that is, not my father. The other men, of course, were on a footing of servants—to me, at any rate. It was only after we got home two days ago, after Echochee and I were alone again, that I kept them away by—by threatening—"

"Don't say what—it hurts me," I interrupted her quickly. "I saw your wonderful courage from our hiding place."

"Everyone was quite friendly up to the time we reached Havana," she continued, in a rather forced, even voice. "We were there three days before your yacht came—though I didn't know it was yours until today—and that afternoon I'd been up in the Prado with Echochee doing a lot of shopping. We always bought every conceivable thing on those semi-yearly trips. Well, when we got back on board my father rather balked about taking me off again to dinner, but I held him to it because he'd previously promised. I think that he had grown so sensate to dangers that he felt one then, but couldn't locate it."

"Because we were anchored so close to you?"

"I don't really know. But it was something. It wasn't a pleasant dinner from the outset, because I resented his devilish mood and was disgusted with him for being afraid. That doesn't sound very nice," she added, half apologetically, "but, you know, there had always been something subtly antagonistic within me that—oh, I can't express it, but I'd never felt very close to him, ever since I can remember. It was largely my fault, I suppose. But I'd had glimpses of his frightfully cruel nature. Then Echochee, who came to nurse me when I was little, always hated him, and I adored her—so, of course, her influence counted. You really think she's coming through all right?"

"Downright sure of it," I declared, in solemn earnest. After a few moments of silence, I asked gently: "Do you mind telling me more?"

She gave a slight start as though the question had brought her from some deep thought, but smiled, saying:

"Certainly, I don't. When your two friends left you in the café my father became terribly excited. I asked him what on earth was the trouble—but smiling, for that was a subterfuge he always demanded of me in public places—and he whispered that he thought the shorter man was a police agent from his lost republic."

"Lost republic?"

"Yes. You see, my father had been its President—in South America, you know—until the revolution compelled us to fly." This was said resignedly.

"Oh," I murmured. "When was that?"

"Years ago. I just remember being carried off one night in a great hurry."

"Tell me the rest about Havana?" I asked, trying to appear calm.

"It's all rather awful," she sighed. "I hadn't noticed your friends more than to get a glimpse of them as they left, but saw you alone at the table. Pretty soon our captain, Jess,"—she may have given a slight shudder, I wasn't sure—"came up and verified my father's suspicions, and then I thought he surely would lose his mind. I was already becoming frightened, especially as the creature, Jess, impertinently leered at me, and my father didn't knock him down for it. He had never dared look at me before, except most deferentially, and suddenly I felt that I was nearing something awful. I can't explain it. It just came to me all of a sudden, you know, with desperate certainty, and—and I wanted to run away."

"Were you trying to tell me that?"

She flushed, but answered steadily:

"Yes. I thought you looked like a man who'd help a girl out of a mean place."

"By Jove, that's the biggest compliment I've ever had!"

"I only had a chance to write a little," she ignored my outburst, "but hoped you'd guess and tell your friend, the police agent."

"I didn't guess that," I admitted, somewhat crestfallen. "But we knew you were in danger."

"I should never have left that café if I'd known more myself, then," she said, tensely. "I'd have stood up and called to you—to every man there!"

"And I'd have brought you out in spite of hell," I cried. "Don't tell me there was anything much worse!"

Her cheeks were still aflame with anger, but she smiled, saying in a lower tone:

"Nothing worse than threats. When we got aboard the yacht my father came to me and said, point-blank before those men, that—that—oh, I can't!" She buried her face in her hands—and it was all I could do to keep from putting my arms about her and whispering that everything was now all right. But she had started out to tell me, and was determined to see it through. "He said that he'd promised our captain, that creature Jess, that I should—should—"

"Never mind," I murmured. "I know about it—he said you'd have to marry the scoundrel."

"Oh," she exclaimed. "I'd never heard anything so cold-blooded and damnable in all my life! The creature stood leering at me over his shoulder, and I knew he'd been using threats because my father, himself, was almost paralyzed with fear. And then I lost my head—in blind rage, I suppose. I must have talked like a common fish woman, but my one desire was to see them cringe. So I told about leaving the message for you, pretending to've written a great deal more—twisting the knife all I knew how, and being thoroughly catty. It must have been a disgusting exhibition," she gave a sigh of despair, as if for that uncontrollable outburst of temper.

"I hope you rubbed it in good," I growled.

"Well, I didn't, because my father became so insane with fear that he actually struck me, and rushed ashore in the frantic hope that you might not have seen my message. He would have killed you had he met you then. It was in those few minutes that the little love I ever had for him turned to loathing—and that's a frightful thing to say about one's father, so I hope you won't remember it."

"We have a very mutual respect for each other in loathing that gentleman," I announced. "But tell me quickly—were you safe after that?"

"Oh, yes, for I began to temporize. Echochee wanted to kill them, of course—that being her only solution. But I hoped we might manage to escape if they could be put off a few days."

"And you were in the small boat when they tied on the bomb?"

"Heavens, yes. But I'd no idea it was your yacht, even then—although I thought I recognized your friends taking pictures the morning we left Havana, and was about to call to them when my father, always suspicious, burst into my room."

"It must have been hellish," I growled.

"It was all of that. And especially as always before he'd tried to be kind—at least, he was extremely deferential. That night at Key West he and the captain left in a small boat, and when they came back I was ordered into it. I think he must have been crazy, really, for he said that he was going to show me what they did to traitors—that was my new name then, you know—and shoved a package of something in my face. The captain cursed him for it—and I'd never before heard him treated with the slightest disrespect, but when I found out what the thing was I hoped it would blow up and destroy us all. I only thank God that it didn't go off and kill—my rescuer," she murmured.

"Then you did call that it wasn't fair?"

"I had to protest! Oh, but he was a demon then," she added, and I clenched my fists, remembering what Gates had said. "But he used to be kind," she added, sadly, "and I ought to remember him for that, don't you suppose so? We have a wonderful library on the islands, and when I was very young he began my education. Do you know," she looked up, "I still remember my first lesson in grammar? He taught me by the days!"

"Quite a remarkable thing, that, to remember so far back," I smiled, whereupon she made a little grimace. "How do you mean—by the days?"

"I was taught a tomorrow, not alone because I could recognize today but because I remembered yesterday, and was shown how these were the past, present, and future tenses of our lives; that the present participle is Living, and the infinitive is—"

"To love?" I suggested.

"To live," she said evenly, and I bit my tongue. "He made me study awfully hard, but I rather liked it as there wasn't much else to do except play with Echochee, and she became tiresome occasionally. Later he started me at the piano, and the violin, and I loved to work after that. For he's quite a remarkable musician, really! I suppose our library must have a thousand books, and I've read nearly all of them—besides stacks of the modern ones we always brought from our semi-annual cruises 'to the world'—as he used to call those trips. Don't you simply adore Blasco?"

"I suppose you mean Ibañez," I said, rather pleased at being able to air this familiarity with literary personages.

"Ibañez, then," she casually agreed, "if you prefer calling him by his mother's name."—And, not knowing upon what hazy path this would lead me, I laughingly admitted:

"Well, I've only tackled one of his things, and haven't even finished that yet." Adding, with perhaps a slightly malicious desire to bring her superior knowledge to bay: "You read him in the original, I suppose?"

"Not freely enough to be quite relaxing. But on our cruise last summer we got a very good translation in French—really, much better than the English, I think."

Again I laughed, as a light entered my muddled outlook because of this astonishing information that accounted for much I had not been able to reconcile with her isolated life. From the moment she had mimicked the cook I had been kept in a state of wonderment. I had felt her superiority; I had marveled at the cultivation that clung about her as a royal robe. Now it was explained. Music, literature, languages!

"That night you protested about the bomb," I asked, "did you hear me call?"

Could it have been that some of the animation left her face as she answered slowly:

"Oh, was it you? I heard someone call to a person named Sylvia."

"But—isn't that your name?"

"Oh," she laughed, "I haven't nearly so pretty a name as that!"

I was crazy to be the judge, but asked, instead:

"Did your—father ever explain why he was afraid of detectives?"

"Nothing more than that he was fearfully hunted and persecuted. When I was almost a baby he had to run away because of a political plot. He escaped with me after," her voice lowered, "my mother had been killed by the revolutionists, and we've been hiding here ever since, awaiting the message that will bring him back to be President again; although while the other party is in power its agents would arrest him—and it's been in power for years. Do you know," she looked at me frankly, "I've never forgiven him for letting them kill my mother! Throughout all of my childhood I used to hold indignation meetings with myself and consign him to every imaginable punishment—both for that, and running away without avenging her."

She was quiet then. This news of the South American republic showed what an accomplished liar old Efaw Kotee could be. Very plausible, indeed, and an adequate excuse for keeping her in a potential prison.

"I fear that I've been terribly outspoken," she said at last, with a wistful expression that held both laughter and apology.

"You've been wonderful," I whispered, deliberately turning away my head and gazing out across the prairie. I could not have met her eyes just then.

CHAPTER XIX
ENLIGHTENING A PRINCESS

As gently as I could, after I felt that my voice might be trusted not to betray itself, I told her of Monsieur Dragot's deductions, who we thought she really was—not the daughter of that old scoundrel, at all. I let her see the record of his crimes, her mother's discovery of the plates, the kidnaping, and, unless something most recent and unexpected had happened, the queen regent of Azuria was waiting at this minute for the little princess to return.

She had been sitting very still, like a child with parted lips enchantingly absorbed by a fairy tale. When I finished she turned her wondering eyes to mine, and gasped:

"It can't be true!"

"I think it is," I said. "I mean that it is so far as Monsieur can judge from the threads of evidence he holds, and what you've told me makes his theory more convincing."

"Oh—and I've called this man Father for so long! You don't suppose he still might be, somehow?"

"There's no somehow about it," I had to smile at this question. "He either is, or isn't; in the same indefeasible sense that white isn't black."

"I didn't mean that he might be just partly, of course," she said so quietly and seriously that I burst out laughing. "But it's awfully hard to understand, all at once! That must account for the subtle antagonism I felt for him. It really accounts for so much!—for the way he encouraged me to spend money, heaps and heaps of it! Why, I've everything I can think of—from Havana, New Orleans and Vera Cruz!"

"He wanted you to spend his large bills so he could get good money in change," I suggested.

"That's obvious now, but suppose I'd been arrested and sent to prison!"

"I won't suppose anything of the kind," I declared, so vigorously that she laughed.

"I do feel like a thief, though," she added soberly. "Why, everything I possess has been bought fraudulently."

"You couldn't help it! Chuck 'em away, if it'll make you feel better!"

"I can't chuck 'em all away," and this time we both laughed.

"You can as soon as we reach New York, and—and—" But as I did not know how to finish this, I stopped; for what had been in my mind was: "When you and I share all I own!"—and, of course, that wouldn't have done to say aloud.

For perhaps a minute she, also, was silent. Then she turned, with the frankest, sweetest manner I have ever seen, and said in a voice of mellifluent charm:

"Do you know that you've been just awfully splendid?"

I knew that my face got very red, but I tried to answer casually enough:

"The splendid things were done by Tommy, Gates, Smilax, and the other fellows. You'll like Tommy, and Monsieur knows—did I tell you he knows your mother?"

"Don't," she whispered. "You make me feel like I'm being led into a new world, with new people, and new customs, and new things!" Now her eyes widened as if making a discovery, as she added: "My fa—, that is, Mr. Graham, must actually have recognized Monsieur Dragot!"

"There's no other deduction," I agreed. "Our case is proved almost beyond a doubt. Don't call that fellow your father again, or even Mr. Graham. Smilax and I have a name we'll share with you."

"What?"

"Efaw Kotee."

Her laughter rippled through the wood, as she cried:

"How perfectly lovely! I know what it means!"

"Then you speak Seminole, Miss—Miss—but you say it isn't Sylvia?"

An expression of happy mischief in her face made it adorable.

"No, it isn't Sylvia. It's Doloria—you see, my life has been sad!"

"One wouldn't say so to look at you now. And I think Doloria's a thousand times prettier than Sylvia! Doloria! Just Doloria—like that?" For I wanted an excuse to keep on saying it.

"I—I suppose so," she hesitated. "Of course, it's always had Graham after it, but—what did your Monsieur Dragot say my last name was?"

"He didn't say."

"Then I haven't any."

"Oh, well, you needn't bother about that. Any time it gets lonesome you can hitch on Bronx—that is, I mean, only in case, you know."

I could have bitten out my tongue for this! I don't know what fiends possessed me to be such an unmitigated ass! It was as unfair as poison—an insult to the only precepts I have ever genuinely felt proud of: the code of playing fair. Before I could pretend to have been making a silly joke she brushed away my contrition by asking:

"Why Bronx? What does that mean?"

Glory be! I had forgotten that she could not know my name! But now I had to deny myself, cast my birthright to the winds, or else let her see that I was a miserable cad who could not be trusted as protector to a girl thrown upon his care.

And, on the other hand, it was decidedly repulsive to tell a lie—especially to her who seemed by her magnetic gaze to challenge the truth right out of a fellow. But conscience is, after all, only a name for our hidden prosecutor, judge and jury, and our sentences are light or heavy depending upon how many witnesses we can persuade to perjure themselves. No man lives who has not at some time used bribery in the mythical court room of his heart. Among women, of course, it is the accepted mode of legal procedure; and this gave me hope to believe that she might be somewhat forgiving when she found me out.

"Why Bronx?" she was asking again.

"Oh," I laughed, "it's a usual name in my part of the country, that's all—like Smith, and Jones."

I thought this would satisfy, but it gave her another thought, instead.

"Your name isn't Jackachobee, of course?"

"As far as Jack, yes. Every one calls me Jack."

A little while before this my cigarette case had fallen, to the ground by us. She had picked it up, and was even now turning it idly between her fingers.

"I see it here," she said, looking more closely at the monogram. "'J. B.' What does the B stand for, Mr.—Mr. Jack?"

"Brown," I answered desperately, and could feel every ancestor of a long and honorable line of Bronxes turning over in their graves. For I detest Brown. It's a good name, an exceptionally fine and distinguished name, the name not only of dear relatives but of very good friends. Yet it just so happened that at this particular moment I detested it—or was it the lie behind it? So to repair my self-esteem I blurted somewhat incoherently: "Bangs!"—having known a rather decent chap named Bangs.

"Is it spelled with a hyphen?" she glanced up rather quizzically. "Brown-Bangs?"

Her mind seemed to have flown lightly beyond me, anticipating the extent of my confusion, for the smile about her mouth, while enigmatic, suggested—enticingly suggested—mischief.

"Of course," I answered. "Brown-Bangs; Brown-Bangs!" And I wondered how many witnesses I should have to bribe now! I wished that in the first place I had said: "It would be unfair to tell you what isn't so, and dangerous to tell you what is!" But she would have guessed the truth by that, to a certainty. Sinners always find comfort in good resolutions, so I resolved to be more circumspect in the future. A gentleman's duty in my position was to be over circumspect; very much over circumspect, indeed!

Somewhat indifferently she laid the cigarette case back upon the ground, happening to put it near a little vine with lavender flowers, shaped like pon-pons; and in doing this it also happened that one of its tiny briars clung to her hand.

"Watch," she cried, gaily leaning forward. "Watch the leaves! We call this the 'shame-face vine,' because whenever it sticks any one every leaf on that particular stem is overcome with remorse!"

To my amazement the nine delicate leaves on the offending stem began to hang their heads and curl up, for all the world expressive of deep humility. It was another of the million or so lessons to be found in Nature for any one who sees with the right kind of eyes. Of course, I could have hung my head for that lie about the Browns, although curling up—at least, after the manner of the shame-face vine—would have required a contortionist.

"A well named little weed," I laughed. "But what wouldn't be penitent after hurting such a pretty hand!"

"I was just wondering," she said, ignoring this banality—for which in my heart I thanked her—"if there are weeds that show embarrassment for people who tell fibs?"

Now there was no possible way for her to have learned my name!

"You don't think there was any fibbing when I said you were a sure-'nough princess, do you?"

"Oh, please, let's not talk of that again," she entreated. "I don't want to be a princess just yet, because it's still very satisfying to have been taken away from that awful place. I'm so humbly thankful to you," she almost whispered, "that just Cinderella without the slipper will suit me nicely."

Beloved of the gods! If she wasn't at that moment princess, queen and all the royal families made into one!

"But I must tell you this much," I insisted gently, "and then we won't speak of it again until you wish. Monsieur says your mother is only Regent until you come; that your destiny is marked out for you, that by every law of God and man you've got to go back and take up the Cross where you left it seventeen years ago,—that you're booked to marry a Prince, I think. And he's armed with an iron-bound authority to take you. He says you've no possible escape—though, of course, you won't want any. I have to tell you this," I continued more hastily, for it was an extremely difficult thing to say, "because I'm only an ordinary kind of American chap, as bad as the worst and as good as the best, but your court in Azuria would have forty duck fits if it knew we were playing together in the woods without a chaperone. Suppose you make me your Chancellor, or something like that—chancellor of your Oasian possessions! Then I can report for orders and escort you about with all propriety, and we can talk and laugh occasionally without having some big soldier stick me in the back with his halberd."

She had been listening attentively, gravely, to everything I said until this last, when she burst into a scream of laughter, rocking herself to and fro in a transport of merriment.

"You're the funniest thing I ever saw!—but so be it, Mr. Jack Brown-Bangs, et cetera, et cetera! I make you my Royal Chancellor, responsible for the welfare of our Oasis!"

"And for the protection of Your Serenity," I bowed, really feeling as if I'd been knighted.

"Thank you," she said gravely. "I couldn't ask for a braver protector. But, Chancellor," she looked at me with serious eyes, "why did you say I must take up my Cross? It sounded like such a direful prophecy."

My lips refused to speak. As a matter of fact, I had been thinking more about my own Cross; how I should have to carry it after she went away until my heart broke beneath its cruel weight.

"That was a careless way of meaning something else," I tried to answer lightly.

"You shouldn't say evasive things. It leads to speaking with two tongues, which Echochee has taught me is wrong."

"Well, it couldn't be a direful prophecy, anyhow, when your mother and your throne are waiting just around the corner, as it were. The direful part of your life has passed, and most appropriately your name has changed from Doloria to Princess—though, of the two, I prefer Doloria."

"When it means sorrow?"

"It only means sorrow to those you leave. You've paid dearly enough to find nothing but happiness now for the rest of your life. It's written in the sky."

"You're a comforting Chancellor," she was still looking at me calmly, "and I'm already beginning to forget." And gently she laid her hand on the back of my own which rested between us.

My blood bounded with an unreasoning pleasure, yet her movement had been neither temperamental nor sentimental; it was instinctive—one of those honest impulses that knows no sex. Did she realize, by some divine insight, that this frankness, this absence of finical conventions, this whole-hearted camaraderie, would hold me more sternly to my path of duty than anything else she might have done? Did the instinct of her sex whisper that each man's heart, however light and worldly, is the possessor of a trusty loadstone which draws the best of him to a woman's aid when her honor is placed unreservedly into his hands? This speaks, of course, of men and not of human beasts; still, a woman is not put to the peril of looking into the heart of a human beast to discover that he is a beast—she can read it, without glasses, in his face!

"Shall we look over the rest of your estate?" I asked. And I kept the hand until she had been helped up, then released it naturally as we started on the tour of inspection.

We finally came to my pool, and I asked her advice in choosing a nearby spot where I should build a lean-to; since our kitchen site, that until now had been the location of my bailiwick, was by right of conquest hers, a place where she should be able to approach without the precaution of whistling like a plover—a thing she couldn't do, anyway! So we marked a spot and started on, taking some time to encircle the pool that, was rather large and, upon this side, densely fringed with a riot of tropical vines and jungle stuff. Yet, when we had gone but a little way, she stopped, looked vaguely troubled, and said:

"You won't be as near to me here as you were at the kitchen. I was so tired last night that I didn't think very much about those men, because our servants were leading them off. But don't you think it's possible that some of them might wander back here on their way home?"

"There's hardly one chance in a thousand," I assured her.

"I know. But that one chance would be dreadful if—if—" she stopped, and added wistfully: "I *would* like to feel in the nights that you are nearer to me!"

I turned to look at something else—at anything but her! Yet if my eyes required a subterfuge my heart did not, and it thrilled as if some wild musicians were tugging at its strings making them sound impassioned harmonies. But, even as I stood swayed by the madness of the moment, I felt that a great, an unseen, presence had pinned a decoration upon my honor—not because it had already proved itself, but in order that it might do so.

We therefore stopped and chose a new place on the side nearer her spring, and that being settled—a most important selection, we pretended it to be—she looked up at me, crying happily:

"After luncheon I'll come and help you build it!—and then you'll cut a path straight from my tent to yours so, should there be any danger, I can run to you without stumbling!"

For another moment, with eyes closed, I visualized my new decoration.

Luncheon, I thought, was even an improvement over breakfast. Nor did I take so long to wash the dishes afterwards.

CHAPTER XX
SLEEPING BENEATH GOD'S TENT

That afternoon we built the lean-to. I had had some fair ideas about building a lean-to, but Doloria was in possession of a practical knowledge gathered on camping trips that she and Echochee had made—for these, I judged, constituted one of her chief recreations since childhood. She knew how to twist ropes of bark for tying the poles, and how to interlay the palm fronds so they would neither leak nor be lifted by the wind. She took the keenest pleasure in it, too, and I can safely say that never in my life have I enjoyed building anything as much as that lean-to. When it was finished I stepped back and, in a burst of admiration, cried:

"It's a palace? I can't ever get along without you!"

A wave of color came into her face, as instantaneous as I believe it was unexpected, though she said in a matter of fact tone:

"There are other little things to be done, but we'll finish them to-morrow."

"It's already the coziest place in the world," I insisted. "Now I'm going to cut that path, and then we'll have—" but I checked myself and looked at her in some concern. She had worked over hard for me—I had not realized it while we were busy; so now I begged: "Won't you let me cook the dinner? I'm afraid you're about dead!"

"Oh, really I'm not. But I'm hungry and so are you, and—" a little curve came into the corners of her mouth that was very tantalizing, "I think I'd better cook it."

"I was hoping you would," I admitted shamelessly, "even if you are tired."

"Purely a selfish decision on my part, I assure you," she smiled. "I haven't forgotten the breakfast you attempted."

"Very well. I'll cut you a nice straight path for a nice big feed!"

"And don't leave anything in it, will you, Chancellor! It would be dreadful to come running to you in the dark, and stumble and—and bump my nose!"

"Dreadful!" I cried. "It would be the end of the world!"

"Or the end of you," she laughed. "Now get to work, and then you can build the kitchen fire. Don't you think we might have dinner a little earlier to-night?"

With this she left me; but how sweetly confidential and domestic that had sounded: "Don't you think we might have dinner a little earlier to-night?"

I found her again, sitting on a fallen log and gazing wistfully across the prairie toward the east, not back in the direction of Efaw Kotee's den, and I felt that she was thinking of Azuria—her Azuria. What visions its existence must have opened to her, whose life had been always passionate after dreams and utterly bored with realities! Yet what were her dreams?

She saw me and arose slowly, passing one hand across her eyes as if brushing away the fancies; then I watched an expression almost of tenderness as she came up to me.

"It isn't quite fair to interrupt," I said, "when you were having such a peaceful time of it; but the fire's ready, and our supply of buttonwood shrinks."

"Was I having such a peaceful time of it?" she asked, wonderingly. "Perhaps it might have been if I knew Echochee and your man are safe. Anyway, I'm glad the fire's ready; I've been expecting you to call me."

"I wish I could give you the same assurance about them that I feel myself. Try to think I'm right, won't you?"

"Yes, really I will, good Chancellor," she smiled.

On the way back we passed my pool, where she kneeled ingenuously to bathe her hands and arms, as chastely innocent as a mermaid.

"Have you such a thing as a towel?" she laughed. "Mine are in the tent!"

I got it, and walked slowly on. And I realized again, what I had once before noted, that overly refined proprieties—I do not mean proprieties of the essential kind—cannot endure between man and maid cast alone in a wilderness. They become frail, insipid; and mar, rather than perfect, the harmony of existence. Contraversely, their absence adds a deeper luster, strikes the tuning-fork that hums with the true note of life. Sorry the man who does not feel a sympathetic vibration! A woman is not exactly at her best when bathing her face above a porcelain bowl, and to be the constant, daily witness of such ablutions would, in my limited experience, engender a slight unrest among the tuneful Nine. Yet let her gracefully lean above a woodland pool, roll back her sleeves and open the collar of her shooting shirt, and she becomes a personification of glory to him who waits near the fire he has built for their evening meal. But she must have looked danger in the face with him, slept near him beneath the stars; knowing, should she be affrighted in the night, that her call will bring his reassuring answer, but also knowing that the voice is all that will ever come unbidden to her side. And thus is the Cave-man in him gloriously aroused to guard her from Nature's wild, while the poetry of their intercourse guards her from himself. What more beautiful existence than to live alone in a forest with the girl you love!

I thought that after dinner it might be well to sit again beside the fort where we could watch the prairie. There is a comforting sense of security that comes to one at nightfall when one has looked in all directions and found all things well. So for a while she left me to the orgy of washing dishes, but when I had turned the last plate top down upon our kitchen log to dry, I saw her returning.

She came humming a tune, a catchy tune—I recognized it at once—that the mandolins had tinkled in the Havana café, and from the mischievous curves about the corners of her mouth I knew that her mood was adorable. So I caught up the tune, whistling softly, and crossed to her holding out my hands.

"It's a corking fox-trot," I said, for the moment stopping our orchestra. "Let's dance it!"

But she drew back, laughing outright.

"I don't know how!"

"Don't dance?" I must have looked my amazement, for she answered:

"I've often danced, all alone, when I just couldn't help it; but there hasn't been any one to teach me your kind!"

"I will," I cried delightedly. "We'll begin with that fox-trot!"

"We'd look awfully silly," she replied. "Besides, the name of your dance is atrocious."

I felt rather thankful that I hadn't suggested the shimmy.

"That may get you out of it now," I announced, "but when we reach the yacht I'm going to teach you ten hours a day. Understand?—ten hours a day!"

Again came the tantalizing expression, as she daintily caught her skirt and made me a royal curtsey, saying:

"It's beyond all measure charming of you, Chancellor. But shall I be so difficult?"

"Don't joke about a wonderful prospect," I answered. "You're difficult because of your grace, not the lack of it—if that's what you mean!" But from her indifferent way of dismissing the subject I judged it was not what she had meant, at all.

The sun must have set while we were encircling my pool. Then we passed on into a still denser growth, following a crooked path that led to the fort—entering a mysterious shadow-land that twilights have the trick of producing when overhead foliage shuts out the afterglow and the serene forest gloom is painted in tones of gray. The soft earth we trod was dark, and the water lay phantom-like in its black bowl. Except for the few times I held aside a swinging wildwood vine for her to pass, we might have been two drifting spirits—so quietly did we move, and so unknowingly were we affected by the hour, the place.

At the edge of our forest, where that long ago prairie fire had blighted a grove of palm trees that subsequently fell upon each other like an entangled pile of jackstraws, she took my hand to get across and, freed from the clinging shadows, we ran out beneath the sky—then gasped in amazement at its splendor.

It was not a sunset, not an afterglow in the usual sense of afterglows, but a sky of deep, smouldering red equally distributed from horizon to horizon; as though everywhere below the world a conflagration raged. I could not at first speak for the grandeur of it, and when I turned to her words were again checked by the look upon her face. For this dull, permeating glow—this enchantment from the heavens—touched her brow, her cheeks, her parted lips, with a light that aroused in me a thousand devils and a thousand gods; it lingered over her hair as if striving to concentrate itself into a halo there; and in her eyes that gazed afar were suggested the awakening of deeper fires, of wilder mysteries.

"God, what a sky," I at last exclaimed, through sheer panic at the imminence of crying aloud my love for her.

"What a sky, O God," she whispered, delicately turning my profane outburst to a sigh of thankfulness.

But, better than she, I knew the meaning of that sky. I knew that down over the western edge of the world blazed a huge funeral pyre on which my past was being changed to harmless ashes; while in the east flames were already lighted beneath the on-coming crucible of destiny, from whose purifying heat a new love arose. Farther into obscurity would sink the one; up and on would come the other; and so the sky was now roseate unto its zenith, reflecting the glory of these miracles. I followed the look of her eyes and saw, high against the red, a lone crane flying majestically homeward to the seclusion of his swamp; and it typified my own belated heart that, without questioning the whence or why, unerringly obeyed a silent voice which called it to another sanctuary.

I wanted to tell her this, but dared not. And so we stood, spellbound, while the night brought out the blue—and the young moon changed from red to silver—and the stars came down to take their places. Then slowly we passed on and sat by the fort, leaning our backs against it; in meditation looking across the prairie that had become so changed a place to us.

The night grew sweet with the purity of untouched wilderness as, shoulder to shoulder, we sat talking in low tones of Smilax and Echochee. She had wondered about them no few times that day, and now I, too, felt some concern. Yet the Everglades lay far eastward and, for any reason giving up Big Cove, I knew he would plunge as deeply into it as his pursuers dared follow. To-morrow would be time enough to worry, I assured her, so we talked about Monsieur, the Azurian throne, and—I could not help it—of another Chancellor who would build her kitchen fires. But I tried to keep all bitterness from my words. In the vague light I could see that her face was serious, and very tender. Then for a time we sat without speaking.

Perhaps it was the place, the charm; perhaps a magic was working stronger than I knew; but words came to my lips that I stubbornly refused to speak. I fought against them; they, too, fought with grim insistence; so as a compromise, looking straight ahead and pretending to jest even while I accused, I said:

"You've been listening!"

"Listening?" Her eyes opened prettily, alert as they always were to parry banter with banter.

"Yes, listening—at the keyhole like a common gossip. A nice pastime for a Princess, surely!"

"At the—keyhole?" She was proceeding warily now; her mind, as in a game of hide-and-seek, was on tiptoe, in expectation of discovering me at every step.

"Yes," I repeated. "And you heard my heart admitting that it's happy—to've found something it was hungry for."

For the briefest instant I thought a tremor ran through her shoulder, as if a little chilly sensation had rippled her nerves. But it was a silly idea, because she lightly replied:

"Corn cakes, maybe. It ought to feel quite stuffed after the seven you had for dinner."

"Six," I corrected.

"Seven," she insisted.

"But I know!"

"So do I," she laughed, "that you stole one from my plate when you thought I wasn't looking."

"I needed that one."

"I never doubted it," she agreed.

Wild words again sprang to my lips, but this time I ruthlessly strangled them. Yet I wanted to say: "I took from you because you stole from me!" And I wanted to ask—O, shades of suffering Dante, how I longed to ask!—if her dear heart were hungering, too, that she should have needed my own to feed it!—if that were her excuse for thievery!

But already I had overstepped my resolution, although not feeling desperately contrite about it after the sleight-of-hand way that a declaration of love had been changed into the accusation of filching a corn cake. Yet it had been a narrow escape and I thanked my gods for the chance of pulling up, of again getting the right perspective.

To tell her anything at all before Echochee came would be the act of an utterly selfish cad, for if she did not want my love—and there was little enough reason to suppose that she did—her position would be intolerable. In such an eventuality never again could we sit beside the fort on nights like this, no longer would she want a cleared path leading to her bailiwick. We would be as two estranged creatures doomed to live near yet apart; each a daily witness of the other's unhappiness; neither able by word or deed to give relief. Ah, I was glad she did not even suspect that I cared a whit for her! I lit my pipe and in moody silence smoked.

A pipe stem is a safe thing for man to grip his teeth upon when silence is a virtue. Here in our forest I was master, the undisputed superior force; and I wondered with a fascinating wonder how that ancestor, who climbed down from his tree at nightfall, would have been greeting her! I visualized his cunning face, now peering at me through the ages, leering at me with bared tusks, bidding me take what was my own by right of might! I felt the savage splendor of it. The wildness of this place, its solitude, its distance from mankind, supported me. The cry of a night bird out on the prairie told that it, too, was preying, or being preyed upon; and, as if being stirred by this, a panther sent his wail across the night. I listened for a mate to answer, but she did not. A large, whitish moth flying out of the shadows passed clumsily within a few inches of my face, its wings swishing as a bird's; and it, too, was without a mate.

Then, as in the following silence I continued to listen, some far off words came back to me. They came as the scent of lavender comes when rain is pattering on the shingles, and some one opens the old trunk that, ever since you can remember, has stood back under the rafters of the sloping roof; the hallowed old trunk where a veil of yellowing lace is stored—a piece of white satin, a blue or gray faded uniform, and maybe a wee shoe, and a lock of hair. Every one who has leaned above that trunk—and thank God they are legion!—has also listened to a voice coming faintly through the past. And so words out of a lesser past now came to me, as they were meant to be written on a torn wine card: "I am in danger!"

She had been in danger of a brute, and had offered the safety of her keeping to me. And the vision of my savage ancestor, though retreating sullenly, faded into nothing. Then I felt her body press against me softly and, looking down, I saw that she had fallen asleep, with her head—precious, trusting thing—resting against my shoulder.

For an hour I sat motionless, fearing to awake her. Finally one of my legs went to sleep, and soon my other leg. Yet it was a welcome discomfort because endured for her. And I suppose the numbness must eventually have crept the length of my body, for, I, too, slept; awaking, I did not know how much later, to find her gone.

Then I stumbled back to my lean-to, but did not go inside. This was not the night, nor mine the mood, to shut high heaven from my eyes, my thoughts, the lambent flame of my love? So I chose the open, and lay on my back gazing up into the silhouetted palm fronds, catching glimpses of a star that here or there peeped through at me, steeping my thoughts in solitude.

For it was that hushed hour of betwixt and between, when crickets, tree-toads and other little creatures of the darkness have wearied themselves to rest; yet also before the daylight life has stirred from its own deep sleep. The silent hour, this is; the one hour in the round of time when nature seems to be absolutely poised in breathless space; when the pendulum of night hangs dead, and dawn is still a great way over the hill. I shared its mysticism, feeling also a rich contentment that she, too, was lying near me somewhere in this same solitude; dreaming, with her cheek upon her arm; her hair kissed by the same dew that cooled my face. I could not, of course, reach out my hand and touch her, but the path led straight; and along this now my heart went begging—impoverished rascal! He went on tiptoe, begging; while I continued to watch for the elusive star, and my soul looked into the level eyes of God.

CHAPTER XXI
PLANTING A MEMORY

A searching look next morning over the prairie revealed no sign of enemies, or of Smilax. Somewhat thoughtful over his continued absence I went to the kitchen and laid the fire, but did not light it because our stock of buttonwood had become reduced to a few small sticks and scraps that would scarcely more than cook one meal, and the use of other woods might at this time be an unwise experiment. So with an eye to prudence I withheld the match until Her Serene Highness should arrive.

When she did not come nor answer to my call, I set out to see what might have detained her, conscious of a vague dread yet not seriously giving in to it; but, after visiting the fort, this grew into an unreasoning fear, and I began to run. It seemed so easy now to understand how some of Efaw Kotee's henchmen could have discovered us, slipped up during the night and overpowered her! What had been a remote possibility yesterday, to-day grew into a certainty. With this obsession torturing me I dashed across the Oasis, finally coming out of the forest at its extreme eastern tip.

Then I saw her but a few yards away. Perhaps the brisk wind, rustling the palms and prairie grass, drowned the noise of my impetuous rush, for she did not turn.

Her face was toward the east, looking above an orange sun that still clung to the horizon. Instinctively I felt that she was thinking of Azuria, that the pictures of it which I had drawn were recrossing before her dreamy vision, forming a panorama of splendor that called more surely than in March the Canadian flats call the Southern water bird. This gave her eyes, her uplifted face, her slightly parted lips, a new glory, and I involuntarily exclaimed:

"Doloria of the Golden Dawn!"

She knew then that I was there and, without turning, reached back one hand to me. Impulsively I took it, raised it to my lips, but afraid to hold it longer I stepped aside as if awaiting her commands. When I had done that she looked over her shoulder, gave a little sigh, and said sweetly:

"Chancellor, I wish you'd convince me that our people are safe, and then help me settle a grave question of state!"

"I think they'll be coming to-day, and—"

"Oh, I hope so!" she clasped her hands.

"As for the state question," I continued, "I'll settle it quickly, if you'll let me."

"No, I'm afraid you can't! No, Chancellor," she gave a little laugh, "you can't be trusted to settle that, at all!" Then firmly, almost severely, putting back into its place a wave of hair that had been coquetting with the breeze, she asked: "Is the fire ready?"

"Ready to light," I answered. "I came to find you."

"Then let's go, for it isn't good to ponder over questions of state before breakfast."

"What is it?" I asked, as we turned back. "Why won't you trust me to settle it?"

Another laugh, more full of pathos, was my answer; nor would she speak again—because of some mischief in her mind, I believed—until, preparing the ambrosial corncakes, she rather abruptly exclaimed:

"I wonder if you deserve any breakfast this morning?"

"Why?" I cried, in feigned alarm.

"Because of your impoliteness."

"My impoliteness was doubtless the need of breakfast. But when was I impolite? I don't remember, honest!"

"Of course, you don't; how could you," she went on rather indifferently. "Were you not such a capable Chancellor I might be more offended. I am tryingly stupid at times, but to be in the very middle of a sentence and discover that the man I'm talking to is fast asleep, is humiliating, to say the least."

Did she think there was a chance of putting over that atrocious yarn on me—of bluffing me into an admission that I had been the first to fall asleep?

"You may be right," I said, with the utmost gravity, "but I did it only in justice to you. You were talking, true enough, but in *your* sleep; saying things that—well, no gentleman could have remained awake, in the circumstances."

"I didn't," she cried, darting me a look of uncertainty. "Echochee says I never do!"

"Echochee wasn't here last night," I casually replied, poking the coals of her fire closer. "I hope you understand that I didn't listen intentionally; for, of course, you'd never have told me all those things—"

"Stop it," she commanded; and, when I had stopped, there was an ominous silence.

But I would not look at her and indifferently pretended to be busy. I confess that I was deriving a purely masculine enjoyment out of this, and intended to push my counter bluff so vigorously that she would be driven to admit her own. Therefore, after I thought the silence had become sufficiently impressive, I yielded to an impulse that many men find irresistible—I made an egregious ass of myself.

"Lots of people," said I, sliding out upon thin ice with the braggadocio of him who rocks the boat, "chatter like magpies when dozing in an uncomfortable position. Police recognize this, and often arrange a suspect's cell so he'll have to sleep sitting up, then they listen and take down his inmost thoughts. That's the way you chattered last night."

"Chattered!" she caught her breath.

"Yes; just rippled along, you know, telling everything you've been thinking these last couple of days. Some of it was rather interesting. Shall I poke up the fire again?"

"Rather interesting!" She sprang around and faced me with blazing eyes, the picture of embarrassment and fury. "You consider the things I've been thinking the last couple of days 'rather interesting!' Oh," she cried, dashing the pan of corn meal batter to the ground, "you're damnable—I hate you!" There was a whirl of a skirt, the twinkle of a little booted foot, and, by Jove, she had gone flying off like the wind; while I, feeling about the size of a june-bug, stood first on one leg and then the other, wondering what the devil she had been thinking these last couple of days.

Now, when a fellow has made a blatant ass of himself, I hold that the quickest road to salvation is "own up and shut up." If he's forgiven, life may flow on as formerly. If he isn't, he has recourse to the pose of having been grossly misunderstood, and eventually work himself into quite a creditable reproduction of a martyred nobleman. If he's good at that kind of thing, a girl will grow sorry and forgive him in spite of herself. I got this from Tommy, one day, and Tommy knows a lot about women—really, an awful lot.

But the most detestable part of my present muddle was that I had hurt her—I, who would have bartered my life to shield her from hurts! Feeling thoroughly contrite I went quickly in pursuit, looking ahead and on both sides for a glimpse of the dress that meant the world to me. Regardless of boundaries, regardless of everything but to implore an instant forgiveness at whatever cost, I rushed impetuously on, calling her name.

Then I came up with her at the side of the bubbling spring. She was lying prone upon the bank, her face buried in her arms that were crossed beneath it. And, having found her, I could not advance. Something about the lovely grace of her body held me enthralled. Furthermore, I had no right to be here; I was an interloper, a prowler! There were but two things to do, and do at once, to wit, make myself humble and scarce.

"Doloria," I said.

She did not move, perhaps she had not heard, so I kneeled and took one of her hands, whereupon she sprang to her feet looking at me strangely, wildly.

"You've no right here," she cried. "You've broken faith!"

"No, please no," I said quickly. "I'm too desperate to care where I am when you're angry! Since you called me damnable—said you hated me—the world's turned black; so I'm not deliberately trespassing—only lost, because you've taken away your smile!"

"*You* took it away," she retorted. "You'd murder any girl's smile by such—brutality!"

"Brutality!" I gasped.

"Truthfulness," she stamped her foot.

"But I wasn't truthful," I hurried to tell her. "I lied like the devil to call your bluff—wanted to make you own up because—well, you'd lied a little, too! I never dreamed my joke would hurt you. Great God," I now cried passionately, "to think of hurting you who are my life and breath and—" I caught myself, stopping short and looking at her; then slowly adding: "You didn't say a word in your sleep, I swear it. It was beautiful of you to trust me that way, and—and if you'll rescue our breakfast I'll never be such an idiot again."

She had partly turned away at my impassioned outburst, but the assurance I gave that Somnus had been dumb brought a hint of the fascinating curve to her lips. Yet her eyes still expressed doubt, and I was growing desperate enough even to humor her incredulity, hoping thereby to discover another road to favor, when she asked:

"You're not just saying that?"

"On my honor it's true—every word! I'm sorry, Princess!"

Again she turned away her face, looking across the spring and murmuring, as though to someone there:

"It's because he's hungry, I suppose,"—then whirled and held out both hands to me, in that sweet way of hers. "It's I who am cruel, Chancellor. Come, poor man, I'll feed you; you look as glum as Pharaoh—was Pharaoh glum? I'll beat you to the kitchen!" And she bounded away, almost before the challenge had been given.

Straight she sped with astonishing swiftness, skimming over fallen logs, darting this way and that through festoons of vines, with the grace of a frightened doe. In freedom of motion she was as some wild thing of forest birth, suggesting the spirits of the wind, the dappled sunlight, the dancing waters; yet never lacking an ineffable refinement that added both charm and mystery.

Each of us was breathing fast when, shoulder to shoulder, we reached the fire, she claiming the race without the slightest show of embarrassment.

"But I was holding back," I said, finding combativeness a very fair outlet to pursue, and adding: "You had the start, too!"

"In a race any one has the start who's able to get it," she asserted. "Besides, I set the pace, and all you had to do was follow. I slowed up toward the end, anyway."

The impertinence of it!

"You slowed up because you had to! And I don't believe you were angry a while ago, either!"

"Don't you?" she asked, slowly.

"Not so very," I compromised, seeing the danger signal. "I think you were just making a jolly chump of me, that's all. I don't so much mind making one of myself, but it's rotten having other people do it for me!"

"I suppose," she said indifferently, raising her arms to tuck in a lock of hair, "that if it's worthwhile making the distinction, you might be allowed a choice."

For the pure deviltry of this remark I looked around for something to throw at her, and then saw our fire—a tragic picture of dead ashes which the wind was blowing over a now cold skillet.

"See," I cried, "what our family row has led to! Fire out, breakfast ruined, and here I am due at the office in half an hour!"

"Oh, Jack," she looked at me gravely, putting an end to our banter—and for the first time calling me Jack, though I believe she did it unconsciously—"haven't we any more buttonwood? This is serious, isn't it!"

"Not so very, perhaps. We can try another kind."

"Will it be safe?" she asked, uncertainly.

"With a small fire of very dry hardwood, and this rising wind, what little smoke there is won't hold together long enough to be seen."

"But it'll blow right toward their camp! The wind's changed since yesterday!"

"That's more than two miles off, and they're probably still after Smilax. I'll make a very small fire."

This, indeed, seemed to work well enough, and by the time a new breakfast was ready our uncertainties had become shadows of no consequence.

"But you *do* know I was angry, don't you?" she asked, out of a clear sky, with an unexpectedness that made me throw back my head and laugh.

"You bet I do! And you beat me in the race, too; and you're the best cook on our block!"

"It seems to be the same old story," she smiled, with affected sorrow, "that food must always be the price of masculine tractability. Ah, the long drawn out tragedy of woman's existence, that she must forever be stuffing man with things to eat, as reptiles are stuffed, to keep him facile!"

"You fail to observe, my little snake charmer," I replied, "that you omitted to say good things to eat. I'm never facile after Smilax feeds me."—Though I owe Smilax an apology for this!

"He must have run great risks of being bitten."

"Oh, no; I'm not the biting kind of snake! I'm a constrictor—I hug!"

"Mercy!" She gave a little gasp, then, turned and went indifferently toward the spring.

Whistling happily I finished the dishes. But I finished them with the promise of a better cleansing next time, and soon was calling her.

She came to me humming the song I had been whistling—an unconscious bit of flattery on her part, but it added to my pleasure. There is, after all, so much to be gained by hitching your wagon to a star, that I tried to believe she deliberately intended it. I would have hitched up oftener to that same star, except for the fact that stars sometimes get hot and furious at too many liberties, and switch their tails and kick the wagons of well-meaning people to smithereens. That it may be better to have had a stellar joy-ride and be sent to hell for speeding than keep your boots forever in the clay, I will neither affirm nor deny; but the prudent man hitcheth to the moon!

As we went toward the fort she turned to me, asking:

"Don't you think they should have been here sooner? Do you fear anything you won't tell me?" Her eyes were anxious, and I saw how insistent this worry had been.

"Everything depends on how far Smilax had to go," I answered. "He'd never dream of coming back until the men gave up—and they might chase him half across the state! So a few extra days doesn't mean anything. They can't catch him, that's certain; and he and Echochee'll only stay away as long as they're pursued. They'll come through, I believe it sincerely; and your Chancellor, sweet Princess, will guard you with his life—with ten lives, if he had them."

"I know that," she murmured, "and shan't worry if you tell me not to."

"Then cheer up! Smilax is a past-master of the swamps and woods, take my word for it!"

"I really suppose Echochee knows a great deal about them, too," she said, after a pause, "for when she was sixteen she had to leave the Reservation with her husband and hide him in the Everglades. She learned a great deal, then."

"Why did she have to do that?"

"He'd fought and killed another Indian, and the officers were expected. But in the fight he received a cut that made him blind. For ten years Echochee fed and clothed him, hunting alligators and watching her chance of slipping the skins to a market. By extreme stinting she finally saved enough to 'buy him loose'—her optimistic way of saying 'pay a lawyer for his defense.' Think, after being outcasts all that time, of leading a blind husband through half a hundred miles of wilderness, with the savings of ten years to wager on a chance of having him cleared!"

"I hope he was," I declared.

"In a sense he was, yes. He knew where she kept the money, and while she was in the lawyer's office persuading him to take the case, her husband stole it and sneaked away."

I uttered a cry at this hideous ingratitude, and she glanced at me, gravely adding:

"Then he got drunk and was run over by a train; so, in a sense, Echochee freed him, after all."

"Oh, the magnanimous courage of a woman's devotion!" I stopped and looked at her. "It's always the same, irrespective of tribe and nation. She's dauntless, world-defying, utterly self-sacrificing. I hope to God, Doloria, that you won't be among those who squeeze their hearts dry! You've lived away from the world and may not know how plentiful these are; but no day passes without its toll of some woman being silently crucified in her losing fight to save a besotted biped—the lord of her earthly temple. It's only by a streak of luck when their stage is cleared, as Echochee's was!"

"That may be all right for clearing the stage," she murmured, "but it doesn't heal the hearts of those who were made to suffer."

I had not fathomed the penetration of her sympathy, being satisfied, man like, to let a swift revenge wipe the slate. She seemed to be contemplating what I had said, and when she again spoke her voice was tender as though it had come unbidden from a wistful reverie.

"I suppose you're right, Jack. The world I've known, only through books, must be full of such cruelties. I rather dread having to go into it. It seems a pity that I can't always live in—in—" then, with a smile, she asked: "Do you ever dream? I don't mean when you're asleep, but awake—wide awake?"

"I rather think I'm dreaming now," I admitted, for a great contentment had fallen about us as we walked beneath the solemn trees.

The silence that followed was again stirred by her voice, saying:

"You mustn't think me childish, but I've always had a secret gateway to a place—my Secret world—where everything is make-believe, and nothing can be but truth and beauty. Often when Echochee was tiresome, or I was tired, I used to slip away and go there."

"I wish you'd take me—won't you?"

"Oh, I can't," she quickly answered, stooping for a flower in our path, holding it in both hands and leaning her face above it.

"Yes," at last I said, "I've a place like that; but I don't know whether I live there in make-believe, or throwing off the make-believe we have to wear in the world you're going to, I live honestly with myself. If you won't take me to yours, sometime maybe you'll come to mine!"

Now, I had no intention of making love to her. We were talking only about secret worlds and day-dreams.

"I'm afraid it might be difficult," she answered, dropping the flower and walking a shade more slowly. "Our lives—yours and mine—are cast along such opposite lines, it seems!"

"That's what Secret worlds are for," I told her, "—that, no matter how far apart we are, our spirits may come and meet; live again, as we've lived here; be happy again—as I've been." I turned, saying with a laugh that was meant to convey an impression of insouciance—yet failing rather miserably: "These two big pines here, Princess, actually make the gateway to my pool—which is, in fact, my Secret world, because you helped me build my home there. So, you see, it wouldn't be very difficult, as you were about to enter without knowing it. Oh, I wish I could tell you more about it!" And I then became silent, too helplessly afraid to go on.

A brighter color had come into her throat and cheeks, but she was smiling whimsically as she said:

"Then we must go around—find another path to the fort—mustn't we!"

She had stopped before me, poised delicately, almost swaying; and for several seconds our eyes, that must have been charged with some untranslatable excitement, held fast. Mine would not let go, and hers I believe could not. Her hands, idly at her sides, were turned palms forward, unconsciously suggestive of supplication.

"Do you know what you remind me of when you stand that way?" I asked.

"No," She looked away now, laughing lightly—though it was more subtly than suddenly done. "What?"

"Of a fairy that's flown from a butterfly moon, just alighting at my threshold and asking to come in."

"Wouldn't a fairy be unseemly forward to come to a young man's threshold and ask admittance?"

"Not admittance, but admission—to my dreams, where nothing is real but you and beauty."

"Dreams are for the old, the young shall see visions!—isn't there a quotation like that?" she asked, smiling.

"You're not playing fair," I laughed—for I was afraid not to laugh, wanting desperately to say that I was seeing the vision now that would be my dream forever!

"I'll play fair if I know the rules," she also laughed. "You haven't told them to me!"

"We'll make them up as we go along!"

"But what are we going to play?"

"Make-believe," I eagerly cried. "That we're exploring our Secret world where we'll come after,"—there was no laugh in my voice now—"you've gone to Azuria, and I'm here alone."

She gave my face a quick, searching look.

"And we only have to pass between these two big trees?" she asked, half lightly, half timidly.

"Only through that gateway, and we're in our world!"

"Why should I go, I wonder?" The question was whispered, almost unconsciously, and catching the tone of it I also whispered:

"To plant a memory, Doloria, that will grow and bloom as long as we live; where each of us may come—when we're lonely."

What forces, intangible, supernal, were at work here no man can tell. Philosophers stumble, fools blunder, and the truth dances on ahead through Life's woodland of mysteries—one instant revealing itself in a golden shaft of sunlight, hiding the next with smothered laughter in the black shadow of a fern, while seekers after it tramp past in grumbling blindness.

At this moment our wood seemed rich with mystic presage. Pleadingly my hands went out to her, and trustfully she put hers into them. Slowly I backed between the two big trees, our eyes held as two charmed beings. Everything about me called to her, everything in her urged compliance; and I knew, as did she, that something strange was happening. Yet when I halted she did not falter, but came on, bravely, sweetly, into my arms.

That she should have done this was as inevitable as it was gloriously true. We could no more have continued to stroll side by side through our Oasis, commenting on the seasons, sometimes rapturous over a sunset or the call of a bird, than we could have rubbed a lamp and brought the *Whim* sailing to us over the sea of grass. Static existences only prevail with static people, and there was too much surgingly dynamic about this twenty year old girl to have encouraged it here. I say, too, with candor that any man of twenty-six whose blood is red is—with the great out-of-doors abetting—not insulated for or against currents. Throw these two alone in a primitive world where their tent is the sky, and a spark must eventually jump across the gradually lessening distance. It is thus that wild things mate—and their mating is incorruptible.

But now as my arms tightened and my face leaned to hers, she gave a half fearful cry and sprang tremblingly back, pressing both hands to her breast, breathing quickly and staring at me with wide eyes.

"Chancellor," she gasped, "this is madness, don't you know it?"

The quick alarm in her voice sobered me and I answered "Yes," for there was nothing else to say. And a moment later when, in an even tone and at a conventional distance, she suggested: "Shall we go on to the fort?" I did not reply, but walked mutely at her side.

Our contact had been too instantaneous for me to collect myself at once, and I wondered how she was managing to do so—or if she were bluffing. For this sudden serene-mindedness she now displayed was quite too enigmatic for my comprehension.

"We planted the memory that will be mine forever," I whispered, trying to see her face which she kept partially hid by keeping half a step ahead of me. "I'll never forget our—"

"Oh," she cried, on the verge of tears, I thought, "don't ever speak to me of it again—ever!"

"It's nothing we ought to regret—it wasn't your fault," I persisted,—

"That's just it—it was my fault, it was," she interrupted passionately, and somehow her hand found mine and pressed it. Was there ever any one more square? "I knew we were going to—do that, and I didn't try to stop it. You'll think that I'm—I'm—"

"The most glorious girl who ever lived," I cried, taking full possession of her hand now.

"Won't you please be honest?" she asked, quite seriously. "I am; and I give you my word I'd never have done it if it hadn't seemed so real—I mean, our planting the memory."

She turned then, and to my relief she was half smiling. For an instant the longing to hold her again showed in my face, but she stopped me with a look. This time it was done with the intention of stopping me, and I stopped. Yet the smile had not left her face as she said, in a tone of sweet confidence:

"Let's be above-the-board-honest with each other in all things, Jack; it makes for long friendships, Echochee says—and there's nothing finer, anyhow, than to freely admit a mistake. So it wasn't your fault any more than mine; we've both been very naughty spirits, and we mustn't be again." She paused, adding: "After all, I suppose it does make our secret world just a little—"

I waited, and when she did not continue, asked:

"A little what?"

Still she hesitated.

"Be honest," I warned.

She smiled again, looking at me frankly.

"Well, a little sweeter, to feel that we're equally to blame; that that's why we can't ever go there again."

"Eden up-to-date?" I laughed.

"Y-yes, I suppose so; and the flaming sword has smote us, so we have to be circumspect forever and ever."

"But Eve wasn't! The flaming sword didn't phaze her a minute!"

"I've had lots of time to improve on Eve," she replied archly.

"That's God's truth," I cried.

A rippling laugh burst from her lips—a ringing, happy laugh that was heard, I swear, in listening heaven. She seemed obsessed by a strange excitement—perhaps like my own, that sprang from a deep, inordinate sense of pleasure.

We were getting on toward the fort, walking inside the edge of our Oasis near that place where the fallen palms lay in a confused tangle. I had her hand and was helping her over this network of logs when she suddenly sprang before me with dazzling quickness; facing outward, and holding back her arms to keep me in check.

It was an act instinctive of protection, yet scarcely had I time to wonder at it when a whining, crackling sound, that might have come from anywhere, dashed past our heads. Men who have heard a high-power bullet splitting the air do not forget the sound, which is as quickly recognized a second time as the rattling of a diamond-back.

Immediately following it came the crack of a rifle, and guided by this I saw, above the prairie grass four hundred yards away, the head and shoulders of a man. At that instant he fired again.

CHAPTER XXII
I LOVE YOU

To be transported instantly from the essence of happiness to the brink of tragedy—and a tragedy wherein the whole of one's world goes tottering—engenders a confusion of mind that for a moment leaves one helpless. And thus it was that the second bullet flashed by us before I sufficiently gathered my wits to act, to realize that some returning member of Efaw Kotee's band had stumbled on our little paradise.

I caught Doloria and swung her behind me, at the same time drawing my automatic and sending two quick shots, aimed high, toward the scoundrel who was making ready to try his hand again. Almost at once he disappeared, though I knew he had not been hit for it was extremely doubtful if, at that range, a revolver bullet could reach him at all. For the sake of caution he was merely crouching in the grass, and waiting.

Then I became swept by an inordinate anger; a natural enough feeling in a man whose life has been sneakingly attempted, but let a life that is a million times more precious than his own be so fired upon and he will pass the limit of human rage. With an oath I pushed her down into a niche of temporary safety, saying:

"Stay there till I come back!"

Immediately I began to scramble over the network of fallen logs; my intention being to reach the high grass and, dropping to my hands and knees, crawl out to meet him—as, in all probability, he was now crawling toward us. But before I got free of the entanglements she had sprung after me and caught my arm, crying:

"It's insane for you to go out there—with only your automatic against his rifle! Come back!"

"Go back yourself," I said sternly, shaking off her grasp. "Crouch in the hole, as I told you! Quick!"

"I won't—unless you do, too! For the love of God—he'll *kill* you!" This last she screamed, frantically catching hold of me again as the man fired a third shot and we felt the breath of his bullet on our faces.

Both of us knew that this was no time for argument, and she began tugging at my belt like a wild thing, bracing herself to keep me back and showing no disposition to obey. So without ceremony I picked her up intending to shove her down between the logs.

"You shan't," she gasped. "He'll kill you if you go—if you don't he'll leave!"

But I was too terrified for her sake to listen—too determined that the fellow should not get back and tell his gang.

"Do as I say," I commanded, giving her a shake.

She had stopped speaking and was desperately using her strength. I, also, had grown desperate. Our position was too unwarrantably exposed to tolerate this further, and urgently I began to pry open her fingers when, by some twist of her own or awkwardness on my part, I slipped and fell out backwards into a deep, narrow slit between the logs, drawing her down with me and wedging my shoulders as if they were held in a vise.

It might have been a serious fall—for her, I mean—had not providentially she landed atop of me; but now, trying to arise, I found that I had measured neither her strength of purpose nor of muscle. Her determination had not been cooled by this mishap, rather had it become more aroused with the consciousness of her advantage; for, in answer to my first movement, she caught my cheeks and passionately shook me. Her eyes, scarcely half a foot away, stared down into mine with a frightened, pleading, commanding look. They were open wider than usual, giving the impression that this was the first test of physical encounter she had ever experienced.

"You're safe here!—you shan't move!" she was whispering wildly.

"I must," I declared. "He's got to be stopped, I tell you!"

I did not want to hurt her, yet at all hazards that man had to be killed, and I began really to struggle.

"No—no!" she panted, pushing down my partially raised head with a jolt that made me see stars. For she was fighting this time, with the ferocity of a tigress, and I, held by her weight, found the task of freeing myself no easy one. I tried working loose one shoulder, growling between my teeth:

"I *will* get out of here!"

"You won't—you won't!" She reiterated this as if sheer force of mind could make me yield. And then her hair, uncoiling, fell softly over my face and closed my eyes.

There is a mesmeric force about the human hair, a woman's hair, resting on a man's upturned face—although I do not mean this in a sentimental sense. It is a natural law; as a wild bird can be put into a state of mimic sleep by laying it on its back and pressing its eyes with feathers.

The frenzy of Doloria's clutching fingers that still held my cheeks, and the pressure of her body whose excited breathing wedged me even tighter down between the logs, had been to us no more than incidents in the desperate struggle we were making, each for the other's safety. But, blinded by her hair, for the moment I desisted and, taking quick advantage of this, she whispered:

"If you've any wish to please me, listen! I know those men by heart—each is an arrant coward when alone. So he won't crawl closer. By the time he brings the others back we'll be inside the fort!"

"That's just it," I retorted. "The fort's no good at night—they'll rush it! He's got to be stopped, Doloria!"

"Jack, do this for me, please?" she begged. Her lips were very near. "If we have to die, we will—but I can't see you go out on that prairie alone—I simply can't!" And I grew still.

Soon I felt her hands upon my chest as she pushed herself up to look over the logs. By this movement the blindfold was partially lifted and I could see her—her body curved backward, as a mermaid that raises itself at arm's length upon the shore. Her lips were parted, her eyes were steady and level as they gazed searchingly across the sea of grass—as many a nymph, no doubt, hiding from a company of swashbuckling gnomes, must have peeped out to see if her glade were safe before venturing from the wood. In another moment she had left me and run a few steps toward the prairie, crying:

"Look! He's 'way, 'way off!"

"I can't look," I called after her. "You've put me here for life!"

Indeed, I was so completely held that the first result of my twisting seemed only to make me lose ground. She came back, this time laughing without control—but I knew the sign; my nerves, too, had recently been drunk on relaxation from a strain. Tucking up her hair with a few quick movements she held down both hands to me and, after more squirming, I worked myself out. But our enemy had by this time disappeared.

"If that fellow's back, the others are, too," I said, with some display of temper. "You've made the very devil of a mess!"

"I suppose I have," she looked demurely away. There was nothing of the tigress, nothing of the willful little fighter, now.

"The consequence is," I continued, "that we have to decide between two darned slim chances, for they'll be coming back within an hour. We can stay here, or run for it! What do you think?" But as she remained silent, gazing across the prairie, I kept irritably on: "If it's run, we can't reach the forests north, south or east without being seen—and you know what a fight in the open means against such odds. We might hide in the grass and travel at night, but if their woodcraft's worth a hang they'll read our trail on this kind of ground like an electric sign. There's an Indian in their crowd, too. If we stay, the fort'll keep them off till night—and there's always a hope of Smilax turning up. They mightn't rush us after dark, either."

I could see that the fort was our best chance, but still I wanted her opinion. Something about the way she stood, having no word to say, rather awed me, and going softly I looked around at her face. Her cheeks were wet and her lips were trembling with convulsive sobs. Oh, how I hated myself then!

"Good God," I cried, throwing my arms about her, "see what I've done!"

But she put her palms against my shoulders and held me off, saying brokenly:

"You haven't done anything."

"I have," I cried again. "I've hurt you—hurt the one I love most in all the world!"

"Don't," she said, more startled now than at any time when she had been facing a greater danger. "Quick! Please—let's get the things we need for the fort!" And she sprang away from me, running toward the pool.

In a very few minutes we were back with the rifles, an ample supply of cartridges, our canteens, and a blanket I had brought in case we decided to slip away at night. Helping her over the parapet I followed, and we stood looking intently for a sign of foes, but the waving grass spoke only of a brisk wind. It might be a half an hour before Efaw Kotee's band could get within range of us. Twice I whispered her name, but she would not answer, so I turned her around until she had to face me.

"I have the right to speak now," I said gently, "because this may be the last of things. The next few hours will decide. You understand, don't you, and know that my words are their own excuse?"

There was a serious, calm mystery in her look that answered mine with simple courage, as she whispered:

"Yes, I understand."

"We can't die," I drew her close to me, "because I love you—I love you!"

For a quick moment, and then gone, a light shone in her eyes—as though some fire raging below had been swept through the entirety of her being. Her fingers that had been clutching my shoulders relaxed, and very softly her arms crept around my neck, as she murmured: "No more than I do you!"

It might have been a minute or a year that we drifted in a rapturously agonizing kiss; but slowly her eyes opened, her lips sighed and, touching them to my cheek, she whispered my name over and over again.

"We'll win to-day," I cried, giving the prairie a searching look above her head, "and after that there's a kingdom waiting for you here!"

"I can feel it beating," she whispered adorably. "But if we—" She could not say it, but let her moist lips cling to mine as if challenging Death to part us.

Who dares measure time when Cupid perches on the clock! 'Twas a wise providence that gave severe St. Gregory the making of our calendar, and not St. Anthony, else some minutes might be spun to days, and hours squeezed to the fraction of a second.

But the ever present danger had not at any time quite ceased to pierce the mist of our paradise. She knew I was keeping a careful watch, even while I held her. Now she drew away, and crossed her arms upon the parapet.

"When things begin to happen," I said, "you must sit on the ground. I won't risk your lovely head above the wall!"

"Why?" she asked. "Aren't two rifles better than one?"

"Yes," I admitted, "but I can't shoot unless you're safe."

"Then don't think of me, at all, for I promise to do whatever you say. Look," she pointed suddenly. "There they are!—I believe every one of them! Oh, I wonder if they've killed Echochee!"

I, too, wondered; for surely here was the gang that had pursued them—quite a mile out on the prairie, to be sure, but unquestionably Efaw Kotee's band, showing as a black smudge above the grass. Whether this pack of human wolves had lost the trail of Smilax I would not try to guess, for it was enough to know that they had found our own.

They were still too far off to be counted, but I felt that Doloria had been right in saying every man of them. That would mean eight if Jess and the old chief were along, furious devils demanding their revenge, mad to surround us and take their own good time about placing a shot where it would do the work. It was only fair that she should know the odds, so I put my arm around her, saying:

"When they get nearer, they'll scatter out. Some will stay in front, hiding in the grass and shooting enough to keep us busy, and others will circle to the trees behind us. It's going to be a close call, sweetheart, but they'll never get in while I'm up."

"I know that," she answered gently. "We may as well be brave and speak of it with indifference; it's easier that way; so I want to tell you that if you—you—" but her voice did choke, yet she raised her chin and calmly finished, "are killed, I'll follow right away. It's infinitely preferable to being taken," she hastily added, seeing my look of horror. "So wait for me just a little while, and I'll catch up with you."

Was there ever such courage! Looking back into her eyes I saw a light that by its own vital force was self-translated, requiring no words, nor the sight of her fingers grasping the handle of that small revolver at her waist, to tell of her determination. In spite of myself I shuddered; yet she was so calm, so wonderful in her abiding faith of catching up with me on that Long Trail that knows no turning back, that my heart, too, burned with a flame more enduring than the love of mortals. Without a word I took the small revolver from her hand, and in its place put mine of larger, more reliable, caliber. Understanding, she looked gratefully up at me, her eyes filling with tears even as she smiled and whispered:

"Now I can do it without being afraid."

"By the God above us," I groaned in my agony, "you'll never have to! For your sake I'll beat off twice that many men!"

"Then don't think of it again, my ferocious, terrible Chancellor," she laughed a little—but I knew, with a sob tearing at my throat, that her playful mood, intended as a tonic for my nerves, was the bravest thing she had yet done. "Look, Jack! They're doing something!"

"They're spreading out," I said, tensely.

Her excitement suddenly died. In its place came a pathetic look of wistfulness as she raised her face to mine and, with a quick sob, whispered:

"Oh, very own mine, try to let me cook your dinner again to-night?"

CHAPTER XXIII
THE ATTACK

When after this I looked across the parapet I was as a man of highly tempered steel. The compact mass had begun to disintegrate, spreading in both directions until their flanks must have been an eighth of a mile apart. Then they advanced.

On a guess I judged their line to be quite fifteen hundred yards away because each unit looked about the size of a pea; and, as these represented the upper halves of men, the distance was too great to open fire. So I raised my sight to a thousand yards and waited. My nerves were steady with a purpose deep-set in me, for I was about to shoot for the greatest trophy of my life, so when the line had advanced a third of the way I took careful aim, and fired. A second passed; then my target disappeared.

"Is he hit or hiding?" Doloria asked excitedly, adding with a little gasp: "He's hit, for some are going to him—see?"

"I believe he is," I agreed, taking another careful aim at one who had not started to his comrade's assistance. He, too, disappeared, and immediately afterwards all of them ducked from view.

"That's awkward," I growled. "They'll do some crawling up, now!"

"They won't dare come close after that," she cried, "for I know you hit one!" Yet this might have been what Echochee would have called "good-medicine-talk," and while standing ready I warned her not to be too sure, as both men might have dropped only for safety.

It will not seem strange that we both felt some disappointment over the probability of this, if one stops to consider what lurked in the other side of the scales for us.

Heads soon began to bob up nearer, now accompanied by quickly fired shots, and I ordered Doloria to the ground. But with relief I noticed that these shots went wild, many times hitting too far away to be heard at all, so our position obviously was as yet undiscovered. The morning sun shone directly in the men's eyes, while the protective coloration of our fort blended most elusively into the background of somber forest.

At the bobbing heads I continued to fire with what quickness I could, sometimes sending a second, third and fourth shot purposely low to probe the grass where it seemed that a man might be crouching. I could not reasonably have expected to register a hit by this, but it kept them in check, and that was our chief concern. From the beginning I realized that if they got near enough to rush us the night would close over a very silent little fort.

Suddenly Doloria gave a cry that froze my blood, for I thought it meant an attack from the rear.

"Quick—quick! Your matches! Oh, not to have thought of it before!" But this last was added while I dug into my pockets for the precious box.

"You can't do it," I exclaimed.

"I can! Keep them down, and I'll crawl! They won't see me!"

There was wisdom here, and I yielded. Nimbly she climbed the wall, dropped to her hands and knees, and crawled to the prairie. In another minute a string of smoke appeared; then with a bunch of grass alight she flew from place to place, stooping as she ran, and leaving in her wake a trail of fire. Almost as quickly she was back at my side, breathing fast.

"You glorious genius, we'll win out yet," I yelled.

The grass was dry and tall and thick, and the wind was blowing smartly. Fire asks for no better playground, and with incredible swiftness a wall of flame sprang up, crackling and roaring as it spread out fan-wise.

She knew, as did I, that the men would back-fire. But while this would save them from the flames it would at the same time remove their cover, and my rifle could then have a whole man to bite at instead of merely his head and shoulders, or less. They would have no alternative now but to come forward quickly or retreat. I think Doloria realized that anything might be about to happen, for she laid the other rifle in position on the parapet, rather casually asking:

"Will it matter if I stand on the canteens? They raise me just high enough!"

Why should she not be given a chance to fight for her life—at least, until they located our point of concealment and began to concentrate their fire on it. That this would inevitably happen might be a matter of minutes, but until then I thought she had every right to stay. There's no denying, too, that I knew her value.

What was going on behind the wall of racing flame we could not tell. But now it rose majestically, leapt skyward and sank to insignificance. The back-fire had met our own; they had gripped, flared up, and died. Likewise were our forces about to clash, and perhaps burn out with the heat of human passion.

Staring through the smoke we counted seven men running to the rear. They well enough knew the danger of being without cover, and were intending first to get beyond our range and then bring the fight back by some other means. Shooting fast I heard Doloria give several quick gasps of excitement as I knocked up the ash dust close to them, and although, their number was not reduced we gained a feeling of greater security to find the fort more impregnable than I had prophesied.

But our budding hope lasted about as long as it took us to conceive it. One of the fellows suddenly changed his direction, waving as he ran, and the others dashed after him. Then we, too, saw the discovery he had made, and it filled me with a sense of desperation.

This was a long, low line of green, indicating a ditch, or slough, edged with saw-palmettoes and bay bushes, that began at some indefinite northwestward point and diagonally crossed the prairie until it passed around our Oasis scarcely more than a hundred feet away. Heretofore, completely hidden by the tall grass, I had had no idea of its existence, and neither had the men, until Doloria's torch changed the prairie to a charred waste. In reality it was the outlet from our spring, and I knew that it must be fairly wide because the fire had not jumped it.

To Efaw Kotee's band it offered both an immediate cover and a place from which to carry on the fight; moreover, by following it toward us, they could reach the Oasis and eventually creep up behind so near that a well-directed shot in my head would be only a question of persistence and time.

Doloria must have understood this, and for the first time she began to fire, yet at nearly a thousand yards, when one's target not only moves but looks small and black upon a blackened background, and is made further elusive by a haze of smoke, only luck can hit it. Still we played that luck to the last card, until one by one the men made safe and disappeared. Then she laid her rifle on the parapet, and I think took a long breath. For a moment neither of us spoke, each being afraid of saying too much, perhaps.

Beginning to fill the magazine, she finally announced:

"They're seven, Jack. You hit that first one, a while ago."

"No," I replied, "or we'd see him on the ground now. He merely ducked, like the others."

"But there were eight the night I escaped!"

"Then Smilax got one during the chase—which shows that he and Echochee haven't been killed." But during this our eyes never left the ditch and our rifles were ready to blaze away at the first sign of movement.

"Why?" she asked.

"Because if he had to make a last stand there wouldn't be as many as seven men here now." And I firmly believed it, knowing how savagely our two servants would account for themselves. I think she agreed with me.

An ominous silence lay about us. I felt sure that the scoundrels were crawling up along the ditch, and told her this. She nodded. Minutes passed.

At one point, about two hundred yards out, there was a spot where the saw-palmettoes and bay bushes thinned to almost nothing. Sooner or later the enemy would have to cross this, and I watched it without blinking because it would offer our best—if not, indeed, last—chance to hold them. So when finally a stooping figure showed itself I opened a vigorous fire. He drew back, or fell back, and the silence again enveloped us, to be shattered an instant later by a fusillade of shots that made the air thick with crackling whines. The location of our fort was known.

"Down, down!" I yelled.

"I am," she answered, obeying as the best of soldiers. "I'll load for you!"

We were being showered with lead by now, and between the wasplike things speeding overhead and their "sput-sput" as they hit the logs, I dared expose no more than my eyes and forehead while emptying rifle after rifle. In the fleeting movement of handing one down and taking the other I saw Doloria sitting near my feet, with several opened boxes of cartridges on the ground beside her. We had plenty of ammunition, so I did not wait for human targets but fired rapidly into every probable place of concealment—just hoping.

This must have begun to touch them up, for one now made a dash across the open space and dived into good cover, from which he started an instant reply to me. There had been only time for a quick shot at him, as the opening was scarcely ten feet wide. Another tried and made it, but the third stumbled. Whether he accidentally fell or was wounded, I had no way of knowing, yet he was able, at least, to continue the fight because there seemed to be no let up in their volume of fire. Then, to my chagrin, a fourth got across, and, following him, the last three tried together—successfully.

In the best of conditions these men would have been very hard to hit, yet I offer no excuses. My aim, of course, had greatly suffered. Disregard for the nicest accuracy in marksmanship may be expected when an enemy is pouring a hundred shots a minute at a certain point, and you happen to be that point.

Again their rifles became silent. There seemed, indeed, no reason to keep them speaking, as the road to the Oasis was clear. When the trees back of us should be reached more shots would ring out, closer, always getting closer; eventually would come the hand-to-hand fight, and then—forgetfulness. Yet I swore with a burning rage in my heart that whoever of those fiends were left to gloat over their victory would remember until their dying day the price I had collected for it.

"Where are they?" Doloria asked, in a voice that trembled slightly. The strain of waiting below was greater than that of seeing what went on outside.

Grimly I told her how matters stood with us, and we, also, became silent.

The next move appeared in the direction of our kitchen, when several shadowy forms began to dart from tree to tree. The same plan was being adopted as that which they had used at the ditch: one man, his advance covered by a hot fire from the others, would stoop and run forward to a previously selected place, then a second, third, and so on, each beginning to shoot from the new position, as he got to it. These tactics might successfully be repeated until the last barrier of trees, not more than twenty yards from us, was gained. But now a fellow showed himself a moment too long and I thought I dropped him, because a howl of rage went up from his mates.

I was keeping the two rifles very busy by this time, and Doloria could scarcely load one before the other was being passed to her. Each side had resorted to the expediency of rising, firing and ducking down again. They were too near for me to risk an inch of head for more than the necessary fraction of a second, and sometimes, in my haste, I aimed at nothing at all. A vigorous fire, whether effective or not, would hold off their rush. But when I peeped over the next time a rifle, protruding from around a tree, showed me that one, at least, had reached the nearest point of cover. I banged at it and ducked, as several shots whizzed over me. It was rather discouraging work, this of being forced to keep down! Another brief silence on their part was suggestive of a new move, and I felt sure that they were preparing for a charge.

Calling this to Doloria, I began to bob up at different places along the wall, trying in a frenzy to check them, and for the moment was successful. Then I heard her give a cry, as a bullet split the stock of the rifle she was loading.

"Some one's in a tree shooting down at us! Look out!" she called, rolling over to get beneath the nearer wall.

Upon hearing this I gave up trying to dodge, and stood to the parapet determined to drop as many as possible before being dropped myself; for if their number were materially reduced she might be able, as a last resort, to come off victor with the automatic. And spurred by this intention I faced them so resolutely that they were compelled to hug their cover. But a second shot from the tree, slanting downward, struck the surface of the sand filling we had used between our walls; it hit a few inches directly in front of my face, knocking up a shower of grit that, for the moment, completely blinded me.

I must have wheeled around with my arm across my eyes, because the men believed that I'd been done for, and with a triumphant howl started forward. Doloria, too, thought the end had come, and gave one despairing cry that I shall remember if I live a thousand years. Through my blurred vision I got a glimpse of her face, a blending of courage and horror and purpose, as she raised the automatic to her temple.

And then by some divine insight I sprang and snatched it away. The howls of triumph had ceased; no leering enemy appeared above our parapet. The smart in my eyes was passing enough for me to see four of them running southward across the prairie with the speed of deer, and suddenly I knew that, without realizing it, I had just been hearing other rifle shots. Whirling about, I saw emerging from a near-by point in the ditch several figures, shouting and waving their hats.

"Tommy," I yelled, "Gates, Echochee, Smilax!" I did not name them all, but turned quickly as Doloria flew into my arms. "We're saved, sweetheart! The dice have rolled for us!"

She was crying a little, clinging to my neck, talking fast, but saying only one thing. And although Tommy afterwards declared that for a time there was such a silence in the fort that he believed we had been killed, I consider this but one of his verbal extravagances; for it seemed only a second after he waved before we were on the parapet waving back to him.

Yet, in the midst of my wildest cheer I stopped. It stuck in my throat, it dried up as the fountain of my gladness seemed suddenly to have gone dry, and I looked at her. There must have been a great pain in my eyes—not physical, for that was transient and had passed—because she touched them, whispering:

"What is it?"

"See what I'm cheering for," I answered huskily. "Our escape only means death to our dreams—it's good-bye to the Oasis!"

"Why?" she asked, her face turning slightly pale.

"Because the minute those people get here you won't be my Doloria of the Golden Dawn any more, but Princess Doloria of Azuria!"

She caught hold of my sleeve and gasped, a little hysterically:

"But, Jack, suppose I don't *want* to be Princess Doloria!"

Our friends had covered half the distance, and I hurriedly said:

"You can't help yourself! You don't know the power that man, Dragot, has! Will you run off with me to-night?" For I could not dismiss the obsession that Monsieur would prevail. "He came especially armed with government orders to find you and take you back. And I'm only afraid your heart's too straight to refuse him, even if you could, when he puts it up to your conscience! Oh, Doloria—please don't cry!"

"I won't," she answered tremulously, "if you stop talking that way!"

I was sorry, and quickly told her that everything would come out all right—that my love was stronger than all the powers of all the governments under the sun. Then I helped her down on the prairie side, for the others were nearly up to us, approaching with bared heads. There was a fantastic note in our situation that deeply affected me. What could have been more bizarre than an Azurian princess holding court upon the edge of a Florida prairie? This, emphasized by our escape from death, added color to the fabric of unreality whose warp was romance, and whose woof was the mystifying surge of human impulses. So my vacillating spirits rebounded to the pinnacle of happiness and, raising my hand, I announced in a loud voice:

"Gentlemen, Her Serene Highness, Doloria, Princess of Azuria!"

Except for Echochee, they stopped and in frank amazement gazed at her. Flushed by the excitements that had made this day memorable, she was indeed the most adorable sovereign before whom knights had e'er sworn fealty. But the old Indian woman, with an undisguised croon of delight, went straight to her side, folded her in aged, brown arms of iron, and faced the waiting men with a look of defiance. She did not comprehend all that was passing, but distinctly wanted it understood that no one should touch her child.

After that they were all about her, even Bilkins and the two sailors asking to shake hands and hear from her own lips the story of what had happened. She recognized Gates as "the splendid captain who found the bomb," and he blushed like a little boy. Monsieur, of course, could not bring himself to treat her with anything less than royal deference, so he kneeled and kissed her hand. I saw her look at the back of it when he arose, and then search his face—he had left a tear which she seemed unwilling to brush off. Tommy, not content with one hand, took both; and these he shook until she burst out laughing. As a matter of fact, we were all laughing a few degrees immoderately. Then, without warning, the strain became too much. Her eyes suddenly filled, her lips began to tremble. Turning impulsively, she put an arm across Echochee's shoulders and together they walked toward the spring, leaving us silent.

Old Gates rubbed his chin and looked up at the sky, saying huskily:

"My word, it's going to rain!" And, although there was no cloud in sight, Tommy said he thought so, too.

Thus the spell was broken and, with a more dismal duty to be performed, we sent for Smilax to bring the camp spade—leaving Monsieur to find Doloria and talk with her, for I had excused him from the contract Tommy made aboard the *Whim*, wanting to remove uncertainties as soon as possible.

Gates entered a careful record in his notebook of identification marks on the three men we found dead. Our joint statement would be sufficient for the law in such a case as this, especially as Monsieur knew there was a price on Efaw Kotee's head, and doubtless on the heads of all who served him.

When Smilax approached the last man he pointed down with grim satisfaction, saying:

"Him bust black boy's head!"

It was Jess, who would have bullied the old chief into giving up my princess! Well, our account was closed. But of Efaw Kotee there was no clue. I felt sure he was not among those who escaped, simply because he could not have run so fast; and Smilax was certain he did not follow with the chase.

Our gruesome task finished, we turned back. For the moment I wanted to be alone, with my thoughts, my happiness, my uncertainty of Monsieur's power of persuasion, my heaviness of spirit caused by the work behind us. But Tommy ran up and slipped his arm through mine, saying with exaggerated carelessness:

"I'm glad that crescendo of horrors is over—if you'll allow a kind of musical term; but I've got music in my soul to-day."

"It's a funny time for music," I grumbled, "—except funeral marches."

"By the way, did you find out about that other funeral march?"

"No, I forgot," I confessed. "Don't bother me, Tommy; I feel like the devil."

"I know it," he gave my arm a squeeze—for Tommy possessed that characteristic making for a community of mind and spirit that did not wait for explanations. "I know it," he repeated, "but you *look* a whole lot better—really like your old self! Now, what's the trouble? If you're worrying about the ruins we created back there, cut it out! I'm not bothered over the one or two I might have got! Fact is, nobody knows which of us hit which, anyway. So what is it? I'm not asking, merely insisting!"

So I told him pretty much everything, as one chum can to another.

"You mean she may listen to the little gezabo and go back?" he asked.

"I mean just that. She will if she thinks it has a bigger claim on her. I know how square she is!"

"Besides being square," he said thoughtfully, "there's also something in the make-up of woman that I've never understood: her apparent hankering after sacrifice. When it comes to a show-down between heart and conscience, she'll follow the conscience ten to one—if she's straight. Look at it," he swept his arm toward the prairie, as if innumerable instances were in sight of us. "See the sweet-faced old ladies who never wrote 'Mrs.' before their names—not that they've missed anything, God knows, but just look at 'em! All because some over-finicky parent didn't approve, no doubt! And see the heart starvation stamped on 'daughter's' face, because 'father' was nearly bankrupt and she *did* write 'Mrs.' to save him! Taking them in retrospect, it's a question if the thing they called sacrifice wasn't plain damn foolishness. Why, hell, Jack, d'you mean to say that the professor and his musty European customs—oh, I can't be profane enough!—the English language is trifling and inadequate! But I'm going to take a hand in this courtship, myself!"

"For a gregarious animal, Tommy, you're something of a wonder," I began to laugh, because it was like myrrh and frankincense blown upon my doubts and fears to hear him talk.

We went quietly on after this. Our boots made no noise in the soft earth, and thus silently we approached the fort; then halted. For on the farther side, hidden by the walls, a man was speaking in tones of earnestness, yet at that very instant a voice interrupted him.

"I wish you wouldn't persist in talking now," it said irritably, "I'm too unhappy over the lives which most have been lost, and—"

"But Your Serenity must realize that lives are nothing. The new destiny that—"

"Oh, I know what you'd say," the voice cried. "But don't give me any more arguments, for Heaven's sake! They're utterly useless and, besides, you might convince me!"

Softly we tiptoed away and, when at a safe distance I stopped to rub my arm where Tommy's fingers had been digging into it, he whispered:

"That didn't sound sacrificy, did it?"

"The old fellow hasn't struck his pace, yet," I answered doubtfully.

"Well," Tommy looked back toward the fort, "the pressure's high enough for one day. She needs another rescuing. You go and speed up the grub."

So, whistling the Charpentier love song, he left me.

CHAPTER XXIV
GERMAN CRUELTY

At the kitchen fire Echochee was busily preparing food for a company now swelled to ten, and Smilax had dropped in rank to an assistant. I saw from her activity that this was not a fortunate moment to interrupt, yet there are some few things in life more important than a well-turned meal, and I therefore advanced, wishing to speak in the presence of our two sailors who hovered near with lips that all but drewled in anticipation of the feast.

"I want to remind each of you," I said, "not to tell the princess that any one was killed. Let it go that a few were scratched, and the rest got away. You get the idea? I don't want her shocked."

My men understood at once, but Echochee, never taking her eyes from the sizzling skillets, asked:

"What you mean—'shocked'?"

"I mean horrified, terrified—sorry," I answered, rather put to it how else to explain.

"Ugh! She already sorry; cry some, say ve'y bad. Me say ve'y good. She all right now. You through?"

And, since I was through, she gave another grunt, leaving me with the suspicion that she thought I was a very small boy.

When finally the others came in sight Doloria walked at the side of Tommy, while Monsieur followed in some discomfiture of mind. His hair was tousled, and his eyes were thoughtful. From this, and the grin on Tommy's face, I judged that all was not going well for him and, in a more happy frame of mind, I went out to meet them.

"Mr. Davis has been telling me a strange story," she smiled at me.

"He's full of strange stories," I warned her. "Don't take him seriously—ever!"

"But I know he was serious this time—weren't you?" The corners of her mouth were tell-tales of merriment as she turned to him.

"Shall we let Jack in on it?" he asked, the grin on his face widening.

"Do you think we'd better?" She was laughing outright now, with an alluring spirit of confidence; so I knew that she approved my estimate of Tommy and had taken him into her heart as for many years he had lived in mine.

But women always loved Tommy—perhaps because he loved them. If some far-reaching providence had not endowed him with a well-developed sense of honor to go hand in hand with his attractiveness, more girls would have looked after him through tears than toward him with gladness. Whatever his loves and secret affairs, he always played above the board and never cheated; so they could trust him if he won, and pet him if he lost. Taken altogether, he was rather a lucky beggar, who learned early in life that the golden key which unlocks a woman's heart is Secrecy—and this they seemed to know by some divine, or devilish, insight.

Before he now had a chance to answer her question, Monsieur caught up with us.

"Ah, my boy Jack," he grasped my hands, forgetting his ill humor to beam on me. "For lack of opportunity I have not expressed my gratitude! Azuria is your debtor! I, who have the authority, say it!"

"Thank you," I replied, "but that debt was cancelled early this morning when its Princess saved me from assassination."

"Good Lord," Tommy cried, in despair, "he's spilled the beans! Jack, you bone-head, we—"

"Be quiet, sir," she commanded, turning beautifully pink and giving me ten thousand messages in a single look.

"Then come on," Tommy said, beginning to draw her away by the hand, "let's go off and think up another!"

"My boy Tommy," the professor sternly reproved him, "she is of royal blood!"

"You said something that time," he imperturbably replied. "Come on, Princess!" And laughingly she went with him.

"*Pardieu*," the old fellow pulled at his beard, "that sex is like a cyclone—the nearer I get the faster I am twisted! But just as her mother was at that age—yes, quite!" He sighed.

"Is she going back with you?" I asked, feeling a malicious joy in the question after the last look she gave me.

"*Certainement*, there is no other way! Thus far I have not tried to persuade her, but merely presented a few minor facts. Yes, she will go."

I confess that my malicious joy sank somewhat.

"You are a gentleman," he continued, "and that presupposes a delicate sense of honor. I know how you feel toward her—yet would you have her remain with you if she one day regretted it? Great things rest on her return, I assure you. Let us start even! You have had two days to persuade her your way; let me have two days to persuade her mine! After that, we fight in the open—you and I!"

There was something straightforward in his appeal that impressed me. I had had two days, and it would be giving her destiny, those great things he spoke of, a square deal to comply. I had misgivings, of course, but these were overruled by—why deny it?—the masculine conceit that becomes assertive after a few feminine favors. At any rate, it was a fair sporting proposition, and I said:

"All right, for two days—provided I explain to her how we made this bargain."

He smiled and hugged me as of yore, crying:

"Almost you would make me sorry when I win! So we fight to the last ditch, eh?"

"To the last ditch," I smiled, shaking hands with him.

But hardly had the agreement been sealed before I regretted it. Tommy's dissertation on sacrifice worried me. And yet, what man with red blood and two wide-open eyes in his heart would have refused to play the cards Monsieur thus honestly laid out? It would be unfair to Doloria's future if I pugnaciously held to the advantage these few days had brought; for it is one thing to start in an open race with men, and run and burst your heart to be first across the goal which means a woman's arms, but quite another to take her unawares in a wilderness and, upon the spot, claim her before she knows what the surrender may involve. In years to follow a time might come when she would look at me through shadows—shadows that grow dark with perplexity over some irrevocable step—and I did not want to sow a seed to ripen into one of these. It is distracting enough for a man to bury his existing ghosts, but sheer madness deliberately to raise a crop of new ones.

In this case I did not so much fear a race with other men in forms of rivals. I had reached my goal, her arms, and nothing could undo that. But her conscience—who dares claim the conscience of another! For two days, then, Monsieur could fight it out alone with her, and if his arguments prevailed—well, I would set about destroying them.

After luncheon, with a brevity that she must have understood meant torture, I explained the compact, saying that I could ask for no more promises until two days had passed; and when she would have replied that her promise had been given I warned her that Monsieur had not even begun to show his power. She seemed a little frightened at this and, but for the sterling mark indubitably pressed upon her sense of right, I think she might have consented to fly from him.

"For two days, then, I'm not to see you," she said simply.

"No," I cried. "But for two days I can't tell you how I love you; how you're the very breath of my life, the control of my brain and body and soul, how I'll finally win you against everything! I'll see you, and be with you, but for two long, weary, interminable days I can't tell you that!"

"Mightn't you," she smiled, a wee bit naughtily, "remind me each morning of those things you must not tell me during the two long, weary, interminable days? Then you wouldn't be so likely to forget, and break your contract."

"Temptress! I wish we'd walked to the fort!" For, while we stood out of hearing, we were still in sight of the others.

"So do I," she laughed now, her eyes expressive of a most fascinating wickedness, a daredeviltry born of the knowledge that the proximity of outsiders made her safe. Tommy says that girls often take this unfair advantage of a fellow. Then Monsieur, believing the time for explanations should be up, came toward us.

At three o'clock our cavalcade started across the prairie for Efaw Kotee's settlement. Tommy and Monsieur were keen to see it, and especially was the latter keyed up to ransack the place for proofs and information. Smilax led, keeping away from the graves. Doloria had made no reference to casualties, accepting them as an unfortunate necessity, and only once asked about the old chief's fate.

I looked back at the Oasis growing small behind us and a great sorrow came over me. It was not easy to leave the place where I had found such happiness, the place sacred to our vows, our first dwelling together beneath God's tent! It lay green and peaceful, but now upon a blackened sea. And, like that flame-swept land, so was my flame-swept heart; the fire of a resistless passion had passed over it, leaving amid the ashes one spot of beauty. She, also, had stopped to look at it and, as she turned away, our eyes met.

When we approached the islands I went forward with Tommy and Smilax, leaving Gates to command the rear guard composed of his two sailors, Bilkins and Monsieur. Echochee, supremely content to have found Doloria, remained at her side.

Four of the attacking party had escaped and might well have returned to their houses. We favored the theory, too, that Efaw Kotee had remained there, expecting his band to capture us; so, if the fugitives were with him, they could by now have prepared a formidable resistance. We therefore went warily up to a certain point and waited while Smilax crawled forward to reconnoiter.

He returned saying that three punts were on our side, from which he believed the men had not come back but were still putting as much distance between themselves and us as possible. Tommy thought the punts might mean a trap and, although Smilax shook his head in doubt at this, we brought up one of the sailors to cover our crossing in case of an attack. Then, scrambling down the steep bank, in less than a minute we stood upon the island stronghold. No shot had been fired, no sign of life existed anywhere. Running to the nearest cabin we hastily searched it, and ran to the next, and in this way came finally to the old chief's bungalow. Here we halted, as if some horrible magic had turned us to stone.

Efaw Kotee, naked to the waist, a few dried smears of blood around his mouth, was there to meet us. His lips munched the air, as a very old man who interminably chews on nothing, and his chest rose convulsively, then rested several seconds before renewing its struggle for breath. He was repulsive beyond all human description; for, stretched as an animal skin to dry, legs and arms pulled wide apart with buckskin thongs, he had been fastened head down on the wall beside his door. Yet this was not all. Hanging at the end of a string—in fact, now resting inertly against his cheek—was the scarlet, black and yellow ringed body of a coral snake, the deadly elaps. Its head had been severed and lay upon the floor directly underneath.

In a flash I read the story: a duel of teeth between this captive reptile and the semi-crucified man; the one in anger wounding, the other snapping in his frenzy to sever that venomous head—his only means of escape from it. From the way the thongs had cut into his wrists and ankles I knew the struggle had been wild, yet much of this may have come from the insanity later kindled by the poison. But that period of torment now had passed. Strength was exhausted, and life dangled by the merest thread.

I heard Tommy draw in his breath. With a shiver Smilax turned away. Better than we he understood what the old man had endured. Together we cut the pitiable victim down, carried him inside and laid him on a kind of divan.

"Who did this?" Tommy kneeled and called in a loud voice close to his ear, hoping to reach a consciousness that had receded far into the shadows.

"I know who did it," I interrupted. "Quick! While there's time let me ask something we're not so sure about!" And, taking Tommy's place, I called: "Is Doloria the princess of Azuria?"

It was so obviously my duty to see that she learned the truth from one who knew, that I may be forgiven this apparent disregard for the sufferer in our hands. But he showed no sign of having heard, although I called again and again in a more commanding voice. His mouth had not munched the air since we put him down, and Tommy, listening for a heart beat, looked up quietly, saying:

"Must have died on the way in."

"If we'd only come an hour ago," I exclaimed.

"No," Smilax shook his head, "him only squeal ve'y bad for last twelve hour. Me reckon some men come back last night; say he plan Lady run-'way; tie him up; tie on snake. No, him no talk hour ago. Coral snake bite make him ve'y crazy bad."

Tommy had arisen and was walking softly back and forth across the room. Finally he stopped, saying over his shoulder:

"I'll give odds there's more in this old desk than he could have told in a week! Here's a safe, too, stuck back in an alcove, that looks like it might hold a ton! You won't have any trouble finding out things!"

I had not yet noticed the room, but now looked with interest at these places that promised to reveal so much. The room itself was large and expressive of luxury, without being luxuriously furnished. The fireplace, mantel, and furniture were of a good, home-made mission type, constructed from gyminda, Florida's nearest approach to ebony; but the floor was covered with really beautiful rugs. Around the walls were built-in book shelves, mantel high, filled with the volumes Doloria had told me of. The piano was there, not an up-right as we had found on the *Orchid*, but a handsome grand, bearing one of the best names. A violin case lay upon it, while near by was a music stand. Altogether, these living quarters of Efaw Kotee showed a taste I would have expected. Instinctively I crossed to the desk, but Tommy stopped me, saying:

"Not while that's in here, old fellow," he jerked his head toward the divan. "In no other circumstances would he take it from us lying down, and it's kind of rubbing it in, don't you think so?"

"If you feel that way about it," I agreed. "But to rob a girl of seventeen years or so of life isn't a crime that merits much sympathy."

"I reckon he pretty well paid up for it during last night and to-day," he said softly.

"Whether he did or not, I don't owe him anything," I retorted, in no charitable vein, that I hope was caused by our excitement and excessive strain.

"You owe him a dog-gone lot," Tommy emphatically replied. "Look at those books, at that piano, at what is suggested by the violin case, at the refinement of this room—and then picture what might have been here! Take another view, and consider what a fine chance you'd have had to meet her if that old codger hadn't turned scamp off there in Azuria! Anyway, we've got to clean up the signs of this butchery before she comes."

In an adjoining room we laid Efaw Kotee upon his own bed. The sheet that Tommy got out of a press to spread over him was, I noticed, of beautiful linen, and I felt softened toward the uncouth frame which, in this wilderness, had still demanded the refinements of life.

Locking the door, we passed back to the living room and thence to the landing where, at our direction, the sailor signaled Gates to bring up his waiting party. As Doloria once more stepped upon the island I saw her eyes grow moist with tears.

We told her that the chief had been found dying, that now he was dead and the place deserted; but after she and Echochee had been rowed across to their own home and the two sailors posted to guard against a possible return of the outlaws, Monsieur and Gates accompanied us to the place of awful murder where we explained what we had found.

Monsieur passed into the smaller room, but came out shaking his head and murmuring:

"The face is much changed, yet I recognize enough to feel reasonably sure it is he."

More positive proofs came when, with breathless interest, we went through the contents of the desk, taking things out in order and putting them aside after minute examination. The first of these was a seal, and the professor, bending over it, uttered a cry of surprise:

"The royal seal of Azuria! What deviltry could he have been contemplating when he stole this!"

Then came a blank sheet of note paper, stamped with a gold peak, surmounted by a gold crown and three lavender ostrich plumes—the Azurian royal crest. These two things alone were strong pieces of evidence for the professor's sanguine expectation. There was nothing further of importance, so we turned to the safe which seemed impassively challenging us to get at its secrets, for the door stood fastened and the combination was unknown.

Monsieur kneeled, placed his ear against it, and began slowly to turn the knob, listening intently for the little metal hammers, or tumblers, of the lock to fall clicking into place.

"I never supposed he knew enough for that," Tommy whispered. "It's a regular crook's way!"

At last, very much disgusted, he gave up after explaining that he could have succeeded in an hour or so, but preferred to use dynamite because it was quicker.

"Undoubtedly it's quicker," Tommy said, "but unless you've cracked safes that way before, we may as well say good-bye to the bungalow!"

Gates thought that the door, being of ancient pattern, might yield to a sledge, and Smilax went in search of one. Finding none of sufficient size, he returned with an anvil, swinging it by its spike. I remember the muscles of his arm that held it, the poise of his body as he raised it above his head and gathered every ounce of power to hurl it upon the combination knob. It made a superb picture of primordial man pitted against the sciences. After each resounding blow we tried to throw the lever, and at last the battered door swung out.

Here was a find worth coming far to see—packages upon packages of greenbacks, all counterfeit, but they made a show, nevertheless. There were also plates for printing francs, pounds and rubles, as well as those from which the American bills had been made. While Monsieur was studying one of these more carefully, Tommy reached past him and drew out a large bundle wrapped in heavy brown paper, securely tied and sealed. He cut the strings and opened it, then gave a whistle of surprise, asking:

"Are these counterfeit, too?"

"*Mon Dieu*, no!" the old fellow gasped, and I, also, caught my breath; for in the bundle were hundreds of unregistered French bonds, of the highest denomination.

Opening one, I looked at the last coupon, announcing that it bore a date of about seventeen years ago, whereupon Monsieur cried:

"Ah, I see it! This accounts for the royal seal we found! Here, at last, is the perpetrator of that grand swindle, lying peacefully behind the door and not caring what we discover! But he has taken his rue with the spoils!—he dared not enjoy these because of the lees he saw in the pleasure cup!"

"Chop that off," Tommy told him. "If you've an inspiration about this stuff, come across with it!"

"Ah-ha, that man—that *capitaine* Jess! His name is Karl Schartzmann, a shrewd, rascally German who vanished after the *coup d'état*!"

"What swindle, Monsieur?—what *coup d'état*? Whom do these belong to?" I was really losing patience; and Tommy murmured:

"Jack, didn't it strike you that only a German mind could have conceived that revenge on Efaw Kotee?"

"It was certainly true to German form," I admitted, without reluctance.

"The Bank of France!—who else?" Monsieur was saying. "As one of the trusted, I know! Listen: the dead man behind us, and the one called Jess, with our Azurian consul in Paris—all scoundrels—hatched a swindle to sell, through forged state authority and a farcical secret diplomacy, a portion of Azuria to France. This, you may remember, came near upsetting the Balkans in 1903. Their crafty scheme lay ready to be sprung when Efaw Kotee—we will call him that—had to kidnap the princess in self-defense. From that time but fragmentary facts came dribbling in from secret agents, as follows:

"First: Two weeks after the kidnaping a foreigner bought a schooner yacht in New York, fitted it up with great masses of household effects, and sailed, his papers designating Guayra, Venezuela.

"Second: Still two weeks later Karl Schartzmann and our consul in Paris transferred the secret bill of sale and left with their arms full of bonds. When France discovered the fraud they were well away.

"Third: Still two weeks later a schooner yacht, afterward supposed to be the one bought in New York, dropped anchor at Guayra and stayed until two men, arriving by steamer, went aboard; whereupon she sailed.

"This is all we definitely discovered, except that before sailing crafty inquiries were made into extradition treaties between France and South American countries—and found, in every instance, to be unfriendly to swindlers.

"I now see how it was with them. Fearing everywhere the press of France's vengeance, shunning telegraph wires, they were driven to the solitude of these islands where, as solitude has a way of treating the criminal mind, their shyness grew to fear, their fear to terror. They did not dare go out except at rare intervals, nor dared they realize on the bonds. It is clear to me at last!"

It was also clear to me, at last inerrantly clear, that Doloria and the little princess were the same.

"Whew!" Tommy gave a whistle. "I feel as woozy as an old warped mirror! Did France offer a reward for this stuff?"

"*Certainement!* And you drew it out!—it is yours, my boy!"

"Like hell it is," he laughed. "I move it goes as prize money to Smilax, Echochee, and the crew!"

Late that evening we buried Efaw Kotee under the mangroves, and did not tell Doloria. No one knows, who has never seen it, the desolation of laying a shrouded figure in a mangrove-covered oyster bar at twilight, where water follows each slushy lift of the spade! I feared for her to witness it, and therefore, Tommy reading the service, the old chief was buried without a woman's sympathy. But, in a measure, he had our own. He held a claim on it for having faced a certain responsibility to Doloria; for having, with the skill of a master, developed the talents God had given her; for having kept her from growing up like a weed.

At ten o'clock that night when, by prearrangement, Tommy and I paddled across to bring Monsieur back from the little island, she was standing with him on the landing. The moon was nearing full, bathing her in a silvery light, and I saw from the droop of her body that she was tired.

"Good night," I said, arising in the punt and putting out my hand.

"Good night," she murmured wearily; but her fingers were cold and did not answer the pressure of my own. I had touched Efaw Kotee's hand only a few hours before, and it had been cold with the same inert, mysterious coldness. I shivered.

CHAPTER XXV
A FLYING THRONE

Early next morning Monsieur was taken to the little island, and I felt that his interview would be long and solemn—perhaps stormy. I hoped so. He came back for luncheon and immediately left again, having given us no intimation of his progress. I did not know what Doloria might be suffering from these visits, but they made me so abominably restive that during the afternoon I took a pine and crossed to the mainland, half-heartedly intending to look for deer. It was nearly sundown when I returned.

"We're packing, sir," said the sailor who tied my punt.

"Packing? Why?"

"Orders, sir."

Without loss of time I hunted up Tommy, finding him and Bilkins busy at carpentry.

"What's in the wind?" I brusquely demanded, forgetting that Tommy was rather particular about the way people addressed him.

"Rain," he imperturbably replied; or did he mean reign, and was employing a vulgar pun to apprize me of Doloria's decision! So I delivered a ten-second philippic on the poverty of some intellects, whereupon he left off working and regarded me with amusement.

"Fact is, Lord Chesterfield, I don't know what's in the wind," he said, "but we're leaving for Little Cove to-morrow at dawn. Bilkins and I are making a portable throne—in other words, a chair suspended from poles so Doloria won't have to walk. Professor came over about five o'clock in a rattling hurry and splendid humor. He's packing Efaw Kotee's effects now. Smilax left two hours ago with orders for the *Whim* to be there and take us off. Add it up for yourself."

"Orders," I angrily exclaimed, for this impertinence on the part of Monsieur was going too far. "He settles with me, that's all!—and the *Whim* stays in Big Cove till I send for her!"

He grinned, then whistled softly.

"So there's no use knicking my knuckles any more on this portable throne?"

"Not the slightest," I told him.

"Love's first tiff," he sighed, laying down the hammer and beginning to fill his pipe.

"Love's what?"

"Tootsie-wootsie tiff, I believe I said"—this between puffs as the match flared high and low over the bowl. "You understand, of course, that Doloria gave the order."

"Confound you, why didn't you say so! What's happened? Did a message come?"

"Sure." He stopped smoking and looked at me. "A big limousine drove up with a note and flowers."

"Be serious," I thundered. "This isn't any time to joke!"

"When you talk about a paucity of intellect," he laughed softly, "it's a wonder you don't bite yourself."

"Oh, Tommy, please let up; I'm sorry, honest—I'm wretched, too!"

His manner changed then. Putting his arm through mine, he led me outside, going toward our landing.

"This is just the time to joke, old man," he said, when we reached it. "She made up her mind to leave, *pronto*! Why? Conscience said obey Monsieur, but heart said nixy! What's to do then? Start home quick, of course, before little heart gives old conscience the solar plexus! That's how I size it up!"

"But I don't see anything to joke about," I said gloomily.

"Well, let me shuffle again—now take a look! When Smilax left with her order, I sent a note to the mate, telling him to bring both yachts down. Then we'll have to split the crew, and in the mix-up I'll see that you and she get on the *Whim*, while Monsieur sails on—But I see you get me! If you can't stifle her conscience before we reach Miami, you're a mud-hen."

"Great guns," I whispered, grabbing him by the arms, "we might sail—"

"All over the Gulf," he chuckled, giving me a push toward the water. "There's your Hellespont, son, as sure as Leander was a gentleman! Cross it now and tell her it's all right about that order!"

"My two days aren't up yet; I'm bound."

"That's nothing. Wait!"

He was off to the old chief's bungalow and reappeared with Monsieur, whose broad smile was anything but reassuring.

"You wish to relieve her uncertainty about that order?" he asked, coming up. "Certainly, my boy Jack, go and say what you please."

"What I please?" I asked pointedly.

"Why not what you please? She goes with me to Azuria—we have arranged it. You could not dissuade her now. Even could you, she knows she can not resist my authority. Yes, go and say what you like."

He was laughing by this time, at his success rather than my discomfiture, but Tommy saw that I was making little distinction between the two and wisely led him away.

As I stepped upon the little island Echochee came down to meet me.

"How's your Lady?" I asked.

"You go see," she answered in a low voice, pointing to the open door.

As I entered the commodious living room Doloria looked up, but did not smile. She was reclining on a *chaise-longue,* beneath a shaded lamp whose rays still blended with the light of a dying afterglow. Her hunting costume had been discarded for a flimsy kind of an exquisite thing of blue—hardly a dress, although it had a lot of lace and seemed to fit her perfectly. It was open at the throat like some dresses, and the sleeves fell away from her arms; but I had seen one instinctive movement she made to pull it closer which might have indicated embarrassment.

"I've come with Monsieur's permission," I said, bowing over her hand.

"With Monsieur's permission," she repeated after me. "We seem to do nothing but with Monsieur's permission."

I saw that she was nervous and very much upset, so replied as gently as I could:

"But this visit involved my promise, otherwise I wouldn't have asked him. I want to tell you that it's all right about the yacht—your sending for her, I mean. She'll be on hand to-morrow."

"Thanks, Chancellor." Her tone had changed to one of complete weariness. "Now leave me, please."

"Leave you," I exclaimed. "I'll do nothing of the kind! The two-day ban is off, and Monsieur has told me I can say anything I please!"

"And having his permission to say anything you please, did you rehearse it before him, too?"

This left me helpless, fervently wishing I'd had more of Tommy's experience with girls' moods. He knew a lot about them, and would have understood just what to do. But I felt suddenly enraged—not at her, but at everything, and cried:

"I don't give a damn for him or his permission! He shan't take you away!"

For the first time she smiled, and held out her hands to me, saying:

"That's good-medicine-talk, Jack. I like it even if it won't cure me. Say it again—that you don't give a damn for him!"

I would have said something in an entirely different way had not Echochee been moving about the next room, but I kneeled, leaning over her, keeping her hand and whispering:

"He shan't dominate our lives! You're going back with me—don't you know you are?"

"Don't make me sorry you came, Jack," she said softly. "I must go with him. So let's talk of other things and keep our last evening here from being a horror."

"I've got to talk about it, as I've got to breathe and think and move and love you! It's all one! It's my existence, and if you went away it would be like tearing me to pieces!"

"Oh, but don't you see that I must," she cried despairingly. "I didn't close my eyes all night, thinking, thinking, thinking! It was agony. It's agony now. But my decision's been through the fire, Jack, and I know I'm right!"

"No decision counts for anything against all you mean to me!"

"Oh, Jack, I'm so sorry!" she moaned, looking at me without dissimulation and letting me see that her face was marked by a solemnity and tragedy that wrung my heart. "God," she whispered, putting her hand to my forehead, "how I suffer while I see your tortured eyes!"

"Then out of sorrow, pity, tell me what the fellow said," I implored, nearly beside myself. "Let me know the strength of your duty, so my own strength can have a chance. It isn't fair to make a beggar of me when I might be fighting for happiness! Let me see his weapons so I can strike back; then, if I lose, I'll lose standing up—and the future," I added, less impetuously, "isn't so gray to the man who loses standing up."

She had turned away with a quick gesture of anguish and seemed to be crying, but when she looked at me again there were no signs of tears.

"He says others have demands and rights, and the many must outweigh the few."

"That depends on the greatness of each side's claims," I began, when she interrupted by continuing:

"My conscience decided that—it had no choice; every claim has been weighed—accurately." Her voice trembled a little, and I thought she was trying to make it harsh. "He said that you and I were thrown out from separate spheres, opposite poles. By chance our orbits happened to cross, and you rendered me this tremendous service. But it was only a part of the foreordination—only to make my path easier to a greater duty ahead, a greater destiny to be fulfilled. Now this commands—he says. The call of my birthright has come, and I must answer. He says that neither of us will mind it in a little while, as memories pa—pass." She wavered at last, and again turned away her face.

"But you don't believe that stuff?" I cried.

"Oh, his words are so unanswerable—when he speaks them! Then he has the authority to command me!"

"They're not unanswerable," I said hotly. "*You* haven't weighed our happiness against this unknown voice of your people, your birthright—he did it for you! His cold logic read the scales—not your heart or your conscience! He's built a wall around you like a cistern, and you can't see out. If it was ordained for us to face death, then by the same law we've got to face life! Sweetheart, don't you see what I mean?"

"I've seen all that from the beginning, dear," she murmured, putting one hand on my hair and stroking it. "But nothing can prevail against what you call his cold logic. He's certain that he's right, and he has the power to make me go."

"Oh, if I only had the brains to out-argue him!" My voice choked, and I bowed my head in her lap.

For a while we were silent. Her hand continued to stroke my hair, and soon her fingers strayed to my temple and gently pressed it—as if she knew that my head burned and ached, and wanted to make it well.

"You don't have to argue, always my own," I heard her whisper. "There's something stronger than words pleading for you."

I looked up quietly, saying:

"Let's run away to-night! Let's have another rescue, and go back to our Oasis—" But she stopped me by putting her hand over my mouth, although she was breathing fast and the color had flown to her cheeks.

"Don't, don't," she gasped. "I've thought of that so many times!"

"To-night," I begged. "You know I'll always make you happy?"

"Happy?" Her eyes, half closed, held mine with a look that did not try to hide its longing. "There'd be no happiness on earth like that of being entirely yours at our Oasis!"

"Then, sweetheart—"

"No, Jack," she now sat straighter. "I was dreaming. Besides, he'd follow with every officer in Florida. Don't you understand, dear, that he has the *right*? I'm helpless to refuse! I can't—possibly! It's simply awful, but it's got to be."

Yet I believed that she had been on the point of yielding, and was about to urge still further when Monsieur's voice, speaking to Echochee, brought me to my feet.

"Well, my boy Jack," he exclaimed, entering with a cheeriness I found detestable, "we shall leave her now, eh? She has packing to do, and must get early to rest."

His protectorate seemed to brook no opposition, and an angry retort sprang to my lips which remained unspoken when I saw the pallor of Doloria's face.

"Yes," she said, without animation, "I must pack. See you to-morrow—on the march."

So, ignoring him, I passed out. But a better humor came to me as I thought of Tommy's scheme about the *Orchid*, and coming upon Echochee at the landing I asked—lightly for her benefit, yet quite seriously for myself:

"Is there any magic in your tribe that can bring a troubled princess sleep and pleasant dreams?"

I knew that she was searching my face with her black little eyes that glistened like a snake's, as she answered slowly:

"Injun maiden find plenty good dream when her head lay on breast of sleeping brave."

"I didn't mean just that," I stammered, feeling my cheeks grow hot. For, albeit, Doloria had slept part of a night with her head against my shoulder when we fared alone in the purity of our wilderness, now, since others of the world were touching elbows with us, Echochee's words knocked me rather into a self-conscious heap. But such is the bitter tithe we must toss into the maw of civilization which, despite its multitude of admitted blessings, breeds also the false! And I stepped into the punt wishing that this daughter of our oldest American family could be divinely appointed arbiter of our customs.

Smilax returned with word that both yachts would be at Little Cove, and one by one the lights in our camp went out. But I sat late at Efaw Kotee's desk writing a ten-page telegram and a fifty-page letter to my father. Both of these I would despatch from Key West—the wire telling him to bring the Mater to Miami where the letter would await them; and I urged them both, as they loved me, to pick up a certain darling of the gods named Nell. Only I made it stronger and more explicit than that, and knew they would comply if such a thing were humanly possible. But this pet scheme I intended to keep from Tommy. It would repay him for his masterly scheme of sailing both yachts homeward.

The next morning after an early breakfast our cavalcade set forth, each man carrying a pack except the two sailors on whose shoulders rested the poles of Doloria's chair. But in this chair sat a very sad little princess—this morning particularly, as she was leaving a nominal home for a new and mystifying adventure. Whatever else Efaw Kotee had been to her, at least he stood in her memory of father; and however irrevocably she may have turned against him, the very fact that she found it necessary to do so was a grievous disappointment.

All that had passed. Strangers had come, and in a few days she was being borne to the other half of the world. To her mother!—what did she know of a mother? To a throne!—but with an unknown prince to rule beside her? And these were entirely apart from the longings she might leave on this side of the world. Surely, if she needed sympathy at any time it was now as the march began.

Although Monsieur had taken a position close to her, and evidently meant to keep it, before we had gone very far I fell in alongside with them, asking:

"How do you find the march? Tiring?"

"Oh, no, not in Tommy's flying throne, as he calls it,"—and in an undertone she added: "I wish it were the only throne I had to occupy."

But the professor, overhearing this—for little escaped him now—cleared his throat and stepped nearer.

"She is mistaken, my boy Jack," he said suavely. "The march is quite fatiguing, and I must insist that she conserve her strength. There will be no more conversation."

Taken aback by this, I was on the point of giving him a jolly good blowing up, but her ready acquiescence caused me to desist. Really, I began to wonder if he had her hypnotized; and, furious—indeed, quite a good deal hurt—by the cool way she obeyed him and began to ignore me, I marched grimly ahead.

As, three hours later, we neared the cove I saw Tommy sauntering back. His manner seemed an augury of trouble, and I hurried on to him, asking:

"What's happened?"

"The *Orchid* isn't there," he turned and fell into step with me. "While getting her out of Big Cove she fouled on a bar. She's still on it, poor dear. So Monsieur sails with us, after all."

For several minutes I stood still in my tracks and swore, stopping only when Doloria's chair came in sight.

"I'm glad you got that out of your system," Tommy grinned. "Now get busy on a new line of attack. We've only three more days, and you'll have to work fast. Surprise her, upset her, then cinch her before she knows what's what. That's the way!" And he hurried back to pay his respects.

The mate and his fellows, even to Pete the cook, escorted us happily down to the small boats. They were honestly glad, and made no pretense of disguising their admiration for Doloria, to the increasing wrath of Echochee.

If ever the men of my own boat crew were on their mettle it was when they sat with oars straight up while I helped her into the gig and took my place at her side—for this was an honor I could not yield to Monsieur, etiquette demanding that, when going aboard, the owner must be her personal escort. With a nod to them they snapped into stroke and we shot away, leaving the old fellow much disgruntled.

At the top of the gangway she hesitated in pretty wonderment before stepping on deck, for the *Whim* was a smart craft and our sailors had not been idle these few days past.

"Everything's so unreal," she murmured. "My house of cards has come tumbling down about my ears, until I think it must be a dreadful dream."

"To be transported to a sure-enough throne is certainly dreamlike," I said, arranging the cushions in a chair. "But I hardly think you'll find anything dreadful about it."

"You don't?" she asked pointedly.

"No," I answered. "The dreadful part's for me."

I knew this was not true, or only partially true, but considered it justifiable after Tommy's warning—and Tommy knew a lot about women. I remembered him saying once that a girl's determination could be changed in two ways: by opposition, and by coöperation. I had tried opposition, so now I would pretend to fall resignedly in with Monsieur's plan, taking it for granted that her future promised nothing but idyllic happiness, that memories would pass, and all that kind of thing. I would become an enigma to her—for this, also, had been one of Tommy's diverse methods of success.

Some day, confessing how my triumph had been achieved, we both would laugh over it, and then she would have to admit that Tommy was not the only one who knew a thing or two about women.

So reasoning, I started in at once. For a while she stared at me, her eyes growing wider and wider. Then she arose and went to the rail, remarking coolly:

"Please signal to have Echochee and Monsieur Dragot brought out at once." And that was the only thing she would say.

To hell with what Tommy knew about women! She would not so much as look at me again, and when that wretched old rag of a shriveled-up squaw, incarnate fiend of a watchful guardian, arrived my princess retired to her stateroom, nor did she appear again the entire day. What Tommy knew about women, indeed!

The rest of us lunched in moody silence, except Monsieur who grew loquacious to the point of making himself an ass. He was not on the crest of popularity, anyway. Previously, in order to give Doloria more freedom, Tommy and I decided to sleep on deck and use Gates's quarters for a dressing room. But when this proposition was also opened to the professor he flatly refused to join with us. The truth of the matter was that he had determined upon a plan—singularly popular among pedagogues—of watchful waiting; he had made up his mind that Doloria and I should not see each other again except in his presence. He may have told her this—I rather suspected it.

As we sat in the cockpit smoking, he became down-right obnoxious by excessive jocularity. It can be disgustingly overdone. Believing that his triumph was assured, he sputtered and giggled with small regard for my presence, and the farther he went the madder I got. Despite his former protestations of fair play, I now began to nurse a suspicion of this befousled little gimcrack; but I'd not thought that Tommy would grow a distemper of any magnitude until the professor, rubbing his hands, announced:

"*Mon Capitaine* says we do not sail for an hour. Let us take a small boat and fish around the mangroves! Maybe a snapper, eh?—or a sheep's-head!"

I was silent. Tommy puffed indifferently at his pipe.

"Come," he cried again. "Let us make a fishing party!"

"The trouble with fishing parties is," Tommy drawled, "that there's always some damn fool along who wants to fish."—Which was, I think, not only the best thing Tommy ever said but, in the circumstances, the best that could have been said.

The professor sat down again rather suddenly and blinked at us.

"So! Then we do not fish," he murmured, and after another thoughtful pause went below.

"I don't suppose we ought to insult him," I suggested, not intending any one to think I meant it.

"I don't care what we do to him," Tommy savagely retorted. "All the good you've got out of this cruise will go to the bow-wows. I won't have it, I tell you! Let's chuck him overboard!"

"Chuck over your grouch," I laughed, although his proposition interested me.

"Oh, I haven't any grouch," he turned away; but swung back, asking: "Are you going to give up?"

"Most certainly not!"

"Then why don't you get busy?"

"Get busy! D'you expect me to go downstairs and drag her out of her room?"

"Yes—do anything! She isn't staying there from choice!" (But I knew better than that.) "If I slug the gezabo you might ask her up. Shall I?"

"Show an idea, man! You know she wouldn't see me!"

"What if she wouldn't! Bring her out, anyhow! Good Lord, Jack, if you're an example of lovers up North, then I say God pity Yankee girls!"

"Well, what would you do, Mr. Know-so-much?" I asked, my temper blowing up. "If she told you she'd stayed awake nights fighting it out and reached the conclusion, absolutely and without peradventure of changing her mind, that her destiny's in Azuria, what would you do then—you who know such a hell of a lot about women?" I just had to say that; it kept irritating me.

"I don't claim any knowledge of the genus," he said, looking mildly at the horizon—and wanting to laugh, I thought. "But a modicum of brain would show you she hasn't thought it out, at all. How could she in forty-eight hours, being confronted for the first time in her life with the two most glowing things in a girl's fancy—love or a throne? She's dazzled, not decided."

"She's worse," I growled. "She's hurt—that's one reason she won't come up! And allow me to say that what you know about women wouldn't fill a gnat's eye!" I seemed to be hypped on this, and couldn't get away from it.

"Well, if you've spilled the beans you'll have to pick 'em up pretty quick, for we'll be home in three days. Just be sure you don't intimate that Azuria can be less than a perfect hell to her, for that would ruin your chances forever!" And with this parting injunction, that drove terror to my heart, he walked aft to join Gates.

Going to the companionway door, I peered into the cabin. The wretched Dragot, bedecked in smoking jacket and spectacles, looking uncommonly like a monkey, I thought, was lounging behind a book. He knew that the nearer uncertainty approaches a certainty the more fatal will be the result of its upsetting; that, whereas a scheme jumbled in its infancy may recover, the slightest maladjustment on the threshold of success often spells irrevocable ruin. He was taking no chances.

CHAPTER XXVI
A TREASURE BOX

Late that afternoon we got under way, setting our course for Key West. But it was a glum company aboard. The Princess remained in her stateroom; Tommy's grouch for Monsieur had grown out of all proportion, so the professor's gay mood lost much of its bloom; Echochee, whenever she left her mistress, scowled at us as though we were pirates; Gates, knowing that my plans had become miserably pied, grumbled over trifles; Bilkins sniffled, and the mate walked about with curses fairly bristling from him like pin-feathers. Heaven knows how wretched I was! If a group of people were ever out of tune, we had struck the original discord. Of us all, the cook maintained both equanimity and cuisine in perfect taste, else I hesitate to think what might have been the fate of the good yacht, *Whim*.

Sometime during the night we reached Key West, and early next morning Gates called me to go ashore. I had requested this. There were the telegram and letter to be sent; and candy, flowers, fruits, magazines, souvenirs, and anything suitable I might find, to lay at Doloria's shrine. Had it not been for the stubbornness of a fellow who insisted that he was under contract, I would have had a moving picture show aboard for her.

By eight o'clock we were again away, sailing lazily eastward before a light breeze. Three days of this inert weather, or possibly less, should bring us to Miami. There Monsieur had expressed his intention of wiring the Roumanian, or some other, consul; then he would entrain with my little Princess, and—well, that would be the end.

All that day we poked along. Surreptitiously I had sent several notes down by Bilkins, but the only reply they got was an angry negative shake of Echochee's head. The old Indian would divulge nothing beyond the fact that her Lady was well. I then thought of knocking at Doloria's door to get a word with her, but the professor, always in the cabin on guard, sat where he could frustrate any such plan. He had stayed there the previous night until a late hour, and was back at his post quite an hour before breakfast.

She did not appear at luncheon, nor during the long and wearisome afternoon.

The next day was a counterpart of its forerunner, except that it got more on my nerves. I had pegged through it in the hope that she might at least dine with us—for this was to be our last dinner on the *Whim*, Gates saying we would land about the following noon. But, happening upon Echochee and asking her this, she almost snapped my head off in saying that her mistress had no such intention.

Growing more desperate as the afternoon waned, I tried again to approach Doloria's stateroom from the far end of the passageway, but Monsieur, glancing over his book, arose and came toward me. The expression in his face plainly said that if I attempted to force him aside he would command her to keep her door locked—and I knew that she would obey. Therefore, ready to abandon hope, I wandered up and sought a secluded place along the rail where, unobserved by steersman and forward watch, I could swear a little, and look more glum, and feel quite natural. It was here that Tommy passed me on his way to the cabin.

"Time for dinner," he said, stopping and laying down something that had been under his arm.

"Don't want any dinner," I growled.

His face, for the first time in three days, broke into a beatific smile, and for a moment I was disposed to punch it, thinking, of course, that he meant to guy me. But he saw this intention and sprang back, holding his palms outward in an attitude of alert protest; yet the smile continued, now to be followed by a low, pleased laugh.

"Don't get mad," he gurgled. "I'm not laughing at you—only at things."

"In the circumstances I consider that personal," I glared at him.

"Well, you needn't, honest! To-night I'm presenting the gezabo with a treasure box, and had really intended asking you to keep away from dinner. That's why I'm laughing—your unintentional acquiescence is a good omen!"

"Treasure box of what?" I demanded, knowing this was some of his tomfoolishness, and irritated that he should have any heart for it.

"Keep your head down," he winked good-humoredly. "You'll know soon enough."

"Tommy," I now excitedly caught him by the arms, "you've got a scheme! What is it, old man? Tell me quick!" I shook him happily, for there was something about his mysterious air that began to inspire me with hope.

"Very simple, son; very simple," he chuckled. "Surprisingly simple, and that's why it'll get across. You sit in the cockpit and observe without being observed, but I'll need your help in one thing: when you see me get up and walk around my chair, you beat it, *pronto*, for this very spot where we are now—and wait here. Understand? It's a nice secluded spot, so you just wait till I come."

"Yes, but—"

"Never mind! Just do what your Uncle Tom says. Now it's dinner time and I reckon Monsieur's starved—he always is! So I'll take my treasure box—oh, by the way, you're not supposed to be in the cockpit, so don't stir around!"

As he picked the thing up I saw that it was a little iron safe about ten inches square—everybody knows the kind. Although small, it was heavy and quite complete, possessing a combination lock of no small merit. In the captain's quarters that Tommy and I now used as a dressing room I had noticed a safe similar to this, and asked if it were the same, whereupon he laughed, saying:

"Yes. Gates keeps his pipes in it, but I got him to flip the combination on 'em for to-night. Well, here goes!" And a few minutes later as he descended the stairs, I, with repressed excitement, stepped back to the cockpit, taking a chair where I could see without being seen.

The dinner had scarcely begun when Monsieur, looking about, asked:

"Where's my boy Jack?"

"Where's Jack?" Tommy repeated, in a voice unnecessarily loud, I thought. "Didn't you know about Jack? Why, he's in bad shape—maybe die, for all I know!"

I must say that the professor looked genuinely concerned, and would have left at once to doctor me had not Tommy sternly interposed. Across the carpeted floor of the dim passageway that led past the staterooms I now saw a thin streak of light, as if some one had quietly opened a door an inch or so. Since this happened to come from Doloria's room, I suspected the Indian woman of listening.

"Don't you go near him or he'll jump overboard, I tell you," Tommy was saying. "He wouldn't let you, and you couldn't help him, anyhow; no one can, poor old Jack! When the Princess stopped speaking to him, and he saw the game was up,—well, his heart kind of broke!"

"*Pardieu,* I am sorry—I am sorry," the professor shook his head.

"Don't let's talk about it," Tommy replied, as dolefully as the loud tone would permit. "I can't look at his suffering—really I can't! It almost kills me! And there's no remedy, now!" And, when finally the conversation had been diverted to other channels, the streak of light disappeared.

Sometime later Tommy, with, a fine show of indifference, said over his demitasse:

"By the way, if we land to-morrow this is your last chance to open that treasure box."

"Treasure box?"

"Yes, the little safe I found tucked down in Efaw Kotee's trunk. Jack and I intended to tackle it to-night, but since he's knocked out I've lost interest."

"I had not heard of this," the professor cried, his eyes sparkling with all manner of hope and enthusiasm.

"Oh, you heard of it, but just forgot. Anyhow, here it is." He lifted it from the floor and placed it on the table. "You're welcome to its secrets; I'm satisfied to get home with a whole skin." Whereupon he reached for a recent Key West newspaper, tilted back his chair and settled down to read.

Monsieur's fingers closed feverishly around the little safe as though it might have held the secret of perpetual youth. After examining it minutely, he sprawled over and prepared to open it by listening for the little metal tumblers to fall into their notches while he slowly turned the combination knob. Tommy, I guessed at once, had neatly anticipated this after seeing him try it on the big safe in Efaw Kotee's house and hearing his boast that he could have accomplished it in time. Now, just as he got his ear flattened to the iron door and was almost choking for breath in an agony of listening, the newspaper began to rustle.

"It gets my goat," Tommy irritably exclaimed, "to have a front-page story carried to the inside, where half the time I can't find it!"

Monsieur, raising his head, politely waited for the noise to cease, as no one could hear the delicate sounds he sought with a newspaper carrying on that way about his head. Yet, when quiet had been once more restored and he was ready to try again, Tommy began another hunt for news.

"Think you can work it?" he casually asked, over his shoulder.

"I—I might, with less noise," the professor suggested.

"Hope my paper doesn't bother you. This is the only place I have to read since I gave up my room, you know."

Several times more, as Monsieur was holding his breath momentarily expecting the mystery of the combination to dissolve, the paper seemed to be stricken with an ague, till at last, hugging the safe to his chest, he indignantly stalked down the passageway and slammed the door of his room after him.

Tommy now arose and walked around his chair, and as I was leaving for my appointed place I saw him start on tiptoe in the direction of Doloria's stateroom.

Ten minutes later he appeared in the cockpit, helped her to the deck, and together they approached. Yet as they drew near the place I was standing she stopped, looking at me in pretty surprise, but came forward again with hands outstretched, saying:

"Oh, Jack, I thought you were terribly, dangerously ill!" And before I could reply Tommy was gurgling, with a fatuous grin:

"Why, hullo, Jack! I see you're up!"

"Are you better?" she asked, letting her hands rest in mine.

"D'you know," here Tommy interposed, not giving me a chance to answer, "that old whiz-bang devil told Doloria that if she spoke to you, or answered your notes, he'd have you jailed for interfering with a foreign country's accredited agent? Sure, he did! He stuffed her poor little head full of trumped-up international law that hadn't a grain of truth in it—to scare her, see? She was afraid to budge!"

"He did that?" I cried.

"Oh, yes, but it doesn't matter now," she said hurriedly. "Are you really better?"

"Dear me, dear me"—it was Tommy again—"I've come up without my cigarettes! You'll excuse me?" He bowed to her, and left without awaiting the royal consent.

The silence was a trifle awkward when he went, and our eyes seemed to be glued to the spot where he disappeared; but now I turned to her.

"I suppose Echochee was listening to his conversation with Monsieur, and told you. Tommy's full of ideas, but this is his masterpiece because it unlocked your prison."

"It was I who listened—purposely," she said, without a trace of embarrassment, but laughed a little strangely as she asked: "You weren't ill, at all?"

"Yes, I honestly was—with unhappiness; but not as near dead as he pretended."

"And you're in no danger by talking to me?"

"The greatest danger—but not from man-made prisons."

"Oh, it feels so good to be up in this fresh air," she said irrelevantly, raising her face to the sky and taking a deep breath.

"He was a scoundrel to keep you shut in down there," I declared; and then she told me of the old fellow's fabrications, really such atrocious lies that for a while I was undecided whether to thrash him or laugh. As it turned out, I laughed; because she did.

She had moved to the rail and rested her arms on it, leaning over and looking pensively down at the water. I, also, went to stand by her, but, in turning, my eyes happened to glance through one of the cabin portlights at Tommy. He was seated comfortably in a deep chair, Doloria's box of candy stood on the table within easy reach, the newspaper was in his hands, a cigarette hung from his lips, and Echochee was just bringing him the basket of fruit I had taken so much care at Key West to have made attractive.

"Picture of Tommy hurrying down for his cigarettes," I whispered. "Peep at him!"

As she leaned forward and the light fell on her serious face, the attractive curves of mischief, always so maddening, touched the corners of her mouth.

"Isn't he a dear," she murmured. "And there's nothing in the safe but the captain's old pipes?"

"That's all. Tommy's waiting to soothe the professor when he makes that discovery, and keep him from coming on deck."

She laughed guardedly, but there was no great spirit of fun in either of us, and again we turned back to our contemplation of the water, for a long time looking down at it in moody silence. I instinctively felt that she had not altered her decision.

In the distance off our starboard bow a hairlike line of slowly brightening silver, forerunner of the climbing moon, touched the far horizon. It resembled a shining lake upon a great dark waste, and I told her it was my love trying to light my life that had turned to night without her.

I know we were subdued by the witchery that comes with watching for the moon, because when its dome appeared her fingers gently tightened on my sleeve; nor did we speak until it stood serenely balanced upon the world's edge, sending to our feet a silvery pathway that twinkled on the waves. And then, by the merest accident of our position as the yacht changed its course among the keys, two far-off pine trees, appearing to move out side by side across the sea, stopped in the center of the moon. She caught her breath at the unusual beauty of this. That sigh from her, and the mystic night, all but drove me mad. My senses swayed with the throb of some vast indwelling orchestra.

"Let's take the silvery path," I whispered, putting my arms about her. "Look, it leads to the gate of our Secret world, where we first found happiness!"

"Oh, dear Jack," she pleaded—but I would not be stopped, and words stumbled over each other in my agony to persuade her.

"It's Fate—your destiny! I can't change it, neither can you! It spoke to us beneath our two big pines on the Oasis; it's speaking to-night—saying you shall never leave me!"

"Oh, but Jack, that's so impossible! He'll *make* me go!"

I saw the glitter of tears upon her cheeks, and answered fiercely:

"He can't, when I love you as I do!"—and whispered over and over: "Sweetheart, sweetheart, I love you!"

She had not moved. The moon, by this time high enough to have mustered its forces, frosted the yacht into the semblance of a dream-ship, and we might, indeed, have been sailing upon some phantom lake in fairyland. My eyes were pleading for hers until she raised them—and then they could not turn away. Held and blended by a mesmeric force, they began to give and answer question for question, secret for secret. I saw the quick pulsations in her throat, which seemed to be beating in my veins, instead.

"Oh, Jack," she whispered, laughing tremulously, with a subdued madness that was made for such a night as this, "let me go back to Echochee!"

But I could only answer as I had before:

"I love you—I love you!"

"Darling, darling Jack," she begged, taking my cheeks in her palms, "you mustn't—you really mustn't! Let me go, dear!—Oh, I believe my throne is—is tottering!"

"And my reason with it!" I cried, drawing her quickly, passionately, up to me.

For a long time a silvery yacht glided across a silvery sea, while in far-off Azuria a throne did totter and fall; but ten thousand loyal subjects smiled in their sleep that night at a strangely happy dream, wherein their little Princess was pressing upon the lips of an unknown beggar the seal of her eternal sovereignty.

When again we thought of the moon it had climbed surprisingly high, making our shadow on the spotless deck seem like a black rug beneath our feet.

"Is it awfully late?" she whispered.

"The moon's still up, sweetheart," I said.

"Is it, dear?" she murmured, adorably sighing her contentment at this evidence that the night must yet be very young, indeed.

And, finally, when moving stealthily like two happy thieves we went down into the cabin, she blew a kiss to the sleeping Thomas Jefferson Davis, then gave both hands impulsively to me, and disappeared into her room. After the door had closed, and I felt she would not open it again, I shook Tommy's shoulder. He blinked at me, mumbling:

"Must have been asleep."

"Must have been," I grinned down at him.

And, when he saw my grin, he sat straight up and grinned back at me—for it is in this way that men sometimes understand each other.

CHAPTER XXVII
THE FINAL HOCUS-POCUS

Doloria breakfasted in her room, but from the galley I sent a note on her tray, among other important things saying that I was about to break the news to Monsieur. In her reply, surreptitiously delivered by Echochee, who was smiling, she wrote—among still more important things—"for Heaven's sake, break it into tiny little pieces!" With this in mind, although having no idea how I should succeed, I came up by way of the fo'castle and walked aft to where Tommy and he were smoking.

The open safe and three or four pipes belonging to Gates lay on the floor between them, while the old skipper who had taken the wheel was silently convulsed with laughter as he watched the puzzled expression on Monsieur's face and the innocence on Tommy's. My opportunity seeming favorable, I said:

"Professor, last night the Princess decided to give up Azuria. She's promised to stay here and rule me; so I'm giving notice that neither you, nor any one else, can take her."

He listened to this with more tolerance than surprise, giving Tommy a look that implied his distress to see my prostration taking the form of hallucinations. But Tommy added:

"It's on the square. Jack's put one over, and all he asks is your blessing. Give it like a good sport, and, we'll drink their health."

"You are cut-upping," he gasped, staring with wide eyes—that perceptibly narrowed as he glanced down at the pipes.

"Call it what you please," Tommy imperturbably replied, though I knew that he was not at all sure of his ground, "but the Princess and Jack are going to be married, and I rather fancy I'm to be best man. It would be right decent of you, as the special emissary plenipotentiary extraordinary fat-and-hairy agent from Azuria, to give the bride away. I'm only suggesting it."

But the professor was on his feet, sputtering and waving his arms in a torrent of rage.

"It shall not be, it shall not be!" he cried. Then suddenly he began to laugh, looking at us with a superior air of cunning that made my flesh creep.

"Why, you are as pigmies with your childish schemes! You suppose I have gone this far without arranging everything to circumvent you, or anything you could do? Bah!"

"Circumvent till you're black in the face, you beloved old rag doll," Tommy gave a mirthless chuckle, "but the Princess doesn't go back with you—and that's a cinch. She's going home with me, to visit my sister. Don't you try to follow her, either, for I'm giving it to you straight that you'd last about seventeen seconds in Kentucky. Yes, Professor, I'd say that in Jefferson county seventeen seconds would be a right venerable age for you!"

"That shows what small children you are," he laughed contemptuously. "The minute we touch land I order the first police to arrest her—and on my authority he will not dare refuse! She is still a subject of Azuria, and not of age according to its laws! Then I will lay the matter with our representatives in Washington, and your President, fearing to disturb the consummation of his League of Nations, will return her, of course! This for your threats!" He snapped his finger at us and began to fill his pipe.

Who'd ever have thought the League of Nations would treat me that way? Tommy saw murder rising in my heart and gave me a warning look. Yet I could see from his puckered forehead that he was pretty well up against a stone wall. Our only hope of success, so far as my mentality could work it out, was instantaneous manslaughter.

Finally, amid a complete silence and under the professor's supercilious smile, Tommy got up and went below. Had I tried to enter the cabin, the old fellow would have followed me.

A sailor passed aft and whispered to Gates, who surrendered the wheel, went forward and disappeared. Ten minutes later he came back and took a seat near us; affecting to be at his ease, but making a very poor go at it. Soon after him came Tommy, carrying open in his hands a large book, calf-bound and old. For on the cabin shelves my father kept a lot of truck in the way of old books that no one ever read. I saw, also, that Tommy and Gates had reached an understanding.

Of course, I was bursting to know what those conspirators had up their sleeves. Tommy stood in the middle of the cockpit, looking serious and thoughtful. Now, in an impressive voice, he said:

"Monsieur, Gates has been good enough to get out his copy of American Marine Law, pertaining to the obligations and powers of captains of American vessels sailing upon salt water. Perhaps, after this brief preamble, it would be tautological for me to continue with what your overly acute mind must have by this time grasped; nevertheless, you will pardon me if I read you a paragraph, that goes as follows: 'In cases of emergency, where it is evident that a vessel can not in the required time reach a port wherein there may with certainty be found a civil officer of the United States of America, or the captain of such vessel in any other circumstances deems the request of the principals a proper one and of sufficient warrant, he is thereby, and is hereby, endowed with the right to perform the ceremony of marriage according to the civil code of said United States, and such ceremony, properly attested by two witnesses, shall constitute the bonds of holy matrimony before the world.'"

At the beginning of this Monsieur had sprung up, but before Tommy concluded he again sank into his chair, breathing fast and blinking.

"Gates," Tommy asked, "do you consider the request of these principals a proper one and of sufficient warrant?"

"I do, sir," Gates answered.

"You consider that the emergency in every way justifies you to perform this ceremony of marriage?"

"I do, sir."

"Then, Jack," he turned to me, "suppose we say high noon. It's a fashionable hour, and gives you a little while to primp up."

I gasped at him, unable to believe my ears; but before I could speak Monsieur was again raving.

"It shall not!" he yelled. "I say it shall not; for now I, too, play a card!" And drawing from his pocket a paper, discolored by wear and age, he flourished it in our faces, crying: "By this authority I claim her as my ward; both of us Azurians; and in the name of my country I forbid the marriage!"

"Gates," Tommy asked, without batting an eye at Monsieur's grandiloquent outburst—which seemed to me the absolute frustration of our plan, "we don't know this man. He's a tramp we picked up at Key West. Do you recognize his credentials, or would you say they're forgeries?"

"They look like forgeries to me, Mr. Thomas," the old skipper answered at once, not being within ten feet of Monsieur and his paper. "If I'm mistaken, sir, I'll apologize when we get ashore, but I carn't see any reason why the ceremony shouldn't take place at high noon. If that's too early, Mr. Jack, we can sail back to Key West—or New Oreleans."

"But my authority," the professor cried, seeming on the verge of apoplexy.

Tommy closed the calf-bound book and tossed it over to me, then turned Monsieur good-naturedly around and pointed to the Stars and Stripes flying at our main peak.

"While you're on this yacht, my friend," he laughed, "that's the authority, and *don't you forget it*!"

I glanced at the volume of Marine Law he had tossed to me. It was *Gibbon's* DECLINE AND FALL OF THE ROMAN EMPIRE!

Monsieur's beard began to twitch curiously. I thought at first he was really intending to make the best of things, but suddenly two great tears squeezed from his eyes and rolled lumberingly over his cheeks; then, as an unbridled torrential storm breaks in the tropics, he threw himself face down upon the cushions and wept—piteously.

Tommy and I were thunderstruck. It gives one a weird feeling to see a man shaken with grief. I was helpless and, there's no denying it, just a little remorseful. As quick in sympathy as he was in resource, Tommy crossed and put a hand on the old fellow's shoulder, saying gently:

"Buck up, Professor. This kind of thing won't do, you know!"

Then my surprise was most complete. Sitting now, face buried in his hands, he brokenly told a story that at times brought tears to our own eyes.

When he finished I had visualized a scene begun more than thirty years ago in the Royal Palace of Azuria: an honorable young doctor, Court physician, voluntarily surrendering his appointment because he loved the King's younger daughter—Doloria's aunt; the old ruler's searching eyes that sympathized even while they censured—the aged hand that pressed with understanding even while it took the proffered resignation. Then the young doctor's quick departure; his plunge into the Universities, trusting absorption of the sciences to act as a panacea for his grief. Years later his return to Azuria; their pure love still burning, though unexpressed. At last the kidnaping; the quick preparations for pursuit; and finally the girl, herself, sweet with many confessions, bringing in her own hands the old King's "authority"—this paper before us—which commanded him to return the little Princess by any means he could, his reward being the fulfillment of his heart's desire.

"And now," he moaned, rocking to and fro, "after seventeen years of searching, I have won only to lose!"

Truly, I was touched. Tommy turned quickly away and blinked at the horizon. Yet neither of us knew that all of this time Doloria had been standing in the companionway door. She now crossed swiftly and sat by the weeping man, impulsively drawing his grizzled head to her shoulder as a mother might have comforted a hurt child. But toward me her face was turned, and I saw that her startled eyes spoke into mine the entreating message which distracted her—telling me that we must acknowledge this claim of Monsieur's poor heart before our own could ever be happy; asking me what to do, since his title to happiness came first. Yet all that her lips spoke was the trembling whisper:

"Oh, Jack!"

But he, with a new determination, sat quickly upright. The warmth of a woman's sympathetic arms upon a life that had been without comfort, the quick intuition that she was pleading for him at a great cost to herself, stirred the fineness of his nature, and he cried:

"Never! I have lived this long, and this long suffered, enough to know the irony of that royal barrier! Your aunt and I, dear child, are passing toward the shadows of life, while you and my boy Jack are just starting out. Your happiness shall not be cindered upon a false altar—I swear it!"

"Good old boy," Tommy murmured. "Do you mean that, honest?"

"*Pardieu*, have I not sworn it?"

"And you wouldn't try to muddy the water again if I confessed that our Marine Law was a hocus-pocus?"

"What is that hocus-pocus?"

"A no-such-a-thing."

"*Sacré bleu*! I see! Pipes and iron safes and hocus-pocus! But I do not care!" He turned to Doloria and, taking one of her hands, said: "You, *mon ami*, shall find your heart's best desire. It is I who say it!—I, who have the authority!" The way he clung to that authority was really pathetic.

"It occurs to me, Monsieur," Tommy crossed and looked down at them—and I saw that Doloria read in his eyes the sadness of one who must remain outside while others pass through to happiness—"that you, too, can find your heart's best desire. Jack and our sweet Princess will be leaving for Azuria as soon as passports are procurable. Now, the day they arrive, you might be moseying about the railroad station, borrow her for an hour, and personally conduct her to the palace. The late lamented King's royal authority contained no stipulation about the missing child being returned in a state of single blessedness, therefore the reward is yours. Add that up, and see if it doesn't spell Eureka!"

Doloria turned to Monsieur with a glorious smile and, being nearest, received the first hug as the light of Tommy's reasoning burst upon him. Then he bounded up and hugged me; but Gates and Tommy ran away, the cowards, yet did a lot of laughing from a distance. And now the forward watch called something, at the same time pointing off our port bow. Low upon the water lay Miami.

Excitedly we took turns focusing the binoculars on it, and after a little as we drew fairly near Tommy, with a puzzled look, asked:

"Who are those people on your Colonel's dock?"

"My father, maybe. I wired him to come."

"Boy, I mean the petticoats! Look at 'em—there're two!"

"Can you make out their faces?" I asked, having a good time all to myself; for here was my chance to return an obligation in the matter of courtships which, if not cancelled, would furnish the versatile Tommy with an anecdote I should never outlive.

"Not yet," he mumbled, squinting more closely.

"One's probably the Mater," I suggested.

"I hope so," he smiled, lowering the binoculars. "What was the toast you gave her, Jack?—'if romance and adventure are alive I'll bring them home to you!'—wasn't that it?"

"Yes, and we sailed out on that quest only seventeen days ago. It seems incredible, doesn't it!"

"It sure does," he chuckled, once more raising the glasses. "You've put on seventeen pounds, too,—besides a special chunk of 120, or thereabouts, which you gained the night of the rescue. That's some record, boy! See here," he asked quickly, "who the deuce are those people, anyway! One has a mighty familiar look!" And I could hardly keep from laughing as I answered:

"I think the Mater went by Louisville and picked up Nell—"

"Good Lord, I *see* her," he yelled, so instantly and irrepressibly delirious with joy that he let my binoculars fall overboard, the chump.

But now I saw that Doloria—which was the other name for romance and adventure—had slipped away from Monsieur; she had gone forward and, all alone, was leaning against the foremast, gazing dreamily at this new world and these new people who waited to take her to their hearts. So I forgot Tommy, God bless him!—he may have known a little about women, after all!